What the readers say about *EVERY S*

'Re. your *Every Street* . . I have fc
loved the stream of consciousness ap
reminiscent of James Joyce's Ulysse.
The tale flows easily . . . And as a septuagenarian Mancunian, I can assure any doubting Thomases in the audience or readership that it is written in a genuinely authentic Manchester dialect . . . First class writing, clever, witty composition. I wish you all the very best with your . . . book. It deserves to win the Booker prize . . .[It] depicts in authentic dialect the striving of a young Mancunian' Billy Hopkins, best selling author of *Our Kid, High Hopes, Kate's Story, Going Places, Anything Goes, Tommy's World.*

'May I offer you my heartfelt congratulations and thanks for your great novel. *Every Street in Manchester.* It is a tragicomic masterpiece. I am lost for words to describe the intense pleasure and satisfaction your wonderful creation has given me . . . I have never read a book which was so rich in sustained manic humour and deeply moving and sincere emotion. I feel completely overcome and emotionally drained after reading it for the first time. There is no doubt I shall be reading it several times more . . . The greatness of *Every Street in Manchester* lies not just in its magnificent writing, the fruit of years of blood, sweat and tears, but in its integrity and sincerity . . . Unlike some gifted writers who merely engage the brain, you have brought warm humanity and compassion into this splendid story . . . I could go on and on about its merits – the marvellous spoofs of Bernard Manning and Chuck Berry; the Goon show quality of its wit; the completely natural and hilarious stream of consciousness passages (a big improvement on Joyce's *Ulysses* and Faulkner's *As I Lay Dying*, though no doubt indebted to both). But what constitutes its greatness is the author's loyalty to his roots. He knows the people he is writing about. [They] are real people, though they come out of Bill Keeth's brain . . . Finally, congratulations on the aptness of the Scripture quotations at the beginning of parts one and two . . .'
Fr Brian Se *Story*

'*Every Street in Manchester* . . . is absolutely wonderful – every sentence a tonic – bringing back many memories from my childhood . . . I savour every page. I'm reading it slowly because I don't want it to end. Superb! Excellent!' Martin McCawley, Bolton, Greater Manchester:

'I love the dialog. . . It really puts me back there in my Manchester days. I can't wait to get back to it. It's like a trip home . . . I wish you much success with your book' Barbara Cunningham, Atlanta, Georgia, USA:

'An excellent read . . . I found it hard to put down. It brought back so many memories of how life was as a teenager in the fifties and sixties. All the hopes (and) dreams . . . Places we used to go to, long since gone . . . I can recommend this book for its wit, humour, and down to earth honesty . . . It made me laugh, it made me cry, but most of all it made me happy' Mary Luke, Blackley, Manchester:

'I had a really good laugh' George Krystek, Cheadle.

'Enjoyed the local references . . . [and] the local history bits . . .' Tony Coogan, Middleton.

'Thanks for the book, can't put it down, reading it in bed at 5am this morning . . . makes me laugh out loud . . . love it!' Lynda Goodfellow, Unsworth, Greater Manchester.

'A great read . . . has an honesty and directness which drew me in immediately to a world of times gone by in good old Manchester . . . entertaining from the first page to the last. I loved it' Janet Driver, Santa Monica, California, USA.

'Just wanted to let you know that … what you wrote … is perfect' Kim Caffrey, Shelby Township, Michigan, USA

EVERY STREET IN MANCHESTER

Bill Keeth

Limited Edition Press

First Published in 2005
by
Limited Edition Press,
No2@164, M16 8AW.
http://www.paulspixels.me.uk/

This edition published 2009.

ISBN: 1 85988 065 7

DISCOGRAPHY

'The Flowers of Manchester' is on the album *The Two Beggarmen* (Sweet Folk & Country label: SFA 109), 1980.

'All I Want to Do' by Tony Auton and The Trauma is on the album *Allergic to Rust* (August Moon Records No. 6), 2003.
See http://www.tonyauton.com

All other titles are amply documented in the *Record Collector Rare Record Guide*, the *Guinness Book of British Hit Singles* and *British Record Charts*, 1955-1979 (pub. Macdonald/Futura)

Cover photograph: stone setts, north Manchester

For forty-seven and fifty-nine,

one house hers, the other mine

Preface

Manchester 9, the setting for this story, is a postal district of the city of Manchester in north-west England. It is bounded by the town of Middleton to the north, Queen's Road to the south, the district of Moston to the east, and, to the west, by the right bank of the River Irk. Its main arterial trunk road is Rochdale Road, the A664, which bisects it on a north-south axis.

The River Irk is a tributary of Manchester's main river, the Irwell, and of English letters too inasmuch as it was the Irk which gave birth to a child whom Mrs G. Linnaeus Banks cast upon to its waters in its cradle to be rescued by Simon Clegg, christened Jabez, and awarded the honorific *The Manchester Man*.

What follows is the memoir of a latter day Mancunian, a friend of mine, whom no one could justifiably accuse of being amongst the most articulate of men. So wherever it has seemed that the sheer volume and strength of his various dislikes and enthusiasms have tended to outrun his powers of expression, or where the limited vocabulary at his disposal might otherwise have been too severely put to the test, I have taken it upon myself to act as his editor. Knowing him as I do, of course, I know he will want to take me to task about this when next we meet, though I live in hope that the one extenuating circumstance in the quiver of my defence will go some way towards pacifying him. For whenever my friend (believe me, my very good friend) has been unavailable for comment, it is I who speak.

Incidentally, there never was an equestrian statue at the back of Blackley Library and Institute, nor was there a youth club where my friend has built one. Neither was it the case that any black cab ever plied its trade from the taxi rank described below. These structures are fictitious either in themselves or by reason of their location. Furthermore, an additional safeguard has been installed here in order absolutely and ultimately to preclude any attempt to identify any character as a real person masquerading under a pseudonym – to wit: it is the express intention of the author that this memoir should be read as nothing other than a work of fiction.

Two other factors may be worthy of note.

Saint Joseph of Cupertino, a Franciscan saint believed by some to have enjoyed the gift of bi-location, has consistently failed to put in even a single appearance as patron of any one of its parishes since the Roman Catholic Diocese of Salford was erected on 29 September, 1850. Abraham Lincoln, on the other hand, the 16th President of the United States of America has been called upon to undergo quite considerable relocation both by Mancunians and by his compatriots.

The Lincoln Memorial created by George Grey Barnard and presented to the City of Manchester by Mr and Mrs Charles Phelps Taft of Cincinnati, Ohio (Mr Taft's brother, William Howard Taft, was the 27th President of the U.S.), was ever controversial. Previously sited in Platt Fields, Fallowfield, facing the entrance to Platt Hall, the statue was originally commissioned for Harrisburg, the state capital of Pennsylvania, in Dauphin County, on the Susquehanna River. Today it will be found in Lincoln Square, Manchester, in the county of Lancashire till 1974, in Greater Manchester ever since, and in both instances on the Rivers Irwell, Irk, Medlock, and Tib. What is said to be an exact replica is sited in Lytle Park, Cincinatti, Ohio.

It is perhaps a truism to say that the human mind, never a perfect instrument at the best of times, is even less so in the wrong hands or under pressure. I offer this both by way of explanation and excuse lest the author has included any inaccuracies of which I remain unaware, though I know full well even as I do so that this is another thing a good friend of mine will want to take me to task about when next we meet.

Byron Marlfield,
Principauté de Monaco, 23April 2005

PART ONE

It is certain that thou art one of them;
even thy speech betrays thee.

Mark: 14; 70

1

The Beatles was everywhere that summer, singing 'She Loves You'. Yeah.

I never liked it much, meself. I can't remember the first time I heard it and when you like a song you can always remember the first time you heard it, can't you? Where you was, what you was doing, who you was with. Things like that stick in your mind, don't they? Well, I know they do with me.

Me, I liked that other one. It was more my sort of stuff anyway, rough and ready like me (ha, ha). Oh, you know the one I mean. It sounds like they recorded it on just an ornery tape-recorder in that club what the *Daily Mess* says they always hung out at. They've got this, like, tom-tom going away there and a mouth-organ, and one of them's shouting like he's hurt pretty bad – and the one with the tart's face (what's-his-name? McCarthy?), or maybe it's the other one, I dunno, but whoever it is, he sounds like he's coughing blood in the last throes of consummation. Anyway, that's the one I liked, and I can remember the first time I heard it, dead clear.

Like the first time I ever heard them at all, singing 'Love Me Do' all crackly on Luxembourg one night and this feller on the wireless says: 'Them's the Beetles.'

And I thought:

'Clever that!' (What with beetles being black and that.)

Then this same feller says how they was Livercunians or summat, and I nearly fell flat on me back at the thought of English darkies that sung like that. And I remember running out of our house and across the street to my mate Huge's house, hoping he'd heard them too, and knocking at his front door, bursting to say:

'Hey, Huge, you hear them darkies on Luxembourg just now? Them English darkies that sound like the Yanks on the London label. And there's you and me been pissed off for ages with Bobby Vee and Billy Furry and Vince Igor and them.'

Only I never said it. Because Shirlee was there, and when I seen Shirlee me mouth wouldn't work. All I said was:

'You comin' out, Huge?'

Which he never done anyway, seeing how his mam was there

too, only further back behind him and their Shirlee, and his mam was of the opinion, she said, that I was a looney tune that she wouldn't be a bit surprised if he was took away in a yellow van any day now for knocking on decent folks' doors at all hours of the day and night like someone not right in the head.

But I remember how I felt that night, clear as day. It was like I'd lost about five years off of me age, and me and Huge was fourteen years of age all over again, like when Chuck Berry and Larry Williams and Little Richard and all them was going, and tight pants had just come in and you wouldn't of been seen dead buying owt but the London label except for Presley and Gene Vincent and Bill Haley and Buddy Holly and them. Here's what it felt like: like you was just glad to be alive, like you had the strength of an hundred men. And that's exactly how I felt about that other one the first time I heard it, only more so, and how I feel still now I come to think back.

I was everywhere meself that summer, like the Beatles I suppose, only I wasn't. It just seemed like it because I was in the money, only I wasn't, not like they was, but I had enough for me. Me Uncle Joe had fixed us up with this job on the Gas Board, digging. Digging, you know, and laying new gas pipes (services, they called them) to houses that had leaky old ones. It was just digging, like, but it was tons better than that grocer's shop where I'd been because it was a lovely summer that year and you was out in the fresh air all day long, and you could earn fifteen quid a week if you put Saturday in.

It wasn't that easy at first, mind, what with me Uncle Joe getting us the job and that. I took piles of stick off our gang because of it. See, me Uncle Joe was one of the gaffers down at Gaythorn, so they had us marked down for a gaffer's man, and I had to show them I wasn't, but was just exactly the same as what they was, that is, interested in doing as little as you can possibly get away with for a fair day's pay. And with me build only being sort of medium, like, I had to crack on I was harder than I was, hard as nails – hard as ruddy reinforced rivets, or they'd of never let up. Like, one Friday afternoon when the van from the stores rolls up with all the bits and pieces we needed for the job in hand. (We was working down near the junction of Briscoe Lane and Ten Acres at the time on what they call a sump where all the water and gas oil collects.) And we was off-loading this five gallon drum of oil that we always filled up the road lamps round the hole with before we went off home of a night when didn't it slip right through me hands and come crashing down – THUD – on me foot?

Hey, and I never had no steel toe-caps on neither, just me cousin Line's army boots from the Terriers that he never went to till some jeeps come one Sunday morning and took him. Just ornery army boots in ornery leather. Ouch! It didn't half hurt! I let out one yelp, couldn't help it, and I must of startled this poor old dear that was struggling past us, lugging about two ton of shopping from the Co-op, there, in a couple of paper carrier bags, because she give this little sideways sort of a jump all of a sudden with this look on her face, like, as if her heart had just skipped a beat or summat, and she was gonna up and snuff it right there on the spot, she did.

'You okay?' says Burke's Law, our ganger.

'What?' I said. I don't know how I managed to say this much because me foot was killing us, and I was that scared I'd start crying, I was holding me lips stiff like a ventriloquist.

'You okay?' Burke's Law says again.

'Me? Yeah, why?' I struck a match then and lit this Park Drive I'd stuck in me gob. 'Why?' I said again, taking a real deep drag and exhaling by way of me nose, and hoping against hope that if I did look like a ventriloquist, then I at least looked like a ventriloquist that was also tough.

'Wasser*marrer* wi' yer',' chips in Jed then, sucking up to Burke's Law like he always done. 'You look like you lost a bob and found a tanner.'

'Nowt. Why?' I cleared me throat and gozzed in the diggings like this goalie I seen on telly, playing for Arsenal.

'That paraf*feen*,' says Burke's Law. 'That drum of paraf*feen*. Fell on your foot, dinnit?'

'Nah!' I said, and turned on me heel, and said I was off to splash me boots just so's I could go somewhere where I could hop about, and swear to meself, and rub me foot in private for a bit. Because all the time this is going on Burke's Law and Stan and Jed are staring at me mug like it's gonna give them the first, second, and third in the 3.30 at Newmarket, though it was still only half-past two as yet. Oh, they *known* all right. They known I done me foot in. But what could they do about it if I never let on? Short of stamp on it till I cried uncle, or run a wheelbarrow full of earth over it to make us scream.

Another time Burke's Law says:

'Right, yous three, get stuck in breakin' that corncrete out while I guz and sees what's keepin' the cracker.'

We was working down the bottom end of Heaton Park Road that day, opposite the Hill Top – Burke's Law and Stan and Jed and me – and Burke's Law jumps in this brand new Ford Consul 375 that he has, bright red, and tootles off to Tweedle Hill to use the phone.

'Yeah, pull the other one, it's got bells on,' says Stan, sarky-like soon's Burke's Law disappears. 'Stick a bet on at the bookies, more like; knock back a swift half in the The Fly Norse on Crab Lane.'

'Wellington,' says Jed. 'Wellington's Holts-ies.'

'Fly Norse,' says Stan. 'Fly's Boddies'.

Then after Fly Norse and Wellington's-Holts-ing it for three and half hours or summat, and diverting to the Pleasant and the Pike Fold for another hour and a half, Stan sends Jed off to fetch this horrible rusty old iron spike out of the trailer, and when Jed comes back with it and hands it to Stan, Stan hands it to us, and says for us to hold it on the corncrete with just me two bare hands while he swings this fourteen pound sledge at it.

Judas *Priest*!

Hey, you know how you say you wanna spend a penny? Well, just then I could of spent a couple of bob at least. But I gotta hold o'meself and I done what Stan said. I took that horrible rusty old iron spike that he give us and I held the pointy end of that horrible rusty old iron spike on the corncrete with just me two bare hands like he told us to. And I done it like I never had a care in the world; like it was summat you done every day on the Gas Board; summat I wouldn't of dreampt of missing out on now it was my turn at long last. Oh, and thank you very much indeed, Stan, for giving yours truly this wonderful work experience opportunity, you super-annoo-ated old get! (This being summat Jed called him sometimes to gee him up.) Yeah, I done exactly what Stan said even though me heart was in me mouth and me hands was all shaky and me knees was all trembly like jelly. I done it with a smile on me face too.

Stan never missed, mind. But I am not to know Stan is such a hot shot with a fourteen pound sledge when he kicked off, am I? Besides, he really put us through it before Burke's Law come back with the cracker – they both of them did. They kept saying stuff like:

'Whoa, you better not wiggle it about like that again!' and, 'Oh dearie, dearie me! Thought I'd missed that time for sure!' and, 'Wow! Your mitts was very nearly mincemeat then, believe you me!'

And *then* they couldn't work the cracker for laughing when we got it because it only turns out that, unbeknownst to me, there is also back in the trailer some horrible rusty old iron callipers, for the use of, what is exspecially intended, not as Jed said they was, for grabbing me Uncle Joe by the bollocks and demanding a pay rise, but for shifting nightwatchmen's brassieres that was red hot after having a fire in them overnight, or for holding the pointy end of horrible rusty old iron spikes on corncrete that you want to break up with a sledge-hammer instead of using just your two bare hands to do it. (And you could easy imagine how this must of been a very, very welcome arrangement indeed when they had to break up corncrete in the olden days before noo-matic drills was even invented.)

See, there was loads of stuff like that I had to put up with with Stan and Jed at first. But it was worth it in the end because the money was good, and the work wasn't too bad, and nobody on our gang ever found out I was only a seven-stone weakling that could of easy had sand kicked in his face – or peat, or clay, or tarmac, or broken corncrete, or gravel, or a load of ash out of the nightwatchman's brassiere that he'd had going overnight. And, looking back, it was funny in a way, and it didn't go on for ever neither. Because one day when I'd been there a month or so and

Stan and Jed are larking about as usual, and one of them's just bunged a lump of nightwatchman's coke in me mug of tea, Burke's Law rounds on them sharpish, and says:

'That's enough of that, yous two! Yer can just lay off of him. He grafts just as hard as any of yers.'

Course *he* was a liar. (He must of been to run a brand new Ford Consul 375 on only eighteen quid a week.) Yeah, Burke's Law was a liar because I grafted harder than them two put together. Damn sight harder. I worked like mad that summer. Dug the earth till the mussels in me back'd knot like fists, punned the back-filled earth till me arms ached like they was bruised, shovelled seven kinds of shite till the sweat poured from me forehead to christen the earth I worked. Yeah, I worked dead hard that summer. No one on our gang never worked so hard as me.

And I bet they wondered how I done it, Burke's Law and Stan and Jed. I bet they did. And wouldn't they of died laughing if they known? Because no one never known how I done it. Well, not till now, they didn't. Because here's how I done it; here's exactly how I done it – here's how this seven stone weakling that could of had sand kicked in his face worked harder than Stan and Jed put together: I sung Shirlee's name to meself all that summer long:

'Shir . . . lee, Shir . . . lee, Shir . . . lee, Shir . . . lee.'

Yeah, that's how I done it, see: I sung Shirlee's name to meself all day at work, only silent, like, or whispered at most. I sung Shirlee's name more times than there's flames in a fire, more times than there's stars in the sky, more times than there's fish in the sea. I sung Shirlee's name from Cheetham Hill to Gorton, from Blackley to Baguley, from Harpurhey to Didsbury, from White Moss to Wythenshawe, from Collyhurst to Clayton, and back. I sung Shirlee's name from eight in the morning (when we clocked on) till when we clocked off of a night. I sung Shirlee's name all day and every day, five days a week – and, six, if we put Saturday in.

'*SHIR* – (*banjo, dig deep in the earth*)
LEE (*heave earth up on to the side*),
SHIR – (*punner, up into the light*)
LEE (*down to earth hard as you like*).'

Tell you, over that summer I reckon I must of sown Shirlee's name in three hundred thousand million billion acres of earth. I must of. I was like that Johnny Appleseed bloke I seen this Disney cartoon of that worn this saucepan on his bonce and planted apple trees all over the American frontier and had this heavenly quire with him everywhere he went – only difference being I never had no pan and no quire, and nothing never grown where I sown Shirlee's name in the earth except inside meself, that is, where what I felt about Shirlee grown like one of them sunflowers you see, and got bigger and bigger and bigger till I thought it'd choke me.

And guess what: it was easy to do the work when I sung Shirlee's name to meself, and it seemed only right too. Because ever since I seen Shirlee in their lobby that night I had worshipped the ground she walked on. And it was, like, as if the earth I dug all day long *was* the ground Shirlee walked on, and just to dig that earth sort of brung us closer together. Well, close as I was able to get to her at the time.

See, the earth I dug that summer, the Manchester earth, well, it was only the very same earth that carried the pavements Shirlee walked on, wasn't it? Like, when she'd go to Armistead's bakery on Moston Lane at the top of Conran Street to get her mam's bread of a Saturday, or to Mrs Wykes's record shop, or Percival's the ironmonger's, or to Victory Valet, or The Meadow Creamery, or to Robert Sidlow's grocer's shop, fronting Rochdale Road (him that funded Failsworth Library in his will). And it was this same Manchester earth that carried the 72 bus that took her to work five days a week too, and to Littlewoods and Lewis's of a Saturday afternoon, or to any one of them other stores in town, like Marks and Woolies and Kendals; and to the World Famous Embassy Club of a night, or to the Northern Club, or across to the Domino on Grey Mare Lane, or maybe the Palladium Club on Collyhurst Street. That is, of course, if Shirlee hadn't decided to go to the Plaza that night, or to the Gaumont, or the New Oxford, or the Red Lion in Blackley Village, or the Charlestown, up near The Fourways – or wherever Shirlee wanted to go of a night where she'd laugh and dance and chat to her friends and run her fingers through her hair and straighten her stockings if she needed to and touch up her make-up and brush her hair (a bit impatient now because it wasn't just like she wanted it to be), and maybe pull her face a bit when she was annoyed, or make this funny little hollow sort of a clicking noise with her tongue that she sometimes done when she couldn't think of anything to say, or when she'd just said summat she thought you'd maybe think was daft (and maybe was too), or just look up from what she was doing all of a sudden and give you that smile right out of the blue, the blinding smile, the blinder, face to face. Yeah, and she'd do all that, every bit of it and more, from the moment she got up in the morning till when she went to bed at night in a special way that was special because it was her special way, Shirlee's special way, Shirlee Jameson's special way, just hers and hers alone.

Hey, but once Burke's Law had said: 'Lay off of him,' Stan and Jed had to admit to theirselves I wasn't a gaffer's man after all, but a damn good grafter. And things begun to get better. And know what? That Gas Board job was a piece of cake, dead easy. You clocked on at eight o'clock and then you put a brew on. You dug an hole two foot six deep and *then* you put a brew on. You laid one inch gas pipe (one and half if they had central heating, which wasn't many in them days) and, ho-hum, then you put a brew on and ate your dinner. Then in the afternoon you filled in the hole and took the punner to the backfilled earth till it was flat (except when it was a crossing when you left it proud and let the cars and buses do that) and then . . . well, you know very well what we done then. 'S right, we'd get a brew going again. Then when we'd supped up and if the weather was fine, well, you just took it easy, and maybe kipped down on a bit of grass and got a sun tan while Burke's Law done his timesheet. Oh, and if you seen that bloke's timesheets what he wrote you'd of done no more good. What with his "surveyed site" and "excavated ground" you'd of thought we'd built the Great Pyramid.

Cushy wasn't in it!

'Hey,' I says one time, yawning and stretching, lazy like, and kipping down on this grass verge near the prefabs off Victoria

Avenue East, up past the Berkshire on the right, while Burke's Law done his timesheet. 'Hey,' I said to nobody in particular. 'I don't know why they don't call this the bleedin' Gas *Bored*!' (Joke.)

Hey, and that fifteen quid a week really went somewhere in them days. I had some of the best clothes I've ever had in me life. I had this pair of tight jeans, not skin tight, but tight, you know, in black denim with, like, green stitching down the seams and a label on the outside of the waistband at the back that had this picture of a covered wagon on it, and a pair of blue denim ones too. And I bought, but on the drip, the never-never, from Walter Peart this Italian suit, mohair, they said it was, and it had these dead narrow lapels and was midnight blue and the jacket was that short we called them bum freezers. Used to feel a treat trotting out in that lot, exspecially on a Saturday night with money in me pocket after working mucky all week. And I was out seven nights a week in them days too.

'And where d'y think you've been till this time?' me mam'd say when I got in, if she was still up, that is.

'Clubbin' it,' I'd tell her, cheeky-like. 'Clubbin' it, pubbin' it, grubbin' it and lovin' it!'

I had thousands of girls in them days. Well, maybe not thousands, but plenny. But I never had enough. Because I never got a look-in with Shirlee. Because whenever I seen Shirlee me mouth wouldn't work. And the laugh of it was (though I never thought it was one little bit funny at the time), the laugh of it was when I was with any of them other girls I could of spouted pomes from a rooftop. If I'd known any, that is. Which I don't do, except for Roses are red and violets are blue, and Up the airy mountain, down the rushy glen, which none of them girls was likely to be partial to of a Saturday night on the back row of the Adelphi Cinema on Kenyon Lane, or the Moston Imperial Palace, or the Don, or the Carlton, or the flipping Essoldo, Stretford.

Nor me.

Dunno what it was about Shirlee why me mouth wouldn't work. I couldn't never understand it. See, maybe it was with her being this little bit older than us. Well, a couple of years anyway. Or with Shirlee being Huge's sister that I'd known all me life from when we was kids at school and I used to play out with a bit, and was bossed about by more often than not with her *being* that little bit older. Hey, and let's have it right – that I never even *liked* very much at all: hated, in fact, mostly, and used to call some not very nice names when we was littler.

Like, one time me and Huge set the sand hills alight one hot summer's day when we set fire to this toy dog on wheels that we found and shoved it off the top of Buck's Hill and give the old fogies waiting for the bus at Blackley Office a sheet of flame fifty yards long to look at – and some sirens to listen to too when the fire engines come, which was something Miss Goody-Two-Shoes-Shirlee-Jameson only went and told her mam about, so me and Huge got done.

Or like, one time I wanted to go off logging for the bommy in the last week of the summer holidays and Huge wouldn't come with us because Bonfire Night was still two months off as yet. So Huge went picking blackcurrants with their Shirlee off of the bushes on the allotments at the end of the street which they brung back to their back yard late in the afternoon in this bashed white enamel basin with blue bits showing and this bucket the same, them and about five hundred other kids. And they rolled out some pastry then, putting the pastry in a baking tray with the blackcurrants they'd washed in the sink in their mam's wash house on top, and they was just about ready to put a pastry top on it before shoving it in the oven on Gas Mark Four or summat, when we seen them at it through the open door of their back yard when we come back down their entry with all the stuff we'd managed to snaffle off of the corporation tip and an old Michelin tyre with a rip in it, me and this gawp of a kid called Idle Wild from off Russell Road down near the dustbin works that was the laziest kid in creation. See, what I mean is, it was me done most of the logging while Idle spent his time watching us gormlessly and picking his nose that was blocked up pretty bad instead of runny like it usually was. Yeah, and he only seemed to come to life, Idle, when we found the two frogs, Heckle and Jeckle, in the mud at the side of Lanky's pond at the bottom of Factory Brow (that is to say Factory 'Brew' as they say it round our way).

Heckle was just a baby frog – tiny, he was, sort of mottled green, with these dinky darker patches. But Jeckle, the big frog, was that ugly he might of even been a toad. So it seemed only right that Jeckle should be the one to go over the Jamesons' back yard wall. Which he did do when I slung him over with an overarm action that would of give the Lancashire captain Cyril Washbrook summat to think about if he'd had to face it at Old Trafford. As it was though, Jeckle's soft landing on the other side of the back yard wall: head first in oven-ready blackcurrants, and greeted by five hundred shouts and screams from the gobs of the five hundred spectators present – well, it was this that spurred Idle on to action above and beyond the call of duty. So Idle done no more than made Heckle follow suit, the only difference being, as luck would have it (a 500-1 shot, if you think about it) Heckle landed feet first in the gaping gob of this mate of Shirlee's called Laura Pod, who must of been that startled at seeing Jeckle do a nose dive into the blackcurrant pie from a dizzy height, she was still stood there, Laura, with her gob wide open. So Miss Oh-What-A-Good-Girl-Am-I-Shirlee-Jameson only went and told her mam and my mam about it, and I got the blame for it – hey, for Heckle too!

Then all of a sudden you is grown up like you never thought you was ever gonna be. And the years have flown past and you is just not the same person no more, and every time you blink it is six months later. Hey, and that kid you had used to play out with and done Penny-for-the Guy with, that had the Dalmatian dog called Scamp and a guider his dad had made for him, has flit from the corner house and someone else has moved in that has an H-shaped TV aerial on the roof and a car outside the front door, and maybe a fridge in the kitchen too. Then another car turns up in the street, and another. And soon there is not no longer just a milk float in the street and a van with Union Jack panels selling packets of tea door to door and Dr Dryburn's green Alvis saloon with hubcaps shiny as mirrors. And you yourself is no longer the gawky gargoyle in a stripey tee-shirt and khaki pants held up with a snake belt that's reflected from the hubcaps of Dr Dryburn's green Alvis saloon that's parked up at the kerb while he makes his calls.

Then you blink again, and there's Shirlee Jameson, walking to and from her front door – hey, clip-clopping, more like, in high heels she is now wearing though you're still supposed to be in school uniform (kid!), and more often than not she is not on her own no more, Shirlee, but with different lads that is older than you is (titch!) because Shirlee *is* that bit older than you are anyway . . . And maybe that's why me mouth wouldn't work when I seen her. Like as if I thought she wouldn't never of took us serious – like I didn't never take Shirlee serious till the night I seen her stood in their lobby with Huge and her mum and the Beatles singing in me ears for the very first time, and Shirlee's mam too (though her for the umpteenth), saying I am a looney tune that will be took away in a yellow van any day soon.

Hey, and them boyfriends of Shirlee's – they all looked like football half-backs or something. I'm not kidding. Like, she went with this bloke for ages that was the spit of Paddy Crerand of Man United. The absolute spit. No oil painting, it's true, but who's gonna tell him, eh? Not that Shirlee went short of Greek gods and Adonises, though they worn ornery clothes and not fig leaves, what with Manchester being a bit wet very often, not to say parky too. Hey, and she never went short of pigs, big-headed bastards, Jack-the-lads, cocky buggers, and out-and-out arseholes that she shouldn't never of been seen dead with, girl like Shirlee. Still, that is just my considered opinion, arrived at in consultation with the Green-Eyed Monster, and you is welcome to take it or leave it as you choose. But this Crerand-feller (it wasn't him, of course – he was already spoken for with a tribe of kids or summat), all the kids from round our way used to hang around outside Shirlee's front door with their autograph albums for when he come out, even them that worn Man City scarves. Till Mrs Parbold that lived next door but one to the Jamesons come out one day and said she'd throw a bucket of water over them if they didn't shift, and did as well when they didn't, which made 'em.

I dunno.

Maybe it was summat to do with me why me mouth wouldn't work when I seen Shirlee. I loved that girl, see, and that seemed to make a difference. Yeah, that seemed to make all the difference in the world. See, I might as well admit it right from the start. I loved

Shirlee Jameson, and I only sort of kind of liked all them other girls I used to went out with.

If that.

See, what I mean is this, see. There was some very nice girls amongst them. In fact, they was mostly very nice girls. So there was maybe summat wrong with me why I never liked them better. But even so, there was some of them girls I used to went out with I never liked a bit. No, not one teeny weeny little bit. And here's summat else too. (And N.B. there is nothing in the whole wide world that is dafter than this!) There was one or two of them girls I used to went out with I actually hated. Yeah, hated! Hated from the word go! (Mind you, if you can have love at first sight, why can't you also have hate?) Like, her off Princess Parkway with all her airs and graces that thought it was Lisa Gastoni or summat – Miss Letting-Board-for-Pigeons, 1962 (according to Byron Marlfield, this is). Or her with the silly laugh from over near Failsworth Co-op – The Hunchfront of Newton Heath (Byron again). Hey, no, serious. See, I only went out with them two because they had what Stan and Jed called 'them nice feminine a-cute-rements, for the use of'. See, what it was was this, see: I just known me ogling, lecherous enemies and mates would be jealous as hell of them nice feminine a-cute-rements (whether for the use of or not) precisely because them particular nice feminine a-cute-rements they theirselves did not have clear and present access to, so I was getting me kicks by rubbing their noses in it.

Yeah, I know. Said it was daft, didn't I? There's nowt dafter this side of the wall round Prestwich Hospital. But maybe that's why I was struck dumb whenever I seen Shirlee. Because ever since I seen Shirlee that night, it was like I seen her different than I'd ever seen things before. Like maybe I was using me eyes proper for the first time in the hole of me life. Well, either that or like, as if someone had reached out and give us a fresh pair of eyes with, like . . . WOW! . . . twenny-twenny vision all of a sudden, and these was a very different pair of eyes than the eyes I had always took with us when I'd went shopping for groceries, or clothes, or LP records, or shaving soap, or after shave, or flowers for Mother's Day, or meat. And it was, like, as if this fresh pair of eyes I'd been give was that keen they'd robbed us of me power of speech. (Pity they wasn't dishing out fresh gobs too, I sometimes think.) Because with the gob I was stuck with I'd loved Shirlee Jameson for ten months, two days, twelve hours, and fifty-three minutes before I got the chance I'd been waiting for.

Yeah, I know I said I *never* got a look-in. But I meant *not never for a long time*. Like, for instance, Johnny Kidd meant on 'I'll Never Get Over You', that record of his. Course, you'd have to listen to the lyrics of the song to understand what I mean by that, and the trouble is you can't borry it off of me because it's on HMV, and in them days I'd only buy stuff that was on the London label. But I remember Laura Pod had a copy. That is, she had it till we bent it when we was sat on it one night, well, lay. (Oh, you've been watching too many of them *Carry On* films, haven't you? Still, you can snigger all you want to. Because I'm just making a perfectly innocent statement of fact about a record of Johnny Kidd's – him that got killed in a car crash on Bury New Road, Whitefield, I think it was. Well, somewhere on the north side of Manchester. Radcliffe maybe.)

Funny how it happened too. No, *not* the car crash Johnny Kidd was in. (*For God's sake*!) No, me getting me chance with Shirlee. Not funny ha ha, sort of funny peculiar. Mind you, now I come to think of it, it was flipping funny ha ha too.

2

It was this Saturday in August when I never had no overtime on a/c of Burke's Law was on his holidays. And I can remember being pig sick about it at the time because I needed a few extra quid to make me holiday money up to fifty quid for a few days away somewhere with Byron – Blackpool maybe. Anyroad, waste not, want not's what I say, so I had a lie-in instead, and rolled out of me pit about eleven o'clock and went downstairs and grabbed the *Daily Mess* between two rounds of toast. (Timewise, that is, not mouthwise, ha, ha.)

But, like I say, it was this Saturday in August, so it was what they call the Silly Season when there was just nothing at all happening in England, Ireland, Scotland, or Wales – or anywhere else in the world for that matter, except that the Prime Minister's missis had bought a new hat, and the Royal Family had had a very busy day yesterday because they had all got up, and a lovely tortoiseshell cat called Timmy had had to be rescued by a fireman from up a tree somewhere in Maidstone, Kent, plus a brave dog had been rescued by an heroic policeman from the "Jaws of Death", it said, when this candy floss machine blown up in an amusement arcade on South Shore, Blackpool, though two lazy gets that was skiving off work from a coalmine in Bradford (Bradford, Manchester, that is, not the Yorkshire one) had got blown to smithereens. (Hey, and serve them right too, or so it seemed.) Oh, yes, and this itsy-bitsy volcano had erupted on a Pacific island somewhere, but there was nowt to worry about, really there wasn't. ("No Problem Atoll", Our Own Correspondent said.) Because it was a French island anyway and not many natives had snuffed it, and – ooh yes! – the temperature *here* was in the nineties at the moment. (See full page photo of brave dog: a Cocker spaniel with its tongue hanging out, it was that hot.) But there might be some bursts of thunder and lightning overnight.

Which there had been, and also an heavy downpour of rain that me mam was not one little bit surprised I hadn't heard it (she said). Because I must of been frazzled as a Franciscan with all the booze I'd thrown down me neck in the tap room of the Alliance last night, aided and abetted by that good-for-nothing Byron Marlfield. And whatever her, that is, me mam's (six foot two inch, Irish jigging, one-day-in-the-year-shamrock-sporting) brother Joe, who had got us the job on the Gas Board, would think about us throwing all me hard-earned money away on booze, she just didn't know. Him (me Uncle Joe, that is) with one lad (their Cletus) going in for the priesthood, and the other, Linus (him that lent us the army boots) a pillar of the local business community. (Tyre bay, bit of servicing, and a Manchester Hackney plate.) This last as she shoves me bacon and eggs in front of us on a dinner plate she's give a pretty mean bit of off-spin to that would of probably wrong-footed Peter May, stood at the crease in his whites, wishing he'd had the foresight to wrap a bit of Blackley tape from Connolly's Cables in Blackley Village round the handle of his cricket bat before he'd went out to face the Aussies at Old Trafford.

Said nowt, me. Though me Uncle Joe was not Irish at all, but English as a Bury black pudding with an Eccles cake on top – his great-grandfather (me mam's too), Mr Malachi Methuselah Finbarr Fingal Bunratty or summat (my great, great-) having jumped ship thirty-odd miles down what was now the East Lancs Road more than one hundred and sixteen years ago, seeing how (whatever the rights and wrongs of the situation) he very much preferred a bag of chip shop chips, with or without salt and vinegar, to no spuds at all, and had went on to earn his living with the LNER railway company until an LNER locomotive cut his life short in Thompson Street Goods Yard, Manchester, so that Malachi Methuselah Finbarr Fingal Bunratty, 1826-1885 (on whom Sweet Jesus, Have Mercy), was now lay at rest in good (though very, very untidy) English earth in St Joseph's Cemetery, Moston. Hey, and I never said a dicky-bird about me cousin Line neither (that is, me Uncle Joe's son Linus), who was the sort of pillar of the local business community that was known on the street as The (Menagerie) Line, and not on a/c of his courage neither (though this was not in question) but, rather, on a/c of his M.O. (as Sgt. Joe Friday on *Dragnet* might of put it). Nah, said nowt, me. Grabbed me knife and fork, shook the salt pot over me egg, undone the top of the Tiger sauce, shook the sauce bottle likewise, and settled down to eat me breakfast as if in complete nodding agreement with the Old Girl about me Uncle Joe's two lines, menagerie and descent.

Folded the *Mess* in half, propped it up between the teapot, the milk jug, and the sugar bowl, munching away all the while, and I must of been maybe halfway through me bacon and eggs, tucking in to this stack of toast that me mam had bowled a googly with from the Scullery End that would of easy skittled Colin Cowdrey for a duck, when I seen in the paper where this Gipsy Petulant is going on about your horrorscopes. So (yeah, I know it's daft but) just for something to do, like, I run me finger down the page to where it said "Scorpio" (moody and tempestuous, that's me, ha, ha). And you could of knocked us down with a feather because how the hell that Fleet Street gippo known about me and me troubles I'll never know. But she did, you know, because it said summat like this:

"Today's the day to make that contact what you've dreampt of. An absent friend leaves you room for manoeuvre. Unfortunate circumstance pays unexpected dividend."

Yeah, that's exactly what it said. And it was me to a tee, wasn't it? Course, it was. Well, apart from the "unfortunate circumstance" bit, and that could of been a misprint. Or it might of been meant for someone living at John O'Groats or Lands End, or even on that Pacific island where the twidgy volcano was. (The *Mess* is circulated worldwide, you know.) But as for the rest of it, well, it was me up and dressed. Because my mate Huge had only gone and drove his mam and dad down to Torquay in his dad's A35 to see his Auntie Vera that kept a guest house in St Marychurch and who'd been took poorly all of a sudden. Yeah, and their Shirlee, Shirlee Jameson – *my* Shirlee, was only across the street there in their empty house all on her todd. In fact, it couldn't of been better because it was me lucky day, see, when I couldn't not put a foot wrong. Not with this Fleet Street gippo on me side. All I had to do was march across the street, knock at

Shirlee's door and give her some of that Me, Tarzan, you, Jane stuff, and I'd be home and dry. And know what? I couldn't do it. I froze stiff as a board just thinking about doing it. I was on to a flipping Fleet Street gippo-backed cert, and I still couldn't do it.

Barmy!

It was like as if I could of dug Shirlee's name right round the Equator, across the Sahara Desert, over the Atlas Mountains and back again via the Kalahari Desert and the Great Rift Valley, but I couldn't never say it to her face.

'Yer bloody fool!' I said, pushing the paper away from us that hard it fell on the floor on the new Axminster carpet that me mam had had fitted now I was bringing better money in.

'Oi, mind your flamin' manners!' says the Old Feller, who's just come in for his breakfast after faffing about with his glads in the back garden in the wake of the storm. And with this he plonks hisself down at the table, snatching up the paper and the last round of toast.

'Not talkin' to you,' I said.

'Well, who *are* yer talkin' to? 'Cause there's no bugger else here.'

Look, I'd better make it clear from the start so it's be out of the way and done with: there'd been a bit of bad blood between me and me dad for some time. Well, ever since I was born really, when he just happened to notice I'd had the bare-faced cheek (hey, literally!) to be born not wearing a Man City strip, but just an ornery birthday suit like everyone else. And this proved to be a shock to his system that me dad never fully recovered from. Besides which, I had only went and made things worser by going to watch the cricket at Towncroft with Byron. (This bloke called Dolly was turning out for Middleton at the time; and a bloke called Roy Gilchrist who'd skittle them for fun – Byron being a big fan of both.)

See, barring his blood and his politics, me dad was a Blue through and through, and he hated anything to do with cricket. So Old Trafford was in his bad books twice-over. And I think it must have occurred to me dad on the morning of me lucky day that he hadn't yet done enough to subdue the natives (yours truly, that is) who earlier that same week had laughed long and loud at his barmiest Blue boast yet. Namely: 'Man United' (according to me dad, this is) 'Man United couldn't even of *played* any home matches after the War, never mind *won* any, if Man City hadn't out of the goodness of their hearts very kindly let them play at Maine Road when City was playing away!'

So, I had only went and commented, sarky-like: 'Oh, and it is news to me too, dad, that bomb damage caused at Old Trafford by the Luftwaffe during the Blitz might maybe count as goals against with the English FA.'

So, he had come at it like he usually done, like a dog after a rabbit; and on the morning of me lucky day he starts in on us again. He leans back in his chair like he always done, making the back of it creak like Hornblower's ship out in mid-Atlantic, twists hisself round, and bawls through the open door into the scullery, spitting Hovis crumbs like speech marks on a/c of this half a slice of toast he's still chewing at the time.

'There's a nutter in here, talkin' to hisself.'

So I was up and out then, up and out of there before me mam can chip in with *her* four-pennorth (one of Roy Gilchrist's beamers at least, using the pantry in the run-up). Yeah, I was up and out of there, and out of the house, and before I known where I was, I was across the street and stood at Shirlee's door – like as if I done what I wanted when I got me mad up. And even then I very nearly turned on me heels and went back home again till I thought how daft I'd look with all the kids playing out and the milkman collecting his money door to door and the Corona mineral lorry doing its rounds and Mrs Parbold, next door but one to the Jamesons, scrubbing her front door step and window-sill with a donkey-stone. So I brung me hand up out of me trouser pocket and knocked three times at Shirlee's door – dot-dash-dot – soft-like.

There was no answer at first, and I was glad in a way. But I'd just sort of half-turned to go back home again when I heard these muffled footsteps coming down their lobby and the front door swung open and I seen Shirlee stood there in her fluffy pink slippers and her dressing gown with this scent of Worcester apples all around her. And then, oh, she smiles at us – not the blinder, but nice, you know, but with a sort of a question behind it, like, as if to say: ‘What do you want?’ I mean, it wasn’t a sneery sort of a smile. No, not what I really and truly deserved, like: ‘Well, what do *you* want, stood there like the right gormless ha’porth that you are?’

‘Now’s me-*chance*-me-*chance*-me-*chance*-me-*chance*-me-*chance*,’ went the runaway train of me heart. ‘Me-lucky-*day*-lucky-*day*-lucky-*day*-lucky-*day*-lucky-*day*!’ Then me lips come into play, but dead slow, and, about ten years later, me mouth too. ‘Is . . . er . . . ’s Huge in?’

Shirlee looks, like, a bit took aback.

Hey, maybe it *had* took ten years to get them words out. Maybe it had took twenny – and I had just that minute woke up from a deep sleep like Rip Van Winkle, and Shirlee just didn’t recognise us no more on a/c of I looked different from what I normally done, with scruffy tangled hair and raggedy clothes and this great long straggly beard. (Oh, fun-*nee,* no that is *not* how I normally look! *Looked*, rather: show you a photo in a minute to prove it!)

‘Eugene’s away,’ Shirlee says at last. ‘He took mum and dad. Thought he told you?’

‘Oh yeah,’ I said. ‘He did do. Sorry, I forgot.’

‘You got a minute?’

‘What?’

‘You got a minute?’ Shirlee says again.

‘Why?’

She takes this, like, little electrical screwdriver out of her dressing gown pocket. ‘The kettle’s gone funny. You wouldn’t have a look at it, would you?

‘Sure,’ I said, and followed her in. ‘Where’s the fuse box?’

‘Cubby-hole under the stairs.’ She points to this little doorway at the bottom end of the lobby and closes the front door. She starts messing about with her hair then, going: ‘Oh, I must look a right mess!’ It sounds almost as if she thinks this maybe has summat to do with why the kettle’s gone kaput.

Hey, I’ve pulled the cubby-hole door open, kicked this sausage dog draught-excluder thing out of the way, flicked the light on in there, and I’m stood just inside the cubby-hole, sort of half-in and half-out with the little electrical screwdriver she’s give us in me hand and the scent of Worcester apples in me nostrils – and this scent of Worcester apples wafts just this teeny bit stronger as Shirlee goes past us and through to the living-room and across to this big gilt bevel-edged mirror hanging widthways on the chimney breast. Ah, she looks no sort of a mess at all, but pretty as a picture as she puts her hands up to her hair again and starts to fix it in front of the mirror, sort of frowning a bit, and with her head tilted slightly forward like you never could of drawn it if you tried, which makes me heart go – bump! – just the once, exspecially when the sleeves of her dressing gown come sliding right the way back from her wrists and over her elbows to just short of her shoulders. Oh, real pale, her arms is and sort of downy too where they catch the light from the morning sun through the sash window overlooking their back yard.

'Fuse wire in here, too?' I said, diving into the cubby hole dead business-like at this point because all of a sudden Shirlee's stopped what she's doing and, for one split second, I seen her look straight at us in the mirror. So I known she couldn't help but notice I'd been stood there gawping like a good un. ('Still, a good un's better than a bad un any day of the week,' as me Grandma Alma would sometimes say to cheer us up if I was down in the dumps maybe.)

'Found it,' I said, meaning the fuse wire. 'Maybe let's have a look at the plug first, eh?'

I went out into the lobby again and through the living-room to the kitchen and unscrewed the plug on the kettle and Shirlee follows us in. All it was was the red wire had worked itself loose.

'Something always happens when they go away,' says Shirlee. 'It was the washer last time. No, the immersion. The washer was the time before.'

'Murphy's Law.'

'What?'

'Murphy's Law,' I said. 'If anything can go wrong, it will go wrong.'

'Ooh, I know the feeling, don't I just?' She's smiling again, nothing brilliant, not the blinder, just comfy.

'When're they back then?' I asked her, re-tightening the plug.

'Sunday night. Monday dinner maybe. Why?'

'Give it a try now,' I said.

'Why?'

'You won't know if it works otherwise.'

She come across and got the kettle and took it to the sink and half-filled it with water and brung it back and plugged it in, reaching past us to do so, and I caught a hint of this different scent then, like fresh baked bread, but oh-so faint.

'No. Why'd you ask when they're back?'

'Just askin',' I said.

'Yeah,' she says, and when the kettle begun to show signs of life: 'Fancy a cuppa?'

'Sure, why not?' I was gonna say when me mouth says: 'Nah, got things to do.'

So, there I was, stood outside Shirlee's house once more with the door slammed shut behind us – out on the street again, with the kids playing out and the milkman and the Corona lorry gone on their way and Mrs Parbold gone back in with her scrubbing brush and donkey-stone for another week, and needing a good kicking up the backside. No, not Mrs Parbold (I'd like to see the man who'd try); me, I'm talking about. I mean, how daft can you get? There I am on me exspecially lucky day, like that Fleet Street gippo said, and I'd had this perfect opportunity, being, like, a knight errand in Shirlee's house, with Huge away and her mam and dad away and Shirlee all on her own for the weekend, and I'd only gone and botched it up because me mouth wouldn't work. I don't mind telling you I felt like banging me head against Mrs Parbold's flipping donkey-stoned window sill. Not that I done that, of course. But here's what I done instead. I went back home and locked meself in the bathroom and settled for two of the esses: the shave and shampoo. And I dried meself off and got dressed up in me best clobber.

Look, here's that photo I was saying about. Yours truly in the clothes he stood up in on the afternoon of his lucky day. It wasn't took that afternoon. I mean, I've got the same clothes on is what I mean, but Byron took this snap with that Kodak Brownie of his up near the running track on the top fields in Boggart Hole Clough one day – Whit Sunday, that year, I think it was, when it was really sunny. (I'll scruffy-tangled-hair-and-raggedy-clothes you!) Yeah, that's me, there: 19 years of age and never been kissed. Well, not by Shirlee anyway, and that's what counted as far as I was concerned. See, that there's that new suit I had, the midnight blue one from Walter Peart's. And I've got one of them stiff collars on too – see? Them ones you needed collar studs with that you had to get them cleaned at the Chinese laundry down on Conran Street across from Burgess Street School. Hey, and there's that knitted tie I used to have, bit of a lighter blue than midnight, though not royal, that I used to tug dead hard at after I'd tied it so's I got this dinky little knot. See it? . . . Yeah, hardly see it, can you? And me black socks you can't see at all due to me trouser legs are hiding them. (Always worn black socks because they went with anything I worn.) Then there's them Chelsea boots I had . . . You betcha, that shiny you could see your face in them. Hey, and look here – *dah, dah-h-h* – me fully-fledged Beatle haircut. (Me lugholes never seen the light of day for twenny years or more.) Gone a bit to seed nowadays, the hair, of course. But anyway, that's *mwa mem* (as Shirlee used to say, acting daft, pretending she was French), that's *mwa mem* when I went out of our house on the afternoon of me lucky day. Yeah, that's the lad that combed his hair three hundred thousand million billion times before he went out, shone his shoes till they sparkled, straightened his tie with this dead dinky little knot in it, went out of the house, and walked down the street in his Walter Peart suit, smart as a whip, thinking he'd maybe catch the bus down to town and mooch about for a bit and do a bit of shopping, and maybe drown his sorrows if he felt like.

Now, down at the end of our street there was these roadworks that day where three fellers that was contractors for the Lecky was hard at it, digging this trench and laying cable in it; and, being in the same line of business meself, I couldn't help but watch them with a professional eye as I walked past. And guess what. Them Lecky fellers worked ten times as hard as our gang ever done. Even me!

See, the Lecky trench wasn't nowhere as deep or as wide as the ones we dug, but it was miles longer. It started up near the Halfway House at the corner of Cheetham Hill Road, and come all the way down Delaunays Road past Crumpsall Hospital gates and past Connolly's Cables and the ICI in Blackley Village. Then it done a right turn at Ye Golden Lion and then a left, and come all the way up the hill to the end of our street. Yeah, it was at least a mile long, the Lecky trench – and they hadn't finished yet. Tommy Senior, the landlord of the Alliance, said they was going all the way down to town with it – four more miles down Rochdale Road to town! Hey, and you know how our gang sometimes done a road crossing where you've got just stone and gravel to deal with? Well, crossings pure and simple is what them Lecky fellers was doing all day long. Because the Lecky trench was *all* in the road, every last bit of it. Yeah, and them three fellers working for the Lecky was only going to have to stone-and-gravel it all the way down Rochdale Road to town.

Mind you, they wasn't working as fast as our gang sometimes done. Yeah, there is that. They couldn't of done, seeing how hard the going was and how far they had to go. See, what them Lecky fellers was doing was never ending, with none of them short spurts of fast digging like our gang sometimes done where someone would give you a turn after a bit, and when you'd finished you could maybe sit down and have a rest. No, them three Lecky fellers was at it non-stop, but slower, like I say – like as if they was going:

'Sh-sh-sh-ir-ir-ir-lee-ee-ee, Sh-sh-sh-ir-ir-ir-lee-ee-ee,

Only all day long.

They'd got this transistor radio with them and there was music blaring out of it, real tinny, but enough to give them a sort of a rhythm to graft to. Maybe a slowish rythmn. Because a slowish rythmn was what best suited their type of work. Like, for instance, suppose it was 'The Song of the Vulgar Boatmen' on the tranny, say. Well, okay, that'd do just fine, and thank you very much, Mr Classical DJ because this is exactly the sort of a rhythm the Lecky fellers was grafting to. But, even if the tune was summat a bit more lively, like, maybe 'The Bum of the Flightle Bee' – well, like it or lump it, the rhythm they'd graft to would *still* be the 'Vulgar Boatmen'. ('Hey, an' here's me banjo if you *don't* like it, pal. Let's see *you* bossa-nova it through stone and gravel four miles down Rochdale Road to town!') But, of course, I mention these classical numbers only by way of example. Because them three Lecky fellers was in no danger of being serenaded by Sir John Buy-Me-Brolly and the Manchester Alley Orchestra. Well, not unless they was ambushed by them when they finally dug their way into Peter Street and was dragged kicking and screaming into the Free Trade Hall and made to have it.

'Make a refreshing change, that,' says Byron Marlfield, slinging his first arrow and getting double top on the Manchester board in the vault when I mentioned this to him in the Alliance one night. 'Seeing how Manchester people were once dragged kicking and screaming from that exact same spot.'

'Eh?'

'Pee to loo, 18.19,' says Byron, talking, like, gibberish, as far as I could make out, and bagging double ten. (We had sunk a fair few, it should be said, though I couldn't imagine for the life of me why he'd want to log the last time he splashed his boots.)

'What?'

'Horror to hunt,' says Byron, slinging his third arrow and getting sweet FA for his trouble.

I said I known nowt about it, me, though I did say one dog to one fox might be just that bit fairer.

Be that as it may though, the reason why them Lecky fellers wasn't never gonna be serenaded by the Manchester Alley orchestra – as I was saying before Byron Marlfield interrupted us – was because the tranny wasn't tuned in to the BBC Third Programme, but to Radio Caroline out on the high seas (Byron: 'the high C's'). So what them three Lecky fellers was listening to was pop music, pure and simple. That is, they was listening to pop music, pure and simple, whenever the flipping yattering DJ would shut his flipping yattering gob and let them listen to pop music, pure and simple. Like he shut his flipping yattering gob for about two seconds flat when I walked past the Lecky trench that afternoon and seen they was grafting in time to 'Keep Your Hands

Off My Baby' by Little Eva, this being a record on the London label that I'd shelled out six bob for at Mrs Wykes' record shop a couple of months back. Which is how I come to be singing this exact same song under me breath as I walked past the Lecky trench that day, though the words I was singing wasn't exactly the same Goffin/King lyrics that Little Eva done.

'Sh . . . ir-ir-ir . . . lee,' I was going. 'Sh . . . ir-ir-ir-ir-ir . . . lee . . .' – when Shirlee herself pipes up:

'Ooh, and there's me thinking you hadn't seen me for a moment.'

Yeah, *Shirlee pipes up*!

Because, all of a sudden, she's right there beside us: Shirlee Jameson, my Shirlee. And guess what. It was exactly like Shirlee said it was. Because I *hadn't* seen her. Well, not until she spoke. Because as per usual, where Shirlee was concerned, I'd been a million miles away, singing her name to meself like I'd already sung it three hundred thousand million billion times that summer.

'Yeah, seen you soon's you come round the corner,' I said.

We was stood right at the top of the brow by now, a few yards past the Lecky trench next to this opening in the fence where a little path drops down through the trees to this bus shelter by the gates of Boggart Hole Clough at the foot of a hill that the A to Z lists as Rochdale Road, the A664, but local people call Valentine Brow.

'You going for the bus?' says Shirlee.

'Yeah, I'm goin' to town.'

'Mm, me too.'

But as we turned on to the little path and made to go down it, I heard the most ear-splitting wolf whistle I've ever heard in the hole of me life. It come from one of the three fellers in the Lecky trench and was followed by a voice, rough as a bear's botty that echoed through the plantation, tree to tree.

'Ah, will yez get a look a' that now, Kevin?'

'Yoo-oo-oo-oo-oo-oo-oo-hoo-oo-oo-oo!' shrills this Kevin by way of reply.

The Whistler give us another blast – even shriller.

Ah, me heart begun to rattle like a steam hammer, twenny to the dozen: Kin-*Paddies*-kin-*Paddies*-kin-*Paddies*-kin-*Paddies*-kin-*Pa*.

I was stood stock still now, glancing round at them, eyes narrowing, and just blazing inside. I was that mad I nearly blown me top there and then.

KER-BLANG!

'Come on,' says Shirlee when she seen I was mad, and she links her arm in mine, giving us this fussy forwards sort of a tug. 'Just ignore them.'

Ah, what sound advice from them sweet lips! Exspecially since Shirlee in her nice creamy summer dress is linking her arm in mine now, and we is together at long last, sort of cosy and perfumed and neat and combed and clean – and just a few steps removed from the safety of the bus shelter at the foot of Valentine Brow. (Oh, and, Shirlee, my sweet, isn't that a bright blue and cream Daimler-engined No. 17 Rochdale bus I see there, parked up in neutral while the driver goes to clip his timesheet at the Tram Office?) And it was considerate advice too, seeing I am just a seven stone weakling and them Lecky fellers never needed no help from Charles Atlas and, besides, is team-handed and ready for action in their work clothes' and not trussed up in a smart midnight blue Italian suit that isn't even paid for yet. But summat just snapped inside us then:

CR-ICK-ICK-*ACK*!

Yeah, something just sort of snapped.

It was, like, as if Gipsy Petulant and all them *Daily Mess* reporters had got this special coach laid on from Fleet Street, London, and was sat up in the Manchester poplar trees in the plantation on either side of the little path, because there wasn't nowt else happening in England, Ireland, Scotland, or Wales, or anywhere else in the world during the Silly Season. But up in the branches of them poplar trees they could at least get a grandstand view of me botching up me lucky day, and laugh their flipping Fleet Street heads off because me mouth wouldn't work and I was scared of me own shadow maybe. Besides, it was a welcome change from brave dogs and fluffy little cats that was stuck up trees, and the Prime Minister's wife's titfer, and Her Majesty's domestic arrangements, and titchy flipping volcanoes that wasn't never gonna devastate nobody unless you was very, very lucky indeed.

'You wait here, Shirlee!' I told her.

Oh, I spoke her name three hundred thousand million billion times more rougher than I'd sung it all summer – three hundred thousand million billion times more rougher than I ever wanted to or should of. Pulled away from her too. Let me little legs take us back to the Lecky trench at the, hey, left-*right*, left-*right*, left-*right* quick march, where they stopped – TEN-*SHUN* – just short of this feller, Kevin, what's leant on his banjo now, having a quiet drag on the fag end of a Sweet Afton cigarette. And me throat racked up a full barrel-load of phlegm that I gozzed like a goalie in the space between his boots.

'Hey, Mick!' I said to this Kevin. 'You the ganger, Mick?' I said.

'I am not,' says Kevin, cool as they come. And he calls over his shoulder to this feller that's stood in the trench between him and The Whistler.

'Ah, now, Pat-Jo, darlin', dare's a feller here dat's after askin' f'yer.'

And out of the trench climbs this griller with a griller's chest and a griller's legs and a griller's arms and knuckles.

Agh! I nearly died. And Gipsy Petulant fell off her perch, she was laughing that much, and them *Daily Mess* reporters begun clicking away like mad on them cameras they'd brung, seeing how this was a very silly Silly Season indeed, because, now me mouth was working, it just wouldn't stop.

'You the ganger?' it said again.

'Oi em,' grunts The Griller.

'Right-ho, Shay-mus,' says me mouth. 'Yer can tell this cowboy to shut 'is kin cake-'ole – an' as for 'im – kin bast . . .'

I glared round his shoulder at The Whistler, doing me level best to rack up enough phlegm to gozz again. But me mouth had give up on us now, and me throat gone dry as a bone.

'Oh,' sung The Whistler above this great burst of static from the tranny. 'Will ye not give dat one a puck in de mouth?'

Then this cannon ball shot in from the sun and hit me full in the mug, and the sun shattered like a greenhouse roof and went out.

When I come to there was blood in me mouth from a gap in me teeth where there hadn't been, and I was sat in the mud in me good suit that wasn't even paid for yet, with me hands caked in the stuff. Me flipping head – me head was swimming, like I didn't even know what day it was. I tried standing up, but I fell back down again, and got muddier still. So I leant back on me elbows, taking me own good time about it now. And looking round then, as much as I could look round, I seen there was just this one fleck of blood high up on Shirlee's cheek near her ear.

'I'm sorry,' I was trying to tell her when what come out was: 'Shir . . . lee . . .'

'Jaze, Mary-Ann, Joe's!' goes The Whistler. 'De feller's babblin' like a bairn!'

Oh, dearie, dearie me! What Shirlee shouted at The Whistler then just don't bear repeating. Though me she comes back to, gifting one glimpse of the blinder, and starts dabbing at me stupid ugly mug with this hanky from me breast pocket and talking real quiet in a whisper almost. Like, as if me and her are the only ones on the Old Road, Blackley, on this Saturday afternoon in August, 1963, and we're throwing a private party that no one else is even invited to.

'It's all right,' says Shirlee, and some other stuff I can't remember now. 'It's all right,' says Shirlee. 'You'll be fine, you'll see.'

'Shir . . . lee,' was all I could say by way of reply. Then like a right boring get, I said it again.'

'For Goth sake, shut de feller up,' groans this Kevin, and slings his banjo the full width of the Old Road so's it give a loud clang against this garden wall and gate and brung this nosey old biddy to the window of her downstairs front room from behind her curtains that had been twitching for a bit.

And it was right then I heard that song I was saying about, coming out of the tranny in the Lecky trench. A Beatles' B-side it was: 'Thank You, Girl', that you probably heard way back in the Year Dot. And if you never heard it, well, tough. Because you can't borry it off of me seeing it's on Parlophone, like all of theirs. Except for what's on Apple, and one that's on Polydor, I think.

See, that's how it is when you like a song. You can remember every little thing about the first time you heard it except for odd bits and pieces that slip your mind till you think on. Like, for instance, it was me that was coughing blood, wasn't it? Not that McCarthy feller like I said it was. Hey, and another thing too – it wasn't consummation.

3

Look, that's the blinder, there, see. Well, it is *almost*, though not quite. Because she'll of been a bit mithered, Shirlee, with me catching her like that, coming out of the side door of Kendals with her bags and her brolly and her gloves in her hand now the rain had stopped at long last, and it had gone a bit warmer, out, since she told us she'd catch up with us later. See, she wouldn't have been expecting to see us outside Kendals in the first place, but over the way in Parsonage Gardens where I'd been when she'd left us to do her bit of shopping, and where I told her I'd be if she wanted us. Still, it's a nice photo, I think. Well, I'm fond of it anyway, exspecially with it being the first photo I took of Shirlee – and the first one I took with that Kodak Brownie camera I bought at Dixons that same afternoon on what I'd managed to sort the flash out a lot easier than I thought I'd of done – which is why I wasn't still sat on that bench in Parsonage Gardens, having a drag, like I told her I'd be, but outside Kendals instead, flashing away like a good un. (Hey, now, none of that *Carry On* stuff if you don't mind, please! I'm trying to be serious here.)

But, it's a good photo, isn't it? Okay, okay-y, so it's *not* the blinder, not really. But it *nearly* is; and everything else about it is just about perfect, I think. I mean, can you see there, how her coat and scarf have got this sort of a little swerve to them, so you can easy tell she's walking towards us? And her hair has too, hasn't it? Got this, like, this little bit of a swerve to it, and she's got her left hand, there, holding on to her Kendals bag and her brolly and her gloves that she don't need now the rain's stopped. And with her right hand having just let go of that big heavy glass shop door they have there, well, it's sort of swinging forward, her right hand, and – well, I don't know much about these things, but I think that gives it a sort of a balance, say – exspecially with the way she's turning towards us and walking towards us too. Hey, and can you see the way her head's sort of tilted there, like you couldn't never of drawn it if you tried? Oh, she always did take a good photo, Shirlee. Miles better than them Members-Of-The-Public-Is-Warned-This-Man-Is-Armed-And-Dangerous faces that I always seem to pull.

Shirlee never liked this photo though. No. And what it was was this, see: can you see there, where I've caught her with Kendals shop doorway right behind her? Well, can you see how she just happens to be stood right underneath where they've got the word "entrance" etched in the glass above the door in big capital letters. Look, there: "ENTRANCE"? See it? Can you see what I mean? Well, that's where I've sort of messed things up a bit, I suppose. Because with Shirlee being just this bit further forward towards us, well, you could say (and Shirlee certainly did), yeah, you could say it looks like the letter "A" in the word "ENTRANCE" is not etched in the glass above the shop door, but is perched almost exactly smack-bang centre on top of Shirlee's head.

'Things like that mean a lot to a tart,' is what Huge thinks one time me and him was looking through this batch of photos. (After our Suzanne's christening, this was, when everyone else had gone off home, and Shirlee and her mum and mine were in the kitchen washing up, and her dad had took Noreen Jessop and her lot down to Central Station.) 'Yeah, something like that happened to me one time, time I was working down in Teignmouth, had digs with me Auntie Vera. Remember? Time she took bad and I stayed down Torquay, well, St Marychurch actually. Got a job that hotel in Teignmouth, came home end of the season, back next year, same place, went back '65, Dee Jay-ing, but Paignton that trip. 'Flowers in the Rain', first record played on Radio One. 'Keep On Running', first record played on Dee-Jay U.E. Jay's Away-Day UK. Used it as a signature tune ever after. I'd follow it up with 'Hang On Sloopy', 'Twist and Shout', and 'La Bamba' – which'd give us five minutes for a fag, cuppa, and a bit of a breather because I'd've only just got back from servicing whatever tart it was I was hanging out of that particular week. Boss thought I was working me bollocks off, giving value for money, which I was in a way, I suppose. Ha, ha, ha, ha, ha, ha, ha, ha, ha, ha. Never dawned on the silly bugger them last three records are the same kin tune, well, practically. Same chords anyway – well, almost. Hey, but Mandy Teignmouth – had this tart down in Teignmouth, Mandy. Right little goer, she was. Hey, 'goer'? Did I say '*goer*'? Think they musta named that Indian holiday resort after her. Goa, you know, ha, ha, ha, ha, ha, ha, ha, ha, ha. Get it? Prob'ly needed Sanatogen, we kept it up much longer. Hey, ha, ha, ha, ha, ha, ha, ha, ha: kept it up much longer. Ha, ha, ha, ha, ha, ha, ha. Anyway, there we are, me and Mandy, on this, what's it called? Some beach down there. What's it called now? Ah, don't matter. This beach down there that's got these, like, orangey-coloured cliffs all around it, well, not *all* round it, of course, because the sea's splashing away there somewhere, I suppose. But it's got these, like, orangey-coloured cliffs on three sides of it, this beach. Watcombe, that's it. Watcombe Beach. And I take this snap of Miss Mandy Teignmouth on Watcombe Beach, get it developed – and she only goes stark raving bonkers. Starkers, I've seen her; raving bonkers, never. Stark raving bonkers, she went. Never seen owt like it. See, with these orangey-coloured cliffs and that in the background, it looks like she's got, like, long orangey extensions on the end of her natural long blonde hair. Extensions, that tart had seen some, I can tell you. Ha, ha, ha, ha, ha, ha. But not hair-do extensions – never needed none, length it was, and even if she had've done she wouldn't have gone for orangey-coloured ones, would she? Would she, now? Nah, not with long blonde hair, she wouldn't. No, wait a minute, hang about a bit. No, that was Bindi Babbacombe was the natural blonde: Mandy Teignmouth had, like, reddish hair. Them extensions would've suited Mandy Teignmouth just fine, might not've even noticed them. Yeah, it was Bindi Babbacombe went mad. Fact, she went that flipping mad she chucked us on the spot. Chucked us, she did, bitch! Girl *musta* been mad. Screw loose, I reckon. Never know with some of them. Hey, I was devastated, me. Don't think I wasn't, pal. Devastated, I was, heartbroke! Yeah! Yeah, must've took us till two o'cock (hey, Freudian slip there, boy, ha, ha, ha, ha, ha). Yeah, must've took us till two o'clock next morning before I made a complete recovery, by which time, ha, ha, ha, ha . . . Hey, you ever heard couple of places down Torbay called Brixham and Dawlish? Loads of tarts down there in the summer. Now, these two tarts . . . What's their names, now? Wendy? Wanda? . . . Dora? Dodie? . . . Ah, never mind, eh? Another time . . . Point I'm trying to make is this: you take a photo of a tart, see, and it's almost as if it gets some idea in its head that you're some sort of expert photographer or somethin'. Kin professional, like David Bailey or someone. Then if you goes and makes a mistake when you're just taking a snap of it, it thinks you've deliberately messed up. Otherwise how come its natural charm and Brigitte-Bardot-buggerin' beauty never shone through, like it fully expected it to – even if it was hanging rag-arsed off the end of a derrick in downtown Beirut at the time, kin demolition ball aimed at its stupid kin head, pin off a hand grenade in it's kin teeth, grenade itself, due to explode in two seconds flat got lodged down it's kin tights somehow. Yeah, how come you never made it look any better than you did, eh? And all the time you, you poor sod, you never pretended to be David Bailey or owt. Because if truth be told, you're just some cunt clickin' away with a Kodak that don't know a lens from a letter box. Kin tarts!'

All Shirlee said about it was this: 'Oh, it looks like I'm wearing a dunce's cap.' (Meaning this photo; meaning the letter "A" in "ENTRANCE".)

'More like a witch's hat,' I told her. (Ooh, was that a mistake!)

'That's just as bad.'

'No, it's not.'

'It *is*.'

'White witch. No it's not, Shirlee.' I picked the photo up then, pointing to where it says "ENTRANCE". 'You're not seein' it right. That's all.'

'Not seeing it right?

'Yeah. It says what you do to us.'

'Do to us?'

'Do to me.'

She still gives us a funny look though.

'Well, *read* it,' I said. 'Go on, read it.'

'*En*trance,' says Shirlee, and shrugs.

'Oh, that's what it says, is it, Miss-I-Finished-the-*Daily-Mess*-Crossword-on-Me-Tea-Break-Today-with-No-Help-from-Penny-Kirkham? That's all it says, is it?'

'Oh, of course: en-*trance*!' When the penny finally drops Shirlee begins waggling her fingers about, like she's putting the fluence on us like some TV magician, David Nixon or someone. 'You are feeling sleepy,' she tells us. 'You are feeling . . . very sleepy . . .'

Hey, I was too, funnily enough. I'd had a pretty busy day at work, and a week of busy days leading up to it. Still, this in no way prevented us from suggesting to Shirlee that she might want to entrance us a bit more and just a bit closer maybe. It was Christmastime after all, our second Christmas together, and the big gilt bevel-edged mirror in their living-room that held the two of us together was shining bright with the lights on the tree and the tinsel and the greetings cards and all the coloured decorations around the room. It was a touch too bright for my liking in view of the way I was hoping Shirlee might want to entrance us before her mum and dad come home to put our magic on hold, with a pot of PG tips and a couple of Jacob's Club biscuits and the smell of Champion thick sliced bread toasting under the high-level grill and news of Mrs Parbold winning a tenner on the bingo at Barnes Green Club.

We'd been going out together just over twelve months or so the day I took this snap of Shirlee outside Kendals. And if someone was to tell us I could have me choice of all the times we spent together down the years, me and her, I honestly think I'd choose that Saturday afternoon we was in town when the rain changed to sunlight with a touch of winter weather in its tail and we done nothing more exciting than a bit of personal shopping, me for the camera and Shirlee for that nice camel coat of hers she's got in the Kendals bag in the photograph – and a bit of window shopping too for a third-finger-left-hand nice feminine a-cute-rement, though not too serious in that respect, at least not yet. Because the jewellers' we looked at that afternoon was on King Street and off it, and the prices was a bit out of our range. Did I say: a *bit*? Heck! We grabbed a pie and a pint in the Rising Sun and didn't have enough left over for the grill we'd planned on having for our tea in the Berni Inn they used to have up on Peter Street near the Theatre Royal. We ended up buying a couple of hot dogs off a street vendor instead – and with me sloshing ketchup down the front of me coat like a fool, and having to leave it in for dry-cleaning, and going back home on the top deck of the 60 bus in just me suit jacket, smoking a Senior Service cigarette for afters and hugging Shirlee every now and then to keep warm.

Must seem barmy, that: picking that Saturday afternoon as summat special, exspecially when you consider there was umpteen special occasions me and Shirlee shared in the years we spent together – in them ten years, nine weeks, two days, two and a half hours we spent together. But there's some of them special occasions I wouldn't want to pick as special anyway. Like our wedding reception, where me cousin Harry that played for Newton Heath Loco set us back a few quid when he demo-ed this terrific backwards overhead kick he was famous for that lofted the mirrored ball across the dance floor before it was caught on the volley by Johnno, this bloke on Shirlee's side: Shirlee's side of the family, I mean. I mean, we wasn't playing 5-a-side with Shirlee in goal, you know! And Johnno what turned out for Stalybridge Celtic only sent the ball over the bar, that is, the drinks bar, demolishing the top shelf (apart from a bottle of Rebel Yell) and the stewardess's bee-hive hair-do . . . Or, like when little legs was born, our Suzanne, and we couldn't get a taxi for love nor money because there'd only been a torrential downpour that had caused other waters to break as well as the ones we was concerned about, said waters being the River Irk that had burst its banks in Blackley Village. Which meant we had to access Crumpsall Hospital via three Selnec bus routes that took us on a grand tour of Moston, Broadhurst, Lightbowne, New Moston, Higher Blackley, Heaton Park, and the top end of Crumpsall. And even then we had to leg it to the Maternity Suite from the bus stop at the top of Delaunays Road . . . And like our Suzanne's christening where the scuffle broke out over the cream doughnut, and Charlie Forrester, the other gatecrasher, the doughnut nicker's pal (being rat-legged after supping Shirlee's dad's Party Seven all to hisself) threw up in the ratter twee . . . Or, like, when we was on honeymoon in Torbay, and it was our first week together, you know, though halfway through that week it turned out to be, for Shirlee, also a time like she had, oh, maybe a dozen times a year, thank you very much. Still, not to worry, eh, because some drunk set the fire alarm off at half past two in the morning, and we spent another forty uneventful minutes or so in the car park of the Stalag Dunroamin Guest House with fifty of our fellow holidaymakers that was also not having a very good time in their pyjamas, or out of them. . . . Or when we got our own back on Frau Schweinhundt, the Gestapo boss, that run the place. That is, when we come back in good spirits from a night out at a pub called the Hunter's Moon on the last night of our stay, and sneaking through the kitchen on our way upstairs so as to avoid Prancer and Dancer, Frau Schweinhundt's Doberman pinschers, we helped ourselves to one bite each out of half a dozen cooked chickens hanging there in readiness for the next day's dinner . . . and when I nipped out a bit earlier than usual next morning for a *Daily Mess*, and nicked the gnome with the fishing rod off of the front patio and slung it on the roof of one of the carriages of the funicular railway serving Oddicombe Beach.

I mean, all them times was good times when you look back, I suppose. But that afternoon we was in Manchester, shopping, was – well, just a nice private special celebration sort of a day, whereas with most of the other special occasions in your life, quite apart from the things that *can* go wrong and *do* go wrong, well, I've very often found those official special celebration days get gummed up with all sorts of people that you'd rather not to be in the company of anyway, not if you was given any say in the matter. Or, even if you like them people at the time, there is very often one or two of them that you never see again in the hole of your life – Penny Kirkham, Shirlee's maid of honour, coming to mind in that respect. I slagged her off for years, Penny. Yeah, big mates, they was, her and Shirlee, real big mates from work, but the last we seen of Penny was on our wedding day. Socially, I mean – me and Shirlee as a couple – though I did see Penny meself a bit more recently than that, but me on me todd. I mean, not with Shirlee. And that was (what?) seven years in the future, counting forward from the day we got wed. So what the hell happened to Penny Kirkham for all the years in between is what I wanna know. Fell off the planet, or summat?

Still, maybe I'd better say exactly what it was we was celebrating in private in town on that Saturday afternoon in 1964.

Dah-dahhhh! Being free, that's what. Yeah, just being free. Because all of a sudden, seeing I was no longer working for the Gas Board, I was free from having to work every Saturday God sent. Simple as that, it was. We was celebrating being able to be in town together on a Saturday afternoon and just please our flipping selves. Because it was one of the first Saturdays I'd been off in yonks, having just been took on at Rapishaw Gap. Okay, Shirlee had had to work the Saturday morning, which was unusual for her (so maybe that made it different too). But I'd arranged to meet her after work outside the Burton's branch on the corner of Great Ancoats Street and Oldham Street, up near New Cross.

We was both at Rapishaw Gap by this time, her in the office and me on the vans. That cold weather the winter before had put us right off the Gas Board, nesh sod that I am. (Please note, there is no way I am a winter person, and if you ever spot us holidaying in apres-ski, please telephone the dog-catcher, for I will have gone mad and am likely to bite.) See, the trouble is the Gas Board is at its busiest in the winter. On the one hand they're selling gas like mad for heating and cooking, and on the other, they've got three hundred thousand million billion blokes like me, running around trying to fix three hundred thousand million billion and *one* gas leaks that spring up all over Manchester.

So, what's wrong with that, you may ask. You've in full-time work; you've got all the overtime you'll ever need (seven days a week if you want it); the money's good – you can live like a king if you want to. What's wrong with that, eh? Well, nowt, I don't suppose – and there's nowt wrong with the Gas Board neither, or with working outside just as long as it's a nice summer's day. But an hibernophobe like me (now, that's Byron for you: I think he made it up) an hibernophobe like me can't hack it – working outside in the cold all day long; good for nothing but kipping in front of the fire of a night after work. Till somebody wakes you up to tell you it's time for bed. Yeah, what use is that to a girl like Shirlee that wants to be took out of a night after work and you the bloke that wants to take her? Which I did do (take her out), and oftener too (soon's I got the job at Rapishaw Gap).

Got it with Shirlee's help, of course. Because Shirlee was already working there. She had been since leaving school, except for a couple of weeks at some solicitor's in town. Yeah, Shirlee worked in the offices at Rapishaw Gap, and she got us this job on the vans – driver's mate with the prospect of a driving job in the future if I suited Rapishaw Gap and Rapishaw Gap suited me. It did do too, suited us right down to the ground, and I suited Rapishaw Gap too. Well, till they had to let us go after . . . Well, till they had to let us go.

Rapishaw Gap runs vans that carry catalogue goods out of a warehouse on every street in Manchester. (Or, did do.) And I bet *that* had you going, didn't it? Bet you thought, like:

'Wow! what sort of an outfit is it that has a warehouse on *every* street in Manchester?'

A flipping big one, mate, I'll tell you that for nowt. Not that Rapishaw Gap was that big, not as yet it wasn't, though it was big enough. But that every street in Manchester stuff is just an old Manpudlian joke about a street called Every Street down near Pin Mill Brow where Rapishaw Gap's warehouse was, and its transport depot too.

But like I say, Rapishaw Gap runs deliveries all over the north of England as far as Tyneside and over into Scotland. You've maybe clocked them vans of theirs on the road – bright yellow two-tonners with a sign on the side saying:

ANOTHER GIFT WRAP
FROM RAPISHAW GAP

They had another depot in Wales near Wrexham that seen to deliveries down as far as Bristol and across to East Anglia, and another in Wiltshire that covered everything south of the Bristol Channel and across to the South-East. Oh, yeah, Rapishaw Gap suited us fine. In any case, Shirlee said her mum always had said I'd be took away in a yellow van one day, and that day had finally arrived so I might as well make the best of it (ha, ha).

Course, the nice thing about working at Rapishaw Gap for me (apart from the heater in the van, and the money, of course, which was okay, I suppose, though not as good as the Gas) was the hours was more regular – and it wasn't seven days a week neither. Oh, you could get stranded out on the road at times due to breakdowns or the weather. But those times was very few and far between because they kept their vans in good nick, Rapishaw Gap. Fact, in all the time I worked there, I reckon I was only ever stuck out on the road and couldn't get home till next day maybe four or five times in all – no, six if you count that snarl up on the A59 near Harrogate one Easter, which meant I didn't get home till half past one in the morning, which *is* next day, strictly speaking, I suppose.

'You get a problem like that, or a breakdown can't be fixed, find a B and B overnight and bill it,' Eric Alport, the transport manager told us.

Rapishaw Gap wasn't known for its generosity ('What business is,' said me dad, 'except to its board of directors?') But this was a concession Eric had stuck his neck out for.

'He trust us?' I asked Biffo that drove the van I was on.

'Who? Eric? Far as he can throw you, pal,' says Biffo, swinging out on to Ashton New Road and clogging it through Bradford towards Grey Mare Lane. 'Nah, he just don't want you shaggin' the van by drivin' back hell for leather after some delay in Dundee, or smashin' it up even, just 'cause you're on a promise with the missis. Cheaper in the long run, you stop over, come back next day. Besides –' Biffo lit one of them Capstan Full Strength of his with this table lighter he kept in the van, like flipping Aladdin's lamp or summat. He inhaled and exhaled, coughed and coughed again. 'Besides, you give us a bell, I can always nip round your place, give the missus a seein' to as a favour.'

But, like I say, you hardly ever got stuck like that. Mostly, you worked 9 till 5, nice and steady, with Saturday and Sunday off, except now and then when things picked up according to season. Which was the reason Shirlee had had to work on the morning of the day I met her in town to go shopping. Things was picking up for Christmas at her end, though there wasn't nowt ready for delivery as yet, which is why I'd had the Saturday off but Shirlee hadn't.

Oh, when you have to work Saturday week in, week out it gets that way that all you can think about is having it off. (Oh, now don't start that *Carry On* stuff again. You know very well what I mean, so don't pretend you don't.) Or, it might be Sunday you always have to work, or it could be any other day of the week. But let's suppose it's a Saturday like it was with me, well, it got that way I would of killed to have Saturday off. Well, not killed, but you know what I mean.

'Funny thing is too,' I said to Line that time I done a few tracks on that black cab of his. 'When I had to work Saturday, I flippin' hated it, but now I don't have to work Saturday, I don't mind workin' it.'

'Know exactly what you mean,' says Line. 'I'm the same about Sundays. Used to open the shop of a Sunday, and nine times out of ten I'd have to drag meself into work. Now I've give over openin' to the public of a Sunday, you'll usually find us in the tyre bay of a Sunday. Till the pub's open anyway. Few repairs, puncture or two, new tyres. And I don't mind at all. What it is is this, kid: it's the havin' to that hurts, the kin havin' to. Mind you, if the havin' to or the not kin havin' to ever kin interferes with me enjoyment of the Sunday licensin' laws such as they are in this country, I'm like a bear with a sore head, believe you me.'

I did believe him, the gut on him. Even so I thought it best not to make no joke about Lines having sore heads same as bears

So there's us, me and Shirlee, on one of the very first Saturdays I didn't have to go into work of a Saturday, a little over twelve months or so after we first went out together, walking through Manchester city centre. Down Oldham Street to Piccadilly and along Market Street, where we done a bit of shopping, me for the camera, Shirlee for some bits and pieces in Marks and that. Then:

Across
Cross Street,
over
From the Korova,
Old Bank Street,
Flag-flanked street,
Takes us from there
To St Ann's Square.
(Hey, the boy's a poet
And he don't know it!)

But P.S: I cheated a bit. Because the Korova Milk Bar was not really called the Korova. That's just something Byron Marlfield used to call it, that milk bar that used to stand on Cross Street next to where the *Manchester Evening News* offices was once upon a time, near where you have, I mean, *had*, the Bodega at the time I'm talking about.

Come rain (okay – mostly, says Byron Marlfield), come shine (which is more often than visiting cricket teams like to pretend it is: Byron), Manchester will take you to its heart through St Ann's Square via a passageway beside the church. From here, King, John Dalton, Mulberry, Brazennose, Queen, and Lloyd are the names of six streets you'll cross; St Ann's, Dalton, Mulberry, St James's Square: passages, entries, and a dog-leg taking you, street to street, sheltered from the weather in the main till you come to the Rising Sun with its front door in one street and its back door in the next. Which was as far as me and Shirlee got that day, across the street from where there's a statue of Abraham Lincoln nowadays: 'a reminder of the Cotton Famine,' (Byron again!) 'when the city of Manchester declared a war of its own on the Confederacy of slave states'.

"*The vast progress which you have made in the short space of twenty months fills us with hope that every stain on your freedom will shortly be removed and that the erasure of that foul blot on civilisation and Christianity, chattel slavery, during your Presidency, will cause the name of Abraham Lincoln to be honoured and revered by posterity. We are certain that such a glorious consummation will cement Great Britain and the United States in close and enduring regards* [. . .]" Free Trade Hall Meeting, 31 December, 1862, Chairman: Abel Heywood.

Yeah, like Byron says, that's exactly what it says on one side of the Lincoln Memorial that stands today where me and Shirlee stood on that Saturday afternoon all them years ago. Abraham Lincoln's reply is written on the other side:

"*I know and deeply deplore the suffering which the working people of Manchester are called to endure in this crisis, an instance of sublime Christian heroism which has not been surpassed in any age or any country* [. . .]"

Replete now (hey, get that – something else Byron Marlfield says when he's had a good blow out, though he'll usually belch and fart right after saying it, and I hope you'll understand if I don't do that with a young lady present), replete now after a pie and a pint in the Rising Sun, we wandered across Deansgate to the Victoria on Hardman Street to sit amongt printers and TV technicians for an hour or so, watching the bar staff playing footsie with them electric beer pumps they had in there, dishing up Tetley's mild and Walker's bitter, with me and Shirlee playing that same game, but different. You can be pretty lonely in a crowd, but very private too, if you choose to be.

'WHY HAVE YE'S TOOK OLIVER CROMWELL FROM OUTSIDE EXCHANGE STATION?' bawled this feller with a Six Counties' accent. 'AND WHERE HAVE YE'S POT HAM?'

'I can assure you, my dear chap . . .' This bloke with a plummy voice was stood on an ammunition box with a Crombie overcoat and a small crowd gathered around him. 'My dear chap, I can assure you I have not, ah, taken your friend Oliver anywhere. And as for my, ah, potting ham . . .' Plummy Voice was using a PA system, so he didn't need to shout.

Someone near the front of the crowd chuckled, a fat lady with a blue rinse hurried away towards Blackfriars Street, and a couple with a baby in a Silver Cross pram made a bee-line for the main shopping centre on Market Street. A dozen or so – me and Shirlee amongst them – was all that was left.

'As for my potting ham . . .' Plummy Voice winked at Shirlee, or maybe at the feller behind us in a red and white bobble hat. 'As for my *potting ham*, my dear sir, I would point out to you if I may, that my grocery requirements are quite adequately catered for by Marks and Spencer, and in any case, I find their potted beef is more to my taste.'

A couple of folk chuckled. But most of us just shuffled our feet, raising little clouds of dust from the clinker underfoot on this bomb site on the corner of Deansgate and St Mary's Gate that they used to call Speakers' Corner, and where the British Airways and American Express offices stand today.

'That's tellin' him, Ferdinand,' said this feller near the back in a gargly sort of voice right back in his throat that made it sound like he was miles away, outside Lewis's department store at the top end of Market Street maybe, and no matter how loud he shouted, you'd only ever be able to hear a whisper on a/c of the distance.

The Six Counties heckler pulled a wine bottle from his overcoat pocket, tugged the cork out with his teeth, spat it out, lifted the bottle to his lips, took a good long swig – and then a longer one. There was no label on the bottle to speak of. You could hear the liquid swilling about inside it in an echoey bottom-of-the-well sort of a way.

'Lanry laundry bleach,' I told Shirlee. 'Your mum's got some in her wash house. Not a dipso, is she?'

Shirlee shushes us, pinching me arm, hard.

'WHY HAVE YE'S TOOK EXCHANGE STATION?' bawled the heckler, bottle in hand. He looked the spitting image of the old feller, front left in that L S Lowry painting, *A Procession, 1938* that me Grandma Alma had on her front room wall – only difference being Lowry's feller don't have a Lanry bottle in his hand. 'AND WHERE HAVE YE'S POT . . .?'

'My dear, dear chap,' said Plummy Voice in an, oh, so patient tone of voice, like an MP that's up for election, and don't mind waiting a week or two before he nails your hat on for you. 'My dear, dear *chap*, I have not tuh, ah, taken Exchange Station anywhere. What's more, I'll prove it to you. If the right honourable gentleman would do me the great kindness of looking yonder, ladies and gentlemen.' Plummy Voice pointed grandly over the heads of the crowd.

And everyone in that little crowd (hey, me and Shirlee too) turned to look where Plummy Voice pointed: past St Mary's Gate and Cateaton Street – every one of us straining to catch a glimpse of Exchange Station on the far bank of the River Irwell, which flowed under Blackfriars Street like molten lead the colour of night. That's all we got for our trouble too – a glimpse. When we looked back at Plummy Voice, me and Shirlee got a fit of the giggles and begun edging away.

'Lo, there it stands, sir,' Plummy Voice announced clear as the tannoy on Exchange Station itself. 'Behold, Exchange Station in all its glory. Not the eighth wonder of the world, it's true – that distinction, as I am reliably informed by no less a personage than Lord Rothschild himself, sir, that distinction, having been unanimously accorded to Compound Interest in the opinion of them, ah, those that know. So there you have it, sir. Compound Interest: the eighth wonder of the world, both ancient and modern. Though I am prepared to grant you this, sir: Exchange Station, Manchester, gateway to the metropolis, must run The Palace of Verse-high, Paris, France, a very close ninth indeed.'

The feller behind us in the red and white bobble hat begun a slow hand clap, and begun to sing:

'And did those feet in anc-i-e-nt times walk u-pon Exchange Sta-a-tion?'

'AH, BUT YE'S GUANO TAKE IT . . . ' The heckler come back, waving the Lanry bottle like a dagger. 'YE'S GUANO TAKE IT. LIKE YE TOOK THE TRAMS OFF US. DAMN-BLAST-AND-BUGGER-IT! LIKE YE'S TOOK EVERY DAMNED . . .'

'Matt Busby for prime minister!' shouted the gargler from Lewis's doorway at the far end of Market Street, which brung a raggedy cheer from the Man U supporter behind us.

'My dear, dear chap . . .'

'WHY HAVE YE'S TOOK . . .?'

(*Cheers*)

'My dear, dear chap . . .'

We left them to it then and tootled across the road to get a couple of hot dogs from this vendor, there – one with; one without, but loads of ketchup (mine). Which is when it happened. See, I'd just lifted me hot dog to me lips and was straining forward ready for that first bite when I seen this lorry stood at the lights. A two tonner, it was, like ours at Rapishaw Gap, but off-white in colour, not yellow. And there was this dirty big advert on the side of it that shown this, like, big corncrete building and loads of office blocks and that, all big and grey and and empty and sad-looking, and there was some jazzy-coloured lettering on it too that said:

POSTERS ADD COLOUR TO THE ENVIRONMENT

Well, I felt a bit choked when I seen that. Till I seen that someone had wrote "BOLLOCKS" in the dust underneath it. And I started laughing then – which is how I ended up sloshing tomato ketchup down the front of me coat like a fool. Because what I seen what someone had wrote in the dust underneath the lettering on the side of that lorry stood at the lights on St Mary's Gate that afternoon – well, it whizzed us right back to what me dad said when Eddie Bliss got killed earlier in the year. Further. Took us right back to when I first got to know Eddie Bliss at school.

4

I was in what they called Standard 4 at St Joey's in them days and Eddie Bliss was in the top class, Standard 8, out in the prefabs. So, what with the difference in our ages and that, you wouldn't rightly say me and Eddie was mates. We was more like acquaintances, I suppose, and even that's not the right word to say what me and Eddie was. See, Eddie Bliss was quite a bit older than us, and a bit of an hard case too, and I hadn't achieved me full potential yet, that is, seven-stone weakling, once removed. But I known Eddie Bliss and he known me. We wasn't what you'd call bosum pals or owt. But we was mates in a way, and here's how it all come about.

It was this Monday morning in February when it was chucking it down, and all the kids in our class come in wellies and Ozzy never come at all on a/c of he was poorly. And they must of been stuck for teachers with Ozzy being off. Because Old Hopalong, who had this club foot he got in WWII, escaping from Colditz with Huge's American marine uncle (Huge said), Old Hopalong, he couldn't never teach kids, but could only belt them when they was sent to his office. So after a lot of um-ing and ah-ing with Old Hopalong and Miss Tyrant (her that wouldn't let the Down's Syndrome kid go to the puppet show because she never brung her penny), kin basket Tyrant, and Old Hopalong stood in the doorway of our class with Miss Tyrant (her that stood Huge in the waste paper basket on his sixth birthday, saying in this screechy-teacher voice of hers: 'You can just stay there till playtime, Eugene Jameson because you is rubbish and that's exactly where you belong, like that stuck-up sister of yours that's in Miss Troup's class in the Girls' school now.' (Oh-ho, do not get me going on that subject, Miss kin twice-basket Tyrant), saying Ozzy was a lazy basket who wouldn't of caught noomonia if he hadn't been daft enough to ref that football match against Burgess Street in the pouring rain.

Then they split us up's what they done then and we all got sent to different classes. And me and Huge got sent to Unzo's out in the prefabs, which was great in a way because them prefabs had an iron stove in the corner that they'd let kids stoke up with coke if they behaved theirselves. But in another way it was rotten because

Unzo sat us next to Eddie Bliss and Huge got sat next to George Ireland (Judd-oh) who was cock o' the school, and meaner than all the teachers that ever learned us in the hole of me life.

Still, I never had no time to worry about Huge because I had enough worries of me own. Because Eddie Bliss was tough enough, and even though Judd-oh could of took him, he couldn't of took him easy. Nah, Judd-oh would of had his work cut out with Eddie and would of only won one of them Prick victories like Byron says they sometimes done in the olden days, where they maybe slugged it out for ages and got no outright winner. Summat else too: Eddie Bliss was captain of the school togger team, so even if Judd-oh had of took him, he wouldn't of been that popular with the rest of kids or with Ozzy that run the team, or with Old Hopalong hisself for that matter. And Old Hopalong could make your life hell if he wanted to. Like he done with Huge that time his mum told him to make sure and ask Old Hopalong about his gabardine raincoat that had went missing at the swimming gala at Harpurhey Baths. And Old Hopalong really put Huge through it for that, because that raincoat of his never did turn up.

Hey, Eddie Bliss! I once seen him, I once seen him kick the ball that flipping hard he only scored a goal from the half-way line. That's when we was playing Holy Tripeshop in the cup. Right in the top left hand corner of the net, it went. Made it look easy, he did. And all our kids that was stood on the touchline behind the nets, annoying the Holy Tripeshop goalie – all our kids jumped up and down and cheered like they done it theirselves. Oh, Eddie Bliss was tough all right. Ask any of them kids that went to St Joey's and they'd say the same. And if them kids that went to St Joey's said you was tough, then you really *was* tough. St Joey's was that tough you daren't let on you had a mother.

So, there I was on this Monday morning in February – dead titchy, with arms like giblets in tisher paper and knobbly knees peeping out of me hopsack short pants, sat next to Eddie Bliss, the well-known hard case and togger player, hoping he wouldn't even look at us too hard. I kept thinking to meself: Please don't let Eddie Bliss find out about me liberty bodice that me mam makes me wear as well as a vest, case I catch me death-of-a-cold and what I have to keep making excuses about so Ozzy won't take us to the baths of a Friday and them other kids find out. (Hey, even Huge would of laughed at us for that and I'd of had to kick his head in again.)

And there's Eddie Bliss sat next to us, sort of big and hairy. Almost a feller, he was. Even smelt like a feller – sweaty and damp (on a/c of the rain) and smoky too (on a/c of he'd been having a drag in the bogs before school begun). And he had this comic in his pocket, Eddie, one of them with the printed stories in and only one drawring to a page. Four of them, there was at one time: the *Hotspur*, the *Rover*, the *Adventure,* and the *Wizard* – all published by D. C. Thomson of Dundee for kids that was too grown up for the *Dandy* and *Beano*, but not quite ready for the *Daily Mess.*

I think it was the *Wizard* Eddie had in his pocket that morning, folded in four. Anyway, it was that one where they had this story about a runner called Wilson that worn, they was either jet black or very, very dirty long johns and a thermal vest; and this Wilson had been born about AD 1750 or summat, but was still running in track events all over the country. Yeah, and he looked like he was just a sprightly young feller, Wilson, and not two hundred years old or summat because Wilson had discovered the secret of eternal youth. That is – well, according to Wilson, that is – all you have to do to make sure you stay in peak condition for two hundred years-plus is to let every single muscle in your body relax completely in between every step you take. Which is why I like to have a good workout every chance I get with (what me dad called) me Egyptian gymnastics. That is, flat on me back, pushing up the zeds with me hands clasped behind me head. It's a lifestyle I share with Wilson, see, and we're nobbut lads, the pair of us. True, only Wilson remains in peak condition, though I'm peaky enough for what I do, which is as little as I can get away with doing, being Burke's Law/Gas Board.

Eddie had this packet of fags too, sort of half-in and half-out of his blazer pocket next to the *Adventure* – a packet of five Players Medium, like you could get in them days with a picture of a sailor's hairy mug on the front and a couple of boats, bobbing about out at sea, and the name of the sailor's ship, "HERO", slap-bang in the middle of his cap. Yeah, and it was almost as if Eddie was daring Unzo to say summat about them cigs, or maybe he wasn't; maybe it was an oversight on Eddie's part. Not that Unzo had clocked the fags, of course, because me and Eddie was sat right at the back of the class. Besides, Unzo had more important things on his mind.

Yeah, he was up there at the front, Unzo, sat on that tall chair of his, tilting it back on its two back legs like he always done, so he could lean back on the blackboard and get this white chalk line across his shoulders like he always had that made Unzo stink like the inside of an empty cupboard that no one had opened for years. And he was giving it out, Unzo, about how the British Isles would fit three hundred thousand million billion times into the Gulf of Carpenter that's out in Australia. Or summat. Though he never said who was gonna tow them all the way out there just to play jigsaws with. And, I seen Eddie Bliss wasn't taking a blind bit of notice of Unzo, or of me, neither, so I started drawring on this bit of paper that Unzo had dished out with a pencil when we first come in.

Hey, I drawn this feller riding a motor-bike, but he wasn't riding it down Rochdale Road to work like you seen them with their butties in their army-bags, looking for little kids they could knock down. Nah, this feller I drawn was a dirt-track rider like I seen at Belle Vue Speedway one Saturday night when our greengrocer give us a free ticket that he had. He was coming round this left hand bend dead fast, this feller I drawn, and staring straight at you, but leaning right over to one side with his boot kicking up clouds of dust that'd choke you. Which it does do. Which is why you never get this close-up view in real life. Well, not unless you worn goggles yourself or stand there gormless like I done that time. And even then you only seen it for a split second because them speedway bikes throws up about two lorry loads of cinders in your eyes and mouth and hair and your choking on dust for a week

But he looked great, this feller I drawn, and you could easy tell he was one of them Belle Vue Aces because I drawn him with the front of his shirt like a playing card. Oh, I was dead pleased with that drawring I done, and I was going: brrrmmm, brrrmmm,

brrrmmm, brrrmmm like I always done when I done a good drawring. Unless I drawn cowwies when I'd go pkh-eeeeeeow-w-w-w, like it was a bullet bouncing off a boulder; or, Japs and Americans when I went ak-ak-ak-ak-ak; or, planes when I went mmm-mmm-mmm-mmm-mmm-mmm-mmm-mmm-mmm, or, mmm-mmm-MMM-MMMMM-MMMMMM-MMM-MM-MMM-pkkk-KKK-KKK-HHHOO-OOORRR, depending on if they was crashing or not. And while I'm going brrrmmm, brrrmmm, brrrmmm, brrrmmm for the three hundred thousand million billionth time, Eddie Bliss (no messing), he snatched me pencil right out of me hand and grabbed me drawring too.

Agh! me heart give one bump under me liberty bodice and the hairs on me neck stood right up. And I leant right over to one side, pulling meself away from him and screwing me eyes up tight, waiting for him to land us one for making a racket, or snap me pencil at least. And when I done that – leant away from him – I seen there was this bit of a carving in the wood on top of the desk, and it dawned on us that it must of been this that had made me drawring go a bit wobbly here and there. Because some kid had been hard at work with a pen knife because there was some writing that said:

WILF McGUINNESS, 1950 – UNITED FOR THE CUP.

(He was a local lad, Wilf – played for England youth team till Man U signed him; later on for a bit he was manager of Man U too.)

'It's a forgery, that,' says Eddie Bliss when he seen us gawping.

'Par-ding?'

'You heard us.'

'It's a forgery?'

'Yeah.'

'A *forg*-ery?' I tasted the word, sweet and long-lasting like a gob stopper. (At ten years of age I thought I was Scotland Yard, the FBI, Interpol, and Walter Street Police Station, all rolled into one.) 'A *forg-ery*?'

Eddie nods. 'Yep – there's four things as give it away too.'

'Like what?'

'Well, he never went to St Joey's for starters, did he, Wilf? He went to Mount Caramel. And he was always a Blue till he went professional. And he didn't go professional till . . . well, I don't know when he went professional, but it was later than 1950, I know that. Besides, there's no way Wilf McGuinness would have wasted his time carvin' umpteen letters in a school desk.'

'An' four?'

'What?'

'Thought you said there's four things. You only said three.'

'Oh, Ozzy learned you to count, has he? We'll make a boxing referee of you yet. You just see if we don't.'

'What?'

'Never mind. Anyway, the other thing's this, see. See that full stop there?' Eddie points to where it say: "United for the Cup".

'Ye-e-ah.' I was nodding me head now, like this horse I seen pulling a coal cart up Moston Lane.

'That's a dead giveaway, that.'

'Why?'

'Because it proves he never done it.'

'Why?'

'Because Wilf McGuinness never known a full stop from a full-time whistle.'

'How d'*you* know?' I said, not getting the joke.

'Because I know him, see. Lives round the corner from us.'

'Oh,' I said, and then: 'OH!' because I seen then that while we'd been nattering Eddie had sorted out all the wobbly bits on me drawring.

'Now, get them hands washed. Go on.'

So, I done what Eddie said then. I put me hand up and asked Unzo: 'Please, sir, may I leave the room, sir?' And I run across the yard and down to the sinks in the main school, and zoomed back to me place in about two minutes flat where I'd of normally spun an errand like that out to a good twenny. But I was in that much of a hurry to get back to me place I scraped the leg of me chair on the classroom floor, and Unzo looks up and across at us like a crocodile that has just woke up from a deep sleep in the mud of the riverbank and is getting ready to bite.

'All right, let's have a look-see.'

I shown Eddie me hands, the backs of them too.

'Get them dirty finger nails cleaned out.' He taps me thumb and Peter Pointer; and when I'd done that, using me hanky, he says: 'Now rest your drawring paper on something hard, but soft.' And Eddie lifts the lid of his desk then, takes a couple of books out, one of them a school atlas that he opens at page seven where he settles me drawring down on The British Isles (Physical).

'And sharpen that pencil of yours too.'

Then he took me pencil, Eddie Bliss, and he sharpened it with this dinky little penknife he had so's he got this lovely sharp point on it with the wood round the point all chunky and handy-looking, and he blown all the wood-shavings and bits of lead off of his desk, leaving just the oily, woody smell of them hanging round, and he set to work and tidied me drawring up while Unzo was giving out about how many six foot Aussies can lie in a line, top to tail, on the Stuart Highway that runs from Alice Springs to Darwen without being run over by a road train, getting sunstroke, being bitten by three hundred thousand million billion snakes, and then it's the spiders' turn.

First off, Eddie shown us how to make it look like there's a jet of steam zooming out of a motor bike's exhaust, so real you can almost hear it. Well, I thought what I drawn was good, but what Eddie done was better. Yeah, what Eddie done was more like them drawrings you got in the *Lion* and the *Tiger* – exspecially when he drawn this scarf that covered the feller's gob up, and behind his goggles, his eyes sort of hard and keen like it was Sergeant "Tough" Luck of the Legion off of the middle pages of the *Eagle* that was riding this motor bike at Belle Vue Speedway, Manchester. And he went back to the feller's scarf then, Eddie, and drawn it trailing away behind him, getting smaller and smaller and smaller in the distance and wriggling like a snake, so you could tell the feller was really shifting and no mistake. And last of all, Eddie drawn these, like, little creases in the feller's pants round the crutch and at the knees, so they looked like these was real legs the feller had that he could stand up on any time he needed to or chose to, and not like the legs of some robot that needed someone else to operate them, like, maybe the Mekon, who looked like Unzo, and was the boss of the Treens that was the enemies of Dan Dare and Digby and Sir Hubert Guest and Professor Peabody on the first two pages of the *Eagle*. Hey, and when he'd finished, Eddie Bliss, he cut this chunk at an angle out of the pencil point with one clean downward chop of his pen knife, and right in the middle of the paper underneath the drawring he wrote two words in them flashy German letters like you got on the front page of the paper where it said *Daily Mess*, except that it said this:

TONY DINCH

'Hey,' I said.

'What?'

'How'd you know me name?'

'I know Miss Dinch.'

'*Who*?'

'Miss Dinch. I go errands for her sometimes.'

'*Who*?'

'Miss Dinch off Glen Avenue. Her house backs on to the Clough.'

'Oh,' I said when I twigged he meant me Grandma Alma. 'How come I never seen yer then?'

''Cause you prob'ly go around with your eyes glued to your own belly button like a lot of people. But I seen you all right.'

'What? Today, yer mean?'

'No, I seen you hundreds of times. You're always round at her house, aren't you? Bike parked up at the back door while you're in there feeding your fat face. Besides I'd know you anywhere, description she give us – ugly little kid, squint, buck teeth, sticky-out ears, bandy legs, wart on the end of his nose –'

'She *never*,' I said, 'She never, she never, she never, she never, she *never*.' (Though when I was a kid, of course, I'd of give me right arm to have a squint and buck teeth. Because a buck-toothed skenning get struck fear into other kids and you didn't get messed about the same.)

Eddie starts to sing then:

'Oh, Dinchy, you're a funny un:
You've a face like a pickled onion.
Got a nose like a squashed tomato,
And legs like two pegs . . .'

And Unzo slung the board duster the full length of the classroom, and it missed Eddie's head by about a three hundred thousand million billionth of an inch, and went – THUD – against the back wall, leaving a dusty mark below the crucifix.

'BLISS!' roars Unzo, coming up on his feet, big like Godziller.

In the quiet the rain beat the windows like a drum.

'Sir?'

'Get yez book open, Bliss, 'fore ye feel me fist.'

So, Eddie opened this other book he'd got out of his desk and flicked through a page or two till Unzo looks away again and gets back to his Sicilian gymnastics (halfway to Egypt, eh?), and tells us how to dig an artisan well when you was out in the Gibson Desert and stuck for water as you was bound to be some day. And it was just as well Unzo had better things on his mind just then because it wasn't no schoolbook Eddie had on his desk but this book called *Hollywood Greats*. And on this page – well, two pages really – that Eddie stopped to look at I seen this picture of three hundred thousand million billion fellers, there was, all togged out like Romans in curtains and frocks and kilts and coal scuttle helmets with paint brushes on the top. And they was all stood about on the deck of this boat that was creaking under their weight where one feller, a big fat slob in fancy armour and a breastplate with tits was marching about shouting orders at everyone else, but exspecially to these angry-looking fellers dressed in babies' nappies that was swinging these whips about like mad. And underneath all that lot, under the lot of them, the fat slob and the soldiers and the fellers with the whips, underneath all that lot, there was even more fellers that was galley slaves, sweating and moaning and chained up and pulling on these oars and getting nowhere fast. And underneath the picture there was some print that said:

But get this. Right under the fat slob's nose there was just this one little feller all on his todd who was doing none of them things the others was doing – the Romans, the boss Roman, the whippers, and the slaves. Nah, this one little feller was sort of leant on the side of the boat, looking out to sea with his gob wide open, like he was yawning his head off – hey, and maybe dreaming about when Senior Service cigarettes would be invented in about two thousand years time because he was just gasping for a drag right now, this feller, because he was so fed up with it all. Yeah, really fed up, he looked – one-hundred-per-cent fed up. And some kid had drawn a speech bubble, like it was coming out of the feller's gob, and had wrote in it in that dirty blue school ink they used to have, like, as if the feller was saying:

'BLIMEY! WOT A MOB!'

When Eddie seen us looking, he grins. 'Only kidding, Dinchy. Miss Dinch – well, where you're concerned, she thinks the sun shines where the sun don't shine. God knows why, and He won't split.'

Well, I'd give over drawring by then and I spent the rest of the time till the bell trying to think of all the places where the sun don't shine: the Arctic in winter; the Sahara at night; the bottom of Moston Pit all year round; St Joseph of Cupertino's School on a Monday morning in February when it's chucking it down; in our coal shed – in our house of a Saturday night when Man City have gone and lost again.

But ever after that day I'd been in Unzo's class – well, while Eddie Bliss was still at school, that is, and I'd maybe be out in the yard playing staggy or rally-voh or just stood around shivering, and I'd see Eddie Bliss in passing, he'd usually call across to us, like:

'Ozzy learned you to draw yet, kid? or: 'Hey, up, Dinchy, how's tricks?' Or, he'd smile at us or wink – or smile *and* wink; or just say hello.

It wasn't much, I know, but it meant a lot to us at the time. Because it give us a kind of protection, see. Like I had some sort of magical power that nobody known about over the great Eddie Bliss that everyone did. Or like I was maybe a younger relation of Eddie's that he would beat up any smart Aleck kid that messed Dinchy about. And it was just like that the day Eddie left school for good. Yeah, just like that, it was, only different.

It was this Thursday morning when it was really windy like March going out like a line and not a lamb, only it was the middle of April, of course. But when we come out to play the wind had dropped, but it was still dead cold and there was piles of kids shuffling about in their boots and blowing on their hands to keep warm, and loads more kids stood with their backsides to the prefab wall where the heat from the stove come through. And the air was that crisp just then that when you breathed in it seemed to freeze your lungs, and when you breathed out again, it was like you was exhaling cigarette smoke. It was that bright and clear, in fact, you could have seen for miles – all the way to Blackpool and out to sea and halfway round the world, except for the brick wall round the school yard and the houses on James Street and the works on Hemsley Street where they brewed smelly oil all day long. But what you *could* do, it was that clear and still – what you could do was shout, and your voice would bounce back at you and ring in your ears like a bell. Which is what me and Huge was doing, shouting our heads off – me in the far corner of the yard where the wall come in past the telegraph pole to meet the wall of the girls' bogs and Huge over by the prefab wall, toasting his bum. I shouted:

'St Joey's convicks never get owt to eat:
Dry bread an' wa'er once or twice a week;
If yer very lucky, a lickle slice 'o meat:
St Joey's convicks never get owt to eat.'

And Huge shouts back:

'DON'T eat Horrocks's BREAD:
It makes yer SHIT the BED,
It's no BLOODY WONDER
You FART like thunder.
DON'T . . .'

And just as Huge come to that bit, there, summat dead heavy hit us – SLAP-BANG – in the middle of me back, and I fell flat on me face, scrawping me chin on the tarmac. I thought it was some kid being funny at first so I rolled over and shouted: 'Watch it!' But it wasn't a kid. It was this Alsatian guard dog called Kim out of the smelly oil works, and it was stood right over us with its snout about an inch away from me face, baring its teeth and snapping and snarling and slavvering at the mouth. (Only it wasn't really doing that last bit; it just sounds better.) Oh, I was really scared, I was. I was that scared I was sort of froze to the ground with me mind going like the clappers, like:

'I'm just a little kid and don't wanna die. Please, don't let it bite us and I won't never ride round here on me way to me Grandma Alma's and throw stones at it through the railings again. And please send Unzo that's on playground duty and ought to stop mad dogs bitin' little kids. Amen.'

Course to make matters worser there was now piles of kids pushing and shoving round us in a circle, like they done when there was a scrap. Hey, and this wasn't no Oh-Okey-Cokey-Cokey kind of circle neither, but a circle like the dog couldn't never of got out of even if it wanted to with everyone hemming us in and yelling and screaming and making the dog madder than it was because they was just glad it had got me and not them.

But as I was lay there, helpless and scared, and squinting lengthwise through me tootsies under the belly of the dog, I seen Eddie Bliss burst into the centre of that circle of kids and come walking towards us real slow. (Just his calves and his feet, this, like the only grown-up in a Tom and Jerry cartoon on TV.) And he done this quick sort of a skip and a run then, Eddie, like he'd do before he took a penalty shot and – BLAM – he kicked that dog up the backside so hard its knackers must have jammed in its throat. Oh, it give one yelp, real pitiful, the dog, and scooted across the playground and out of the gate with its back legs trailing behind it, like they couldn't keep up

'BLISS!' Unzo's voice comes blaring across the yard like a foghorn out at sea with Unzo trailing behind it. 'Break's over, Bliss.'

'Sir?'

'Your lunch, Bliss.' Unzo pokes Eddie's shoulder. 'Get rid of your lunch, Bliss.'

Eddie looks, like, a bit puzzled then. Till he looks down and seen he's got this round of toast in his mitt.

'Well, Bliss?'

Eddie looks at Unzo.

'Get rid of it, Bliss.'

'Sir . . .'

'Throw it *away*, Bliss.' Unzo sounds like he's spelling the words. Then he shouts: 'THROW THE TOAST AWAY, BLISS!'

'My mother . . .'

'*THERE WAS AN OLD WOMAN OF GORTON*,' pipes up Huge from the prefab wall.

'WELL, BLISS?'

'My mother made this toast,' says Eddie.

'*WHO HAD A BIG TIT AN' A SHORT UN . . .*'

Quick as that, it was. Unzo's straining round now, trying to see who's shouting rude words in St Joseph of Cupertino's schoolyard . . .

'*BUT TO MAKE UP FOR THAT*
SHE HAD A FAT . . .'

And Eddie Bliss was gone, gone for good – over the wall, toast in his mouth, and legging it. Past the smelly oil works he went, across James Street to the convent wall, past the statue on horseback, across Lewis Rec and the putting greens – never to see St Joey's school yard again, or be seen by it, where three hundred thousand million billion gobs now sung like they was one:

'*AN' A FART LIKE A FIVE-HUNDRED NORTON!*'

*

I never seen Eddie Bliss for yonks after that. But I heard plenny. Like, when I was in Mr Irlam's class that had Unzo's class when he left, he said Eddie had joined the Navy, though the Merchant, not the Royal. Still, he got out of that quick enough. Because when I left school and had me first job at Hugh Fay's, I used to deliver groceries to their house on Glen Avenue, and his mam said Eddie had wrote her from Australia, and shown us this photo he'd had took on top of Air's Rock or summat in the middle of the Australian Setback. And Eddie wasn't doing no jigsaw puzzle neither, but was swigging a bottle of Coke, happy as Larry with his arm round this fair dinkum sheila. Another time I bumped into Charlie Forrester doing a Hughie in the gents at the Red Lion. And Charlie reckoned he'd heard Eddie was playing togger out at Yankee Stadium. But Charlie was three-parts pissed at the time (hence the Hughie). So I'm not too sure about that. In any case it must of been about the same time that Huge come up with this story about how Eddie had got a boat of his own and set sail for the Canneries with a crew of naked tarts. But as Byron Marlfield said: 'Well, that's Huge all over for you, isn't it? Wouldn't be much use to him in a Gale Force 10 off Cape Trafalgar, would they now?' But Eddie turned up back home again then and stayed at his mam's for a bit. And then I heard this other tale about how he'd got this concession off some shoe firm up the Rossendale valley somewhere and was wholesaleing carpet slippers out in Brazil. There again, Idle Wild said he known it for a fact that Eddie Bliss had got this entertainment job on the Queen Mary. Thing is, I never known nowt for sure. Because I never seen Eddie Bliss meself for – what? – nine or ten years maybe. Because I never seen Eddie Bliss again till one Friday night I was in Bernard Manning's World Famous Embassy Club with Shirlee.Yeah, and me and Shirlee had been going out together for six months or so by then and was already being spoke of as 'an item' by Penny Kirkham that Shirlee worked with.

5

Once upon a time, if you happened to find yourself on Rochdale Road of an evening where Westbourne Grove runs down to meet it just south of Moston Lane, you was faced with two very real dangers. You might get knocked down for a start, because it's a very busy stretch of road, that. Like I knocked this feller down the first Christmas we was married. (Tootling along in traffic, me and Shirlee: normal speed, loads of pedestrians, lots of traffic, street lights, engine noise of Morris Mini Countryman, big feller goes for it when he shouldn't of done – close up, Arthur Mullard's face, Marciano-fisted, Countryman's windscreen, off-side bottom corner dislodged. Didn't only spoil his Christmas, I can tell you.) Or if you wasn't lucky enough to get run down crossing Rochdale Road, you might turn up late at the World Famous Embassy Club, find there was a full house, have trouble getting a seat, and make the fatal mistake of asking a waiter to help you find somewhere to sit while Bernard Manning was in middle of his act. Like we done that Friday night, the Friday night I'm on about – me and Shirlee, that is.

As the waiter led us across that little square of dance floor, the World Famous Embassy Club, full house or not, fell eerily silent as the grave. But Manning was not unkind. Well, not to Shirlee, at any rate.

'C'mon, Miss Dolittle, sit y'self down.' (*Titters.*) 'Y' comfy now. Seat to y' liking? Get y' another, y' insist.' (*Boom of PA, echoey voice, nervous laughter: hounds ready for the off.*) 'Thaz very nice dress you're wearin', Eliza, lovely dress. C and A open this late, are they?' (*Checks his watch, looks around the room till it's quiet again.*) 'Must tell the missis. She likes C and A.' (*Louder.*) 'Sez very handy, have pair-er kecks, tell affront frommer back.' (*Laughter.*)

Thinks: 'Now's your chance, Dinchy . . .'

No chance; not a snowballed cat in hell's chance!

'Oi! Professor Higgins!' (*Howls.*) 'Bin keepin' Miss Dolittle lay tin class again, have y'?' (*Booming from PA system, audience is drawn in again.*) 'Just looker tim, will y'? Stater vim. Don't get same classer punter these days. Learnin-ur t'talk proper, yiz.

Wooden thin kit, looker tim, wood y'? Mind you, talks very posh, this feller. Oh, very p-hosh. Seen Professor Higgins, here, talkin' p-hosh, Midland Bank, corner the Avenue.' (*Aside, to some other poor chump who's chanced his arm*: 'Oh, is that so, Mr Magoo? Symond Road, is it? Well, Symond Road, my arse, pieman complained, punter turned out to be queer.') 'Oh, talkin' very p-hosh, he was, with his: "H-o, may H-i have h-ay h-overdraft, h-iff H-i may?" (*Sniggers.*) "H-ay H-overdraft?" kin trainee cashier says turra manager. "Wotz one a them, boss? Zat wotcher get, elephant farts y' face?"' (*Brings the house down.*) . . . 'Feller guz turra doc, big ears, horses hooves, long tail, sez . . .'

Dinchy is dismissed, reprieved, he is let off the hook; he is permitted to sit down at last – left to stew in his own juices. The eyes of three hundred thousand million billion people who are known to Dinchy, at least by sight, are no longer upon him. So the boy sinks down gratefully on to a stool that Shirlee positions for him, where he sits for a moment wonderfully quiet – wonderfully, wonderfully quiet – and pretends everything is just hunky-dory, tickety-boo, and just as it jolly well ought to be, old bean! Dinchy makes as if to pick up a pint of Tetley's bitter that has arrived before him at Shirlee's behest. But – lo! – the hands are far too shaky to undertake this manoeuvre just yet, though they do manage – left hand extricating the wallet from his inside breast pocket; right contriving to open it – to pay for the drinks, said pint of Tetley's bitter for Dinchy and a snowball with a fancy cocktail stick for Shirlee.

'And, your own, pal!' says Dinchy tremulously.

Yes, the lips are working too. They accept the Senior Service cigarette that Dinchy places between them, and – well, leave well alone while you're ahead, thinks Dinchy. Let Shirlee take the box of England's Glory (*England's Glory* being the name of Nelson's flagship at the Battle of the Nile, 1897. – Thank you, Byron!) Yes, leave Shirlee to find a matchstick, strike it, light the cigarette for him. (Thank you, Shirlee.) Inhale: yes, inhale. Ah: again. Yep, the job's a good un!

'Feller guz fruh narmy medical, truss on, guz in, doc writes: M. E. "Medically exempt, eh, doc?" kin feller axe him. "Mid-least!" sez-a-doc. 'Wearer truss baxter-front, can rider kin camel!"'

Puffing away now (inhale, exha-a-le, inhale, exha-a-le), Dinchy surveys the scene, attempts to quantify the extent of the damage done to his street cred, such as it is.

Idle Wild, across the way, accompanied by Dinchy's old flame, Miss Avis Henstone, no less, and half her family from the looks of things. And judging by the face Idle pulls when he catches Dinchy's eye, Idle's still getting his rocks off on what Manning's put Dinchy through. Still, it doesn't seem as if anyone else is taking a blind bit of notice of Dinchy now.

The Hunchfront of Newton Heath with its new beau, Barry Brick-Shithouse-In-A-Suit, works at Paul and Smart's: nowt . . . Gordon Forrester, Charlie's older brother and his mates – in Dinchy's class at school, Gordon, twenty years old and never been kissed: oily fingernails, knuckles to match, half-baked shave, always with a motorbike, never a girl. Nowt . . . Three dozen more like this – blokes Dinchy knows, birds he's knocked about with. Seen it (Dinchy being made a fool of); done it (laughed their stupid heads off); now intent on doing something else.

'Sister Contracepta, zebra crossin', Moss Side, 53 bus, double-decker, fuller koonz, runz-o-vrer . . .'

'I wouldn't even give you a penny for them,' Shirlee tells Dinchy.

'What?'

'Whatever it is you're thinking. You look like people must look when some idiot says: "Cheer up, it might never happen."'

'Which it won't do, of course.' Dinchy gives Shirlee what's supposed to pass for a smile. 'Because it already has.' He shrugs. 'Nah, it's okay. Honest. Just a bit of fun, that. Bit of fun I'd rather of done without, mind. Be someone else's turn next week. Bit unnervin', that's all. Besides, I've had a right day of it today. Spare you the details, but a gas main blew, Queen's Road. Playing dodgems with the traffic all day long. Burke's Law says: "Why the hell the coppers don't . . ."'

'Oh, was that your lot? The traffic was backed up to Livesey Street, coming home.'

Hey, now don't get us wrong (says Dinchy, regaining his equlibrium at last): it was just a bit of fun, that – Manning setting you up. But even so, I was more than happy to be sat at this table near one of the pillars, so I could sort of hide behind the pillar if I needed to, or pretend I hadn't seen anyone who might want to extend the joke. I'd had enough of the limelight for one night – and if it ever looks like they've got around to dishing out that fifteen minutes of fame Andy Warhol reckons is on the cards for everyone, I'll make damned sure I tell 'em I'm only short of another ten. Besides, like I said to Shirlee, me day at work had left us feeling a bit ragged. Yeah, I'd of maybe been better off if I'd stayed at home and kipped in a chair in front of the fire. Except that Shirlee would not then have been keeping us company, of course. Yep, I already known I'd have to find another job, a job that was more suitable for an hibernophobe like me.

'Wotz one a them, boss? Zat wotcher get plane for Rangers?' (Joke.)

Look, let's hold it right there if we can, because every word of this so far is crap.

Fact: me and Shirlee was in the World Famous Embassy Club one Friday night long ago. Fact: Bernard Manning done us before I even got to me seat. Fact: I was knackered after work. Well, what a pity! What a very great pity! Dinchy trots out them mitigating thingumajigs as if born to the job. The guilty party dons his best suit of clothes, places his right hand on the Bible, and swears the evidence he will give will be the truth, the whole truth, and nothing but the truth – then proceeds to tell anything and everything but, so help me, God. Because in amongst all them wotchermakrite circumstances the guilty party is dead set on avoiding the point at issue, namely: *mea culpa, mea culpa, mea maxima culpa.* (Didn't know I had the Latin, did you?) *Through my fault, through my fault, through my own most grievous fault.* (Sunday Missal from the Year Dot, the Ornery of the Mass: Latin with English translation on the opposite page – that's all the Latin I've got. Still, I had you going there for a minute, didn't I? Hey, and here's a bit more while we're about it too: '*Munda cor meum ac labia mea, omnipotens deus.*' Bet you never known Dinchy was such a smart arse. Oh, you did, did you? You had us sussed all along? Well, just for that you can sort your own flipping translation out.) I'll tell you what though: I bet you can easy see that Dinchy is still prefabricating or summat. That is to say, Dinchy is still avoiding the issue, though he's gonna have to face up to it before very long. Hey, and no apologies do I make for this neither because I fully intend to avoid the wotsit for just as long as I can. I can't handle it on me own, see? I'm gonna need Shirlee's help. So I give you a riddle to solve at your leisure:

Q. What is nothing?

A. A bottomless bucket without sides or handle. (The *Beano Annual*, 1952.)

Nah, that's not it, that's thingy again – prefabrication. No, here's the riddle: 'Truth will speak when my truth speaks.'

Now, what the hell's that smart arse Dinchy mean by that, eh?

There's this song I'm keen on called 'Love Is Strange' and it's been around since the 1950s, I suppose. So it's a bit long in the tooth (like me, ha, ha) and it's been done to death by umpteen singers as well. So there must be a few other people who like it too. And though I don't pretend to know everyone who's ever sung 'Love Is Strange', I do know a fair few. Mickey and Sylvia, for starters – that is, Mickey McHouston Baker and Sylvia Vanderpool, to give 'em their Sunday names. Then there's Michael Holliday, Lonnie Donegan, the Everly Brothers, Buddy Holly, Wings (*Wildlife* album, 1971), Laura Greene, Everything But The Girl – and me old mucker, Eddie Bliss, who sung 'Love Is Strange', fronting this group he was with at the World Famous Embassy Club on this Friday night I'm talking about way back in history. Yep, me old mate, Eddie Bliss!

I've got all them recordings of 'Love Is Strange', except for the Eddie Bliss one (because there isn't one). And know what? I couldn't rightly say for the life of me which of them I like the best. See, a couple of them recordings (Wings, Everything But) – well, it's almost like they're singing their own tune, I mean, melody. So maybe they don't count. So more often than not, I think I prefer Buddy Holly's version. But there's an organ on that one that don't suit the song. So then I'll maybe lean towards the Everlys' version. But their version's a bit too up tempo for my liking – like 'The Price of Love', say. And the tempo don't suit it – like Jim

Capaldi singing 'Love Hurts' with a smile on his face. So then I'll be back with Buddy Holly again via Lonnie Donegan's calypso version, Everything But, and Wings. (I never play Michael Holliday or Laura Greene at all. Maybe I should.) But, overall, you know, I reckon I like the Eddie Bliss version best, though forty years down the line, me opinion about that's very likely worthless, and not least because of the way I felt about Eddie Bliss. Besides which, to be perfectly honest, I don't think the best version of 'Love Is Strange' has yet been done – and I don't think it ever *will* be done. Because the song itself's a bit dated now, like 'The Twelfth of Never', say, or 'Fever', which were great songs in their day, though they're now well and truly past their sell-by date.

The Mickey and Sylvia version of 'Love is Strange' is *really* dated. But seeing Mickey McHouston Baker co-wrote the song, I reckon he's perfectly entitled to do whatever the hell he wants to do with it. Though exactly what Mickey Baker wrote, the lyrics or the melody is hard to tell, except that he didn't write both. See, what makes it hard to tell is this, see: British artistes credit Baker, Smith (that's Bessie 'Tootsie' Smith, by the way), while across the Atlantic (with one or two exceptions) the credits are reversed. Hey, but thank you, Warner Brothers, for the *E* Smith, *M* Baker credit on the Everlys Brothers' label!

The exceptions to the transatlantic rule are Laura Greene and Mickey and Sylvia. They both credit Baker, Smith and – wait for it! – Robinson. So who the hell's that, eh? Smokey? Sugar Ray? *Jack*? Well, no. Actually it's none of them; it's a lady called Mabel Robinson. Though why no one else gives her credit for what she done, I'll never know.

Still, how's about that for an anorak hood full of utterly useless information to be going on with for any of you trainspotters out there who've got a few pages left over in your little notebooks and all the time in the world to listen to Dinchy going on with hisself about anything and everything other than what he ought to be going on about?

'I've heard worse, I suppose,' I said when Eddie and them had finished – their set, that is. Because they sung a good half a dozen numbers in all, him and this group he was with. (Can't remember what they was called now: it wasn't The Trauma, I know that.

Because they was on with Tony Auton, and that was at the Bottom Derby on another night.). Yeah, 'Love Is Strange' was just the song they kicked off with.

'Oh, I thought they were pretty good,' says Shirlee. 'I liked that last one. Sort of – well, haunting, I suppose you'd call it. The guitars anyway.'

She meant 'Listen To Me', another Buddy Holly number. They had a copy at the youth club on 78. It was okay, I suppose, but I always preferred the B-side, 'I'm Gonna Love You Too'. Once upon a time it was my favourite Buddy Holly track of all.

'Tell you I went out with him?' says Shirlee.

'Buddy Holly?' I said, and laughed.

'No, silly – Eddie Bliss.'

'Really?' I said. 'No, I never known that, Shirlee.' But I did do. Yeah, Shirlee had been knocking about with Eddie Bliss round about the time I'd met up with Laura Pod again.

Okay, okay-y, so it's out in the open now. And it didn't hurt too much after all, did it? Yeah, it's out in the open now, the reason I done what I done that night in The Embo. I mean, the reason I done what I *never* done!

Later on, it was, right near the death. I'd went to order a couple of drinks at the bar on me way back from splashing me boots, and I was just stood there waiting to be served – over to the right-hand side of the bar, this is, where Manning, Mrs, (Bernard's mother) was manning the till (Joke!), when I suddenly realised I was stood, oh, within maybe an arm's length of Eddie Bliss.

Yeah, right next to him, I was. Well, almost. And him just stood there having a quick bevvy with his mates before shooting off to the Palladium Club on Collyhurst Street that Manning owned too. Not that Eddie had clocked us, of course, being busy nattering to his mates and that. Besides which he probably wouldn't not have recognised us now I was fully grown into me seven stone weakling stature and was clad in another of Mr Peart's creations, a bronze shade, they so described it as, that hid me knobbly knees and that. No, but honest to God, I was stood that close to Eddie Bliss that Friday night in the Embo I could of just reached across and tapped him on the shoulder and said Hello. And Eddie would of spun round, smiling: 'Hey up, Dinchy! How's tricks?' And we'd of been off again like in the old days back at St Joey's. Stocking up with Banana Splits and Trebor Chocstix at Mr Mac's toffee shop on James Street before loosing ourselves on Australasia to didgeridoo it round six foot cobbers lining The Bitumen, or maybe billabong an artisan well of our very own out in the Atherton Tableland, and after that . . .

Well, who knows?

Yeah, who knows, indeed! Because I never done it. No, I never done what I could of done, what I should of done – what I now wish I could say I done. Nope, I never tapped Eddie on the shoulder. Cracked on I never even seen him. Collected our drinks, mine and Shirlee's (a crummy pint of bitter with a crummy flat head on it for me and a crummy snowball with a crummy cocktail stick in it for Shirlee), and I took them back to our crummy table near the crummy pillar where Shirlee was sat waiting for us. Oh, yeah, I kept well out of Eddie's way that night. And as things turned out, of course, kept out of Eddie's way for good.

Oh, why was that? I hear you mutter. Whatever made Dinchy turn his back on his old pal like that? Why ever would Dinchy want to crack on he hadn't not seen his old pal Eddie Bliss who taught him how to draw and only saved his flipping life in St Joey's school yard them many moons ago? Still, Dinchy must have had his reasons, I hear you say. And I thank you for that. Because Dinchy *did* have his reasons. Though this is not to say that Dinchy's reason was *good* reasons. I mean, they was good in one sense, of course, because they was Dinchy's own good reasons. But that don't mean Dinchy's reasons was good, meaning good good – like a dog can be good, or a kid that behaves itself, or like cocoa and toasted tea cakes by the fire of a winter's night is good, or like a saint is good, or God, say. No, every one of Dinchy's good reasons was tied-up with Dinchy making damned sure there was no way in the world he was gonna facil . . . facul . . . felicitate Eddie Bliss becoming reacquainted with Miss Shirlee Veronica Jameson of this parish. And if truth be told, Dinchy was very successful in this. Because Eddie Bliss never did become reacquainted with Miss Shirlee Veronica Jameson of this parish, nor she with him. In fact, Eddie Bliss never become reacquainted with many people at all upon his return from his travels. And there is a very good reason why this should be so. And the very good reason why this should be so is that, almost exactly a fortnight after I seen Eddie Bliss singing 'Love Is Strange' on stage at the World Famous Embassy Club, I seen this report in the *Daily Mess* saying how Eddie Bliss was dead.

Me dad would sit there in the living-room after eating his tea of a night, reading the *Daily Mess* with the back of his chair creaking for England whenever he'd lean back on it or swivel round on it, and call out odd snippets of information to me mam who'd be out in the scullery, doing the washing up. Most of the time it was pretty boring stuff they was interested in, like:

'Hey, I see Harold Greenslime died. Only forty-four, he was. Funeral at Blackley Crem, Thursday, two o'clock. Family flowers only, it says here. Donations to Christie's Hospital, Holt's Radium Institute.'

Or:

'Blood yell! Noola Hooligan got knocked down on Collyhurst Street last night; she's in intensive care at Ancoats.'

Or, just very occasionally, there'd be something of general interest. Like, one night around the time of the Munich Air Crash, me dad's going on like this as usual when all of a sudden, he lets out this cry of disgust:

'Ohhh! Reg Fawlee got off with it, the blighter!'

Reg Fawlee was a local nob who was loaded. He had this engineering place down Hendham Vale somewhere. Couldn't pay his workmen in the thirties, but the War made him. Reg Fawlee had narrowly missed a drunk when his Jag mounted the pavement near the Essoldo one night after he'd been boozing down the Press Club with his mates. The court case had been long awaited.

'His *wife* was drivin',' says me dad, real sarky-like. 'An' a dog ran out in front of her. Aye, an' there's the Police Benevolent Fund a few hundred quid to the good!'

'Hey, where's it say that, dad?' I asked him, getting up and peering over his shoulder.

‘Here.’ He points to the headline.

But all it says is: DIRECTOR ACQUITTED.

‘No,’ I said. ‘Where’s it say about the Police thingy?’

He laughs then, me dad. ‘Oh, it don’t say that. You’ve gotta read between the lines.’

So, I had a go at that on his say-so – reading between the lines. But all I seen was, like, white paper, newspaper with no newsprint on it.

But this night I’m on about in February, 1964, me dad says nowt at all at first, which is unusual to say the least. But I known there was something afoot because the back of his chair’s creaking like Hornblower is westering home south of the Azores. Then the creaking stops all of a sudden and he shoves the paper in front of us, open at this page where the headline says:

DEATH LAKE CLAIMS THIRD VICTIM

The report below it said how Edmund Bliss had ventured out on the ice on what they said was the death lake in Rhodes Woods, Middleton, but there’d been this overnight thaw and the ice had give way, and what with the water being so deep and cold and the scene of previous tragedies (three deaths in ten years now), why, Mr Bliss had drownded, of course. And they shown this photo of Eddie too, the one took in Australia, but with the girl cut off, and you could easy see how he was the kind of nutter (Hey, who but a nutter has a big cheesy grin on his face when he’s just snuffed it?) that wobbled about on top of big rocks and that, swigging Coke and happy as Larry because he’d never of dreampt he could of fell off any minute. And this quack said that even if there’d been someone about on the Sunday morning in question it would of probably done no good because human beings can stand just so long in water that’s freezing, then they always snuff it, though he had known of one or two instances where . . . And a police spokesman said that, in spite of repeated warnings given by the police to the general public, people still done daft things when they seen a bit of ice. Of course, he couldn’t make no comment about this incident in particular other than to say that foul play had been ruled out and the matter was now in the hands of the coroner. But it just seemed sort of wasteful and sad to think of a young life lost in such tragic . . .

They never found the little kid till the Tuesday.

Well, for one thing, said a police spokesman, they'd not been looking for a little kid till late last night because he'd not been reported missing yet, what with his mam thinking he was still at his grandma's and his grandma thinking he'd took hisself off home again. And another thing, the little kid was all tangled up in the weeds at the bottom of the lake whereas Mr Bliss had been found on the surface. Well, yes, the body of the little kid *had* been retrieved not very far away from where the body of Mr Bliss had been fished out yesterday – due to heroic efforts made by the police underwater search unit in the face of sub-zero conditions and near nil visibility. . . And this quack said how modern for-wotsit techniques might help them determine whether the little kid had drownded at approx. the same time as Mr Bliss . . . And the police spokesman come back and made an appeal for any witnesses to come forward, saying the number to ring was . . . Well, ye-e-es, he supposed there might well be some speculation that Mr Bliss had maybe lost his life trying to save the little kid, but the matter was in the hands of the coroner and it was up to him to say whether Mr Bliss was brave or had just come a cropper.

'BOLLOCKS!' says me dad when I put the paper down again, and the back of his chair creaked once or twice, stood at anchor off Spithead. 'If it'd been a boy scout or a vicar's son they'd be fallin' over theirselves to pin a medal on him. Bloody good footballer too!'

'Oh, you mucky pup,' says Shirlee, meaning the ketchup I'd sloshed down the front of me coat when I seen me dad's comment wrote on the side of that van in town that day. 'That'll never come out.'

The girl was to be proved right too. Even dry-cleaned (we left it in that same afternoon at this shop on Corporation Street), even dry-cleaned that coat never did come good again and I had to chuck it away and buy a new one from Burton's on Piccadilly.

Yeah, she really known her onions, Shirlee – well, her tomato ketchup stains anyway. I reckon she'd of easy got an award for Messy-ology or whatever they call it. Hey, and maybe at the self-same ceremony where Dinchy would receive an award that was all his very own. Always provided, of course, that they manage to drag him out from where he's still hiding behind one of the pillars in the World Famous Embassy Club.

'Lazy gennulmen, Professor Higgins, y' know. (*PA system booms, Manning consults his wristwatch, waits for silence.*) Fume innits a-fame owny laz week, talkie h-oh so posh.' (*Titters.*) 'Got hisself h-ay h-overdraft frommer Midland Bank.' (*Laughter.*) 'H-and now he gets h-another h-effing h-accolde, lazy gentleman. Lazy gennulmen, h-iff you please, h-ay big hand for Professor Higgins who's won h-ay h-Oscar – h-ay h-Oscar no less, lazy gennulmen, for being – h-and h-I quote! Where's me specs? . . . H-ay H-oscar for being "H-ay H-extra Special Kind of a Kin Prick" . . . Professor!' (*Laughter, cat calls, pretend applause, the slow hand-clap, booing from Idle's table.*)

6

I told her. Yeah. Well, I had to really. I said: 'Shirlee, I've already got a ring, you know.'

We was coming back from Southport on the train at the time, the Thursday of the Easter holiday week, sat on our own in one of them carriages where the windows opened with this, like, a barber's strap affair, and if you wanted the toilet, well, tough, because there was no corridors and you was just gonna have to hang on till the train got in to Manchester Central, unless you wanted to chance your arm in the toilets on the platform at Wigan Wallgate, hoping you wouldn't get left behind when the train pulled out again.

Shirlee just sort of looks at us.

'Yeah, I've already got a ring,' I said.

'What d'you mean a ring?'

I said: 'A ring, you *know*.'

But it was like she didn't believe us or summat, because she says: 'I've never seen you wearing it.'

'No,' I said. 'I mean a lady's ring – one for a lady.'

Well, she looks at us sort of funny then. 'Oh,' says Shirlee, smiling (not the blinder; amused, like). 'Oh, prithee,' says she (whatever that is when it's owt). 'Prithee, kind sir,' says she, or summat, 'and what are you doing with *that*, may one ask? You got a secret past I don't know about?'

'I might have,' I said.

'Oh, do tell,' says Shirlee.

So, I said: 'Nah! It's me Grandma Alma's that she left us when she died. It's one she had. An old one. I mean, like an antique. It's a nice one though. It'd do for an engagement ring.'

'It'd *do*, would it?'

'I don't mean that the way it sounds. I mean, I want you to have it, if you like it. But if you like it, well, it'd . . .'

'It'd *do*. Yeah, I heard you the first time.'

'I don't mean it like that, I told you. Have a look at it when we get back, see what you think.'

But I already known what Shirlee thought. Oh, too right, I did. The expression on her face told us that much. Yeah, the expression on her face as good as said that Shirlee Veronica Jameson (Miss Keck!) would insist on having an engagement ring that was her very own personal choice, thank you very much (you just see if she didn't) – hey, and it was most unlikely to be any old thing that just happened to be lying around in a drawer back at your house, Dinchy, even if it had used to belong to your Grandma Alma that you always thought the world of, and she you.

'Look, I want you to have it anyway,' I said.

'Why? What's it like?' says Shirlee after a bit.

'Well, it's . . . I dunno.'

'You don't know?'

'Yes . . . I mean, no. What do I know about rings?'

'Well, is it a solitaire, or a cluster, or what?

'Solitaire,' I said, though I wasn't thinking about me Grandma Alma's ring no more.

'What colour's the stone?'

'Yes,' I said.

'*Yes*?'

Just outside the park gates – behind St Joey's school and Blackley Library and Institute (as was) – where I never can remember there being no park gates, just red brick gateposts with pinnacles on top, because they only went and took the park gates away in 1940-summat along with everyone else's park gates and railings and all the pots and pans they could lay their hands on, saying these was just what was needed for the war effort and after they'd made them into bombs and that, they was gonna drop them on Dusseldorf from a dizzy height – well, just outside the park gates that's never been there for as long as I can remember, and a little bit over to the right, where it can be seen from the park, and from right at the other end of Tudor Avenue (what it stands on) and from the opposite side of Rochdale Road by the post box outside Hugh Fay's grocers and Mrs Jones's toffee shop (where I was parked up at the time because Rapishaw Gap had sent Mrs Jones whatever it was she'd ordered out of the Freeman's catalogue), well, just there, where I said, there's this statue of a feller on horseback with its backside to the convent wall. Bloke called Haig. Well, summat to do with whisky, though there's no way it's White Horse, because this gee-gee's been prancing away in that same spot for donkey's years, and the black dogs and the spotty ones have all had a good go at it – and the birdies too. But it's Haig all right – though God knows who Haig was, and He won't split.

He *was* some sort of swank general, of course. Any fool can tell that, because he's wearing this stone uniform with bird-shit coloured epaulettes and a moss green Sam Browne belt and a peaked cap that's almost black and matches his face – hey, and matches the look on his face too, because Haig is frowning, oh, really frowning, in a stony, soldierly sort of a way, like, as if he's just heard the old fogies effing and blinding on the bowling green over in the Rec, or the kids larking about on the tennis courts, and – well, it's enough to make his stony moustache curl (by Jove!) and just as soon as he's drawn a bead on the bounder that's upset him, he's gonna bring that right hand of his crashing down on his stony flank as a signal for the squaddies to let loose with the Maxim gun and a stun grenade or two just to show them that's cavorting in the David Lewis Recreation Ground without a care in the world what it means to be an Englishman, by Crikey!.

"'*He was*,'" says Byron, quoting this IRA bod called Behan talking about his prison doctor, "'*very hard in an English way that tries to be dignified and a member of a master race that would burn a black man alive or put a pregnant woman out the side of the road in the interests of stern duty.*'"

That's Haig!

Well, just there, where – come hail, come snow, come rain and come shine – his nibs is everlastingly on the alert, that's exactly where I seen her that day when I pulled up near the pillar box to drop Mrs Jones's parcel off: Solitaire (as I known her before I known her name), Avis Henstone (as she was when I did) – Mrs Avis Wild, Idle's missis (as she afterwards become).

Through them invisible park gates she comes that day, pushing a trolley that's loaded up with about three hundred thousand million billion kids, a couple of spare ones hanging on at the side, and another one she's carrying, and not in her arms neither. I mean, you could easy tell she was expecting again because she's got this ornery coat on but the buttons fastened sort of funny, like she's got her buttonholes mixed-up, only she hadn't – she was just that big in front. Big in front? Big all over more like. Well, bigger than I remembered her anyway: Solitaire aka Avis Henstone, Dinchy's first love. Correction: she wasn't that – I mean, isn't. Because Dinchy's first is his last is his first, and her name isn't Avis. But Solitaire aka Avis Henstone *was* the first girl I ever went out with. Pinched her, I did too (meaning "stole", not "goosed") off this arsehole called Tough Titty.

I let on to her soon's she got across Rochdale Road with the tribe, exchanged the niceties: 'Hi, Avis. Long time, no see. Got your hands full, there, haven't you?' Etc. etc. (It was pretty obvious she was heading for the pillar box because she had this letter in her hand, ready for posting.) 'Many've y' got now, then?' Meaning kiddies.

Avis laughs. 'Oh, there's only the one's mine. Spike here.' She ruffles the hair of this little mite that's digging deep into it's left nostril with a finger twice the size of it. 'Doing a bit of child-minding at present.'

'Spit 'n' image of him,' I said, glancing from her to the ruffled one. 'Amazin'.' (Though what really was amazing was that I didn't laugh in her face, seeing Spike rooting for gilberts like his dad always done.) 'Er . . . how is, er . . . (hey, and I had to think for a minute: 'What was Idle's flipping name?') How is . . . er . . . Malcolm?.'

'Da-ddy, le-tter,' says the toddling snot-nose.

'All right, chicken,' says Avis, ruffling Spike's hair again.

'*Chef*!' I thought to meself, '*you can clean more than that chicken's insides out before you put it on my plate*!'

'Post daddy's letter in a minute,' says Avis. Then to me, as she lifts the kiddy up to reach the post box: 'He's working away at the moment.'

'*Aye, pull the other one*!' I thought. Because even in the 1960s there wasn't that many places where you couldn't keep in touch with the outside world by phone. Mind you, Idle could of been somewhere like Glasgow or Southampton or Ipswich, and it was his birthday or something and they was posting him a card. Thing is though, it wasn't that kind of an envelope. And in any case, I didn't need Avis to tell us how Idle was doing, or what – or where. See, I known Idle's away address. Yeah, and I known how he come to get put there too. Hey, and I'll tell you something else (and there is nothing more certain than this): I only hope it never occurs to Her Majesty that she ought to take as good care of Tony Dismas Dinch as she was at present taking of Malcolm David "Idle" Wild, late of Russet Road, late Russell.

Casino Royale, the very first James Bond story, made a pretty bad film but a pretty good cartoon strip in the back pages of the *Daily Express*; and Solitaire made a pretty good first Bond-girl too. I used to study them cartoon strips on me tea break at the shop. It was that cartoon strip that learned us to draw, helped by Eddie Bliss, of course, and the Juliet Jones cartoon in the *Evening Chron* and the Superman comics – oh, and anything and everything by R. S. Embleton, who was me hero when I was a kid.

Solitaire in the *Casino Royale* cartoon strip in the *Daily Express* was very much her own woman, as I remember her – an individual, tall and slim and dark and mysterious and mature. Hey, and Solitaire was the name this 16-year-old Hugh Fay grocery delivery lad (Dinchy, as was) borrowed off of Ian Fleming and give to this new girl that worked at the travel agent's at Moston Lane corner, though Dinchy's Solitaire was not quite as tall or slim or mature as the 007 one. But she was pretty – hey, and pretty mysterious too, because Dinchy didn't even know her name as yet. But too late already (as Mrs Feinstein on Hazlebottom Road used to complain when I delivered her groceries of a Saturday dinner), seeing how this trainee garage mechanic from down near Harpurhey Road had got his motty in first and was already going out with Solitaire before Dinchy even known her name was Avis Henstone. So Dinchy never even got a look-in. Well, not for some time, he didn't – not for a month or so. In fact, not till that Friday night at St Joseph of Cupertino's youth club.

Bastard!

No, not Dinchy – oh, and not Miss Avis Henstone, that's for sure. No, Bernard Tiffield, I mean, the aforementioned trainee garage mechanic. Hey, and this is a first (and a last too) because nobody never called Bernard Tiffield Bernard Tiffield, not even his mother (who called him Barney) or his dad (which all the signs are that Titty had never known one). Because Bernard Tiffield was always Tough Titty round our way, or T to his face. And no one (not even Line, who he drove a cab for) was ever on first name terms with Tough Titty. Best he got from Line was Ty, though the 1970s did see this stretched to Tie-Dye for a time.

Ah, but enough of this malarkey! Let's get into the youth club and meet them. Besides, it's pretty cold, stood out here on Mary Street. (Hey, is that snow, or what?)

'Yeah, be with you in a minute, Idle. Not seen Byron, have you?' (Huge, I known, had took this bird we called Trailing Ivy to the Greenhill cinema: nice plush seats, quiet back row.)

Look, I don't know about you, but there's no way I intend to stand out here, shivering. (Yeah, it is, it's snowing. Bound to go a bit warmer now, but it's still cold.) I mean, you're very welcome to tag along with us if you like. See what you're getting into before you join. I'll sign you in, like. I mean – well, it's nowt to write home about, the youth club, but it's better than nowt, and it's somewhere to go when you're stuck, exspecially on a cold winter's night. Don't cost much, neither; couple of bob, say. Hey, and it's just as well too because I don't have much, fiver a week from Hugh Fay's that me mam keeps three quarters of, so I've got maybe thirty bob or so to see us through the week. Which means kids like me will very often say to a bird they've got in tow:

'Meet y' inside, okay?'

Not just tight arsed – tight arsed and flipping skint!

You are dead right, my friend. Never a truer word was said: St Joseph of Cupertino's youth club is nowt if not scruffy. Like an old army hut painted black, and not a nice Valspar gloss black neither. No, it's more of an old engine oil sort of a black – hey, and an old engine oil that's been around the world a few times with Les Hiddens, the Bush Tucker Man, putting it through it's paces, and Les only changed the oil because he had to after that sandstorm north of Cooper's Creek when he broke down looking for some drongo that had to go and dig hisself an artisan well at Menindie that turned out to be crook.

Still, there's loads of kids go to the youth club that I know, see? And, yeah, I know all they do is mooch about most of the time (table tennis, snooker, bit of a kickabout, and – if old Mr Holwick, the caretaker, isn't around, get a card school going with a marked deck they've got), but on a Friday night and Sunday night too, there's a dance from eight till ten, and you'll hear some great music because the kids bring their own 78s, like this one I've got here – and this one you can hear now: 'It'll Be Me' by Jerry Lee Lewis, the flip side of 'Whole Lotta Shakin' Goin' On'.

Hey, listen to him go, Jerry Lee, The Killer: playing that piano of his like he's trying to wrap a parcel of live ferrets. Oh, come on, let's get in there, please. Ten past eight of a Friday night and all I'm doing is stood out here in the cold and the snow, trying to explain that: Well, all right, it's not the Ritz Ballroom or owt, it's nothing posh, but they've got a cloakroom and a bogs and there's refreshments on sale – hey, and there's loads of women. So what more do you want? And what more has the Ritz got to offer? Apart from posh wrappings, and polite bouncers that sez: 'Oh, do h-excuse h-uz, sir!' when they sling you out on your dog teeth to do a close-up personal inspection of the kerbstones on Whitworth Street West.

Oh, just listen to thissen they're playing now: Little Richard belting out 'Lucille' like his throat's been cut.

Look, this, here – just inside the door – this here's Walter Jordan: harmless old git, looks after the door: bald head, specs, sat on a bentwood chair smoking a pipe, uses more Swan Vestas than Three Nuns tobacco. ('Evenin', Walter.') Couple of bob each and we're in.

Uh-oh, this way quick: Colin (three-bags-full-Fr-Elrick-good-man-of-the-parish) Leitrim on his way across. Looks after the Friday and Sunday night dances. Creep!

No, not that way. Room there, that door's closed to the likes of you and me: more good men of the parish – HAH HAH HAH, club within a club, I'll-pat-your-back-and-you-pat-mine: parish football pool tonight, parish pilgrimage of a Thursday, parish-

God-knows-what-all-else the other three nights a week they're banged up in there with the door shut.

Snooker room, hey, *vwala*! (Pardon me French.)

Packet of crisps, Nibbets, Butterkist, Kiaora? Straight ahead, pal. ('Hi, Teresa!') Teresa Mickleton, there, dishes them out: nice old bird, but the birds we is interested in is over this way. And so's the music.

The body of the room (No, I do *not* mean Dot Harrytown, jiving away there, and showing the world as much as a girl dare show on a winter's night), the body of the room – again, *vwala*: a row of ex-cinema seats along each wall, sprung dance floor in between, stage up there, bit of a rake to it, blue velour curtains each side, valence across the top. Hey, and there she blows, up there on the stage, slap-bang in the middle? Yeah, that's it, my friend. An absolute beauty! Like something out of Flash Gordon or summat. Massive old record player – more like a gramophone really, because you have to keep winding it up and changing the needles. Yeah, metal needles, would you believe it? But something else you can do with that old machine that you can't do with your Dansette or Philco turntable at home is vary the speed to just about anything you want almost. Hey, and I don't mean just 16, 33, 45, or 78 rpm, neither, but any in-between speed you want. Yeah, and it's great that:

'Isn't it, Idle?'

Yeah, we like that – me and Idle and Byron and Huge – because if you really like a particular 78, you can slow it right down and really spin it out, so to speak. See, pop songs was all pretty short before the Beatles got going; LP's was pretty mean too till the Beatles bunged fourteen tracks on their first LP – the one where they're hanging over the stairwell in Manchester Square and Ringo's still got his quiff and the songs on it are credited to McCarthy-Lennon. (Yeah, McCarthy-Lennon! Check it out, you don't believe us.) Here, I'll show you what I mean about the speed. See this 78 I brung, I'll get Idle to get Colin to cut this 'Catch A Falling Star' crap and stick it on, then maybe flip over to the B-side.

'Okay, Idle? Yer a pal . . . An' cut the speed back when he puts it on, will you?'

Two ticks, that's all it'll take him, my friend. Kids do it all the time, like requests. So any minute now. I mean, it's not as if we'll have to wait about three hours or something, like you always have to do with that live BBC broadcast in the summer where some kids request a record they like and they send a gopher down to the BBC archives to fetch it and the gopher's gone for a week or summat and they have to send out a search party to find the poor sod and it's a completely different top ten when he gets back and Macmillan's replaced Anthony Eden as PM.

That 78 of mine's 'Johnny B Goode', by the way; and it's got the most exciting guitar intro in the history of the world. Yeah, a real hairs-on-the-back-o'-yer -neck-raiser, it is . . . Oh, all right, have it your own way, But I think you've been spoiled . . . Yeah, of course, I know 'I Saw Her Standing There'. Matter of fact, it's that record that finally got us branching out from buying just the London label, but it didn't come out till '63, did it? First time I heard it was at the Top Ten Club at Belle Vue. Hey, Jimmy Saville used to leave his Roller outside the front door, showing off, and it wouldn't get scratched neither . . . Whaddyer mean, I've been spoiled? . . . Oh, law and order-wise, you mean? Thought you meant pop music-wise for a minute. Because this is 1958 I'm talking about and even Radio Caroline hasn't been invented yet, never mind flipping Radio One. All we've got in '58 is Pete Murray and Jack Jackson on Luxembourg late at night on programmes that are geared up to flogging sheet music, not vinyl. So after all the trouble you've gone to tuning in to the flipping station in the first place (*BONG! Two-Oh-Eight Metres, Medium Wave BONG!*) you've got the airwaves all crackly and whistly at best – and gummed up with a right load of old crap you never wanted to listen to in the first place. See, that sheet music was what organists with arthritis was dead keen to play in the Tower Ballroom, Blackpool, and other venues of the Living Dead. 'Tammy', 'A Certain Smile', 'Volare', 'It's All In The Game' etc. etc. et-boring-cetera . . . Hey, and a Two-Way Family Favourites to you too, chum! Course, songs like that are very suitable in a kind of a way, I suppose, because it was always bedtime when you was tuned in to Luxembourg and songs like 'Tammy' and that would have you pushing up the zeds before you can say . . .

Ah! here it is now! 'Johnny B Goode': and it's only cost us a couple of couple of bob to be stood in St Joseph of Cupertino's youth club, listening to Chuck (Charles Edward Anderson) Berry entertaining us up on stage, hopping around all over the shop like a cripple with the runs and no key to the bogs' door. But better still is the B-side, I think: 'Aroun' And Around'. Sure, it's slower, but (just listen to it!) sort of chunky, and it's got this great guitar riff in it, exspecially where you get this bit in between the singing. Here it comes. Yeah, this is it. Chuck's singing away there – listen! – but, after every few words, the guitar comes in like this:

DAH, dah, da-da

Well, summat like that, only more twangy. Then after a bit, when he's about halfway through, he must of got fed up with singing or summat, Chuck, or maybe he's just knackered, what with all the hopping around he's done, or maybe he's found the key to the bogs' door at long last. (Lovely echo in there, by the way.) But anyroad, whatever it is, Chuck clams up then and just leaves the guitar to it like this:

Bip-a-loom-dip: DAH, dah, da-da

And from here on in, it just keeps on going like that right the way through to the end, except for just this one bit very near the end where you're still expecting it because Chuck has only done it about three hundred thousand million billion times up to now, but this time he don't. Instead he goes . . . Hey, listen; here it is now!

Bip-a-loom-dip: DAH, dah, DIP-bee-yoing-BIP

See what I mean? Yeah, 'Around And Around', we play that over and over again at home – me and Idle and Byron and Huge – and slower as well, which is 45 rpm on me Dansette portable and miles too slow really, though it's better when we use Huge's Philco. See, the Philco's got this arm on it that lets you pile a few records on at the same time, but if you don't wanna do that and just put the one record on and leave the arm right back, well, it'll play that record over and over again without you even touching it . . .

Hey, why're you looking at us like that all of a sudden? . . . Oh, you're not impressed? You're not impressed. eh? Suit yourself: it don't bother me . . . You don't agree with us? Hey, fine by me, chum . . . You don't think a rock song deserves such devotion? Hey, come on, now! I mean, what government was it passed this law says Felix Meddlesome, Billy Wagglejavelin and them have some sort of a monopoly on hairs-on-the-back-o'-yer-neck-raisers. And while we're at it, why is there always someone getting all hoity-toity about music and stuff because kids oughtn't not to like it or be interested in what they like and the things they're interested in? I mean, I must admit to having reservations about some of the newer stuff, like rap, say:

Hey, ol' Mudder Hubbard
She wen' to da cubba
To ge' da po' doggy a bone, huh!
Bu' when she ge' dere
Da cubba wa' bare
So da po' li'l doggy go' none, yeah!

But what do *I* know? Okay, so rap does nowt for me, but that don't mean there's nothing to it. I mean, I dunno. I really don't know. I mean, there might be absolutely nothing there at all. Just some loudmouth bozo, going on with hisself. But maybe there's some really deep message there that's got something important to tell us about our time and place.

Like, maybe there's some old lady in this great country of ours that's so hard-up, she's on her beam ends – hey, so much so she can't afford to feed her pet dog. Yeah, and how about this? She can't even remember what she's got in her kitchen cupboard: she has to go and look! (She got Alzheimer's or something?) Or, maybe someone's broke into the house overnight where she lives all alone in the inner city. (She's a mother, for God's sake: where's the kids? Got theirselves a mortgage and a BMW and moved away?) Hey, and whoever broke into her house last night has took what she had in the cupboard, yeah. Yeah, and very likely that someone was an asylum seeker or something. (Bastard!) Well, not English anyway, that's for sure (bastard foreigners!), or he would of known you can't take a bone on trust no more in case it's British beef.

Hey, and I know it's daft, but if just one teeny weeny bit of that is true, why would anyone in this great country of ours rather sympathise with old Mother Hecuba, say, for having her nose put out of joint at the siege of Troy? (Ooh, how's Dinchy know about that? you say. Because there was a Priam Street, behind Loofe's tailor's shop opposite Queen's Park, Harpurhey, once upon a time, that's why – and when I asked Byron about it, he only give us chapter and verse, as is Byron's wont till the cows come home.)

But it's a free country, pal, and all you gotta do at St Joey's youth club if you don't like someone's musical taste is make your own selection. Simple as that, it is – and you will never be short of pals to advise you neither. So how about that nice Vic Damone with 'On The Street Where You Live'? Oh, and I do hear Pat Boone's very good too. 'April Love' might be more to your taste, though personally, I find it a bit like bunging Hermesetas in me milk coffee when I might have had an espresso and Demerara – and had it black in the first place too!

Course, it's only natural that Idle should get fed up while me and Percy Pooh-Slinger's understudy (what I've very kindly signed into St Joey's youth club) is going at it hammer and tongs there. So Idle shoots off to the bogs where I follow him through after a bit to comb me silken locks for the three hundred thousand million billionth time that day.

You combed it right back, your hair, in them days, then in from the sides at the back. Then you took your comb and shoved the teeth sideways on into the front bit where your quiff was and pulled it out, real gentle, so you got what was a Tony Curtis, I suppose, but what we always called 'a little-bit-o'summat-comin'-out-'ere', which made it look like you had *not* taken great care to comb your hair three hundred thousand million billion times that day, but (hey, surprise!) had found it that way when you rolled out of kip in the grey light of dawn – or at the crack of noon if it was a Saturday.

Yeah, you and James Dean too!

Hey, these bogs I'm talking about in St Joey's youth club – the Gents' – was at the side of the stage but below it, and soon's we come out again I seen Colin Leitrim was not on the stage at that moment, having took hisself off to the refreshment stall for a snack. Hey, and who should be minding the shop, meaning the record player on stage, but Solitaire (as was), Avis Henstone (as I now known her to be), Mrs Avis Wild (as she would become in the near future)? So, with no more ado I hopped up on stage, excused meself to Avis, got me Chuck Berry 78 that had me name wrote on it in case it got nicked, and bunged it on again, replacing the 'Tea For Two Cha-Cha' that Colin Leitrim had left us with. Then I shoved the little lever thing so the turntable spun round at about 70 rpm.

Beep-a-loo-oom-deep: DAH-H-H, dah-h-h, dah-dah
Beep-a-loo-oom-deep: DAH-H-H, dah-h-h, DEEP-be-yoing-BEEP

Being up there with Avis was something of a bonus, of course – until Idle clambers on stage as well and all of a sudden there's this bit of a ding-dong going on between the two of them when Idle says (jokingly!):

'Whyn't yer lend yer dad's razor?'

Which is Idle trying to be funny, and not succeeding. Because what Idle means is, with Avis being very dark and that, you can just about make out this faintish sort of a shadow on her top lip, which to be perfectly honest is something I always found exciting, me. Being, like, a very personal glimpse, so to speak. But this point of view has maybe not occurred to Avis (or maybe it has, and she don't care for its implications). So Avis starts going on at Idle hammer and tongs then.

Hey, but get this. I was just sort of stood there, minding me own business, and thinking: 'Uh-oh, here we go again!' (meaning Idle) – and wondering if I hadn't better do summat about sorting it out when someone (Tough Titty, it was, who'd snook up behind us on the quiet), someone gives us this right old clout on the side of the head, spinning us round so's I lost me footing and fell in a heap in the stage curtains, getting covered in dust and ruining me quiff in the process.

7

I had this crazy dream about it a few nights after. (I've had it the odd time since if I've maybe had indigestion overnight.)

'Now, see here, Bernard,' I'm telling Tough Titty, using his Sunday name and this posh voice I've lent off of this BBC twit with the moustache, waistcoat, and spotty bow tie. 'Now, see here, Bernard, h-old bean, h-if I've, ah, h-offended you h-in h-any way, perhaps, I, ah, might be h-allowed to h-enquire h-as to the cause. But for goodness' sake, Bernard, h-old bean, I, ah, suggest we discuss the matter h-in h-ay, ah, more civilised manner.'

What really happened had went summat like this . . .

The Players

Anthony Dismas Dinch, arsehole of this parish
Bernard Harvey Tiffield, aka Tough Titty, rough house of this parish
Malcolm David Wild, aka Idle, crow-roller and navel-defluffer
Miss Avis Hermione Henstone, aka Solitaire, acknowledged bit of all right
Colin Leitrim, good man of the parish and creep
Byron Marlfield, a scholar and a gentleman

DINCH (*to Titty*): Whassermarrer with you, yer big ape? (*Music plays on for a time, the people nearest to the stage stop and stare. When the record on the turntable finishes, a whisper does the rounds:* 'Scrap!' *Dinchy struggles to his feet, smoothes his hair down. His face is flushed, he struggles to control his breathing.*)

TITTY: Oh, big ape, is it? Well, now, how's about sayin' that again, son, only somewhere where I can do summat about it. Like outside, for instance. (*Dinchy's glaring at Titty. Sheer bravado, it seems. He doesn't seem to be in too much of a hurry to take him up on his offer. Dinch knows it's started to snow now; he wouldn't want to wreck his thumb-length, fleck, Tuxedo-buttoned jacket that took him six months to save up for. He seems a bit happier when Idle steps in to restrain him lest he murder Titty out-of-hand.*)

IDLE: Come on, Dinchy.

TITTY: Yeah, go on yer little runt!

(*Colin Leitrim returns to the stage*).

LEITRIM: All right, all right. That'll do. Break it up now, lads.

DINCH: He started it. Ask anybody. He started it, the big ape

TITTY: Yeah, an' I'll finish it too, son. Come on, any time you say.

LEITRIM: All right, all right. That's enough, I said. (*Leitrim pushes Titty back through sheer weight of years, preventing him from damaging his knuckles on Dinch's top set. Meanwhile, Dinch sets up some curious defence mechanisms: the half-open gob with the stiff upper lip and a bit of a twist to the side (early Presley); a half-squint (Jack Elam); a truculent stance – he appears to be waiting to catch a package jettisoned from the top floor of a tenement building (Marlon Brando:* On The Waterfront*).*

BYRON (*stage right*): Ah, *Waterfront* – Schulberg's allegory about the McCarthy Era, the Un-American Activities Committee hearings being a prime example of the way Nativism is never far below the surface on the American political scene . . .

DINCH (*aside*): Piss off, Byron. You're not even in this. (*To Titty*) Pssst!

TITTY (*uncertainly*): Well, he better leave . . . my woman alone or he's dead.

DINCH: You on about?

AVIS (*to Titty*): Now, let's get one thing straight, here: I'm nobody's woman, me. So you can get that idea right out of your head. And I'll have an apology from you while you're about it too.

BYRON: Ah! *The Disenchanted* – Schulberg again. Best one of all, I always think. His other stuff, well, it's okay, I suppose. But *What Makes Sammy Run, The Harder They Fall* – well, they're more like film treatments than novels in my opinion. But the Scott and Zelda one, sorry, the Manley Halliday, Jere one, *The Disenchanted* – it's got to be the best. See, Schulberg's just a bit of a kid – what? – nineteen, twenty years old, and the studio sends him out to some mid-West college with Fitzgerald (where was it?), Dartmouth, yeah – scripting a movie. Okay, so Budd's daddy's some studio bigwig, so it's a bit like Prince Charles having tiffin with Laurens van der Post, but even so . . .

DINCH: Hey, Byron, you not think that's maybe a bit ana—, anac— . . .

IDLE (*helpfully, with dictionary to hand*): Anaconda?

BYRON: Anachronistic?

TITTY: Yeah, it's only 1958, innit? Jughead's only ten years old as yet.

BYRON: Point taken: I mustn't get ahead of myself. (*Byron stops abruptly, noticing the players on stage, plus the kids on the dance floor are biding their time none too patiently, not to say getting restive. e.g. widespread study of cuticles, some wide-mouthed yawning, a bit of blinking as if trying to stay awake, shuffling of shoe leather on wood, puffing and panting here and there, a solitary stray fart, one pair of arms folded, another pair akimbo, a variety of pained facial expressions, tumbleweed drifts across the dance floor, an owl hoots, the church clock at St Bartholomew's church on Bottomley Side strikes thirteen.*)

TITTY (*to Dinch*): Psst!

DINCH: No, it's you. Go o-on!

TITTY: Yer what?

DINCH: Go on!

TITTY: No, that's me line.

(*Laughter*)

DINCH: Oh, yeah, sorry. Again then.

TITTY (*to Avis*): Yer what?

AVIS: You heard me. I want an apology from you, and I want it now.

TITTY: Well, yer not gettin' one, you hear?

AVIS: Then you know what you can do.

KIDS OFF STAGE: *Oo-oo-oo-ooh!*

TITTY: Yeah, I do, least for starters . . . (*Grabs Dinch's 78 off the turntable, snaps it in two.*)

LEITRIM: Now, there's no need for that, that's sheer vindictiveness.

AVIS: Yeah, you big baby!

TITTY (*to Dinch*): See you outside, son. Jus' pick yer time: I'll be waitin'. Give yer such a kickin' yer mummy won't recognise yer.

DINCH: Oh, ye-ah? You an' whose army?

Yeah, something like that, it went. Dead boring. Seen it three hundred thousand million billion times before, see it three hundred thousand million billion times again. Storm in a teacup; all about nowt. Still, that's more or less what happened on the Friday night Idle scarpered out the bogs' window and I ended up with Avis Henfield.

Mind you, that was later on, after we'd all stood around bored to tears for a day or two when Fr Elrick turned up like he sometimes done and ky-boshed the music and give us this forty-eight hour sermon about how your body is a temple that should be kept in violet – which is not a colour I care for very much, being a bit tarty, I always think. I mean, like I said to Byron:

'What's wrong with all them other colours?'

So Byron says: 'What?'

I said: 'There's seven colours in the plectrum, right? So what's special about violet? It's just another flippin' colour, far as I can see.'

Byron looks at us like he's not heard us right. 'Violet?' he says.

So I told him to go and get his ears washed out, because Fr Elrick just said your body is a temple that should be kept in violet. But Byron wasn't having none of it. So I said: 'Yes, he did, Byron.' Like, I said to Idle: 'You heard him, didn't you?' And Idle says: Yeah, he had done. But maybe Fr Elrick meant the flower, or the footballer that played for Man U that Charlie Forrester got his autograph that time. And Byron laughed out loud then, just the once but dead loud, so Colin Leitrim started tut-tutting for all his worth.

'You *berks*!' says Byron.

'Yer w*hat*?' I said, a bit annoyed with him now.

'You flipping berks!' says Byron, and he says in violet's one word, not two, and he spells it out, and says it's got nothing to do with colours or flowers or Denis Violett that played for Man United, you pair of bleeping pillocks!

'Oh, hasn't it?' I said. 'Well, all right, so what's it mean then, clever 'ole?'

So Byron says in violet means not tampered with.

'What's not tampered with?' says Idle.

And Byron says Nothing's not tampered with, exspecially in Idle's case, or mine too, if it come to that – well, from what he'd heard tonight, it wasn't, seeing how it was pretty obvious something was draining all the sense from our grey matter, if we asked him.

So we did ask him. 'Yer what?' says Idle; and I said: 'Yeah, go on, big 'ead, I know you're dyin' to tell us.'

So Byron give this deep sigh, real sarky-like, and says he's already told us what in violet means, but the trouble with people like me and Idle was we didn't know the Queen's English. And I told him, Yeah, of course, we did; Her Majesty was as English as the rest of us, maybe more so, seeing how her family had come over here a long time before mine had run out of King Edwards. Though Idle thought it was maybe Maris Piper his lot had run out of because his grandad was Scotch and played the bagpipes. Hey, and I'll say this much for Byron: Byron always was a boy who was generous in defeat. Yeah, Byron said No, he couldn't tell us nothing because I known the lot. Yeah, he admitted as much. But I was just as generous as he was in me own way because I said, Nah, the lot I didn't know, as it happened, because I'd no idea what Fr Elrick was going on about and, for all his blather, I didn't think Byron known any more than I did.

'Oh, don't I just?'

'No, you don't,' I said; and Idle says: 'Dinchy's right, you don't know nowt, you. You're just showin' off as usual.'

Now, Byron never could keep his big yap shut when he thought he known something you didn't. So Byron says Fr Elrick as good as said wanking makes you go blind. So I put it to him straight, I did. I said: 'Where's your white stick then?' And Idle says maybe we better have a whip-round and get him a guide dog from Henshaw's, eh? Which is why Byron told us to do something physically impossible, and stormed out of the club.

Okay, maybe we had took it a bit far, me and Idle. But that still didn't stop us sending Byron on his way with a right good earful, that is, me shouting after him to hang on a minute while we seen him across the road. (Cracked on I never seen Tough Titty stood in the porch before the door swung shut, leaving a flurry of snowflakes behind it.) Then we put Byron right out of our minds and took ourselves off to the refreshment stall to get a drink, though there was nowt to be had as it happened, seeing how Teresa Mickleton had scooted off to the stage end of the room where Fr Elrick was dishing out advice she was very much in need of if her specs was owt to go by.

Oh, the refreshment stall was open all right, with the lights on and a tap running all the hot water off and pots draining over by the sink and Teresa's coat and bag and brolly hung up behind the door and the Ascot water heater bubbling away like mad over the sink above the trap-door, and you was gonna be able to get summat to eat and drink in another three hours' time maybe, by which time your belly would think your throat was cut. But right then – well, you might not like it, but you was gonna have to lump it because there was nothing at all to be had.

'Rack 'em up,' says Idle, meaning the balls on the snooker table in the back room. 'I'll hang on till she comes back.'

So I went through into the games room and put a tanner in the slot and turned the knob and the light come on over the table and I got the triangle off the hook and positioned the reds and set the colours up – yellow, green, brown, blue, pink – and I was just getting the black out of the end pocket to put it on the spot, when Idle sticks his head round the door.

'I'm off, Dinchy,' he says, sort of breathless.

'Thought I smelt summat,' I told him, the old joke.

'No, I'm off home.'

'Bleed Nell!' I said, peeved because I'd stuck me money in now.

'It's nearly chuckin'-out time anyway,' says Idle, meaning Titty.

'Why? He's not after you, is he?'

'I'm takin' no chances. You comin' or what?'

'I've put the money in now. Comin' where anyway?'

'The bog's window's open.'

'Nah.' I bent to address the cue ball, but I was already talking to Idle's back.

Don't get us wrong now. I'd no idea how I'd handle Tough Titty, come chucking-out time. But if trick snooker shots could of helped us I'd of been well away. Because I done a few nifty ones after Idle skedaddled.

Hey, I done this one where you smash the white into the reds that hard on the break it flies off the table like a rocket, bounces off the Chubb fire extinguisher, rattles across a few stools, and nearly lands in the waste paper basket near the door, then always has to be retrieved by hand because no matter how you try you just can't seem to manage to hook your toe underneath it to kick it back into play. And I practised that other one where you snooker yourself behind the pink and try to make the white ball jump up in the air and land on the one remaining red, leaving a load of blue chalk stripes on the green baize so it ends up looking like a George Melly stage suit. Yeah, and I perfected this unique trick shot of me own where you pretend you're Gene Vincent at the BBC with a microphone on a stand. Then you swing your leg right over the tip of the cue and snap it in half by accident. But, I'd more or less give over with them more dramatic trick shots, and was concentrating on potting the pink from the D, when Avis Henstone walks in.

'Oh, hello,' she says, when she seen us there.

'Hiya.'

She looks like she's lost and makes as if to go out again.

'Avis.'

'What?'

'You okay?'

There was this right rubbishy record banging away in the main room, 'Hoots Mon' by Lord Rockingham's XI and loads of nutters prancing about, pretending they was Scotch. You could hardly hear yourself think. I put the cue down, and went across to her, shoving the door to.

'Yeah,' says Avis, like maybe she isn't okay.

'You doin'?'

'What?'

'You doin' in here?'

She worn this white blouse-thing with, like, different coloured smocking round the neck and short cuffs the same, and one of them wide skirts with a really deep belt that had four bright little stud-things to fasten it at the front, and on her feet she'd got these, like, little ballerina slippers for dancing.

'Promise you won't laugh?'

'Yeah.'

'I was looking for another way out.'

I laughed in her face. 'You an' me too.

'It's not funny,' she says, looking pained.

'Tell you what is though. Thingy went out the window.'

'Eh?'

'Thingy, me mate.''

'Him that started it, you mean?'

'*People say yes everywhere . . .*' Conway Twitty half-sung in the main room, like he agrees with her.

'Well, yeah. I suppose he did in a way,' I said, meaning Idle.

But Avis don't believe us when I say he meant no harm, honest, because Idle is just trying to be funny and not succeeding. Because Avis thinks it is only funny if Idle breaks his neck when he goes out the window. And it was then I said, wanting to cheer her up (and get in her good books too), that I known a way out of there that Titty wouldn't think of. To which Avis says, Yeah: the window, I have already mentioned that, thank you very much. So I said, Well, if she would insist, though the window I spoke of was in the Gents'; at which point Avis says, Oh, it gets better and better; and laughs. And as soon as she lightens up a bit, she asks if I'm serious, meaning if there really is another way of getting out of there. Well, yeah, I told her, I'm being dead serious because I've had a brainwave, see. About how we can get out, the two of us. So Avis says, How? So I said, How, paleface? And Avis laughs again.

'You do mean a door, don't you?' she says.

'Yeah, a door. You give it one push and walk away free.'

'The fire escape!' says Avis, and the both of us is laughing then. Because the fire escape is slap-bang in the middle of the main room, and short of starting a fire or something, there is no way we're gonna be leaving by the fire escape that night or any other night.

'Nah. There's another way,' I told her, as Cliff Richard in the main room told us we'd better Move it. 'There is, honest.'

'No, there's not. I've looked.'

'Ah, but there is, see.'

So Avis wants to know if it's safe, so I told her to Just watch this space because Dinchy is gonna use it even if she isn't. Anyway, I said, it's a helluva lot safer than going out the front door, and Avis is very welcome to come with us. If she wants to, that is.

She never says nowt for a bit then, Avis. But then she nods her head just the once, and says she'll have to get her things.

So, with Avis gone I wandered through to the refreshment stall and ordered a bottle of Vimto, a carton of Kiaora, a packet of Nibbets, and a packet of Smith's crisps. Then casual as I could, I pulled me wage packet out of me back pocket, ripped it open, and tossed the fiver across.

'Lord love us, son!' Teresa Mickleton waves us away like I'd hoped she would. 'I can't change that. You got nothing less?'

No, I hadn't, I was telling her, when Avis come back with her coat and her boots and her dancing shoes stuffed into this little leather shoulder bag. I said to Avis: 'Not got change of a fiver, have you, love?'

Avis hadn't, of course – just like none of them kids that went to St Joey's youth club would of had change of a fiver. No change for a quid, most of them.

'They'll have change.' I said.

'Sorry, son?'

'The pools fellers,' I said, meaning the good men of the parish, locked away in their little room there. 'They'll have change.'

And Teresa thinks this is a good idea of mine. The pools fellers very likely will have change; and off she goes to serve this kid with a top set like a rabbit who's asking her for a Tizer and a bag of peanuts as, up on stage at the far end of the room, Perez Prado's 'Patricia' hits the bum note it's famous for.

'Will you ask 'em for us, Teresa?' I called across to her. 'They'll only bawl us out if I stick me head round the door,.'

'I can't go off and leave everything just like that,' says Teresa Mickleton.

'*Oh, can't you?*' I felt like saying, but didn't. '*So how come you went an' left everythin' when Fr Elrick was goin' on with hisself there?*'

'Aw, go on, Teresa,' I said, putting it on a bit. 'I've had no tea yet; I'm starvin'. I come straight from work.'

'Tell you what,' says Avis Henstone right out of the blue. 'I'll keep an eye on things till you get back if you like.' Which done the trick.

Teresa smiles, wipes her hands on her pinny, takes it off, and hangs it up on this hook behind the door, saying: 'I don't suppose you'd pull the shutters down for me, would you, pet?' Never even took me fiver neither. Just shows you how decent some folk can be. Present company excepted.

Now, I know – yeah, I do know that one trap-door, eight steps and an emergency exit door don't take that much sorting out. A kiddy could do it. Course, that kiddy would need permission to go in the storeroom in the first place, all the time in the world to play with, an electric light bulb that works, and clear access to the emergency exit door.

As it was, the electric light bulb was all me and Avis had that night. (And thank God for small mercies, is what I say.) Oh, we got the trap-door up easy enough on the word *Quick*! And we found the light switch too, but letting the trap door down again over our heads, we run down the eight steps to find a right mess of crates and sacks and boxes and things blocking our way to the exit. We was at it for ages, clearing a way through, with every noise we made sounding like a gunshot and every footstep on the floor above sounding like they was made by circus elephants in big clumpy boots. But we done it. Yeah, we done it. Because we had to. Hey, and *Quick*! was the word I used again then, ready for the off. To which Avis says: '*What*?' when what she really means is: '*Okay*' as she come towards us on the run, hooking her bag over her shoulder.

Maybe that's what done it. I mean, with her bag swinging loose like that – maybe that's what thrown Avis off balance. Or maybe she just caught her foot on a bit of sacking or one of the boxes that was lying about in there. See, I dunno. Because I never seen her fall. Just felt it. I mean, there's me, stood with me arms outstretched, ready to hit the bar on the door when – WHAM – Avis falls against us and the both of us went flying and fell out headlong into the snow.

Oh, all hell broke loose at once then. There was all sorts of stuff going on in the club now from what we could hear, what with Dumbo and his pals charging about and trumpeting and swinging on the trapeze and some silly tart screaming like the Vikings had got her and the burglar alarm making a noise like the fire brigade had come. So we jumped to our feet and scarpered quick, but not straight across the croft in case we was seen.

I grabbed Avis by the hand and dragged her into the shadow of the wall of the building. We was laughing and breathless and breathing hard all at the same time, and covered in snow from head to foot. Soon's we come to the corner of the building where the street lights on Mary Street might of picked us out, we peeled off to the right and come diagonally across the croft in the shadow of the club thrown by the streetlights. And we just kept on going in a straight line then till we come to this back entry that led through to Factory Lane where we was maybe thirty yards or more away from the club by now. So we stopped to dust the snow off us. Me pockets was full of it and Avis had some in her boots.

All the shouting and barging about had simmered down a bit now and, looking back from where we was stood, I seen someone on the inside messing about with the exit door. They banged it shut and it swung open again, shooting a line of light over the croft like a lighthouse out at sea. Then whoever it was give the door one almighty heave, and it slammed shut for good, taking the light with it and leaving just the croft all lumpy and white in colour except for this raggedy trail coming towards us, sort of black and grey where we'd scuffed up the snow when we run for it.

There was tons of kids piling out of the club by this time and making a right racket out on Mary Street. Three lads – I thought Titty might of been one of them – three lads come round the corner of the building, but they never seen us and just carried on walking towards Rochdale Road. It was exactly two minutes past ten according to my H Samuel Ever Right Watch, and just then – with Avis stood next to us, dusting herself down and making nervous little noises with the effort of it and all the excitement that had gone before – suddenly, just then, it begun to snow again: a dead lazy sort of snowfall with great heavy snowflakes drifting down like torn tisher paper so that, from the entry off Factory Lane where we was stood, everything seemed dead white as if you was looking through lace curtains towards Mary Street where the roofs and the chimneys of the houses and the pitched roof of the club on the skyline stood out like cardboard cut-out castles. A car was making its way down Mary Street with its headlights on full beam and its tyres thumping like heartbeats on the road when I turned towards Avis Henstone and kissed her.

'Hey, there's no messing about with you, is there?' says Avis Henstone, aka Solitaire, aka Mrs Malcolm Wilde, now mother of two.

'I suppose you could say that,' said Anthony Dismas Dinch of this parish, aka Dinchy, to the first girl he'd ever kissed.

8

'Why didn't you say it was an emerald?'

'Dunno,' said Dinchy, meaning he didn't know it was an emerald, he didn't know emerald was Shirlee's birthstone – he didn't know anything about the ring, except it was his Grandma Alma's ring, of course. 'Thought maybe it was jade.'

'No.' She slips it on, tries it on different fingers, looks at it with hand outstretched. 'It needs cleaning, of course, downsizing maybe. Only a bit though. Look.'

Dinchy looked: third finger, left hand – loose; third finger, right hand – not. He stifled a yawn. 'You like it then?'

'Oh, it's lovely.' Shirlee breathes on it now, her lips close to the stone – takes her handkerchief to it, polishes it.

This seemed to make no difference at all as far as Dinchy could see. 'Steady on,' he said. 'You'll summon the genie of the ring.'

'To whisk us to Avalon or Far Cathay.'

'St Marychurch'd do for me.'

'It's nice.'

'Huge said.'

'You don't think it's maybe too old fashioned?'

'St Marychurch?'

'The ring, silly.'

'What?'

'Oh, never mind. It's not a solitaire, by the way.'

'No?'

'No, it's what they call a cluster. There's the one main stone, see, set off by one, two, three, four . . .' She's counting in what Dinchy calls "a fairy whisper": no larynx required, just her lips and the tip of her tongue. 'Seventeen, eighteen, nineteen diamonds. If they *are* diamonds. They could be; they're so tiny.'

'The emerald's you,' Dinchy told her. 'The nineteen's me when . . .'

'Your grandma died?'

'No, I was twenny then, remember? Went out with you in the August, Grandma Alma died the following April.'

'Eight months?'

'Seven. No, you're right – eight. Be nice, you had her ring.'

'We'll get it cleaned, then see. Mm?'

'Sure. There's that place down Shude Hill, there. Near the market, Smithfield.'

'Oh, there are lots of places.'

'Well, yeah, but . . . Hey, and you don't have to have it, you don't want, you know. I mean, I want you to have it, but it doesn't have to be for . . . Well, we'll get it cleaned, but we can always have a look, that little jeweller's shop – where is it now? Penny Kirkham mentioned it.'

She puts her finger to his lips, shushes him. 'All in good time,' she says, her words throatier now. She turns away from him, clears her throat. 'Anyway, we've got till my birthday, haven't we?'

'I can't wait that long,' said Dinchy.

'You can't wait – what? You can't wait a *month*?'

'I can't wait that long,' said Dinchy, straining towards her now, looking for the whisper – throaty or fairy, either would do.

The gate, a wooden slatted one, battleship grey in colour, cuts through the privet hedge into the garden at an angle of forty-five degrees and locks by means of a latch, provided you lift the gate, then shove it back again once you've passed through. A tarmac path leads to the front door of the house – a path that is, quite literally, off-the-back-of-a-lorry. That is to say, the path is a tarmacers' foreigner, flaking at the edges and none too stable underfoot. It runs diagonally across a grassy patch too uneven to be called a lawn, though the grass itself is neatly trimmed and is high-lighted here and there with what a child might describe as boulders, though what to an adult's eyes are nothing more exciting than three chunks of limestone and twice as many lumps of aggregate, painted white.

The front door is lack lustre too, battleship grey like the gate, but the front door is enlivened by three distinctive features: a rectangular letter box, a door knocker in the shape of a turtle, and a two digit numeral – each one of these brass, each one a-gleam with an intensity that is one result of their being polished on a daily basis by the lady of the house. Another result of this daily routine is that the battleship grey of the door has taken on a gunmetal shade here and there where the polishing cloth has caught it.

The downstairs front window of the house, a bay window, features cross-hatched lead, a set of floral curtains with flounces, and an art deco statuette of a lady who dances forever along the interior window ledge towards a plaster cast of a boy from Tuscany who chomps perennially on a bunch of grapes suspended from his right hand. And it is accoutrements such as these which may lead a visiting child to imagine he stands on the threshold of Nutwood where Rupert Bear and chums may be found. Naturally, such a child will never learn any different because for all normal purposes the house is accessed via the back door, not the front, and the lady of the house, Miss Alma Ellen Dinch, invariably makes a point of deflecting the child's enquiries about Rupert, Rosalie, Bill Badger, Edward Trunk and friends with inventions, circumlocutions, and queries of her own.

The back door is where the child's fairy cycle may be found at present, parked up against an old Silver Cross pram, rusted in parts, which Alma Dinch loads with her washing and that of old Mrs Thurrock next door when she goes to the wash house at Harpurhey Baths of a Thursday. Miss Dinch's back door stands ajar, whence the salt-and-peppery smell of potato pie fresh from her oven runs to greet us. We hear voices, music too – a woman's voice and that of a boy, and, in the background, the signature tune of *Workers' Playtime* on the Home service. Though whether the programme is just beginning or drawing to its close, we shall never know. And neither will the boy. For he is with his Grandma Alma once more, as he was so many times in days gone by. Not that Miss Alma Ellen Dinch is really the boy's grandmother, though truly she acts the part. For Alma is mistress of the boy's heart and soul, and stomach, until, that is, there will come a day when this boy, this ingrate, will desert her for another, another of her kind, whose given name is Shirlee.

*

Funny, isn't it? says Dinchy, meaning strange. Funny, isn't it – when it's not the Real Thing for either of yous? Dinchy makes sure he distinguishes the concept of the Real Thing from the right time – that is, too early in life or too late. Because, according to Dinchy, there's no such thing as too early or too late. There's a right reaction or a wrong one, and that's all there is to it. You pays your money, and you takes your choice. Because Love never calls at the wrong time, says Dinchy; though, like an avalanche or a train crash or a lottery win, it can single out the wrong person often enough . . . a woman who wouldn't know a rainy day if it hit her in the face with a wet haddock and a size ten sea boot . . . a man who wouldn't know his ship had come in if the *Marie Celeste* sailed up the Manchester Ship Canal to Trafford Wharf with a full crew singing shanties in the rigging, Aztec gold on the cargo manifest, and, deck-side, Middleton Brass Band playing 'She'll Be Coming Round The Mountain When She Comes'. And that's not one little bit funny, says Dinchy. That's just sad. No, what Dinchy thinks is funny, meaning strange, is when it isn't the Real Thing for either of you. Yeah, that's what Dinchy thinks is funny, meaning strange.

There you are, one minute, says Dinchy. You think this bird's the best thing that ever walked on two legs, then after a bit (and none of your *Carry On* sniggers, please), and not a big bit neither, you just can't wait to get shut of it. Funny, isn't it? Please yourself, says Dinchy: I think it is. You suppose it's the same for them too?

One minute it's all you can think of, says Dinchy, and the next its voice is grating on your lug-holes. She'll be chunnering on there about some stupid pop star or other, or about her even stupider boyfriends what you wonder how she ever managed to get shut of them in the first place if they was so flipping marvellous. And you find yourself saying, Oh yes, Avis, you do very much like her new frock (that you wouldn't of give her a second glance in if she'd worn it the first time you seen her). And you're being called upon to show real concern about her grandad's lumbago (which is about as interesting as watching an action replay of May Day celebrations in Red Square in slow motion).

And you're pretending you like crap records that you don't (no, not in an 'Endless Sleep'-by-Marty-Wilde of a month of 'Only Sixteen'-by-Craig-Douglas flipping Sundays, you don't). And you're having to put up with her daft mates that is even dafter than she is, and couldn't raise an I.Q. of 100 between them if they threw in her pet dog, Fido, the goldfish she won at the fun fair at Heaton Park, and the man from the Prudential who calls round to her house on Beeston Street in his bicycle clips every Tuesday week, pedalling a green Raleigh sit-up-and-beg push bike with a chain-guard on it. Then all of a sudden, says Dinchy, you just can't stand it no more.

Maybe what it is, says Dinchy, is you notice one of her stockings is a bit twisted when she meets you at the corner of Queen's Road near the Milan. Or there's this stray thread of cotton hanging from the hem of her coat when you're stood there in the queue waiting to go in the Avenue cinema one night – or maybe her lipstick's a bit smudgy or summat after you've walked her home from the Embassy Club in the pouring rain. Yeah, it's usually some little thing like that, says Dinchy. Though it's not really a little thing at all if you stop to think about it. Because if it's a little thing like that that drives you barmy, it's a cast iron certainty you don't think much about the girl herself. Because if you did, then she would suit you just fine if she turned up wearing Charlie Cairoli's make-up and bowler hat and wanted to talk about mucking out rabbit hutches all night long. Then all of a sudden, after putting it off for ages, you think: Sod it! And you just have to get shut.

Point I'm trying to make, says Dinchy, is me and Avis finished on a Thursday night three weeks after we begun going out together. Early on, it was, about eightish. So when I'd dumped her I found meself at a bit of a loose end, so I called round to the youth club to see if there was owt doing, and found there was this game of five-a-side football in progress. Nowt serious: just a few lads kicking a Mitre Mouldmaster about, with a free kick given if the ball went above waist height in case you broke a window. There was no pitch marked out or anything. Nah. What they was playing on was what was the dance floor of a Friday and a Sunday night where you've got the old cinema seats screwed to the floorboards down each side, and they'd just slung their coats down for goal posts at each end – mine amongst them when I went and joined in.

Like I say, apart from the waist high rule, there were no real rules to the game. I mean, there was no hand-balling it, of course, or picking the ball up and running with it, or kicking one another where it hurts most and that. But that's about it. I mean, there was no rules about throw-ins, or corners, or off-side – or falling on the floor and pretending you're injured every time a toad's got a wart on its nose so's to impress the ref. There was no ref anyway, so that'd of done you no good in any case. And if the ball shot off to the sides, well, maybe half a dozen of you would run after it, scuffling like mad to hook it back in to play with your foot. I mean, it stands to reason, there couldn't have been no throw-ins or the game would of been stopping and starting all night long and we'd of all been bored to tears. Of course, as things turned out, I'd of been better off if there had been throw-ins, bored to tears or not.

See, right near the end of the game, it was. We'd been playing for the best part of an hour or so, when this kid called Quelch that fancied hisself in goal took his fist to the ball and really smashed it, so it shot up in the air, bounced off the roof at a funny angle, and come down behind the cinema seats on the left hand side of the room, if you was looking at it from the stage end, that is.

Should of been a free kick by rights, but we just carried on playing by common consent, and me and Gibbo and a kid called Maggot and this other kid called Harney, well, we all dived in there after the ball, whirling our feet about like we was testing for landmines in the Gaza Strip and was willing to risk a toe or two. Hey, and with four legs swirling about in these crazy semi-circles, and with some kid maybe changing the leg he was using every now and then and coming at you from a different angle, well, someone was bound to get hurt, and that someone was me.

See, I'd just got me foot on the ball for the three hundred thousand million billionth time, and was just about ready to lob it up and out into play, having spent the best part of five minutes scrabbling about for it in a space that wasn't big enough to open

Old Moore's Almanack in, never mind play flipping football, when someone (Harney, it was) whipped me leg right out from under us, and I fell forward with me full weight – SMACK – on the arm of one of the cinema seats.

Now, the arms on them cinema seats was ideal for resting your elbows on when you was in the Empire bug hut at the top of Factory Lane next door to the Corporation yard and intent on unwrapping a block of Fry's Five Boys chocolate or a Pendleton's Twicer that you'd bought off the usherette. But, being made of wood and dead hard, the arms on them cinema seats was not quite so ideal when you was with a bird that you fancied when they was just a plain nuisance. Hey, and the arms on them cinema seats was even less than ideal when they upped and jabbed you slap-bang between the tits all of a sudden – exspecially if you had fell on them from a great height to allow them to do this.

Ouch! It didn't half hurt. BANG! I went, right on the end of the arm, sunny side up. It got us on that part of me breastbone you'd be fighting over to pull and make a wish with if it was one of Bernard Matthews' turkeys we was talking about and you'd just took it, stuffed and ready-roasted out of your New World Image 100 Mark 2 oven with the family sat round, mad keen to get stuck into their Christmas dinner.

Jeesh! I was doubled up with the pain of it and making a pretty good Prince of Denmark out of the whole situation, moaning and groaning and doing a dying duck act that any ref (if we'd had one, that is) would of easy give us a free kick for. No, I was bad, honest. Hey, I must of been because the others lads wasn't laughing too much at all when I sunk down on one of the cinema seats, rubbing me chest and generally feeling very sorry for meself indeed.

The game more or less fizzled out at that point, what with the cripple on the touchline stealing the limelight from the star players. Besides it was getting late now and everyone was sweaty as pigs and beginning to smell like it too. So one by one, the others grabbed their coats and sloped off, and I done the same, thinking I'd get off home and have a hot bath and get the Elliman's liniment out of the bathroom cabinet and see if that done any good.

Pity I didn't shove off with the others. Because I called in the bogs first to splash me boots, and when I come out again all the other lads had gone. Apart from them three, that is. Three that hadn't been playing five-a-side, three that had only just turned up, as it happened – three that seemed to be more interested in playing three against one maybe. Tough Titty, I mean, and them mates of he's, Cig Heil, and Himmler the Ted.

Straight off, Titty slung a pair of boxing gloves at me feet. A right raggedy pair they was too from out of this tea chest under the stage. The right-hand glove had this two foot long yellow shoelace in it; there was nowt at all in the other one.

'Lace 'em up,' says Titty.

Someone, at the time of Alma Dinch's death in April, 1964 (Alma's niece, her sister Madge's daughter, Noreen Jessop, or so it's generally believed within the family, though Noreen herself continues to deny it), someone in the Dinch family at the time of Alma's death loaned the Squirrel Horn confectionery box containing the Dinch family photographs to Fr Francis X. Elrick, parish priest of St Joseph of Cupertino's parish. Fr Elrick's father, Gus, had been a classmate of Alma Dinch many years before under the tutelage of the Presentation nuns at St Patrick's Infant School, Collyhurst. In addition to this, Fr Elrick's mother and Alma Dinch had belonged to the Agnesians in their early teens in St Patrick's parish, and one of the photographs in the Squirrel Horn confectionery box had shown the two of them lining up in Albert Square, Manchester, for the Whit Walk on Whit Friday, 1905 (the Anglican churches walked on the preceding Monday). But, unlike Fr Elrick's mother, Mairead Offaly, Alma Dinch had never progressed to membership of the Children of Mary in the parish, nor did she subsequently join the Legion of Mary. But, leaving aside for the moment the matter of who was responsible for the loan of the Dinch family photographs to Fr Elrick (and, to be fair to Noreen Jessop, her personal culpability in the matter never has been finally established), the loss of them (for such it would become) was something that each and every member of the Dinch family, individually, at different times, and to greater or less extent, would regret for many years to come.

For Fr Elrick was an uncommonly busy man with much on his mind and an abundance of parochial and diocesan affairs requiring his attention, one consequence of which was that he omitted to return the Dinch family photographs to the Dinch family prior to his own demise due to cardio-respiratory arrest in March, 1967. Moreover, Fr Elrick's executors – his brother-in-law, Simon Larkin, and Mr Oliver Plunkett Darcy, LLB, principal partner of Darcy, Allen, Larkin, Larkin, and O'Brien, a firm of Catholic solicitors well-known in the locality – were quite unaware of any importance attaching to the Squirrel Horn confectionery box they discovered on the bottom shelf of the cupboard below the book case in Fr Elrick's room together with a twice-folded copy of the *Sporting Life* for Tuesday 7 March, 1967; a Fontana paperback edition of Thomas a Kempis' *Imitation of Christ*; a heavy glass tumbler that was a souvenir of a visit to Waterford in the Holy Year, 1950; a three-quarters depleted bottle of Chivas Regal, and its replenishment, unopened as yet, but bearing a label identical to that of its predecessor of the previous week.

'Forget not Holy Mother Church,' are said to have been the only five words ever addressed to Fr Elrick's executors by The Right Reverend Thomas Holland DD, PhD, DSC, DLitt, eighth Bishop of Salford, formerly Bishop of Etenna and Coadjutor to Portsmouth. Nor did Fr Elrick's executors forget her, for on 3 December of the same year (the feast day of St Francis Xavier) the Ecclesiastical Education Fund was endowed with an undisclosed sum of money which represented a tithe on the deceased's estate, and rumours persist to the present day that this was not less than ten figures (provided the one and the two, signifying the solitary ha'penny were counted as separate units).

And neither was the Dinch family forgotten by the executors; for it is impossible to forget what has never been known, and no member of the Dinch family was known to Fr Elrick's brother-in-law, Simon Larkin, or to Mr Oliver Plunkett Darcy, LLB, principal partner of Darcy, Allen, Larkin, Larkin, and O'Brien. Accordingly and in due course, the Squirrel Horn confectionery box containing the Dinch family photographs was passed along by the executors to the Salford Diocesan offices together with a miscellany of items and documents found amongst Fr Elrick's possessions and concerning which the surviving relatives of the deceased had expressed neither interest nor desire. Then subsequent to a brief sojourn on top of a desk in a side office at the Cathedral Offices next to St John's Cathedral on Chapel Street, Salford, the Squirrel Horn confectionery box containing the Dinch family photographs found its way (courtesy of the Reverend Thomas Pavor MA, STL) to the Bishop's residence at Wardley Hall, Worsley, where it would enjoy seven years of blessed anonymity in the company of two spare blankets and a bedspread within a recess of a cupboard in a guest bedroom at the back of the house. It would be a foggy day in November, 1975, before the Squirrel Horn confectionery box containing the Dinch family photographs would next find itself disturbed from its slumber.

It was at this juncture that a visiting friar of liberal views and sentiment, having enjoyed His Lordship's hospitality at table, came across the Squirrel Horn confectionery box prior to retiring for the night and whilst searching for an extra blanket which, assisted by slug of Jim Beam (an alcoholic *vade mecum* the friar invariably had ready to hand), might help dispel the cold of a winter's night in this northern clime. And it was at first sight that Fr Malchus, the friar in question, adjudged the Squirrel Horn confectionery box an ideal temporary container for the impedimenta of his present travels, these being no longer quite so easy to compress within the confines of the friar's overnight bag – a bottle of *Lachryma Christi* (a present from Fr Guardian of the Novitiate House of the English Province, recently returned from Sorrento); two packets of Polo mints; a copy of the *Daily Telegraph*; a copy of the *Craven Herald*; an A-Z of Manchester and Salford; a street plan of downtown LA; 49 blank sheets of A4 Croxley Script plus a fiftieth that bore the legend: *Mortfification and Modern Man* in Pica typeface; a hardback copy of Hilaire Belloc's *James II* (unread, apart from page one); and a paperback copy of Machiavelli's *The Prince* which Fr Malchus had had the good fortune to pick up at a bargain price at Sherratt and Hughes in St Ann's Square to replace the Everyman edition he had inadvertently mislaid on a pilgrimage to Acapulco. Accordingly, the Squirrel Horn confectionery box in question, now bereft of the Dinch family photographs, departed for Canterbury with Fr Malchus together with his personal effects and the friar's confident expectation of speedy advancement within the Order.

The Dinch family photographs themselves remained on the same shelf in the same cupboard of the same bedroom at Wardley Hall for a further five years. Loosely stacked (as Fr Malchus had left them), bestirred, untidier, dustier with each passing year, the Dinch family photographs were disturbed (though only ever so slightly) each and every time one of the cleaners or a visiting religious happened to open that particular cupboard door and close it again. Until, that is, there came a Monday morning towards the end of September, 1979, when the Dinch family photographs could no longer have been retrieved from the shelf of the cupboard in the guest bedroom by anyone having reason to require them. This was due to a simple oversight by a temporary cleaner from a local agency who had been recruited to stand in for one of the Sisters who normally undertook the domestic chores at Wardley Hall, but who were during that week on Retreat at The Cenacle, a Carmelite convent to the south of Manchester city centre where the rule of silence is *de rigeur*.

Elinor Redmayne of Belvedere Road, Salford, mother of three, was a personable and pleasant enough woman, possessed of good looks still, good humour, good kids, and a good lad named Phil. But on the Monday morning in question, towards the end of the month of September and around the middle of hers, Elinor Redmayne (dyspeptic, too, subsequent to a bibulous tenth wedding anniversary celebration with Phil that had taken in The Paddock, The Flemish Weaver, The Kettledrum, The Brass Tally, and two packets of Kershaw's king prawns and a tray of Donnelly's whelks in addition to a tenth Bacardi and Coke), Elinor Redmayne was feeling a little out of sorts in general, and out of sorts in particular with DDs, PPs, Monsignori, and her own PMT.

And so it came to pass that, at four minutes past noon precisely, Elinor Redmayne opened the cupboard door in the guest bedroom in the course of doing her rounds, took the Dinch family photographs from the shelf where she found them, shuffled them into some semblance of good order, and placed them in an empty Kwik Save bag. The mistake Elinor made (and it was only a mistake after all) was to use for said purpose a Kwik Save bag identical to the one she had brought into the bedroom with her and which was already acting as a receptacle for the accumulated broadsheets of a weekend at Wardley Hall and which Elinor had cleared from a downstairs lounge: *The Times*, *The Guardian*, the *Daily Telegraph*, *The Sunday Times*, *The Observer*, the *Sunday Telegraph, The Scotsman*, and a solitary tabloid, the Scottish *Sunday Mail*.

Elinor Redmayne then took the wrong Kwik Save bag and dumped it in one of the bins round the back of the hall whence the Dinch family photographs in the Kwik Save bag that now contained them were trundled on their way to the Salford Council incinerator accompanied by the remnants, animal and vegetable, of a dinner given by His Lordship the previous Saturday evening for His Grace, Archbishop (later Cardinal) Thomas Winning of Glasgow, who that day had addressed a meeting of the Catholic Teachers' Association in a northern suburb of the city of Manchester. The accumulated newspapers of that weekend at Wardley Hall in late September, 1979, remained secure in the other Kwik Save bag on the shelf in the cupboard of the guest bedroom where Elinor Redmayne had shut them away in the company of a couple of spare blankets, a bedspread, and a solitary Polo mint that was some three years past its sell-by date.

Its sheer size alone had saved the photograph of the charabanc trip from sharing the same fate as the rest of the Dinch family photographs. The photograph of the charabanc trip, a professional job of work executed by Estalls of Collyhurst is the size of three postcards laid end to end. The obverse side, in fact, in addition to indicating the name of the photographer, delineates three separate spaces where three different addresses together with three conflicting messages might be written, and to which three individual postage stamps might be attached. And a mischief maker who felt so inclined might have been able to drop the photograph of the charabanc trip, thus completed, into a post box, thereby presenting Newton Street sorting office with a jocular talking point, and some unfortunate postman with a headache until he realised he was being got at.

The photograph of the charabanc trip was simply too big to fit in the Squirrel Horn confectionery box with the rest of the Dinch family photographs, and it had always been kept separately in a large manila envelope with a stiffened back. And somehow or other, when Alma Dinch passed away and her emerald ring was passed across to Dinchy, the photograph of the charabanc trip came too.

It was a nuisance to store, Dinchy would find. It had always been a nuisance in that way, but apart from the ring that came into Dinchy's possession at that time (and a Colibri cigarette lighter that had fallen from Alma's pocket on Clough Road and been lost), the photograph of the charabanc trip was the only tangible evidence that remained of Alma Ellen Dinch's seventy-one year sojourn in this vale of tears.

The open-topped charabanc in the photograph is a credit to Gus Elrick, who sits at the wheel glaring at us in a not unfriendly fashion, his right eyebrow inclining towards an unexecuted wink. The bodywork of his coach is in pristine condition and reflects the figures of several bystanders who await the chara's departure for a destination unknown, though it is obviously a wedding they are going to. The passengers are all ladies and every one of them, bar one, wears a buttonhole – a carnation pinned to the right, its bloom inverted. Alma Ellen Dinch, age 25 at the time, is the odd one out: no buttonhole has she, though apparently this will not be for long.

A child of five or six years of age with the face of a cherub, reaches towards his Auntie Alma, handing to her a flower he has received from his mother, Beatrice, who in turn has received it from her mother-in-law, Alice, who seems to be in the process of distributing buttonholes to all and sundry. Alma's hand, her left hand, is extended towards the cherub in the act of receiving the bloom.

All this is taking place on a sunny day in the summer of 1918 outside the White Lion public house, now demolished, which stood at the junction of Sudell Street and Stonehewer Street, Collyhurst.

Alma Dinch sits next to her sister Madge to the near side rear of the chara. Both of them are smiling, Madge a little more broadly – and Madge is wearing a hat, as are most of the other twenty-eight ladies on board. Alma is bare headed. A pretty girl, her hair short and styled, her left hand – poised to receive the buttonhole from her nephew, Alfie, seems delicate as the flower for which she reaches. And surely a ring is discernible on the third finger of that hand, an engagement ring, an emerald cluster perhaps, gifted, not as a birthstone, but to mark the month the gift was made: May, 1918 – the last time Frank Sidney enjoyed some home leave: Corporal Frank Sidney, as he then was, of "D" Company, the 18th Battalion, The King's (Liverpool Regiment), Alma's intended, who is destined never to return from his present posting. For Frank Sidney (Sergeant Frank Sidney, as he was at the time of his death) died on Sunday, 10 November, 1918, at the 48th Casualty Clearing Station in the village of Busigny, Departement du Nord, France, from wounds sustained effecting the rescue of an officer during a skirmish in the previous week.

The headstone of Frank Sidney's grave is one of 750 such headstones in Busigny Communal Cemetery Extension on the road to Bertry, north-east of St Quentin. But it is the only headstone inscribed with a military rank inferior to the occupant's status, "Corporal" being the rank inscribed on the headstone commemorating Sergeant Frank Sidney, late of Middlewood Street, Harpurhey, Manchester 9. Though Sergeant Frank Sidney would remain, of course, plain Frank in the heart and mind of Miss Alma Ellen Dinch, late of Glen Avenue, Blackley, and he was not any the less valued for that.

Apart from eight miserable weeks she spent as a junior in the offices of Darcy, Allen, Larkin, Larkin and O'Brien on Valette Street, off King Street, Manchester 2, Shirlee Jameson had worked in the office at Rapishaw Gap since leaving school. And until she and Dinchy bought the Mini Countryman some eighteen months or so after they started going out together she had travelled to and from Rapishaw Gap's offices by bus, preferably by the number 72 or 72X, neither one of which went into Cannon Street or High

Street like the other buses running down Rochdale Road. The 72 service ran along Great Ancoats Street before turning off into Newton Street, which meant Shirlee didn't have as far to walk to get to work in the morning and, even more importantly, didn't have as far to walk to catch a bus on her homeward journey after the clocks were put back at the end of October. Before they'd bought the Countryman, and once Dinchy had got the job on the vans at Rapishaw Gap, they'd travel down to town together by bus, though their finishing times rarely coincided, so Shirlee still travelled home alone more often than not, and she still caught the 72 or the 72X. Penny Kirkham would usually accompany her as far as the top end of Newton Street before going off to catch her own bus to Fallowfield from the bus station in Piccadilly.

For some reason that Shirlee could not even begin to imagine only the oldest, most rickety sorts of buses were used on the 72 route. It was as if the 72 were a Manchester Corporation Transport Department bus inspector's afterthought, a by-blow of a service cobbled together for the benighted denizens of north Manchester who resolutely refused to avail themselves of the sleek limited stop services serving Langley Estate and Rochdale, and who had been inconsiderate enough to buy housing accommodation that British Rail's Bury line or West Yorkshire line had never deigned to service. Consequently, it could take the 72 as long as forty minutes to get from Great Ancoats Street to Blackley Library where Shirlee got off. Thus it was on this particular Wednesday night in July, 1965.

Lurching and rolling between bus stops, dragging itself onwards in a generally northerly direction, the 72X on which Shirlee was a lower deck passenger spat alighting passengers like the pips of an orange, one at a time, at every bus stop along its route. At Churnet Street it left an entire queue of hopefuls stranded in the rain due to a full complement having been taken on board before it arrived there. But Queen's Road brought a general clear-out, a whole crowd of people getting off to catch the 53 that ran east to west and vice versa – double deckers being banned from other roads heading in an east-west direction due to a series of low railway bridges on Collyhurst Street, Monsall Road, Ten Acres Lane, and Hardman Lane, Failsworth.

'What's the longest bus route in the world?' Eugene had asked her on one occasion Shirlee had arrived home complaining. Unthinkingly, she had fallen for it, responding with a question. 'The 53: Jerusalem to Jamaica,' was the answer Eugene came back with – the 53 ran between termini in Cheetham Hill and Moss Side.

Blackley Library, where Shirlee got off – Turkey Lane, The Foresters, Alfred Street, Moston Lane, the Library – was five stops further on from Queen's Road; and thereafter, apart from Friday night when she would perhaps bring a chippy tea in with her from Chadwick's next to the Alliance, she followed a private routine that would take her as far as seven o'clock. Unless Eugene was home (and nowadays Eugene was away more often than not) Shirlee would have the house to herself till her parents returned from the half past six Mass they attended at St Joseph's church Monday through Thursday (Friday, Saturday and Sunday, they attended Mass at noon).

Opening the front door she had already stepped into the lobby before she remembered she had meant to check to see if the Countryman was parked up across the street. She stepped out again on a pretence of doing something with the milk bottles. No, it wasn't there. She hadn't really expected it to be. Silly really: she knew he'd been up in Cleveland all day. It was twenty-past six now, he must still be on the road. She hoped he'd take care and remember not to . . . No, she didn't. She did not. She hoped nothing of the sort. She hoped . . . well, nothing: she hoped nothing.

She didn't wish him harm, that would be childish. But, equally, there was nothing she hoped for, not one single thing. That was more like it. Yes, that was just the way it was; precisely the way it was. What business was it of hers anyway? How he was, where he was . . . *If* he was? She pulled that face only she knew how to pull when she was annoyed, making a conscious effort to shut him out of her thoughts. It was force of habit, that's all. It was sheer force of habit. How long had it been now? Three, five, seven, fifteen, twenty-one . . . Sugar! Twenty-three months of habit. She stepped inside the lobby, closed the door behind her, sighed.

This is what she must insist on when they had a place of their own: they must have a shower; yes, even if lack of space meant doing without the bath. And there you go again, she thought. What place of their own? What shower? What bath? And who were these people who would have a place of their own? Force of habit, she reminded herself, sheer force of habit.

Her tea was waiting for her in the fridge in the kitchen, ham and cheese salad tonight. She had prepared it as soon as she came in from work. The works canteen at Rapishaw Gap was cheap and cheerful and spotlessly clean, so she and Penny used it on a daily basis. Come teatime, except on a Friday, Shirlee would prepare what little she wanted after the dinner she had had at work and leave it in the fridge to be eaten later in the privacy of her room after she'd had her shower. And she would run the shower until she heard the front door go, or, until – as on this occasion – she heard Vic Jameson complaining about the electricity bill out on the landing:

'You're going to have to pay something towards this, our Shirlee, y' know. There's no need for it. I don't know. Must be like a tropical hell-hole in there.'

Shirlee mouthed the words with him, pulling that face only she knew how to pull. They were always the same words. She pulled a towel from the rail and dabbed at her hair and when her hair was no longer dripping, wrapped a smaller towel around her head, and dried herself off and talced herself and stepped into her slippers and shrugged on the towelling dressing-gown that hung on the back of the door. She opened the small window to let the steam dissipate and hurried across the landing and entered her room. Now, in the cooler air of her room, she began to feel properly dry and nicely chilly. She shook her hair loose prior to drying it. Then for a time, the noise of a Moulinex hairdryer filled the room.

She opened the wardrobe and selected a jumper and jeans to wear. The jumper she'd found on Oldham, the jeans on Newton Heath – markets, that is. She thought they went well together, and she laid them on the bed. She went to the drawer where she kept her small things and his handkerchief was the first thing she saw. The blue one, the pocket handkerchief that twenty-three months before on a Saturday afternoon in August had been covered in blood. It had lain in wait to ensnare her. She picked it up, held it to her cheek, then just as impulsively threw it down like a tainted thing. Almost immediately, she picked it up again, folded it in four and held it to her nose to smell it before replacing it in the drawer. She could smell her new perfume on it. She had had to wash the handkerchief three times and steep it overnight before she got the bloodstains out. She wouldn't imagine he'd want to go around perfumed by Lancôme. She supposed she'd have to wash it again.

'*Au contraire*, *Mam'selle*,' she reminded herself for perhaps the fiftieth time that day: you, Shirlee Jameson will not *have to* anything any more. Because you and your life and your love are all your very own once more to do with as you please. '*D'accord*, *Mam'selle*?'

'Ah . . . *D'accord*.'

9

'Come on, lace 'em up,' says Titty. Which is a laugh in a way. Because how you lace up boxing gloves single-handed is beyond me in much the same way as is the noble art itself. (And while we're on the subject, what's so noble about? I mean, *nobble* I'll have!) Besides, the left-hand glove had no lace in it to be laced up anyway.

Cig Heil offers no help, stood there in his leathers, a Woodbine stuck in his gob that he removes every now and then between fingers that spell out half his attitude to life – HATE, which for the time being extends to flicking cigarette ash on the floor and rubbing it in with his left foot like a dog marking its territory. Meanwhile, Himmler the Ted's off in a world of his own, somewhere west of Wyoming, thumbs looped over this leather belt that's got a metal skull for a buckle and holds his denims up.

I pulled the lace out of the right-hand glove, slung it.

'Come on, come *on*,' says Titty, skipping about as if he known a bit about boxing, touching his nose with his right thumb a couple of times as if checking to see if it was still there.

Heck, I hadn't even started on him yet!

'Whassermarrer wi' yer? I said. Playing for time, and scanning the room for help or an escape route. No help was to be had though; there was no escape route neither. They'd got us blocked in, the three of them, right, left and centre.

Colin Leitrim's miles away at the far end of the room, sat on this table near the refreshment stall, swinging his legs about and chatting to this bloke in a trilby hat sat next to him who's got the tweedy look of a bookies' runner.

'Whassermarrer wi' yer?' I said, louder still, and still to no avail.

'Marrer wi' *me*? says Titty.

'Yeah, I done *you* no 'arm.'

'Oh, *no*?' Titty begins nudging us with his left fist, then his right – like each punch is a speech mark. 'You mean, like . . . *off'rin'* us . . . *outside* the other night an' . . . *never* showin' . . . so's I went an' *caught* . . . me *death-of-a-cold*?'

The old one-two-three-four then.

OUCH!

'Yeah,' says Cig Heil.

'So's I 'ave *to* . . . get the old *lady* . . . *rub* us down wi' . . . Vick *Vaporub* an' . . . tuck us up in *bed* with an . . .'ot *water bottle*.

One-two-three-four again!

OW!

'Yeah,' says Himmler.

'Oh, *no* . . .' says Titty, 'You've not done . . . me no harm. So . . . you can get *that* idea . . . *right* out of yer kin head . . . *twat*!' Punches us, hard.

KINNELL! ENOUGH ALREADY!

'They joinin' in too?' I blurted out in this same half-shouting voice that done us no good before and done us no good now neither.

Titty laughs then, like he's never gonna stop laughing. 'Gonna need 'em, aren't I? Hey,' he spits over his shoulder to Cig Heil and Himmler. 'Grab a seat, yous two.'

And with that they very kindly leave us to it, sprawling like dead men across a couple of the cinema seats where I'd done me chest in earlier. Cig Heil snips the live end off his dimp and flicks the dimp so's it arced across the stage to somewhere I couldn't see where it went but where there was this window banging about in the wind. No sooner's the dimp landed he's got another Woodbine stuck in his gob and a box of England's Glory in his hands, ready to light up again.

So, there I was on that Thursday night long ago, in the middle of the dance floor at St Joey's youth club in the very same spot where three hundred thousand million billion kids would be having a good time tomorrow night, just like they'd had a good time in the past. Yeah, there I was on me todd, having to face up to Tough Titty, who was an evil bastard and hated me guts for summat that I never done and was Idle's fault in the first place.

Agh! Me heart was in me flipping mouth, it was. That's when it wasn't going BOOM-BANG-A-BANG against the bruise on me chest.

THWACK!

Titty's right arm shoots out fast, makes a hard connection with me left shoulder, knocking us sideways. I got me balance back, but not as quick as I'd of liked to. Because the sudden sideways movement fetched up this, like, screech from me chest.

'JEEZOZZ H. KHRI-I-ST!' it went.

THWACK!

Hard again. I was spun round the other way now and come back even slower. Me face was a picture – it must of been. And me poor chest took this loud hailer out, and told this GP off for probing too deeply:

'THE HELL YER DOIN'? I SAID I WAS POORLY, DIDN'T I?'

THWACK! THWACK!

Oh, I turned one way and, straight off, was shoved the other, slipped, nearly went down, only just managed to keep me footing. Me chest got Jeff Chandler on the tannoy in his peaked cap and US Navy whites:

'NOW, HEAR *THIS* . . . NOW, HEAR *THIS* . . .'

THWUNK!

Bull's-eye! He found the mark. Me chest went stereophonic. He must of read the look on me face, Titty.

THWUNK! THWUNK! THWUNK!

Okay, I admit it: there was tears in me eyes.

THWUNK! THWUNK!

Each punch rammed home to the same spot now. I lost count of them. The room was just one splodge of bright colours now, mostly red, with this darker red that kept coming at us . . . kept coming at us . . . kept coming at us time after time after time to bring new, fresher reds to life.

THWUNK!

THWUNK! THWUNK!

THWUNK!

THWUNK! THWUNK! THWUNK!

HWUK!

Look, I've no idea how it happened. Because me arms was just flailing about. But all of a sudden, right out of the blue, I caught Titty this lucky one right in the mush. *Stiff-armed* the bugger! What I'd of give to of seen his face!

THWUNK!

HWUK!

Done it *again*: stiff-arm. Maybe he fell on it.

THWUNK! . . . *HWUK!* . . . THWUNK! . . . *HWUK!* . . . THWUNK!

Oh, here it comes, I thought. Here it comes: The Chop, The Hammer Blow. And I just waited there for Titty to murder us, to knock us to the ground, to beat us into a bloody, writhing pulp. But nowt happened. Well, yeah, it did, of course. But what happened was not exactly what I thought would happen.

See, it had been dead windy all night and there'd been this window banging away on and off behind the stage somewhere, and all of a sudden at that moment the window slammed shut really hard and there was this sound, like, breaking glass, and in the silence that followed I heard this other sound too. Like, this great hoot of helpless laughter, and then another – and *another*! Hey, and get this! Gloves off, Titty grabs us round the shoulder, and hoots again:

'HOOT, HOOT, HOOT, HOOT, HOOT!'

Which is chorused by Cig Heil and Himmler, but in a sniggery sort of way.

'You jammy bugger!' booms Titty, giving us this horrific squeeze that's as bad as a punch, the condition I was in. 'Right, my crash. Get yer a Coke for that.'

WHAT? Had I heard him aright? I blinked, slung the gloves off, rubbed me poor eyes and stared. Was that it, then? Was that *it*? I just couldn't believe me luck. But, yeah, that was it, it seemed. Couple of lucky punches and – hey, presto! – there we is, me and Tough Titty, the best of mates all of a sudden, on our way down to the refreshment stall, Titty ambling, me reeling, with Cig Heil and Himmler loping along behind us. Till we run into Colin Leitrim, that is: off to see about the broken window behind the stage. Hey, and I was that relieved with what's happened (or rather what hasn't) I greet Colin like he's a long lost pal, miserable flipping ha'porth that he is. Whereupon said miserable flipping ha'porth stops dead in his tracks and rounds on us.

'Whoa, just one minute, now,' says he. 'Do you mind telling me what *you're* doing here?'

'Eh?' Titty, this.

'You've got your ticket, young man.'

Well, isn't that just typical? I think to meself. Story of my life. I mean, here's Dinchy with his sworn enemy, Tough Titty, who has very nearly murdered him in full public view, and who is now Dinchy's best mate all of a sudden, intent on treating him to a nice cool drink of Coke – well, maybe a bottle of Tizer because I don't like Coke, or, better still, a Vimto cordial. And now he won't be able to, seeing how he has somehow fell foul of the good men of the parish, the naughty boy. Ah, well, such is life. Some you win and some you lose; sometimes the cookie crumbles, sometimes it bounces too. He who fights another day, lives, but has to run away before he does so. Or summat. Still, if that's the way things is, that's just the way things is and there is no sense worrying about it because there is not a damned thing you can do. At which point I glance at my pal Tough Titty and shrug me shoulders. Me chest insists I done it just the once.

'Well, you might have the c-hommon d-hecency to look at me when I'm speaking to you,' says Colin Leitrim, very hoity-toity now.

Still, the boy Leitrim's not wrong. After all, it's only common courtesy to look at someone who's putting the boot in, exspecially if the boot that is being put in is the official St Joseph of Cupertino's parish youth club boot. I glance at Titty again. Don't hurt too much if I don't shrug at the same time. But this does; this really hurts: Titty *is* looking at Colin; Titty's been looking at Colin all along.

'YOU! I'm speaking to you! Would you mind looking at me when h-I'm speaking to you?'

I glance from Titty to Colin.

'Oh, *thank* you, th-hank *you*,' says Colin, very sarky-like. 'Thank you very much h-indeed.'

'What?' I said.

'I'll give you "what", you cheeky young bugger,' says Colin, tipping the wink to the bookies' runner, like as if to say: 'Just watch us deal with this bit of a kid, but you better be ready to back us up if he gets too stroppy.'

The bookies' runner slides off his perch that he's been buffing with the backside of his cavalry twill pants all night.

'What yer on about?' I said to Colin.

'I'll tell you what I'm h-on about. You've got h-exactly one minute to leave these pre-hemises. You're barred till further notice.'

'Why? What of I done?'

'What *haven't* you done, more like.'

'What's that supposed to mean? If I'm barred you've gotta give us a reason.'

'I don't *have* to h-anything,' says Colin. 'But seeing as you h-ask, and seeing as you've had the dire-bollocking cheek to show your face again, I'll tell you.'

'Well, go on then. I'm waitin'.'

'The last time you was here,' says Colin, 'you vaccuated these premises in an h-unconventual manner.' Or summat.

'Oh, talk English, can't yer?'

So Colin drawn this long, slow breath then, like the very patient good man of the parish he'd like you to think he is, what has been very sorely put to the test by this young scrote, namely Dinchy, and he says: 'The last time you was here, you h-exited through the cellar, setting h-off the burglar h-alarm, and causing h-all sorts of trouble for those of h-us who were left behind to clear h-up h-after you.'

'I never.'

'H-oh, yes you did. Because you was seen.'

''ooever says that's a liar.'

'In h-any case,' says Colin, as if I hadn't spoke. 'That's not the reason you're barred.'

'*Eh*?' I thought. 'Well, go on, then,' I said. 'What is it if it's not that, then?'

Oh, dearie, dearie me, I can't say I didn't ask for it. Because he's off then, Colin, round and round the houses. Oh, on and on and on, he went, about Teresa Mickleton, the old biddy that looked after the refreshment stall at the Friday and Sunday night dances – about how Teresa Mickleton was such a wonderfully kind old lady that done such wonderfully kind and unselfish work in the parish; about how Teresa Mickleton went up to church on her knees every day, pushing a peanut up Cumberland Road with her nose; about how Teresa Mickleton cleaned all the windows in the presbytery, inside and out, once a fortnight, and the stained glass windows in church too, by licking them with her tongue; about how Teresa Mickleton went on pilgrimage to Lourdes three hundred thousand million billion times a year, swimming out through the Bay of Biscay with a cripple on her back; about how Teresa Mickleton was more Catholic than the Pope; about how Teresa Mickleton ate Kit-E-Kat on a Friday instead of meat; about how Teresa Mickleton worn this hairshirt with Weetabix crumbs in it; about how Teresa Mickleton took Duraglit to that halo of hers on a daily basis till it shone; about how Teresa Mickleton slept in a special bed rigged up by Slumberland that had nails and broken glass and barbed wire in it and no covers on with the window wide open, blowing a Force Ten gale; about how Teresa Mickleton worn shoes that was two sizes too small for her, specially constructed by Timpsons with six-inch tacks licking up the insides; about how Teresa Mickleton had this bog seat at home that was really a Norweb hot-plate and a flush that dropped grenades instead of water; about how this wonderfully kind, unselfish and good old lady, Teresa Mickleton, whose feet you was not worthy to touch with a ten foot barge-pole that had been blessed by the Pope, steeped in holy water by Fr Elrick, and made from the True Wood of The Cross in the first place . . . how this good old biddy, Teresa Mickleton, instead of staying at home, knitting vestments and saying the Rosary three hundred thousand million billion times an hour with a rose between her teeth while listening to Verdi's Requiem played backwards on the Third Programme – how this wonderfully kind, unselfish and good old lady, Teresa Mickleton, come to the youth club week in, week out, every Friday and Sunday night to serve ungrateful yobs like me . . . (Oh, there was tons more of this, this being only a snippet.) Yeah, on and on and on, he went, Colin, and I was just sort of nodding off to sleep when he finally gets it off of his chest what he's on about.

'And what thanks does she get? Has her purse nicked for her trouble, that's what.'

'*What*?' I never said it, but I must of looked it: wide-eyed, gormless, gawping gob.

Anyway, Colin takes it for a question: 'Yeah, has her purse nicked by a young scrote like you!'

'I never done it,' was what I wanted to say, what was on the tip of me tongue to say. But summat stopped us. Because I known I'd be wasting me breath.

You know, sometimes where you get a cartoon character in a kid's comic that's messing about in Outer Space, say? Not Superman, or any of them. One of the other ones – Fudge the Elf or Toby Twirl. Hey, and maybe not one of them neither. But one of the funny ones, I mean. Characters that's meant to be funny, like Tiger Tim or Laurel and Hardy. Yeah, one of them, right? And like I say, they're messing about in Outer Space, and they're on their way home at last. Well, how can you tell they're on their way home? Easy! says he. Because there'll usually be a signpost sticking out of the moon or one of the planets or an asterisk, pointing to planet Earth with a big arrow on it, saying: HOME.

Daft, isn't it?

But here's summat just as daft. Two or three times in me life it's been like as if summat has struck us about a situation and made us step back, do a double take, and completely change direction. Like, once upon a time on one of me Wednesday afternoons off from Hugh Fay's when it dawned on us I had to get a different job. And another time I was at this party in Crumpsall (I think, but more about that later), having a ball, till it struck us I wasn't having a ball. Not by a long chalk. And then there was this crummy Thursday night at St Joey's crummy Youth Cub when Colin crummy Leitrim blamed us for nicking Teresa Mickleton's crummy purse and I just couldn't be bothered telling him it wasn't me that done it.

There was no signpost, saying: HOME or owt. It wasn't as daft as that. No, it was more like an idea that made sure I heard it because it just wouldn't go away. If there'd been a signpost, of course, it would of said: EXIT, not HOME, and it would have been stuck right over the door of St Joseph of Cupertino's parish youth club. Because it was like I seen in a flash that the good men of St Joseph of Cupertino's parish made their minds up years ago that it's Brownies and Girl Guides and Venture Scouts and members of parish confraternities that do any good deeds that need doing, and scrotes like yours truly that done the bad ones.

And when the good men of the St Joseph of Cupertino's parish make their minds up about summat, why, them minds of theirs stay made up for ever and ever. Amen.

Even so, I didn't need no exit sign, or an arrow pointing to it, did I? Because Colin Leitrim told us exactly where to go.

'Now, OUT! says he. 'Get h-out that door. And don't never come back. You're lucky Fr Elrick don't want the police brought in.'

'Nah, he wouldn't do, would he?' said I, pausing at the door to blast him with two barrels of wild shot. 'Because then he'd find out who really done it, an' you Holy Joes wouldn't get your hands on the collection plates again.'

So, there I was, kicked out of the youth club in me youth for summat I never done. I mean, for summat worser than I done that I never done. Lost a few mates through it too. Still, it learned us who me real mates was. Because they known I never done it. And it got us Tough Titty for an even better mate because he thought I done it – which I never done, or I would of said so. In any case, I know they say St Joseph of Cupertino had this knack of being in two places at once (a knack similar to what you was expected to have at Hugh Fay's grocer's shop of a Saturday). But this is something I have never personally had the knack of. So how can I of nicked Teresa Mickleton's purse when I'd been in company all the time on the Friday night it went missing – and was only on me todd in the snooker room for a minute or two where Teresa Mickleton's purse never was at any time I known of in all the years she helped out at the youth club?

It never dawned on us till next day that it was Idle done it. Because I just hadn't been thinking straight before. I seen it next day though, with me head being a bit clearer when I was having me break and a cuppa and a Gray Dunn Caramel Wafer round about eleven. Which would explain why Idle shot off early that night. It wasn't because he was scared of Titty (even though he *was* scared of Titty), but because he'd nicked Teresa Mickleton's purse. Right? See, Idle had had the perfect opportunity to nick the purse when I'd went through to the snooker room when Teresa was down the stage end, hanging on to Fr Elrick's every word.

Hey, I should of known it was Idle straight off. Because Idle was always nicking stuff. Yeah, he was in piles of trouble for it when we was at school. Course, it was only small stuff then, like, some kid's ha'penny chew, or your iron dobber, or an handful of HB pencils from the classroom cupboard, or a rubber, or your prize conker, or your elastic band that you used to fire bits of paper at people with, or your lump of pitch that you'd took the trouble to scrape up off the cobblestones on Wilson Road on a hot summer's day and had left lying around for about two seconds instead of it being in your pocket where it kept nice and soft because of your body heat – or your love pin, say. That is, this brass paper fastener less than an inch long that kids used to have in them days when they was at school and would stick it through the lapel of their blazers like a badge, and cross the prongs over on the underside because this meant there was someone they loved.

Yeah, just small stuff like that it was in them days, daft stuff. I mean, far as I know Teresa Mickleton's purse was the first serious item Idle ever nicked – and I suppose even that's just small stuff in the greater scheme of things, no matter how you feel about some scrote doing the dirty on a wonderfully kind and unselfish old lady like Teresa Mickleton, who was helping out at the youth club out of the goodness of her heart and didn't have that much to nick in the first place.

See, Idle was daft in that way. Always nicking stuff, and always nicking small stuff too – a purse, say, or a wallet, or a few quid, or a bike. Yeah, Idle would nick anything that was just lying around your house, or outside in the street, or on display in the local shops – anything that was just waiting to go walkies if someone had a mind to make it go walkies.

I'm talking about an attitude of mind, here. Because Idle Wild was always nicking stuff and never give over nicking stuff And from when he was in his teens, he was always getting caught at it too – even when he never got caught red-handed and thought he'd got clean away.

See, once the cops had his number, and, say, they was a bit bored hanging around Walter Street nick of a night, well, all they had to do to keep theirselves amused was roll up at Idle's house, have a good look around, and drag him off before the beak again with whatever Timex wristwatch, Draper socket set, half-pint tin of Berger's Magicote Non-Drip Gloss, or retail pack of Beech Nut chewing gum (max. contents 48) he'd gone and nicked this time. In fact, Idle was that used to having the police turn up at his front door that one Monday night, thinking it was a police van, he done a runner soon's he seen a white Sherpa pull up. Thing is, this particular Sherpa was not a police van at all, but a minibus he'd booked with Citicars earlier in the day to take him and Avis and other members of the family to Belle Vue dogs to celebrate a small win he'd had on Zetters the previous week.

Now I know you'll probably be at a loss to understand how I put up with Idle as a mate. But he was all right in other ways. Besides, once you know someone's a tea-leaf, you can take steps to guard against it. Oh, they is never your best mate, of course, and they never can be. But when you get right down to it, what's a few bits and bobs between friends? I mean, like Grandma Alma used to say, things that'll go walkies if you don't keep 'em under lock and key all the time is not worth worrying about too much. Because, if they're gonna go walkies, they're gonna go walkies. What you've really gotta be sure to take extra special care of is the things that really matter, the real things in your life, them things that won't never go walkies unless wild horses drag was to drag them off of you.

And another thing while I'm at it. Getting chucked out of St Joey's youth club wasn't no big deal, you know. Because there was loads of youth clubs in them days where the good men of St Joseph of Cupertino's parish didn't have no say in the matter. See, it wasn't like it is now, where there's nowhere for kids to go except the pub whether they're old enough or not. Nah, in them days you could go to a different youth club every night of the week if you wanted. And besides, there is always other churches to go to too, churches where the good men of the parish might just occasionally be exactly what they pretend to be. In any case, them same good men of St Joseph of Cupertino's parish I was well shut of, because they'd of thought no better of the likes of me if I'd of let them crucify us every Friday and once a month on a Sunday for good measure. They'll think no better of Jesus Christ Hisself, some of them, unless He bucks His ideas up, shaves the beard off, gets a short-back-and-sides, talks p-hosh, and wears a three-piece suit from Burton's the Tailor for the Second Coming

I never had no falling out with Idle about it neither, though I don't know how Avis put up with him, with them having the bread snatcher to feed and another on the way. Like she was that day I seen her at the pillar box at Blackley Library with that letter she was posting, pretending Idle was working away – which, OK, I suppose he was in a way, but working for H.M. the Queen, sewing mail bags maybe.

Oh, and how does Dinchy know all this, I hear you ask. Heard it on the grapevine? Read a report it in the *Daily Mess*? Well, yeah, both of them things But I'd of known in any case. See, the last time Idle got nicked I seen them catch him at it.

She would never interrupt him when he was eating. Like you'd do with a dog, she supposed. Wherever did he put it all? Because there was nothing of him, was there? He was nothing but a little scrap of a thing, like the runt of a litter. Friendless, or so it seemed, apart from the two lads: the Marlfield lad and the other one, the cocky little so and so – the one that Alma just couldn't take to for the life of her. What was it about him, Tony? He just kept coming back, didn't he? Yes, that's what it was, she supposed. He just kept on coming back – quite literally now he had the little two-wheeler. But he kept coming back from all the put-downs and the knock-backs is what she really meant. Like the time his dad made fun of him singing in the children's choir at church on Corpus Christi, so he made sure he sang all the more. Oh, dear me, if singing's what you'd call it. *Panis Angelicus* – God help us: a dingo's rendition, all day long, till Alfie gave him a tanner just to shut him up and get him out of the house for a bit, and packed him off to Mr Mac's on James Street for two ounces of Rainbow Crystals and a stick of spanish.

Or that time, Joe Bunratty made some sarky comment about his Coronation mug and the tin of Cadbury's milk chocolate biscuits with the flags of the United Kingdom on the lid that he'd sent off to Bourneville for. Great muscle-bound lummox! Why couldn't he leave the lad alone, spouting all his wrap-the-green-flag-round-me Gaelic League flannel within his hearing? Still, he'd got his come uppance within the week, Big Joe, on Coronation Day when he'd turned up with Alfie after a dinner time session in the Gardeners Arms, Moston, to find the lad had collected – ooh! – two square yards of clover (it must have been at least that) from the CWS sports ground on the corner of Victoria Avenue East and Greengate and somehow or other he'd managed to press each stem individually into the open pores of the foam filling of an old cushion he'd found in Joe's garden shed and rigged a safety-pin fastener on the back of it too. So when the men came back from the pub they'd found him sporting a giant shamrock-thing nearly as big as the lad himself. Oh, and absolutely po-faced he'd been about it too, sitting on the sofa in the Bunratty's front room in the house on Caen Avenue with his cousin, Cleet, his mother and his Auntie Annie, sharing a jug of Robinson's Barley Water, a Battenburg cake, and the sight of Her Majesty climbing into the State Coach on the Ecko TV in the corner of the room. Joe had laughed louder than anyone, of course. He would do. She supposed he had his good points, Big Joe, otherwise he wouldn't have turned up with a bike for the kid in the first place. Okay, so it was a second-hand one he'd come across on his travels somewhere, but he needn't have done it at all, need he?

Alma brushed away the few crumbs on the dresser top and drew them together with the back of a bone-handled bread knife, sweeping them to the edge of the worktop with her cupped right hand, catching them when they fell on to the side plate she held in readiness on a level with the two drawers below. She tipped the crumbs she'd collected into the sink tidy, took the dishcloth, dipped it into the washing up bowl, squeezed it out, and wiped the work top clean. She cleared the kitchen table and the worktop – milk jug, sugar bowl, cruet set, butter dish, a couple of knives, one fork, the Hoe's sauce bottle, a bottle of Chef tomato ketchup, screwing the top back on. She wiped the work top over with the dish cloth once more. All that remained was the bowl containing the wimberry tart and custard that the boy had very nearly polished off. The news came on the radio, so Alma switched it off. It was quiet in the kitchen now apart from an occasional trickling of water inside the cistern and the dull metallic rattling of the teaspoon in the boy's hand as it beat a tattoo on the side of the bowl each time he scooped another spoonful from dish to mouth. She opened the window slightly and the distant echo of children's voices rose to meet her from the path beside the brook in the Clough. The air was cooler now, dampened by a shower of passing rain.

While she waited she opened the left-hand drawer of the worktop, her drawer, the drawer that contained her personal things and items she needed on a regular basis, or ready access to for reference at a moment's notice – her pension book; a book of postage stamps; Basildon Bond envelopes, blue; a Silvine writing pad, lined, white; a ball-point pen; a bottle of Jackson's Febrifuge; an opened packet of Rowntrees Pastilles with four pastilles remaining, one blackcurrant, three green; a hairbrush, pink in colour; a large plastic comb; a pair of rosary beads; a Roman Missal; an old creased photo of her sister Madge; a prescription form; a bottle of Milk of Magnesia; a bottle of Eau de Cologne; a ten packet of Wills' Bristol tipped cigarettes; Frank's ring in its box; an A5 manila envelope containing receipts; a warranty document for the stove; the rent book; the TV rental documents; a picture postcard: 'Greetings from Lytham St Annes'; another postcard, from France; a birthday card she must remember to post by Wednesday at the latest (Noreen Jessop's birthday); an appointment card to see a specialist at Crumpsall Hospital on Tuesday week.

Maybe that was why they got on so well, her and Tony. Frank had had that way about him too: he just kept coming back. She hadn't . . . well, at first she hadn't . . . hadn't wanted to go to Hardcastle Crags with him on that Easter Monday when . . . when he . . . Oh, not now, Alma. Don't let the child see . . . on that Easter Monday . . . When was that? . . . Yes, thirty-four, thirty-six years ago at least. Maybe more . . . Mmm . . . Yes, it *must* be as long ago as that because all it took to stop herself nowadays was the blinking of an eye. Just the blinking of an eye. Provided she caught herself in time, of course. Provided that . . .

Alma removed her pinny and hung it, folded once, across the back of the nearest chair. She returned to the drawer, fussed about doing nothing in particular, took out the ten packet of Bristol cigarettes, took a cigarette out of the packet, and laid the packet on the worktop. There were two cigarettes left in the packet. She'd get another ten packet when she went on the Lane in the morning. She laid her cigarette lighter on the worktop too, the Colibri lighter she had treated herself to three birthdays ago – the lighter that had that odd pulling as opposed to a plunging action. Frank had smoked Capstan, the ones in the blue packet, not the coffin nails – Capstan Full Strength in the brown.

Frank wouldn't let her say no to that first outing. He'd mithered her every day for a week – no, ten, twelve days, it had been. So in the end it seemed the only way she was ever going to be able to stop him asking her on a daily basis for the rest of her natural was to say, Well, yes, all right, but just this once, mind. Then after all that, she'd enjoyed herself and she had continued to enjoy herself whenever they were together. Which wasn't that long a time, of course, because Frank had joined up early on with his pals from the Manchester Ship Canal Company, and almost before they knew it, he was off to Belgium and Italy and France, and anywhere else his regiment and Frank's apparently charmed life decided to take him.

The postcard was in her hands again, almost of its own volition, it seemed. The postcard had arrived four months after they got engaged on Frank's last home leave:

'*Dear Alma,*' she read. '*September, 1918. Much has happened since last we met. Have just arrived back at HQ. Had a lovely journey, weather is glorious. Magnificent scenery passing through the Rhone Valley with Alps in distance. We must come back here on holiday once this is over. Your ever-loving Frank.*'

These were the last words Alma Dinch heard from Frank Sidney, though not the last she heard *of* him. A month later she heard how Frank had been wounded. It was nothing to worry about, she heard too. But something went wrong. Frank rallied, made a comeback. But somehow too, by the 10th of November, 1918 – ah! the last day but one, lad! – Frank Sidney had gone beyond the cares of this life and, in a corporeal sense at least, from Alma's life for good.

Finished at last: get his things.

'Well, you seemed to enjoy that,' she said, removing the dish and the spoon in one sweeping movement, wiping the table where they'd been.

Dinchy smiled up at her. 'You're doin' a Barker's Cafe, grandma.'

Alma's turn to smile now. 'I am, aren't I, chuck? No sooner have you lifted your cup to your mouth than the waitress takes your saucer.'

'You are, grandma. You're doin' a Barker's Cafe? Have you got any biscuits?'

'Oh, where *do* you put it all, my little cockleorum?'

The boy laughed at the name she'd called him. He pointed to the cave of his open mouth. 'You know, grandma, *you* know. It goes down the red lane.'

'I know where it goes all right. But where's it all end up? That's what I want to know. Have you got hollow legs? Is that it? Have you got a pair of hollow legs?'

He glanced down at his thighs, standing up from the table the better to inspect them. He pushed his chair back, making the tubular metal legs scrape on the linoleum on the kitchen floor. 'Hollow legs?' he said. 'Hollow legs, grandma?'

'All the food you put away, is that where it goes? Does all that food end up in your hollow legs? Because you've not grown any bigger since I last saw you. And you've eaten enough to feed a football team. What are you after now?'

'Digestives,' he said, looking round from the open door of the kitchen cupboard with the lid of the red Crawford's Rover Selection biscuit tin from ten Christmases ago in which Alma kept anything in that line that was going. 'Chocolate digestives.'

'I've not been to the shops yet.' She took the biscuit tin and placed it on the worktop. 'Have a Blue Riband instead?'

'Can I have two?'

'You greedy monkey.' Alma handed him two of the remaining three.

He took the two Blue Riband without a word of thanks, though didn't snatch them. He shoved one of them into his right-hand trouser pocket, then unwrapped the other, screwing the cellophane wrapper up in his hand and depositing it in the sink tidy where it immediately unravelled itself.

'Can I watch TV now?'

'No, you can't. There's nothing on anyway. It's only the fish tank or the potter's wheel – chewing gum for the eyes, that's all.'

Alma took one of her two remaining cigarettes and clicked the Colibri lighter. She stood as she always stood when she smoked in the kitchen. Her back to the dresser, her left hand resting lightly upon it above the right-hand drawer, she raised the cigarette to her lips with her right hand, and inhaled. She inhaled more deeply a second time then threw her head back so that, her neck now being fully extended, her parted lips funnelled cigarette smoke vertically towards the ceiling. Thus, Alma Ellen Dinch, spinster of this parish, in her sixtieth year, at rest.

Her television set and ten cigarettes a day were the two luxuries she allowed herself – indeed, the only luxuries her pension would permit her whilst she continued to remain solvent. There were many people, she knew, who couldn't afford even that. Alfie and Helena, for instance, who'd got more to do with their money with the young un to bring up and Nelly herself not being in the best of health. Well, okay – maybe they could have afforded a television set if Alfie had *wanted* to afford a television set, television being just one of those matters of principle that Alfie seemed to be so full of nowadays. Alfie 'didn't believe in TV', he said. By which Alfie meant, Alma suspected, that Alfie had been taken in by some miserable Brains Trust old fogey writing in the *Sunday Tunnelvision* whose theme for the day had been to predict that television would be the end of civilisation as we know it, a pronouncement prompted in all likelihood by the failure of that same miserable Brains Trust old fogey to fill his boots with sufficient shares in television and associated industries at the right time at the right price, so that any subsequent weakness in the share price would work to his own financial advantage. You might as well say, thought Alma, that Mother's Pride white sliced bread would be the downfall of the nation. And, of course, that was another of Alfie's dislikes: white sliced bread. Nelly always had to give him brown or wholemeal, and it always had to be bread she had personally sliced with a bread knife, so there was no way in the world you could make yourself a proper butty with it, an honest-to-goodness corned beef salad butty with all the trimmings, say – hey, and gimme another one of them, please do, and it'll stand me in good stead till it's time for tea.

Alma was under no illusions whatsoever as to what attracted the boy to her: TV and tomato sauce (tomato sauce being another of Alfie's strict no-no principles). She'd watched some old western on TV the other night where someone (Randolph Scott or Bill Boyd – she couldn't remember which) had wandered into a saloon looking for trouble, and had found it by the simple expedient of ordering a glass of milk at the long bar. Alma had laughed at that. Alfie – Alma thought to herself at the time – Alfie could have caused mayhem in the Kardomah with a tomato sauce bottle, or rather, without it.

'A hungry man doesn't need sauce,' Alfie would observe with boring and predictable frequency.

'True, he does not,' thought Alma Ellen Dinch (though she wouldn't have said as much to Alfie for fear of causing trouble). 'And a starving man doesn't need a knife and fork either. But that doesn't mean he should eat like a pig, or think like one.'

At what precise point in time, Alma wondered, had she lost Alfie, the cherub in the charabanc photograph, the Alfie she had raised as her own when Beatrice died of consumption within twelve months of his father Jonathan's death at the Battle of Amiens just three months before Frank Sidney was killed. What had happened to the pleasant, open-faced child she had known – the youngster she had always found so caring, so cheerful, so attentive even?

The years themselves hadn't done the damage, Alma felt sure. It wasn't the luxuriant head of hair she missed, the good looks (almost girlish), the sprightly way he had of carrying himself. Things like that happen to everybody sooner or later. Everybody grows old, deflates into a sort of caricature of a former self, hair departing for good on the one hand, and on the other, growing in clumps within orifices as unattractive as they are inaccessible to clippers. With the passing of the years, Alma supposed, the best you could hope for in this life was to grow old gracefully. Which is precisely what had eluded Alfie. Yes, this is precisely what she, Alma Ellen Dinch, could neither understand not tolerate – the descent of Alfred James Dinch into a dour personalised dogmatism that would brook neither discussion nor dissent; that would accept neither innocent new diversions that made life a bit more bearable, nor the slightest deviation from a rigid strait and narrow of his own prescription that he had himself chosen to tread and now insisted on foisting on those around him.

Alma blamed the thirties and forties for this – those God-awful decades of the devil when everybody knew they had the answer to everything, though those answers were all different and every one of them was wrong, though nobody could possibly know that at the time because nobody was listening to anybody any more, because nobody was talking to anybody any more, because everyone now adjudged it good to bark orders at everybody and weakness to show compassion. Until it was too late, of course, by which time everyone you'd ever known, everyone you'd ever loved, everyone you'd ever cared for was dead. In the camps and in the dressing-stations, in the hospitals and in the mouths of the guns. Jonathan, Frank, Beatrice: three dead in her own family alone from Alma didn't really want to know how many millions of dead there'd been, Because it was just too, too depressing, like night without end. Because that hadn't been the end of it. There were the walking wounded too. The inmates of St Dunstan's; Alma without Frank; Alma's friend from the CWS tobacco factory whose husband returned from the first war, but never returned home; and Alfred James Dinch, a tower of post-war strength (the second war) – Hamer Shawcross in his own mind; Thomas Gradgrind to those around him whose lives he most affected: Alma who raised him, this poor little mite who came to her house, hungry for TV and tomato sauce. Bread and circuses, thought Alma to herself in her kitchen, and laughed. They won't make you a better person, she thought. But they might just stop you going mad.

Not to everyone is there given a second bite of the cherry, thought Alma. And she'd be damned if she'd let the same thing happen to her second little lad, the one who came to her almost daily now he had his bike.

'Lord, grant me only this,' whispered Alma Ellen Dinch, smoking her last but one cigarette in her kitchen that day. 'Neither Shawcross nor Gradgrind let this one be.'

The boy giggled, hearing her mutter these words. 'What say, grandma?'

Alma smiled at him, ruffled his hair. 'Just saying my prayers for a boy on a bike. Now, give me a kiss before you go.'

The day I seen Idle Wild get nicked I'd promised Shirlee I'd pick the tranny up even though Aristos Audio wanted paying for the repair and we thought it should of been done under warranty. And I'd meant to get it at dinner, but what with spending half the dinner hour having a ding-dong with this bozo in accounts after wages went and docked an extra fiver in tax out of me pay, I clean forgot about it.

'H-if wages done it,' says this bozo in accounts in that plummy voice he puts on when he can't get his own way. 'H-if wages done it, h-it must be right.'

'Oh, yeah,' I said, sarky-like. 'Like a lot of other things must be right, only they never is.'

Course, that only made it worser, and, like I say, we had this right old ding-dong and I clean forget about the tranny till about a quarter-past two, by which time I was dropping some Rapishaw Gap gear off on Oldham Road, up near the White Eagle Club, so I bowled round to Aristos Audio and parked up in the car park there.

This Aristos Audio place was upstairs in this old mill building. (I say "was" because they've gone out of business since, and I do wonder why, though not really.) See, this old mill building had been converted into different shops and that: a frozen food shop, a supermarket, a men's clothes shop, a lady's hairdressers, a furniture outlet, a travel agent, a florist, and – up there on the top floor, with the whole floor to itself – *vwala*: Aristos Audio. They'd done it up nice – all modern and that, with new glass counters and showcases and neon signs and lights and heaters and brand-new electrical goods and assistants in smart three-piece suits, so it was clean and warm and not like some Scrooge was running the place. But up in the roof space you could still see the same old iron girders that held the place up from when it was a cotton mill, and underfoot the floorboards was that rough you'd of chucked them on a bonfire rather than use them for your garden shed.

Now, when I went in that afternoon there was only a few folk about, what with it being a Tuesday, this being early closing day in Oldham and thereabouts, but someone had a radio on, blaring away, top blast, with some toffee-nosed geezer on it giving out about how everyone in this great country of ours was gonna have to tighten their belts and pull their fingers out and put their shoulders to the grindstone, not to mention their noses to the wheel. In fact, everyone in this great country of his was gonna have to do everything that this toffee-nosed geezer had no intention of ever doing hisself, being far too busy running his Sussex farm and looking after a string of racehorses up in North Yorkshire somewhere – that's when he wasn't jetting to and from Gay Paree, of course. Then someone must of twiddled the knob because there was this dead loud burst of static before they tuned into Watchtower Radio and Little Richard singing 'Send Me Some Loving', which is the B-side of 'Lucille' (some B-side!), and this wonderful bluesy tenor sax solo scooted right up into the roof space, weaving in and out of the old girders up there till it was time for Little Richard to get things off of his chest once more, cut throat notwithstanding.

And that's exactly when it happened.

All of a sudden I seen this little feller come belting up the aisle towards us between the cookers and fridges like he's going for the hundred yard record. Oh, his little legs was going like the clappers, they was, and making this quick sort of a drumming noise on the floor. And when he got right up close, of course, I seen it was Idle, but he was past us in a flash then. Hey, and clutched in his arms, tight up against his chest, like it was his little baby, the apple of his I, he'd got this electric toaster – one of them nice yellow ones with flowers on the side like Shirlee wanted, and probably Avis did too. And right behind him, hot on his heels, there was these three hundred thousand million billion shop assistants, all chasing him, and all running that bit faster than he was, on account of they wasn't carrying nowt in their arms and could swing them about a bit so's to gain momentum.

I just stood there, me, and watched them, and waited for them to catch him. Which they did do, of course, out on the landing before he could hop on the Down escalator. One of the assistants (the *Daily Mess* said he trained at Watersheddings with Oldham RLFC), well, he done this beautiful flying tackle that brung Idle down. And the next thing you known all them three hundred thousand million billion shop assistants fell on top of him. Except for just this one feller, a big bloke with a bushy moustache, a bright red face and little piggy eyes that held off and left them to it, and come striding back into the shop with his heels clip-clopping like castanets and shouts to this lass behind the counter.

'Get the police, Michele, there's a good gel!'

The others was dragging Idle back in by this time and calling him all sorts of names that wasn't fit for Michele to hear, good girl or not. Hey, and one feller – the littlest one among them – well, he had hold of Idle by the scruff of the neck, sort of holding on to the collar of his jacket and shaking him about so's to make it look like he was trying to make a break for it and was having to be forcibly restrained.

Well, it really got up me nose, that, because Idle was just stood there, sort of dazed, like you would be if all them fellers had fell on top of you. His jacket was all covered in dust, like, and his shirt was out of his pants and halfway up his back, and there was this tiny trickle of blood seeping out of his left nostril. And he was still clutching the toaster in his arms, though it was all smashed and bent now and wasn't no good to no one no more with this sort of a little spring-thing hanging out of it at a funny angle like a cuckoo that had called the time and couldn't get back in the clock.

'What's up, lads?' I said – shouted it more like. 'What's up, lads?' I said, making sure the few customers that was mooching about in Aristos Audio that afternoon give us their full attention. 'What's up, lads? I said, dead loud and sarky-like. 'Forget his change, did he?'

No one said nowt; no one said a dicky bird. They just looked at us like they could smell summat stinking rotten awful, and I was it.

The Mile House where I ended up that day is this little Boddingtons' house on North Street, Cheetham. It's a dinner time sort of a pub, I suppose, because there's a lot of light industry and warehouses in the area and not that many houses. (Acoss Cheetham Hill Road from Elizabeth Street, it is.) But it's a tidy sort of a place (clean and cosy, smashing pint) with a cheerful landlord and a nice tiled lobby and walk-in to the bar. Judging by the name, I reckon it's nobbut a mile from Manchester Town Hall. But it's the sort of pub that, if it was stuck on some hill top out in the country somewhere where it was hard to get to, Jack and Jill Public would be flocking to its doors – hey, and telephoning to book in advance too: 'Oh, please can't you squeeze h-us h-in, pretty please? We've heard there's a simply squiffy BMW car-key fob fight to be had h-in the cocktail lounge h-of a Saturday night.'

Which is not to say there's a cocktail lounge at The Mile House, Cheetham. Hey, there's no Beamers or Mercs neither, though there was the odd Riley Elf or Wolseley Hornet or Austin Cambridge parked outside at one time when there used to be a Kennings British Leyland car dealership at the end of the street, there.

Anyway, I stopped off there for a quiet half hour after I seen Idle get nicked when me next drop had took us down Queen's Road and right on to Cheetham Hill Road to the Polish Club. I'd been charging about like a madman all day, I'd had a barney with accounts, I'd been to pick the tranny up – plus seen Idle get nicked. So I fancied a quiet half hour to cool off. Pie and a pint, that's all. But what I seen behind the bar in the Mile House that day has took us back there the odd time I've thought on about it and had the time to do it.

See, what I seen behind the bar in the Mile House that day put us in mind of a certain lady I always thought the world of – still do. See, what I seen behind the bar in the Mile House that day was a Toby jug. I mean, there must of been three hundred thousand million billion Toby jugs behind the bar in the Mile House that day, and a very nice decorative effect they is too, very suitable for the bar of a pub, except that it's one particular Toby jug I'm talking about.

Look, I don't know whether you know this, but me Grandma Alma that's dead now and that I loved to bits when I was a kid and she me, judging by the way she treated us, well, I don't have a photograph of her, except for this one I've got of her on a coach trip in the olden days when she was pretty young – hey, and pretty too, I suppose. Maybe beautiful. But that's not the Grandma Alma I known. Well, it is, of course, though it isn't really because she looked different when I was growing up and me Grandma Alma was – well, she was growing old. Yeah, she was about forty years older than she was when she had that photograph took on the chara. Still beautiful, of course, though I may be wrong about that, and maybe she was just beautiful to me. But to cut a long story short, the Grandma Alma I known from when I was growing up looked like this face I seen on this Toby jug I'm talking about behind the bar in the Mile House that day. Or vice versa. That is, the face on this Toby Jug I seen behind the bar in the Mile House looked like me Grandma Alma – Miss Alma Ellen Dinch, this being me Grandma Alma's Sunday name.

Now, I know Toby jugs is supposed to be pictures of fellers, but this one I seen behind the bar in the Mile House looked like the face of an old woman – like I say, like me Grandma Alma's face when she was old and had white hair and sad grey-blue eyes and thin, slightly down-turned lips without make-up on and laughter lines under her eyes and at the corners, and this look on her face that was sort of kind and told you she was more likely to say something to cheer you up rather than moan at you – exspecially if things was really bad. And when she done that, me Grandma Alma, she'd maybe start laughing that wheezy laugh of hers that'd bring on another coughing fit if she didn't remember to stop laughing in time.

The barmaid is taking a breather when I clocked this Toby jug I'm on about. She's stood this side of the bar with her left hand resting on the bar and her back against the wall below the clock. She takes this Embassy Number One out of a twenny packet and lights it with a Ronson gas lighter and inhales, throwing her head back and exhaling this column of smoke towards the ceiling.

'Tidy bit of stuff you've got there, love,' I said, meaning the Toby jugs.

'Landlady's.' She takes another drag, exhales again.

'Nice.'

'Depends what you like, I suppose.'

'Cost a bob or two.'

'Well, I know one did, I remember her saying. Dunno which one though.'

'Owt you'd call priceless?'

'Dunno whether you'd say that exactly.'

'Ah, but I would!' I never said, just thought it. Oh, yes sir, yes, sir, indeed – and cross me heart and hope to die. Because there is not nothing in this world that is truer. Just like it's true that pigs can't fly and there's never a pot of gold at the rainbow's end and big boys don't cry. Except that, well, sometimes when you're maybe trying to have a drink and a smoke and a bite to eat and read the paper and hold a conversation with the barmaid and listen to the jukebox all at one and the same time, and you suddenly start thinking about something in the past, something you always took for granted, like – well, maybe cigarette smoke might get in your eyes at a time like that, or maybe an eyelash, say – or a Toby jug.

A kin *Toby jug*?

Time you was back in that yellow van of yours, Dinchy?

Look, we'd been going out for two years or summat when Shirlee fell out with us that time. Okay? What happened was something stupid, something really stupid. See, Shirlee had booked us in to see *West Side Story* at the – oh, I dunno where it was now, but it was somewhere like the Opera House on Quay Street, or the Palace Theatre. But what happened was this, see. I'd been out in South Yorkshire all day and got stuck in traffic in Rotherham and didn't get back till half past eight at night. Course, we've missed the show by that time, so Shirlee gets it into her head I've done it deliberately on purpose because I don't like musicals. And I don't. But I didn't get back too late to see *West Side Story* deliberately on purpose. Honest. I really did get stuck in traffic. But instead of apologising and trying to make it up to her in some way, I ended up saying something I maybe shouldn't of said. Like I say, it was something stupid. Well, okay, Thingy come into it for some reason or other – what's his name? – him that was the spit of Paddy Crerand of Man U. And then Shirlee says something *she* shouldn't of said. (Hey, no way was Miss Letting Board for Pigeons, 1962, Miss Second Hand Dart Board, 1961, like Shirlee said she was. I wasn't having that.) So we fell out, me and Shirlee, and I spent seven days in hell.

*

We had this daft conversation once upon a time – me and Byron, and Huge, where you had to say what you thought heaven was like and what would be hell. Heaven was easy arrived at: it was a full size snooker table and the space to put it (actor Richard Harris, having already baggsed being married to a nymphomaniac whose father owns a pub). We had more of a job on with hell though – I mean, whose hell was best, meaning worst.

I started the ball rolling with eternity on the waltzer at the fairground. Then Huge goes one better (that is, one worse) with eternity on the waltzer in the dentist's chair. Then Byron says: You're in the dentist's chair on the waltzer, right? But you've got to eat tripe and cow heel all day long and listen to never ending Irish diddley-diddley music. So Huge cries point of order on the grounds that Irish diddley-diddley music went on forever anyway. But he was overuled. Well, okay, says Huge, but only if – in the dentist's chair on the waltzer, eating tripe and cow-heel and listening to never-ending Irish diddley-diddley music – you is also gonna have the everlasting stink of Levvies up your nose. (Levvies being this rotten eggs smell the ICI in Blackley Village used to let off at teatime – Levinstein's being the name of the chemical works the ICI had took over). Oh, I pooh-poohed that one like a shot. (Joke.) Yeah, I said it sounded like heaven to me because the hellion in the dentist's chair on the waltzer, eating tripe and cow-heel, listening to never-ending Irish diddley-diddley music, and sniffing Levvies for all eternity had not yet had Denzo wrapped round his hands and feet, and round his head too except for his ears and his mouth and conk.

If stunned silence signifies victory, then Dinchy won the argument. Because Dinchy was the only one who known ("known" being what Dinchy said) that Denzo is a gunge-impregnated bandage the Gas Board wraps round gas leaks they can't attend to just yet and gas pipes they've just renewed and want to make doubly sure of. Denzo, Dinchy said, is mucky stuff on stilts – gungy and khaki-coloured, stickily glue-like and crude. Denzo is where Mother Earth dives full fathom five into the Underworld via the hot mud of Rotorua, N.Z. Denzo, said Dinchy, is so vile to the touch that no one with half a brain, walking upright on two legs, would dream of handling it unless the survival of the planet depends on it and they've been handpicked for the job when the SAS bottled out. Hey, and even then, said Dinchy, you still wouldn't go near it without marigolds (and callipers for preference). Denzo: yuk! said Dinchy. Denzo, said Dinchy, is hell at its high water. No sewer known to man ever coped with cruder cargo. But, as Dinchy confessed when he fell out with Shirlee that time, he'd been wrong about hell. Because hell – Real Hell (according to Dinchy) is not like that at all.

Real Hell, says Dinchy, is not about going off your food. Because he ate like a pig for a week. Real hell, says Dinchy, is not about being Billy-No-Mates. He was out every night bar none. Dinchy – and there are a thousand witnesses to the fact – Dinchy got rat-legged in pubs (three), in clubs (four – and five if you count Joe Bunratty's fiftieth at St Joey's). Any one of those thousand witnesses could vouch for the good time Dinchy had that week. But every one of a thousand witnesses (Dinchy included) would be wrong. Course, no one could be blamed for thinking different, says Dinchy. Because he *seemed* to be having a good time. He heard a good few jokes and a few good jokes, and he laughed long and loud at all of them. He went to Towncroft on the Sunday with Byron, watched the Wood Cup all day, swilled Lees' bitter like a native, ate his third Chicken Vindaloo in twenty-four hours, and threw his socks up behind the White Hart at the bottom of Hollin Lane at precisely 10.45 that night. At work, in the pubs, in the clubs, on the road, around the town (*towns*, rather – Middleton, Machester, Bury, Bolton, and Heywood too), Dinchy was hail-fellow-well-metting it for England, day in, day out, morning, noon and night, every waking hour of his life for a week.

But the real truth of the matter is this (says Dinchy), Real Hell is the real world where nothing is ever more (or less) than it seems. Real Hell (says Dinchy) is a place where every shape is angular and lying in wait to stub your toe or catch your funny-bone or bash your head when you go up or down the stairs. Real Hell is a place where the physical dimension of things can never change and never will. In Real Hell nothing is ever better and nothing can ever be worse. Real Hell is where the Cheviot is forever 2,676 feet high, where baked beans always taste the same as they did the time before, where your watch is never two minutes fast or five minutes slow, where you never forget to put the clock on (or back), where you never get a lousy pint of beer (or a good one), where the week you spend at the seaside is precisely that, a week. Real Hell is a place where it's daytime all day long and night time all of the night. Real Hell is a place where everyone is forever laughing and no one durst be sad. Real Hell is a place where the 72 bus takes exactly forty two point two five minutes to travel from town, but Shirlee is never on it. Real Hell is a place where Shirlee is never at the bus stop at Blackley Library when you drive past looking for her, never at home when you telephone her, never in when you call. Real Hell (says Dinchy) is a place where Bernard Manning's World Famous Embassy Club is filled to bursting three hundred and sixty-five days a year, but Shirlee is never there. Real Hell (says Dinchy) is every street in Manchester where he wished he'd never been born, where he wished he'd never known a girl called Shirlee who he's crazy about, where he drives a yellow van all day every day, and it doesn't ever drive him to the looney bin where he known (Dinchy said 'known') he really belongs.

I was driving me own rig by this time, but I made a point of taking the manifest into the office Monday through Thursday on the off chance I'd see her. Being the driver, all I really needed to do was send my mate in with the manifest – young lad, Ronnie Eshton, who'd started on with us a couple of weeks back. But, like I say, four days on the trot it was me went into the office, though I only ever seen Penny Kirkham there, never Shirlee. On the fifth morning, the Friday morning, I give it up as a bad job and sent Ronnie instead – and then I only had to go and chase him up because he was taking so long about it (we was due in Hexham, Northumberland, before noon), and as soon as I opened the outside door to the office I seen Shirlee coming out of the strong room they have there. So I told Ronnie to get back to the van and check the windscreen washer bottle, and I'd see him in a bit.

'Shirlee, I've gotta see you,' I said.

Shirlee looks around, like, as if to say, like: 'Oh, is that that crane fly-thing that's been flitting about the office all morning annoying everyone? Is it there again, nuisance it is?'

Me heart dropped.

'Oh, what about?' says Shirlee.

'You know what about.'

'Do I?'

'Shirlee, I gotta see you.'

'Gotta?'

'I've got to.' I went across to her then, right up close. 'Don't gimme an English lesson, Shirlee. I've gotta see you.'

She raises her right hand quick then and I thought she was gonna slap us or summat. So I flinched, and she smiles – and she reaches across then and turns back me upper lip, and says:'Oh, we're going to have to get that tooth of yours fixed.'

'I've had it fixed.'

'I mean properly. Penny knows a dentist, does a really good job with crowns.' She calls across to Penny Kirkham at her desk near the filing cabinets. 'Penny, what's the name, that dentist you told me about?'

Hell was just a memory now; this was limbo. In limbo someone like Penny Kirkham is always in the room with you and someone like Ronnie Eshton is always waiting outside the door to be drove up the A1 before dinner, so heaven must wait.

11

By the time he was 21 Byron Marlfield was on his way – over the Pennines mainly, into Yorkshire, West and North, and down to North Wales of a Sunday in this old Bedford van with the sliding front doors he bought at auction at Brighouse; and, within a year or two, in a brand new Ford Transit – new to Byron and new to the commercial fleet market too with room for three up front and a plusher interior than van drivers had been used to up till then. But Byron Marlfield wasn't just on his way mobile. He was on his way money-wise too.

'You are never gonna get anywhere working for someone else,' says Byron that night we was at the Cafe Monico on Union Street, Oldham – me and him, Shirlee and Amanda, celebrating our engagement. 'Well, not unless that someone else is pops, and pops has already made his bundle and is getting ready to pass the business on to the kids. Or unless you're one of the precious few in this great country of ours who happen to find themselves in the marshalling yards for the gravy train.'

'The railways?' I said. 'Me great-great grandfather, Malachi Methuselah Finbarr Fingal Bunratty or summat worked on the railway, and he never got nowhere at all, except well away from the potato blight and killed by a train in Thompson Street Goods Yard, Manchester. The kin railways, Byron?'

'Oxbridge – the Universities of Oxford and Cambridge. It's what John Osborne calls Oxford and Cambridge.'

'He have that pub, the Osborne, next up from Livesey Street on the right?

'John *Osborne*,' says Byron, like it means summat.

Said nowt, me, like maybe it did.

'Young gobshite, straight from school, knows nowt, thinks it knows the lot. Never held a job down in his life, never had to, total lack of nous, utterly devoid of any feelings of compassion for the rest of poor, suffering humanity. Bullshits its way into Oxbridge, gets an accent that won't travel north of Newbury, knuckles down to a bit of work if he's any sense, lands a job at ITN or the BBC news – loads of dough, weekends off, bit of overtime Bank Holidays.'

'Weekends off?'

'Now, don't tell me you never noticed nothing newsworthy ever happens at the weekend, Dinchy. Except sport, of course. Nothing on a Bank Holiday Monday either. Sport again, maybe a traffic jam. Handle that from a chopper, can't you? You never stop to wonder why the television news they're always foaming off at the mouth about whenever the franchises are up for grabs always has to take a back seat till midweek the rest of the time? Come midweek, all the ace newshounds have finally made it back from hunting, shooting and fishing, frigging about in Henley-on-Thames, and jetting to and from Gay Paree. That's why the television news gets held back till midweek. That's why no one who wants to make the headlines ever riots till the pubs throw out of a Sunday night. Stands to reason. No one's interested in rioting unrecorded, are they? You never figured that out, man? Sure, you might get the odd rumpus kicking off in some banana republic, say. But that's foreigners for you, isn't it? Don't play by the rules of the game, old bean; never have, don't-cha know?'

Byron had spent a couple of years in sixth form at North Manchester Grammar School doing his A-levels. For a time then, he turned his hand to the kind of jobs he was now well qualified for with his three hundred thousand million billion O-levels and A-levels: Civil Service (Tax Office and DHSS), District Bank, CIS, Manchester City Council. But in the evening and at weekends, and on Bank Holidays too, he'd been bang at it, working at every kind of part-time job that's known to Manpudlian man – the sorts of jobs that maybe don't need doing till the night time or the weekend. But when them jobs do need doing at the night time or at the weekend, then quite a lot of whatever it is that don't need doing till the night time or the weekend then needs to be done. Like bar work, say, or dishing out newspapers and delivering them. Or maybe the person that normally does that job at the night time or the weekend wants some time off for a change – just like them gravy train travellers that have their bread buttered on both sides and jam on it too, plus their cake and ha'penny as well. Yep, night time, weekends, Bank Holidays – or whenever there was some bod wanting time off from work for a family christening or blow-out, that's when Byron Marlfield would step in and mop up.

Paper rounds, bar work, waiting on, market work, shop work (tailoring, shoes, household provisions), selling ice cream at Old Trafford one time the West Indies was playing (though he never made much doing that, he said – watched the cricket mainly), window cleaning, insurance round, football pool agent etc. etc. etc. See, that was Byron Marlfield's life from the time he first stepped into long pants at the age of thirteen. Then around about the time I got took on at Rapishaw Gap, Byron went independent and made his first bundle – the bundle he made on the knocker. The TV rentals and the properties, them other bundles (what Byron calls his 'steady stream of income'), they come later. But here's how Byron Marlfield set about making his first bundle. Well, as near as I can make it out anyway.

'You gotta think first generation immigrant, man – even if you're not. Hell, especially if you're not!' Yeah, that's how Byron put it at the Cafe Monico that night. 'First off, you get your mind-set right. "Look," you say, "here I am, a newcomer in a free country where there are laws that let me do the things I want to do and laws to protect me from anyone who's unhappy about my doing them. If I live within the law nobody's gonna shoot me dead in the street and the police will not break my door down during the night without good reason. Well, not unless I'm unlucky, they won't. Now, that's not the way things are back in the old country; so it's a way of life I appreciate very much. If I'm sick, a doctor will make me well again. Also, the kids'll get free schooling, and I've no worries about where my next meal is coming from either.

'So I'm safe, right? I've got food to eat, I've got access to medicine, clean accommodation. I've got the basic requirements. But, that's *all* they are – basic requirements, subsistence, if you like. It's not what you'd call a living. And to what extent have I got those basic requirements when I've got 'em? This being a democracy, my subsistence is subject to change precisely because the government is subject to change. Furthermore, what I've always understood to be a socially committed political party – well, that party might renege on its principles when it gets into power. Then a whole chunk of my subsistence can be taken away from me overnight. Which is not much of a problem if I'm young and fit and in work. But what if I'm not so young? What if I'm getting on in life when the government puts the boot in. Now, that's the moment of truth, man. That's the killer, see. Because there's nowt down for old folk in this country whatever government's in power. So there I am, I'm old, I'm out of work, and I can't *get* work, because nobody's gonna give me any work. The 99.99% of my fellow countrymen – those who are permanently excluded from the marshalling yards – hey, you won't give me any work. No, not you, man. And as for the freeloaders aboard the gravy train. Hah! They've never so much as tossed a cob of coal off the tender in the last five-hundred years or so. So there's no way they're gonna start now.'

'What about Oxfam?' I said.

Byron turns and looks at us, like he's come out of a dream and is surprised to see us there. 'Yeah, that's unfair of me. Oxfam does untold good. Individually, I mean. Now, don't get me going, man.'

'Don't get you goin'? You're already goin' to some tune, if you haven't noticed. You sound very bitter, Byron.'

'No . . . no, I'm not bitter at all,' says Byron. 'And I'm sorry if I gave you that impression. No, if anything, I'm grateful to them. You see, my basic needs are going to be taken care of for the time being. And meanwhile, anything I can profitably turn a hand to has got to be better than the filing cabinet future my qualifications have fitted me for. Yeah, all I've gotta do is climb out of this hole they've very kindly dug for me. Mind you, it helps if you've got a good woman behind you.'

Which Byron had, of course: Amanda the Loveable (as he says her name means in Latin). So Byron hit the road while Amanda sorted out the back office, such as it was – terraced house on Ashville Terrace, lock-up garage on Ada Street.

To begin with.

Like I say, this was five years or so before MOnrOvia TV took off – ten years before Colorado. (Byron had dropped the big letter Os by then. Because if you couldn't see Colorado was a TV shop with about three hundred thousand million billion ex-Granada rental colour TVs in the window you was not likely to be a potential customer.) And, come Colorado, Byron and Amanda moved out of Ashville Terrace to the poshest house on Polefield Road, set back behind gates at the end of a drive. Course, that was before Amanda got a yen for Prestbury. But they had to wait till Marlfield Immobilaria was up-and-running before they had enough for that.

'There are twenty-four hours in a day,' says Byron. (Which wasn't exactly news to us, I must say: Unzo had told us that much!) 'You gotta sleep eight; you gotta eat and wash. I intend to sleep six, and no shopping, Amanda'll do all that. No sports either: this is my hobby.' (Byron raised his left buttock and ripped one off: the two girls being in the Ladies' at the time) 'And no farting about either.' Byron burped: he always winded hisself both ends after a good blow-out, and said: 'Replete!' He said so now. 'Replete!' – and ripped another one off.

'Eighteen hours a day is a lot of hours, man, especially if you times it by seven. A hundred and twenty-six hours a week in all. I absolutely refuse to believe you can't make a decent butty working eighteen hours a day, seven days a week. Even if you use half that time for thinking – hell, especially if you use half the time for thinking!

'Besides it won't go on forever. Year or two, three – five years down the line maybe. Depends on a lot of things really. But if you keep your wits about you, if you're just a little bit lucky . . . Well, after a time, the money becomes the muscle. And when it does I can sit back and exercise the grey matter a bit more. Make even more money, pile on the muscle, so to speak. I know it sounds daft, but you can be too busy working to make any real money.'

Oh, I agreed with him about that all right – it sounds daft because it *is* daft. Though I never told Byron that. After all, a feller's entitled to make his own mistakes in his own way. I mean, take MOnrOvia TV, for instance, the TV rental buiness Byron got into up on Moston Lane where he had (what was it now?) summat like three hundred thousand million billion TVs rented out by the time I was doing the Wrexham run when our Suzanne was born. Now, if Byron had only had the sense to get up off his arse every once in a while instead of sitting around thinking all day long, he'd of maybe had three hundred thousand million billion and *ten* TV sets rented out, if you know what I mean.

'Now take yourself, for instance,' Byron says to us in the Café Monico that night, 'I expect you could use a few more of the readies now you're saving up to get wed, and I need a feller I can trust. So how about lending me a hand? Saturday, Sunday, the odd day mid-week if you're free or on lates – Bank Holidays, you're not tied up, Henley-on-Thames or Gay Paree. I mean, you get most weekends off, right? And I wouldn't always need you anyway. Not every weekend. But you're not frightened of driving a van or a bit of graft is what suits me. Run a stall for me – run a couple, you take to it. You think, Shirlee? You gonna let the boy out to play. Fiver a day for starters till we see how it goes?'

Like I say, we was celebrating our engagement at the Café Monico that night. Mine and Shirlee's, I mean. Byron and Amanda's engagement had had to be put on hold till Byron's 'steady stream of income' come on tap five years down the line with MOnrOvia TV.

Anyway, that night we'd ended up at the Cafe Monico, which was this Berni Inn on Union Street, Oldham. Nowt to write home about – grilled steak, gammon, chicken, bottle of plonk – except that Berni steaks have never yet been bettered on the face of this planet. And, in amongst all the chit-chat, Byron had been telling us about his immediate business plans while we smoked a couple of them Henri Winterman cheroots they used to have for sale at the bar there.

Course Shirlee okayed Byron's suggestion as long as it made sense to me, and I filled her in a bit more about it when we got home. It made sense all right. Fiver a day was more than I'd be able to earn anywhere else at the time. It was very nearly as much as I was earning on the vans.

Anyway, that's how I come to be working part-time with Byron during the time me and Shirlee was saving up to get wed. The dosh I got off Byron suited our purpose only too well (in me hand, tax free), and by the time I jacked it when we got wed, Byron's brother, Pearson, had already started to help him out with a stall on the Sunday market outside Queensferry. And Byron had three other brothers waiting in line to get stuck in. (Huey, Dewey, and Louie, as I called them.) But it was me that was with Byron Marlfield when he made his first bundle. Yeah, and here's how he done it too.

We posted leaflets through letter boxes by the thousand, every one of them elastic-banded round a green plastic garden bag.

HELP! HELP! HELP!
HELP US SAVE THE PLANET
HELP US RE-CYCLE YOUR UNWANTED GOODS
books, records, garden tools, household implements,
bric-a-brac, clothing, furniture, toys, shoes,
electrical appliances etc. etc. etc.
IN FACT, ANYTHING THAT'S CLUTTERING UP
YOUR ATTIC,
LOFT, DRAWERS, BLOCKING YOUR GARAGE –
OR JUST GETTING UNDER YOUR FEET
We will gladly take it away
* FREE *
FOR LARGER ITEMS, PLEASE ASK
THE DRIVER TO KNOCK
WE WILL CALL BACK THE SAME TIME TOMORROW
If you have nothing to donate on this occasion,
please leave this bag and leaflet in your letter box.
Thank you.

Course, before we done this, Byron would take an A to Z street map of Greater Manchester and choose his area carefully. What you want, says Byron, is districts where people want to live and prove it by stumping up good money for the privilege. Like, Droylsden, say, or New Moston, Chadderton, Alkrington, Chorlton, Sale, Holcombe Brook, Unsworth, Shaw. These is the sorts of areas you want, says Byron: comfy and convenient – private property that's tidy but not too posh.

Monday morning, if I was on lates at Rapishaw Gap, we'd saturate the area Byron picked with the flyer, then follow it up the very next day.

'Don't give anyone time to get too Sarah Ball about it,' says Byron.

'No one's gonna throw a wobbler,' I said, thinking he meant that Sarah Ball palsy there'd been a programme about on Panorama.

'Leaflet, collect, and away,' says Byron.

'Sounds like the engineer's motto they had at Paul and Smart's when Line worked there,' I told him. '"Span 'er, screw 'er, leave 'er, an' bolt!"'

Course, you had to make sure you picked the right kind of house. Terraced houses – this is the Gospel according to Byron, this – terraced houses don't have that much stuff cluttering the place up for the simple reason that there's not a lot of room for it in the first place. So any clutter, they usually bin it quick; and an house without clutter was no good to us. So terraced houses, we never ever touched. And Byron also says:

'We don't want houses with big drives either, because big drives are knackering, leaflet delivery-wise. Also the owners of houses with big drives are mainly interested in houses with big drives and not Planet Earth.'

And you will often find, says Byron, that there'll be one or two toffee-nosed freeloaders living in houses with big drives who'll maybe start mouthing off about what me and Byron was doing being a rip-off. And not only is this aggro we would much very much prefer to do without, says Byron, but he disagrees very strongly with this point of view.

'Go on, you tell me,' says Byron one day we stopped off at this caff for a brew after some carpet-slippered solicitor-type in Timperley had just been having a go at us when we'd gone to his front door. 'You just tell me how what we're doing on the knocker is any kind of a rip-off. You've got people who are cluttered up with gear the council won't take away for them, or won't take away without charging them for the privilege, and we'll take it away for free. Seems like a good deal to me, man. And then you've got people who've got gear they can't shift themselves because they've haven't got transport, or they haven't got a car that's big enough, or they haven't got the physical strength to load the stuff in the car if they've got a car in the first place. But you and I will do the honours for them – and right willingly too. Seems like a good deal to me, man. Right load of old shite, some of the stuff they leave out too – no good to man nor beast. But we'll take it away without a quibble and dump it for the old dear that it's getting under the feet of. Go on, you tell me: how is this a rip off? Hey, and how is it a rip off when for every hundred garden bags we dish out door to door, we only ever get maybe half a dozen back – eight, nine max, because the other ninety-odd oh-so upright local ratepayers, like Mr Timperley Gobshite Mouth-Almighty LLB have nicked the rest of them to bung their holier-than-thou grass cuttings in? How is this a rip off, man? The shoe's on the other foot if you ask me, man. Seems to me the half dozen bags we do get back are fully paid for by the other eight dozen we're obliged to donate to the hard-done-by horticulturalists of Heckmondwike.'

'We never leafletted Heckmondwike,' I said.

'It's a litter Asian,' says Byron.

'What? Like that Chesterfield we picked up in Dobcross that time? An Ottoman, you mean? Like a divan or summat?'

Garden terraced and semis is just ideal for the job we was doing. Being a bit bigger than a terraced house, but not too big, garden terraced and semis is very often occupied by the sort of person who known there's a very real need to save the planet but has not got around to doing much about it as yet because they've been too busy bringing up the kids and earning a crust, and who may be only too glad you have thought to provide them with the opportunity to contribute. Even so, there's still some types of garden terraced and semis that are definite no-no's.

Council houses are not owner-occupied, so they're a definite non-starter. Also, we had to make damned sure we avoided any house displaying a notice warning hawkers and canvassers they'll be garrotted with the Rottweiler's choke chain if they so much as unlatch the gate. And, last but not least, we always run a mile from any house that displyed a biblical text.

'Biblical text houses,' says Byron, 'are the worst of the lot. In my experience, a house displaying a biblical text will be occupied by Vlad the Impaler, or one of his brethren, who will not hesitate to run you through with a rusty pikestaff, then swear black is white before Mr Justice Hot-Under-The-Collar in the High Court that he only did so, Your Honour, as a last resort when he realised you were intent on practising animal husbandry on his yapping Doberman bitch that he bought on Tib Street for Mother's Day.'

Like I say, we'd distribute Byron's leaflets one day, collect them the next. So we'd be all done and dusted in just over 24 hours. Deliver them 9 o'clock onwards when the kids had gone in school; collect from 10 o'clock next day. One tour on foot, another quick sweep in the van an hour or so later. Like I say, six to eight per cent was the overall return, bag-wise. Money-wise, the sky was the limit.

True, there'd be junk that needed tipping, but not much of it – hey, and we'd tip it too, no mither. As for the rest, well, mostly it'd be clothes: men's, women's, children's. And Amanda would sort these out back at base, wash what was marketable, pack the stuff in suitcases at discount prices ready for market, or mark it up individually for the dress rails that carried the classier gear. Any clothes we couldn't get rid of like that (smaller sizes was a problem: we're a nation of fat gets – well, a nation of second-hand clothes-buying fat gets, at any rate), or oddments, or old-fashioned gear, or raggedy stuff, Amanda would bag it and, as soon as we'd got a van load of it, Byron would take it to a ragman up in Oldham near Mumps Bridge who'd divvy up according to weight.

Generally, you got what you asked for: books, records, tools, bric-a-brac, clothing, furniture, toys, shoes, electrical appliances. If people wanted to know if you'd take owt else, they was not shy of asking you. Apart from builder's rubble and garden waste, not once did Byron say: No!

Fridges, washers, cookers, TVs, lawnmowers, carpets, guitars, piano – you really wouldn't believe what folk will throw away. Take a trip down the local tip, you don't believe us; it's an education. Got too much money, some people. And at the same time, they've got too little. You'll have a man and wife, say, out at work all day long, kids being minded by someone else, and all of a sudden they start acting like money comes easy – yeah, like they're rich as Creasers (this Roman feller Byron told us about).

What they don't seem to realise is it's their lives they're throwing down the rubbish tip along with the old Erika typewriter they don't want no more now they've got a word processor, or the paraffin lamp out of the greenhouse, or the gas mask their grandad worn in the Second World War, or the old Ercol cottage suite they don't want now they've got a new one from DFS. See, all that stuff they thrown out was worth good money to Byron and me.

Any stuff we couldn't move immediately, we'd make an appointment to come back for – and we always kept that appointment. Anything we couldn't shift personally, or knew we wouldn't be able to sell it on, Byron would come to some arrangement with someone else to shift it. Like this Yamaha overstrung piano we had one time. The Davyhulme and Dumplington Operatic Society was looking for a piano, cheap, says this ad in the *Salford Advertiser*. So Byron done a quick deal on this piano we'd been offered, provided the Pirates of Penzance (men only) come team-handed in a pantechnicon and shifted it within forty-eight hours.

Like I say, the only stuff Byron drawn the line at was builder's rubble or garden waste. See, that stuff's a no-no from the start, and householders known better than to ask. And even then, Byron once got a gang of roofers to strip a roof for a feller in Gatley that was gonna have a new one put on – and he got a good back-hander off the feller and off the roofers too. And sometimes too, if there wasn't too much of it, we'd maybe shift a bit of hardcore as a favour for some old girl. See, all the other stuff, the stuff we was perfectly willing to take away – well, that could all be sold on, either by you, or by somebody else.

Best thing we ever got give buckshee was a working TV that happened to be a bit dirty. But it cleaned up a treat and was perfectly serviceable. (Byron stuck it in his bedroom.) Then, there was an Hoover Junior vacuum cleaner, a New World gas cooker, and a Hotpoint larder fridge – every one of them in good working order. (The Hoover was that much of a worker it wouldn't switch off, but we fixed it.) And we got them all gratis, just for the asking. I mean, the fridge, for instance: how's this for a case of penny wise, pound foolish? Feller over in Droylsden asks us to take this fridge away, a worker it was, but he insists on having the plug off it for his new one. No problem. Cut the plug off there and then with a Stanley knife. Stuck a new MK plug on it back home at Byron's place. Sold the self-same fridge, cleaned up, perfect working order through the small ads at the cost of a new plug from Volmax on Great Ancoats Street plus a fee for the small ads in the *Hebers & Tonge Telegraph.* Got top whack for it too! Twenny-five quid – one hundred times the price of the MK plug!

Can deliver! That's the secret. Yep, them's the magic words, says Byron – can deliver! I mean, Byron wasn't only working the markets during the day, you know, he was selling stuff seven nights a week too through the small ads section of the local press – Manchester, Stockport, Oldham, Ashton, Rochdale, Bolton – and doing deliveries anywhere within a twenny, twenny-five mile radius. (Any further, he'd maybe ask for a bit of petrol money, depending on how sweet the deal was.) But them's the magic words, says Byron: Can deliver!

'You do get knock-backs,' says Byron. 'But not all the time. In fact, nine times out of ten you don't have any trouble at all. Not if you describe things properly. The trouble is, of course, the ten knock-backs in every hundred all seem to come in the same week. So it can be a bit dispiriting, that. But only if you let it be. See, that's why you've gotta take the long view – six months, a year. If it's working for you overall, why knock it?'

Believe you me, Byron made a very nice butty out of it. Selling through the small ads seven days a week, out to market four or five days a week, adding a bit of new gear to the second-hand gear he'd collected when he'd visit one or two wholesalers in Cheetham Hill. Crockery, cutlery, mirrors, kitchen tools, bedding, towels, tableware, fancy goods, electrical gear – plugs, connectors, batteries, aerials. Anything bright, anything brash, anything seasonal or topical, anything at bargain basement prices, anything that the people who bought it off him at the right price would eventually run out of or break, and have to come back for some more.

Oh, that stall of Byron's! It looked a treat when he flashed up. (Market men call it a flash, that: the set-up, the way it looks, the Hey-come-on-and-buy, folks!) He just had that way with him,

Byron. Strikes me a lot of people who are dead set on making a load of money seem to think that all they have to do is look after theirselves. Hey, and maybe that's right. What do I know about it, never having had no money to speak of? All I'm saying is this – Byron Marlfield had that way about him where he'd leave the customers feeling like it was them who'd got the good deal. And they had too. I mean, bargain basement prices wasn't in it. But, meanwhile, Byron Marlfield was making a very nice butty for hisself too, thank you very much. Does that make any sense? Because I think it does. And Byron was just the same in later life when other people give him their money to invest. Always give them a square deal, is what I heard.

'Keep your feet on the street,' is the way Byron summed it up one time. 'Business, even big business, is like a market stall. If there's no bargain to be had, there'll be no profit for the boss in the long run. Run a high-priced monopoly? Hey, fine and dandy – till Mr Cheapo-Copycat rolls up and chops your little legs off for you.'

The billies loved it. (Sorry, 'punters': the Billy Bunters.) Byron was usually bombed out.

Bet you think market men are mad. Up at the crack of dawn, out in all weathers, back home after nightfall, needing summat like a Ford Transit in order to do business – which don't cut the same sort of dash with the Joneses as a Ford Cortina Mark One GT with a Blue Mink paint job and a leatherette roof. But market men could be saner than the likes of you and me. Oh, they're up early, it's true, but they've got no boss to worry about, and on a cold winter's day a market man will always be a lot warmer than the billies because he'll make sure he's dressed for it. Layers of clothing is the secret, from the thermal underwear out. Thick socks, thinner socks, thick soles on his shoes, and a bit of wood or a duckboard – even a bit of cardboard, to lift him up off the cold ground. He's set for the day then. Another thing is the brekky. A market man will always shove a full monty breakfast down his neck first chance he gets. Sure, he'll eat all day if you let him, but when business is brisk the billies won't let him. And is he worried about that? Is he heck as like. Because he's making good money and he knows he won't starve with a full monty breakfast inside him and, come nightfall, he'll grab another monster munch at his leisure.

Sometimes a market's quiet, of course, which is obviously something a market man don't want. But there's stacks of things for him to do when it's quiet, like tidying up the stuff the billies messed up last Sunday at that hectic market outside Prestatyn. Or maybe he'll introduce some new gear he's fetched in the van, stuff he'd only have to introduce when he gets home after work – and when he gets home after work, of course, there is absolutely no chance whatsoever that a billy will maybe come up to him while he's doing it, asking him to please relieve him of a fiver for an electric toaster he collected buckshee from a doorstep in Tottington a week last Tuesday in one of the half dozen green garden bags that come good that day.

And Byron, you know, Byron Marlfield ticked over even when a market was quiet. See, as well as his normal stuff, he carried a tea chest with all kinds of stuff that market men need to ply their trade but very often run out of, or forget to get in the first place, or are too bone idle to go shopping for when they have a day off. Permanent black magic markers with a chisel point, card (bright orange, yellow, green and pink), pens, clips and pins, receipt books, price tags, refills for price ticketers, cash bags to strap round your waist, fingerless woolly gloves in the winter. And the other market men got to know Byron had this stuff available and was only too pleased to buy it, and at a premium too when they was desperate enough, that is.

Sundays, we'd more often than not drive out to North Wales during the summer, the two of us, and stop at any of the markets from Queensferry on – Flint, Prestatyn, Rhyl, Abergele, Colwyn Bay, Llandudno, Penmaenmawr. The rest of the year he'd be up in North Yorkshire – Skipton, Settle, Harrogate, Leyburn, or Hawes. Or nearer to home in West Yorkshire – Bradford, Leeds, Huddersfield, Otley, Holmfirth. We'd perhaps do these nearer ones on a weekday. Though sometimes I'd stand a North Wales market for him while Byron drove further on and stood a second one, picking us up on his way back.

One day when we stood Richmond, North Yorkshire, Byron says: 'I came up here when I first started because I didn't want people I knew to see me at it before I knew what I was doing. Then after a bit it got that way it suited me. See, Manchester's done to death market-wise. The billies are spoiled with there being a once in a lifetime bargain on every street corner. So I reckoned I'd be better off sticking a bit of extra fuel in the tank, driving up country, and selling cheap to people who'd maybe appreciate it more.'

Just travelling around with Byron was an education too, you know. Oh, we had the normal laughs and accidents – and booze-ups too when we'd had a good day. And we ate more full monty breakfasts than are good for the heart. But the A635, the road that crosses Saddleworth Moor between Greenfield and Holmfirth always got Byron prattling away to some tune. To this day I don't know what it was about the A635. Maybe it was with us using it more oftener than any other road. I dunno. But there was something about that road, the A635, that always seemed to get Byron going.

Course, it's no ornery road, the A635. It's the sort of road where you can sometimes have really good visibility, and the next time you use it (maybe a mile or so further on even) the visibility's down to nil. It's like a causeway across the moor really, though the only tides that ever wipe it out are hill fog and cloud and mist. Still, there's something about the A635 that's not quite real – a feeling that (and I don't want to labour this point too much) you are not alone, even when you're travelling alone, though who your companions may be, I wouldn't like to say. And that's silly talk, I know, and maybe it's just the sudden arrival and movement of mists and fog in these parts that makes us feel that way. But, looking back, I think Byron felt it too – and felt too the need to keep in touch with another human being whenever we was passing so close to them places where (as Byron says) 'a monster's business had been done with the remains of youngsters that the same monster had done the unspeakable and unimaginable to'. This isn't just hindsight speaking. Because by the time me and Byron was driving between Greenfield and Holmfirth on a regular basis, the police had already done enough digging on Saddleworth Moor to last any normal man a lifetime.

12

February, 1966: Byron Prattle No. 1

We're driving towards Holmfirth one day with Byron prattling on about this school speech day he was at, the year he done his A levels. And he's taking off this big wig alderman going on with hissself up on stage there at the Free Trade Hall on Peter Street.

'"Opportunity, my de-ah boys, is a woman," he's giving it out, this nobhead,' says Byron. '"Opportunity, my de-ah boys, is a woman with a full head of hair except that she's completely bald at the back. You must grasp this woman from the front, my de-ah boys. It's so hard to take her Art Ergo."'

'Art Ergo?' I said.

'Yeah. I only wish,' says Byron, 'I'd had the nerve to challenge his sauce.'

'His *sauce*?'

'Yeah, it's not *Pilgrim's Progress*, as he said it was. Alderman Addlecock either didn't know that, or he was only pretending, being in polite company for once in his life. But callow youth that I was at the time, I had all my work cut out just keeping a straight face. Because I couldn't for the life of me imagine making overtures to a female slap-head – perish the thought Art Ergo!'

'Sounds American,' I said.

'Eh?'

'Art Ergo.'

'It's Latin.'

'What the Romans spoke?'

'Yeah.'

'His sauce Latin too?'

'*Rabby-lay*,' says Byron

'You know, that breakfast's been repeatin' on me all day too. Bacon was a bit greasy, I thought.'

'*Gar-gan-chewer*!' says Byron

'Better out than in's what I say.'

*

April, 1966: Byron Prattle No. 2

Another time, we're heading back towards Greenfield with the sun going down when Byron brings that Pee to Loo stuff up again. But this time he's good enough to explain that he's talking about this rumpus called the Peterloo Massacre that took place in St Peter's Fields, Manchester, where they've built the Free Trade Hall since so everyone can sit down and be butchered in comfort if Orator Hunt ever gets around to putting in another appearance.

'You know, it beggars belief,' I said, 'to think that once upon a time London thought Manchester important enough to send soldiers in to kill us. I mean, you couldn't expect that sort of personal treatment nowadays, could you? Prob'ly just bung the price of petrol up to, oh, ten quid a gallon or summat so you wouldn't be able to afford to get out of the flippin' street, never mind drive all the way down to Peter Street to not even flippin' riot.'

But Byron says it was the local militia that done it, though he took me point. And Byron also says: Now, I mustn't get all bitter and twisted like what he wasn't. Because Byron said, it is only right and proper that London gets the best of everything, being the capital. Right? And anyway, it could be a helluva lot worser. Heck, says Byron, imagine if you was Scotch and got nowt at all from the government except picked on for every barmy bit of legislation they feel like to trying out before they dare foist it on the Home Counties. Oh no, says Byron, I mustn't get all bitter and twisted like what he wasn't.

June, 1966: Byron Prattle No. 3

Market day in Holmfirth again, and we're heading out that way early on as usual when Byron comes out with this load of codswallop, right out of the blue, he does:

'Suppose,' says Byron, 'suppose some terrorists invade the USA, burn Washington DC to the ground, and set fire to the President's house. What would you do with them, Dinchy?'

'You kiddin'?' I said. 'This a joke or somethin'? You mean that film on the telly the other night?' Can't remember what it was called now. Byron ignored us anyway.

'Answer the question,' he says.

'What? They done what, Byron? They burn Washington . . .'

'They burn Washington DC to the ground.'

'An' they set fire to the White House?'

'Well, yes and no. It's not called the White House yet. That comes later. They set fire to the President's house; it's where he lives, right? But it's not called the White House yet. Some folk say it's not called the White House till it gets that dirty with the terrorists setting fire to it they paint it white to cover up the mess they've made. That's when they start calling it the White House, they say. But there's others who say that's just a story. So, okay, it's the White House if you like, but only after the fire, not before it.'

'And they what? What else they do?'

'Ah, you're playing for time, Dinchy. I know you. Look, they've burned the city of Washington to the ground and set fire to the White House. What more you want 'em to do before you sort 'em out? You gonna let 'em get as far as Baltimore? Which they will do in the end, if you don't hurry up. Go on now. Tell us. What're you gonna do with them?

'The puppet . . . the ones that done it?

'The perpetrators, yeah. Now, get on with it. You'll have it dark. What're you gonna do with them, for Pete's sake?'

'Depends,' I said. 'Do I know where they come from?'

'You do.'

'Nook 'em!' I said.

'Whoa, hold ya hosses, Dook,' says Byron, putting on this bit of a drawl, like. 'The bomb's not been invented yet.'

'Well, why'n't you say so? Saturation bombin', then.'

'Sorry. There are no bombs of that kind either.'

'Okay. Scorched earth thingy. Give 'em a taste of their own medicine. Set fire to their country. Burn every house for miles around, the crops in the fields – put 'em out of house an' home. See how they like it.'

'Yea, verily,' says Byron, talking like Count Draclia as we

dropped down to Holmfirth. 'Vengeance is wrought. Dinchy the Destroyer incinerates Greater Manchester.'

'Eh?'

'Or, to be more precise,' says Byron, talking like one of them *Sunday Tunnelvision* reports, 'Dinchy the Destroyer erases from the map of the British Isles that region of north-west England which in the post-industrial age will come to be known as the Greater Manchester conurbation.'

'Pard-ing?'

Byron's laughing his head off as he pulls up at these traffic lights near Harry Ramsden's chippy. 'Washington DC was burned to the ground and what for the sake of convenience we'll call the White House was fired in 1814 during the War of 1812 by a British expeditionary force under the command of Major-General Robert Ross, recently Colonel of a regiment, now better known as the Lancashire Fusiliers.'

'Well, I'll go to the foot of our stairs!' I said.

Byron's still laughing. 'The Twentieth Foot would be most appropriate, Dinchy.'

'Eh?'

'Colonel Ross's regiment. Mind you, he paid a high price for what he'd done. He was killed in action near Baltimore later that same year.'

August, 1966: Byron Prattle No. 4

Hey, the Korova Milk Bar – that name Byron always used for that milk bar on Cross Street, Manchester, near the old *MEN* offices and the Bodega (long gone)! Well, one day Byron tells us he's pinched this name off a milk bar in some book called – hey, get this! – *A Clockwork Orange*. You ever hear such shite?

Which prompts us to treat Byron to some prattle of me own for once. Because I'd heard quite enough of Byron Marlfield's prattle to last us a lifetime, thank you very much. Yeah, I reckoned it was high time I got me own four pennorth in.

*

August, 1966: Dinch Prattle

We was tootling along the A635 in the Transit as per usual. This is the same day, this – the *Clockwork Orange* day, just as soon as Byron has shut his cack about it. Coming back from Holmfirth, five miles short of Greenfield, we was, where this road shoots off to Meltham on the right. And I don't know why it come over us to tell him just then, but tell him I did. And in no uncertain terms too. Yeah. Pulled no punches, me, once I got started. Told him exactly what he could do with them books he was always going on about. Told him where he could stick 'em too, beginning with *A Clockwork Orange*. Always provided they was paperbacks, of course, and he could roll them up pencil fashion. Told him why I'd no time for 'em too.

Well, Byron stamps on the brake pedal dead hard then, and pulls off into this lay-by with a sort of a sliding skid. A red Jag following close behind us nearly slammed up the backside of the Tranny, he done it that quick, and we got this long blast on the horn from Mike Hailwood at the wheel that went from loud to soft, the Jag was going that fast too.

'You are unbelievable, man. You know that? Go on, run that past me again.'

I looked at him, like he was joking or summat.

'Oh, I mean it, man. Run that past me again. I've gotta get my head round this one.'

I shrugged and rolled the passenger window down a touch. I took a cig out of a twenny packet, tapped each end on the packet in turn, lit up, put the spent match in the ashtray, and took a real deep drag. (Senior Service, not me usual Park Drive: we'd had a pretty good day in Holmfirth.) I watched this kestrel hovering high above the track that drops down past Shiny Brook and the reservoirs to Wessenden Lodge.

'Look,' I said. 'You know I can't never get into a book, Byron. It makes me head go wuzzy.'

'Ye-e-ah?' Byron says this real slow, like he's humouring us.

It put us off a bit, that, so I shut up and looked out the window and went to get out to stretch me legs. The kestrel swooped down to earth and disappeared from sight.

'Get on with it,' says Byron. 'We haven't got all day, you know.'

True, it was coming up to five o'clock by this time and me tummy was rumbling a bit. We'd been at it all day with nowt to eat, barring the KitKats and the bacon barms we'd had for breakfast.

'Them books,' I said, 'Them books you're always goin' on about. I know I don't do a lot of readin' but I wouldn't read sequels if I did.'

'Par-ding?'

'Sequels,' I said. 'They're never as good, I don't think.'

'Sequels?

'Yeah.'

'What sequels?'

'*Demetrius and the Gladiators*.'

'*Demet . . .*'

'Sequel, innit? Sequel to *The Robe*. Richard Burton and Jean Simmons have just jossed it with this heavenly quire to help 'em on their way. But Victor Manure's still alive and the Romans nab him and he gets made into a gladiator.'

'*Who* does?'

'Who does what?'

'Who gets . . . Who becomes a gladiator?'

'Victor Manure.'

'Who's he when he's owt?'

'Big bloke, wavy hair, never worn a suit, always in a mini skirt.'

'Whoa . . . whoa, I know *who* you mean. You mean Victor *Mature*. That's who. You're talking shite in more ways than one.'

'No, I'm not.'

'Yes, you are, pal. For starters, I don't have a book called *Demetrius and the Gladiators*.'

'Never said you had, did I?'

'Why bring it up then?'

'Because it's a sequel. Like them books you're always goin' on about.'

'What kin books?'

'The Birkenhead one.'

'The Birkenhead one?'

'*Birkenhead Revisited.*'

Byron pulls his face, like his belly's giving him gyp. 'You mean *Brideshead* by any chance?'

'Yeah, and *Dextry Rides Again.*'

'*Destry Rides Again*?'

'That's it.'

'I know that's it, man.'

'So what're you laughin' at?'

'Hey, who's laughing? What's there to laugh about?'

'Look, Byron, all I'm saying is sequels does me head in. Right? It's a free country, innit? I'm entitled to me own opinion, aren't I? Just like you're perfectly entitled to read whatever the hell you want to read – *Trent's Last Case*, the Goodbye books . . .'

'The *Goodbye* books?'

'*Goodbye to Berlin.*'

'Isherwood.'

'Bless you.'

'Thank you.'

'*Goodbye to All That.*'

'Graves.

'Don't know that one. Sounds scary.'

'Sounds that way to me too, man.'

'Yeah, and the other one . . . Nah, it's gone now. It'll maybe come to us in a minute.'

'Why bother if you don't like it?'

'Because it's annoyin' me, that's why.'

'That'd never do.''

'I know it's Goodbye summat . . . Goodbye somethin' . . . No, it's not. But it's summat like.'

'Right, you finished then?'

'Well, yeah, apart from that one. Why?'

'Wanna ask you something?' Byron winds the driver's window down, lets a load of fresh air in. 'You don't like sequels, right.'

'I already told yer that.'

'Okay, okay. But put me out of my misery, will you? What have sequels and Victor Mature and *Demetrius and the Gladiators* and Old Uncle Tom Cobbley and all got to do with any of the books you've come up with? There's not a one of them's a sequel. Well, apart from *Demetrius*, and that's a film, not a book.'.

'You barmy, or what? You *completely* off your trolley? Every last one of them's a sequel. I mean, take the *Brideshead* one. Where's Brideshead? Go on, where's Brideshead? I don't mean, like, where's Brideshead, like, Blackpool's a town at the seaside. But where's *Brideshead*, the book?

'Par-ding?'

'You heard us. Wash yer flippin' ears out. And while we're on the subject, where's *Destry Rides Out*? Because if Destry rides again, he must of rode somewhere in the first place. You can't just ride again if you've not rode nowhere before. Like you can't revisit Brideshead if you've not never been there beforehand. They've gotta be sequels. It stands out a mile.'

'Plain as the nose on your pikestaff, eh?'

'Key-rect!'

'So let's see if I've got you straight here, Dinchy. What you're saying as I understand it is *Trent's Last Case* must be the sequel to . . . well, *Trent's First Case*? Am I right?'

'Spot on, pal!'

Byron takes a deep breath and breathes out, puffing his cheeks out like he's a bullfrog.

'Hey, don't get us wrong now,' I told him, not wanting to hurt his feelings now we was discussing things on the same level at last. 'I reckon I could dive straight into *Hello to Berlin* if you've got it. I'm interested in other places.'

'I think you are some other place,' says Byron. 'You on that wacky baccy, Stetson Tex ships back from abroad?'

He meant this bloke I'd told him about, one of the gang that worked at Rapishaw Gap: Stetson Tex that always worn a big hat with a brim, Mackie Flowers that always took a bunch of flowers home on pay day, Vinny the Pig that looked like a kin pig, and him who'd been my oppo till he took bad, Biffo – who thought we called him Biffo because he was a big handy feller, which he was, of course, though he was also a Big Ignorant Fucker From Oldham. They called us The Rookie behind me back after I made the mistake of going to work in Line's army boots one day mine was at the mender's.

'And by the way,' I said, because the name of that other book had just come to us all of a sudden. 'It's *A Farewell to Arms*.'

'What is?'

'That other Goodbye book.'

Byron begins banging his head against the driver's door window, making the Tranny rock from side to side.

'You cryin'?'

'Nope. Smoky in here.'

'Yeah, but listen,' I said, 'You can see where I'm comin' from, can't you? I mean, where's *Hello to Arms*, or whatever it's called? Because there must of been one, mustn't there? And while we're on the subject, where's *Hello to All That*? Because, where there's a Goodbye, it stands to reason there must of been an Hello at some time. There must of been. So them two's gotta be sequels as well. And, like I said in the first place, sequels does me head in and I don't want nothin' to do with them.'

The Tranny had stopped rocking about when Byron stopped banging his head against the window, but she shudders a couple of times when he starts her up and shoves her in gear. Then as he pulls out on to the A635 again, up the backside of this green Thames van, he looks across at us, and says:

'Know what, Dinchy? You never spoke a truer word in your life. That last book in particular is something no one in his right mind ever wants to see a sequel to ever again.'

Now, I don't know about you, but I think it's really nice when you come to a meeting of minds with a pal – exspecially after a heated discussion, say, and when the thing you have come to a meeting of minds about is something you is both very interested in, both very knowledgeable about, and both care about very much indeed. So it was nice to know that in his heart of hearts Byron Marlfield felt exactly the same as what I done. Hey, even though I had beat him hands down. Still, credit where credit's due's what I say. Because Byron Marlfield, you know, he always was very decent about things like that. Yeah, I have never once known Byron to hold it against you if you'd bested him in an argument. Mind you, the subject of sequels never has come up again. But just the odd time, say, when someone's maybe mentioned books or films or summat of the sort, and me and Byron have happened to be in the same company . . . Well, to be fair to him, Byron has always took one step back, like, and maybe held his hands up as if to give us the floor. Yeah, and he'll maybe say to whoever it is that's brung the subject up in the first place:

'Whoa, rather you than me, man. You won't catch me winding Dinchy up about that. The boy's mustard, he really is.'

And me? Well, I've never made a point of sticking me oar in neither. Like I say, fair's fair is what I think. I've always been a bit of a soft touch like that. Never do like to kick a man when he's down. Otherwise, I could of told Byron Marlfield where to stick his hardbacks years ago. Hey, and flipping MFI flat-packed, at that!

13

It is certainly Manchester. You can easily tell that because it's smoggy in the way it was invariably smoggy in Manchester from November onwards before the Smoke Control Act of the 1970s brought its overnight cure. The atmosphere is dank, the cobblestones are gritty with dirt, the landmarks in the background dominate the scene in an impressionistic kind of a way. The front elevation of Manchester Town Hall stands to our right with the monument directly opposite, and further back, buildings can be seen running into Albert Square from the top end of Cross Street and on to Princess Street. Yes, we are certainly in Manchester, and we are in rather grand company too. Middle left, a royal prince seeks shelter from the rain and, middle right, larger than life, William Ewart Gladstone, the Liberal Prime Minister and one time MP for Hawarden in Flintshire, disdains to use the horse drawn carriage at his feet and raises his right arm magisterially to flag down a hansom-cab (unseen) approaching from Mount Street. The thousand square yards of fog that separates these two stalwarts is populated with a crowd of lesser worthies: councillors, business folk and the like (be-hatted and be-tailed), though these are only hinted at rather than delineated in detail – as, indeed, is the pedastal-mounted form of John Bright, MP, and nearer towards us still, a veteran car with a yellow boot. (This, I always like to imagine, is the artist's car making its trademark Hitchcock-like appearance. For is not this same car pictured in *Oxford Road* and *York Street*, two of the artist's other works?) Front left an old man, who nowadays would be long retired from work, stoops to the shafts of a plumber's handcart he pushes before him. He is clad in a smog-coloured cap, heavy workboots and an overcoat of a similarly indeterminate shade. The hair beneath the cap is white. The old man makes painfully slow progress across the foreground of the picture. Even so, he will soon be gone.

The title of the painting is *Albert Square,* and the artist is Adolphe Valette (1876-1942), a native of St Etienne, south of Lyons, who taught at the Manchester School of Art from 1906 to 1920, L S Lowry being his most famous pupil. The copy of *Albert*

Square in Dinchy's possession is only a print, of course, and is framed to 14 inches by 16 inches in what Clive Bradley, the proprietor of Manor Arts, Fountain Street, Middleton, calls 'the two inch Ital' (Italian dark wood). It has hung on the wall nearest the kitchen in Dinchy's living-room since he and Shirlee moved in, though the Italian dark wood frame was acquired more recently. Shirlee bought the print for Dinchy when he was still living at home, and in the same week he was despatched to St Joseph of Cupertino's church (to the presbytery, to be exact) with instructions to post the banns of matrimony whilst Shirlee was otherwise occupied at a dressmaker's on Grange Park Road.

'I owe so much to him,' Adolphe Valette's more famous pupil was once heard to say about his mentor. 'For it was he who first showed me the good drawings of the great masters. He was a real teacher, a dedicated teacher.'

Dinchy would never have used words like these, of course. Nor would he have articulated a thought in quite the same way. But he did have a similar regard for the old priest – white hair, stoop, Roman collar, cassock of overcoat length, desert boots, who seemed not unlike the old man in the painting, and opened the door of St Joseph of Cupertino's presbytery to him on the evening of his visit there, Dinchy having rung the day-bell. Fr Human, as the old priest came to be known colloquially amongst the parishioners, was new to St Joseph's, and was not to remain there long. Nevertheless, he was there quite long enough for two conflicting stories to beat the bounds of the parish about him.

One of these stories had it that Fr Human had been imposed on the parish priest, Fr Elrick, from above – though from no further above than His Lordship, Bishop Thomas Holland, DD, PhD, DSC, DLitt, the eighth bishop of Salford, the posting being intended, it was said, to chastise Fr Elrick for insensitivity in his dealings with Fr Richard Bellis, a popular curate, whom he had censured severely for neglecting to lock the side door of the church on the Wednesday of Cheltenham Gold Cup week, Fr Elrick being absent on family business with his McElrick relations from the County Kildare. For upon his return from Gloucestershire

Fr Elrick had discovered candle wax on a carpet by the Lady Altar and just 143 parish hymnals remaining when he knew for a fact he had ordered a full gross from Burns, Oates & Co. so as to obtain the discount rate. Fr Elrick had been further disturbed to learn during the following August (from a teetotal parishioner – a Pioneer, who will be allowed to cling to the shroud of his, her, or its anonymity) that Fr Richard Bellis had been seen to fall from his pushbike outside the Golden Tavern after closing time on the Feast of the Assumption.

Not a drop had passed Fr Bellis' lips that night save for what little transubstantiated wine he had consumed at the Mass he had celebrated earlier in the evening at the Alexian Brothers Nursing Home on St Mary's Road prior to spending an hour with the residents, a further half hour cycling back to St Joseph's by way of Lightbowne Road and Church Lane – which circuitous route had facilitated a promised visit to a lady parishioner who had experienced a difficult seventh delivery despite her being in receipt of the very best medical care at Beech Mount maternity home adjacent to the Cintra Cinema, later Gala Bingo Hall.

But the other story that had gone the rounds said His Lordship was at his wit's end, not to say fed up to the episcopal back teeth with Fr Human, because no PP in the Diocese would take him. For it was felt amongst the senior clergy that Fr Human was a bloody (Dinch Senior's adjective!) nuisance and ought by rights to have taken the sacerdotal equivalent of the Chiltern Hundreds, whatever that might be, but just as long as it included two essential ingredients: Fr Human, and great distance from the Diocese of Salford.

His Lordship, it was suggested at the time, by those who claimed to have knowledge of the ways of the Cathedral Chapter and Diocesan Curia, had tended towards a more dispassionate view. Fr Human's retirement from active service could not be justified on grounds of age: the man wasn't yet seventy. Also, he was dispiritingly hale and hearty, and – in any parish in which he served – he invariably brought a disproportionately large amount of energy to bear on whatever it was that needed to be done. Naturally, there were certain drawbacks, as is ever the case when anything appears to be too good to be true. For Fr Human had become forgetful of late. And in addition to this, he seemed intent upon bringing some of that disproportionately large amount of energy to bear on causes, charitable and political: CND, UNICEF, this New Century-New Start malarkey he was rattling cages about at the moment – causes which no PP in his right mind would have dreamed of touching in a month of Sundays to the tune of a Preston Guild.

And so it had occurred to His Lordship – so the story goes – to remind Fr Elrick of a very great favour he owed to the Diocese, a favour Fr Elrick had owed to the Diocese for some considerable time. Now, the full details of Fr Elrick's obligation to the Diocese of Salford have been lost in the myths of time, and (unless it be a New Jerusalem Bible he were perhaps reading from) His Lordship would not have been so ungracious as to quote chapter and verse. Suffice it to say, then, that the favour Fr Elrick owed to the Diocese of Salford involved one of the many appearances the Manchester United football team has made at Wembley Stadium, one of the many results that have gone in the team's favour, one of the many visits Fr Elrick had made to said venue with his friend, Sammy Faithful, the bookie, in his Rolls Royce Silver Shadow saloon (a car reputed to have been formerly owned by Fanny Craddock and to have a cabinet better informed than the one to be found in Downing Street – though only with regard to top shelf liquor and mixers), and four Sunday morning fixtures that had taken place in St Joseph of Cupertino's parish (namely, the eight o'clock, half past nine, half past ten, and twelve noon Masses) which, subsequent to the Reds' victory on this particular occasion, had perforce been shared between Fathers Bellis and Lancaster, Fr Elrick being indisposed until the following Tuesday.

'I know you, don't I?' were the first words Fr Human addressed to Dinchy when he opened the door of the presbytery to him on the night of his visit.

'I don't think so, Father,' said Dinchy.

'Oh, I know that face from somewhere,' Fr Human insisted. He pointed at Dinchy shakily with the index finger of his right hand as if to confirm the fact that it was Dinchy to whom he was referring, though there was certainly nobody else about at the time.

'No, I don't think you do, Father.'

'Never mind, never mind.' The priest stepped to one side. 'Perhaps you'd better come in.'

Dinchy entered the vestibule and, Fr Human closing the front door with a resounding thud, followed him where he led: across a corridor which was empty save for a radiator and – right at the far end, above a panelled oak door which gave access to the sacristy – a large, wall-mounted wooden crucifix.

'Here we go then.' The priest indicated a small study to his left, his voice booming due to an echo that emphasised every sound – their footsteps, their garments rustling as they walked along, the oak door of the study swinging open, the sound of a telephone which began to ring in another room further along the corridor in the direction of the house.

'*Je* . . . 'Fr Human turned towards the telephone's insistent ring, mouthing this utterance as if inexpertly essaying the French first person singular. '*Je* . . .' He said again with similar enunciative brutality.

For a second he seemed undecided as to what he should do. Then, as if Dinchy were no longer there, the old man – for this is what he seemed to have become all of a sudden – the old man left the room without another word.

Dinchy heard him lumbering along the corridor, heard a door being opened. Obviously, the receiver had been lifted, for the ringing stopped abruptly. Odd, disembodied words – inconsequential, almost alien, distorted by resonance – came echoing along the corridor from the room which Fr Human had entered, and where a telephone conversation was now taking place.

'That's right . . . St Peter Port . . . wood shavings . . . Smithfield Market . . . a chef . . . Friday week . . . ringworm . . . Harpurhey Baths . . . perhaps gold . . . *toot-sweet*!'

Dinchy could not even begin to guess what was going on. Not that he was particularly interested, of course. He had the banns of matrimony to put in and he had promised to pick Shirlee up from the dressmaker's at half past nine.

After a minute or two everything went quiet. A door closed, another door opened. This second door appeared to be even further along the corridor in the direction of the priests' living quarters. This door too was closed. Then came a silence absolute, save for Dinchy's shuffling, finger-clicking, cough, cough again – a silence that continued for . . . well, all Dinchy knew about it was that a good five minutes into the silence he wished he'd thought to check his watch in the first place. But Dinchy retained his composure.

For some reason he had felt comfortable with Fr Human. Perhaps the Roman collar and the cassock had helped him there. Dinchy called to mind the single most useful piece of advice Dinch *père* had given him to date:

'Never trust an artist in a tie, a clergyman in mufti, or a gardener in a posh car'.

This had made more of a positive impression upon him than another snippet of paternal wisdom to the effect that he might consider using eucalyptus-based hair shampoo on the grounds that: 'Norbert Scammerton shampooed with eucalyptus every day of his life and he still had a full head of hair when he died'.

'He just snuffed it, your mate, dad?' Dinchy had enquired on hearing this.

'Oh, no,' said Dinch Senior. 'Nobby got the chop over Bremerhaven during the War.'

The little study where Dinchy now waited was windowless and devoid of any decoration save a picture postcard pinned to the wall opposite the door. This showed the Trevi Fountain, the Spanish Steps and bore the printed greeting: *Arriverderci Roma*. A small chrome crucifix hung alongside it and, on the mantelpiece below, above a hearth where no fire burned, there stood a statue of the Virgin. The room itself was decorated with an off-white wallpaper which Dinchy seemed to remember from the sitting-room at home during the mid-to-late Forties that featured the heads of eight stags, a brace of them above the picture rail in each corner of the room.

The floor of the study was covered in a dark green but otherwise patternless linoleum, and along the skirting of the fireplace wall lay stacks of papers, booklets and books: the parish newsletter for the forthcoming Sunday, 7 August, 1966, several copies of *The*

Harvest magazine, a pictorial magazine called *The Word,* thirty-two parish hymnals, half a dozen church collection plates, and a copy of *Chambers Twentieth Century Dictionary Revised.* Against the right-hand wall stood a bookcase and a bentwood chair. A captain's chair stood with its back to the opposite wall and next to it was a large wooden desk with an open leather briefcase beneath it and upwards of two reams of paper on top. The paper, exclusively foolscap in size, was in such a state of disarray that Dinchy imagined it to have been stirred like a porridge pot, vigorously and over a very long period of time. Most of the remaining floor space apart from the small rectangle of space where Dinchy now stood was taken up by an empty metal waste paper basket that bore an advertisement for Dr Potter's Pink Pills For Pale People.

Dinchy glanced idly at the bookcase, which stood four feet high on legs and held three shelves of books behind a pair of glass sliding doors. In addition to the books inside the bookcase, three lay on the top: Benjamin Graham's *The Intelligent Investor*, Edwin Lefevre's *Reminiscences of a Stock Operator*, and Fred Schwed Junior's *Where Are The Customers' Yachts? – or A Good Hard Look At Wall Street.* The top shelf contained a selection of religious volumes: three Bibles (Douai, King James, and CTS), seventeen back numbers of the Salford Diocesan Almanac, 1950 to 1966 inclusive, two volumes on the history of the Jesuits by James Broderick SJ, *The Life of Christ* by Fulton Sheen, and Butler's *Lives of the Saints* in five volumes. History was the concern of the centre shelf: Geoffrey Barraclough's *History in a Changing World*, Tacitus: *The Histories*, I-III, Livy (Books XX-XXVIII), Josephus, Eusebius (Ecclesiastical Histories, I-X), Wakeman's *Ascendancy of France,* and a couple of other books the titles of which were indecipherable to Dinchy's merely cursory glance. Below these the bottom shelf contained the complete works of Charles Dickens (Hazell, Watson & Viney Ltd.), the works of William Shakespeare in one volume (Frederick Warne & Company, New York), Conan Doyle's *Sir Nigel, The White Company* and, again in one volume, *The Napoleonic Stories,* beginning with *Uncle Bernac*, and a handful of foreign phrase books, four of them Berlitz (French, Spanish, Greek, Italian), the other from a now defunct Dublin publishing house with the title *Gaelic At Home* (1922 edition). This last attracted Dinchy's attention, the city of Dublin being amongst the European capitals Shirlee had expressed a wish to visit. Reaching across, he picked it up and flicked through its pages. What he found on page 33 gave him some cause for alarm. The Gaelic made no sense to him at all; the English translation ran thus.

'Do you know that an ambush took place in O'Connell Street last night?'

'No! What time?'

'Just after we crossed the Liffey by omnibus according to what I hear.'

'We were in luck so. And was anyone killed?'

'One man was killed on the street and a bomb went off in a lorry, wounding three.'

'Was there a hostage at the front of the lorry?'

'I believe there was.'

'And was it Black and Tans or soldiers who were there?'

'Soldiers, I do believe. They had come from setting fire to a building nearby where some fellows had been seen with a Thompson gun. The smoke, I am told, was quite acrid and intense.'

Neither acrid, nor particularly intense was the smoke emanating from the bowl of Fr Human's meerschaum on his return, but it soon filled the little study.

'I'll lay odds you thought I'd forgotten you,' said the priest.

'Not at all, Father,' said Dinchy, a little unconvincingly perhaps as he closed the Gaelic phrasebook and replaced it in the bookcase, shelving with it any plans he might have had for shipping out of Holyhead towards the west.

'Then, I would either have lost my bet or called you a liar,' said the priest. He went across to the bookcase, took the three financial titles from the top of it and placed them in the open briefcase next to the desk, which flashed the metalled initials H. M. on his pulling the flap forward prior to locking it.

'Now, let's see, let's see. The banns of matrimony, am I right? Yes, the banns of matrimony.' Fr Human pulled the captain's chair across to the desk, sat himself down on it, assumed a writing position. 'There's not a lot I forget, Mr, er . . .'

'Dinch,' Dinchy assured him, and coughed apologetically.

'But I do forget often. To make matters worse, I occasionally forget things that others deem important. Still, we soldier on, eh?'

Dinchy smiled encouragement and, he hoped, a sense of urgency. It was already five past nine.

Fr Human pulled a register from the desk drawer, though to position it on the desk top, let alone make a written entry therein, would surely have proved impossible due to the dry ski slope of paper that lay heaped upon it. But the old priest would brook no obstacle in the way of his intent. Laying down the meerschaum on the mantelpiece in such a way as to wreath the statue of the Virgin with the scent of Old Holburn tobacco smoke, he balanced the register across his knees whilst trawling towards him as much desk top strewn paper as could be encompassed within his outstretched arms. Remaining seated and swivelling at the hip towards the waste paper basket, he then jettisoned the lot.

Sadly, the waste paper basket advertising Dr Potter's Pink Pills was on the small side and, though the priest had played basketball in his youth and was still a fair shot, just twenty-eight sheets of foolscap made it. Five hundred and forty-two sheets now carpeted a good portion of the floor that had boasted only linoleum. And it must be said (and perhaps this may go some way towards explaining Fr Human's imminent departure for pastors new) that at least two of the foolscap sheets that now lay on the floor were deemed important by others.

The first of these was a letter from the Bishop's desk that His Lordship had indicated should be read out at all Masses the following Sunday; the second was a tax return requiring Fr F. X. Elrick's immediate attention. A third sheet referred to a matter that Fr Human would himself have judged important. This was a request originating in the parish of St Edmund's, Miles Platting, for confirmation of the baptism at St Joseph of Cupertino's church in July, 1959 of one Noel Grubb, aged 7, whom his peer group had dubbed the Christmas Maggot, and whose parish priest, the more kindly – some said, saintly – Canon McCabe, had hoped to call a first communicant during the approaching Christmas season.

Still, the desk to which Fr Human now turned his attention was three parts clear, enabling him to lift the register from his knees, slam it down on the desktop, heave open the front cover with an elaborate movement reminiscent of the opening of Tower Bridge and, laying the register flat, pull from the interior of his cassock a mottled green fountain pen that had been manufactured by Waterman when Fr Human was a lad.

The meerschaum, Dinchy noticed, was forgotten and, thankfully, out.

'Name?'

'Tony.'

'Your full name.'

'Anthony Dismas Dinch.'

'Procrastination,' said Fr Human as if lost in his own thoughts.

'Par-ding.'

'The thief of time.'

'That's what me dad says.'

'Why, then, I wonder, would he give you the name of a thief. Still, he was the Good Thief, oxymoronic though the concept may be.'

'Sorry.'

'A good thief: a contradiction in terms.'

'Like Red Square.'

'Pardon.'

'It's grey.'

'Oh, I see. Well, the Good Thief . . .'

'Anthony?'

'No, no, Anthony of Padua treasured the Child Jesus. Hm, there's a thought . . . whereas Dismas treasured the Man *in extremis*. "Lord, remember me when Thou comest into Thy kingdom."'

'"This day thou shalt be with Me in Paradise,"' said Dinchy, his old teacher, Vincent Irlam, prompting him quite clearly down the long cluttered corridor of Dinchy's past – amazing him, even more so when tears came and stung his eyes.

'*Lachryma Christi*,' said the priest.

Unthinkingly, unthankfully, Dinchy accepted the linen handkerchief he proferred.

'The tears of Christ,' said the priest ponderously. 'Uncountable. Tears from Christ, unaccountable: unexpected, unheralded, gratuitously impulsive. A gift, Mr Dinch! As, indeed, is the excellent red wine of the same name: *Lachryma Christi*, made from grapes men wrest from the jaws of Vesuvius – itself an impulsive beast. Never unheralded, it's true, though its outbursts do seem to have been largely unexpected in the main.'

Fr Human thrust the handkerchief Dinchy returned to him into a side pocket of his cassock. He began to write in the register with a purpose now, mouthing each word in a quavery voice that belied the solid copperplate adorning the line along which his pen had passed. 'An-thony, Dis-mas, Di-nch.' He glanced up. 'Have we sorted out the day, the time?'

Dinchy reminded him about a telephone call that had pre-dated this visit. It was to be mid-week, a Wednesday to be exact.

'Will it be you, Father?' said Dinchy.

'Mm?'

'Will you be offici . . . Will you be doin' the wedding?'

'Fr Bellis, I understand.'

Oh, thank God, thought Dinchy. Not Fr Elrick, thank God. Was it last Sunday, or the Sunday before, the PP had upset Shirlee when he'd inveighed against 'so-called Catholics who won't baptise the baby till Auntie Betty buys a new hat'? Was it the week before that, or last week, he'd reminisced about his days as a hospital chaplain in Blackburn? And, subsequent to telling of hearing the death bed confession of some life-long, albeit anonymous miscreant, and dispensing absolution, Fr Elrick had revealed to the congregation his personal inner revulsion:

'A-ha, where are your pals down the pub now, eh? Tell me that,' he had said.

'And the name of the young lady?' Fr Human twinkled. 'At least I presume she's young.'

Dinchy told him.

'*Veronica*?' Fr Human looked at Dinchy and made as if to lay down his pen.

'Shirlee Veronica.'

The priest nodded, smiling. 'I told you I knew you, Mr Dinch. Now I know where I know you from.'

Shirlee's name was spoken hesitantly in much the same way as Dinchy's name had been spoken. The handwriting was identically neat. The register was blotted, slammed shut, left where it lay together with the Waterman pen. Then rising from the captain's chair and pushing it back, Fr Human walked to the door of the study, motioning for Dinchy to follow him.

'Come with me, Mr Dinch.'

He led Dinchy along the corridor, their footsteps echoing, and through the panelled door to the sacristy where he flicked on a bank of light switches beside a second panelled door which gave access to the body of the church itself. Strange, thought Dinchy, as the door swung open and the two of them passed through, to see the church bereft of all parishioners bar one.

To their left, above the sanctuary, burned a light within a suspended red glass container: the sign of the Real Presence; over to their right stood a bank of four confessional boxes adjacent to the Lady Altar. Three of these bore a brass shingle above the door on each of which was inscribed the name of a priest: Fr Francis X. Elrick, PP, Fr Richard Bellis, Fr Edmond Lancaster BA. Above the door of the fourth confessional box, the one closest to hand, a plain white postcard was secured with a drawing pin, and on it, written in copperplate script, was the name: Fr Hugh Munn MSc, MCL.

Pausing just long enough to close the door to the sacristy behind him, Fr Hugh (for it is he) plodded across the body of the church towards the opposite side. Arrived at the centre aisle, he turned, faced the altar and genuflected, then continued on his way across the church until he stood before the Pieta in the far aisle.

'What we see here, Mr Dinch, is a monument to poor suffering humanity in general and to Sergeant Frank Sidney in particular – you see his name there? This was presented to the church by his grieving family many years ago – a shore of bitter homecoming that's been washed by the tears of a thousand bereaved women and men.'

Still pretty dusty for all that, it occurred to Dinchy, though he kept the thought to himself.

The priest walked a few steps further until he stood before a plaque on which two figures could be seen – a woman who bore a cloth in her hands, a man who bore a Cross. The Roman numeral VI was etched above this scene. Thirteen similar plaques are to be seen distributed about the walls of St Joseph of Cupertino's Church. They are devotional artefacts known as the Stations of the Cross, each one of them plotting a stage on the *Via Dolorosa*, the Road to Calvary.

When Fr Hugh next spoke his tone was unnecessarily sonorous perhaps, considering his congregation numbered only one. It was as if he were reading from a pre-composed devotion.

'Veronica sees Jesus covered in sweat and blood as he walks along. She hands him a cloth and on it he leaves the impression of his holy countenance.' Fr Hugh turned to Dinchy. '*Vera* is Latin for *true*; *ikon*, the Greek for *image*. And so, we get *true image*: *vera ikon* or, as we say in English, Veronica. Of course, it's almost entirely certain that the story's apocryphal, so we won't argue about that, Mr Dinch.'

Hey, who's arguing? thought Dinchy. He'd no idea what *apocryphal* meant in any case. Vincent Irlam would have been hard pressed to take him that far out into the ocean deep. In Dinchy's case, the coral reef of *Daily Mess* English had remained a distant pipe dream; Dinchy had seemed to be perfectly happy splashing about in the shallows with Dick and Dora.

'And it's of passing interest in any case, the name Veronica serving to jog my memory, that's all.'

Fr Hugh now retreated a few steps before he stopped at the preceding station, the one that was marked with the Roman numeral V. Here were depicted three figures, each of them male. Again Fr Hugh intoned more than somewhat.

'They caught hold of a man called Simon of Cyrene, who was coming in from the country, and they loaded him with the Cross so he should carry it with Jesus.'

Dinchy's face was a picture – puzzlement the subject of the composition.

'Son?'

'Er . . . it's twenny-five past nine, Father. I've promised to pick Shirlee up.'

'Of course, of course.'

Dinchy made as if to go.

'A minute of your time, if you please, Mr Dinch.' Fr Hugh's voice conveyed the authority of command.

Dinchy felt he could do no more than wait.

'You know, I've puzzled about the fifth station all my life, son. But it's only recently the significance of it has dawned on me.'

'Father?' Maybe a bit of prompting would hurry him up.

'The three figures we see here: Jesus Christ, the Roman soldier, Simon of Cyrene . . . By the way, do you know where Cyrene is?'

Dinchy had to admit he did not. His school atlas had been used as a resting-place for a succession of quarto-size drawing papers.

'It's in north Africa – Tunisia, to be exact. But it's in Africa, that's the main thing. You see, that's the key to my understanding of the meaning of the fifth station.'

Dinchy nodded – a slow, deep sort of nod, the sort of nod that swallows a yawn like an oyster and masquerades as consent.

'So we've got Simon from Africa and Jesus from Asia . . .'

'Asia?'

'Yes, Jesus was an Asian. The Holy Land, or Israel as we call it nowadays, it's on the continent of Asia.'

Vincent Irlam had had a similar uphill struggle with Dinchy's geographic perspective. Half the time, the lad had not appeared to know if he was coming or going.

'So, we've got an African, an Asian and . . .'

'A Roman soldier,' said Dinchy, helpfully.

'Our fellow European,' said Fr Hugh.

In the street outside an argument had developed between two cars. A horn sounded, long and hard, and then another horn on a higher note. Then came a revving of engines, a squeal of tyres and another bout of beeping. In the silence that followed Fr Hugh said:

'What we have here, Mr Dinch, is the economic history of the world for the last two thousand years.

'Eh?'

Dinchy had heard about history, he'd heard about the world too, but he had never had to count to two thousand. So Economics was out. Shirlee was the pen pusher; Dinchy left the sums to her. And when it came to big words like *economic*, he'd get his pal Byron on the case.

'It's got to STOP, Mr Dinch! That's if the human race is going to see another two thousand years!'

'Father, I . . .' Dinchy was yawning almost as often as he was breathing now. Fr Hugh had lost him somewhere west of El Alamein. Besides, Dinchy had sneaked a crafty glance at his watch and noticed it was half past nine. He should have been on Grange Park Road picking Shirlee up, not in church listening to . . .

Fr Hugh appeared to be unaware of any urgency whatsoever other than in delivering the message he was intent on getting across. 'Africa and Asia forever getting the dirty end of the financial stick from Europe – well, from people of European descent anyway. That's what the fifth station's all about, Mr Dinch. Well, to my mind, at any rate.'

Dinchy stifled his three thousand million billionth yawn of the evening.

'Ah, when I was a young man, Mr Dinch, how I used to envy Simon of Cyrene helping Jesus to carry the Cross. Of course, nowadays I couldn't carry the Cross if I tried. But the thing is, son, I don't want to do that any more. No, what I want to do nowadays is take the Cross *off* them – take the European Cross *off* Africa and Asia, I mean. I can't do that on my own, of course. But I can help New Century-New Start do it.'

'New Century-New . . .?'

'Are you with us or agin us, Mr Dinch?'

'Me?'

'Yes, you.'

'Doin' what?'

'Well, we want to reduce Third World debt for a start.'

'I've got enough debt of me own to worry about.'

'You have?'

'Yeah. We're buyin' an house.'

'Oh, you've got a mortgage then?'

'Mm.'

'At what rate of interest, may I ask?'

'Dunno, Father. Shirlee sees to that sort of thing.'

'Well, how much have you borrowed then?'

'A thou.'

'A thousand pounds?'

'Over twenny-five years.'

'In the developing countries, if you lend a man £1000 at 10% interest, then he can't pay you back, in just over 7 years' he'll owe you £2000.'

'Two thou?'

'Yes, that's Compound Interest for you, the Rule of 72.'

'Well, he better get it paid off quick, then.'

'Ah, but sometimes he can't, son. The crops fail, there are natural disasters, civil war even. In less than 12 years' time he'll owe you £3000.'

'Three times what he lent off you?'

'Yes. Compound Interest again, the Rule of 115.'

'But that's the banks, Father. You can't expect anything else, can you? I mean, it's not as though it's me personal, is it?'

'Oh, but it *is*, Mr Dinch. Well, let's say, it was.'

Dinchy pulled out a really puzzled look now and stuck it on his face.

Father Hugh smiled. He placed his hand on Dinchy's shoulder and walked him towards the sacristy, using a language that Dinchy would later describe to Byron as Double Dutch.

'*Plus ça change, plus c'est la meme chose*, *Monsieur* Tony Dismas Dinch. The fifth station may look a bit different nowadays, but it's not, I can assure you. And each and every European is an integral part of the injustice it represents.'

Dinchy shrugged, whereupon Fr Hugh stepped back from him, threw out his arms and cried:

'RAPISHAW RAMBLERS GO GO GO! Now, I'm sure I read that headline somewhere recently. Wasn't it in the *Daily Mess* earlier in the year? Yes, yes, I do believe it was. It was on the Saturday of Holy Week, if I remember correctly. There was maybe a dearth of newsworthy items at the time. Because I seem to recall they went so far as to print a half page photograph of the five of you. Yourself and the other local lad . . .

'Byron,' said Dinchy, a big cheesy grin on his face all of a sudden.

'Oh, that's his name, is it? And the Asian student . . .'

'Raj, yeah – and the other two, the Yank and the Aussie.'

In his mind's eye Dinchy visualised the photograph that had appeared on page 3 of the *Daily Mess* that day: the catering caravan in the background, Dinchy with that same big cheesy grin on his face, a fresh cuppa steaming in the polystyrene cup he held in his hand, Byron and Raj heaving the Cross Country Kit upright like Old Glory on Iwo Jima, Milt and Cass waving their burgers in muted triumph.

'Yeah, we raised fifty-odd quid for wotsit,' said Dinchy. 'That New Century-New Start thing. We done over a thou with the rest of the lads from work. Some of the other firms done even more.'

'Well, that's something to be thankful for, I suppose,' said Fr Hugh.

Dinchy laughed. 'Hah! I'd forgotten about that till you said, Father. Yeah, Rapishaw Ramblers, they called us.'

'So they did, son,' said Fr Hugh. 'But I didn't. In fact, I can remember saying to Fr Bellis at the time it looks very much like the same old International Brigade to me.'

14

'He had this dirty big chopper. You should of seen it . . .'

'I beg your pardon?' says Amanda, her cocktail cherry stopping just short of her gob.

'An helicopter,' I said. 'It come thunderin' in from the south over Bleaklow.'

'Over what?' Shirlee plonks her menu down on the table.

'It's this dirty big hill overlookin' Longdendale.'

'The Woodhead Pass, the road through to Sheffield.' Byron picks up Shirlee's menu along with the other three.'It's making that much noise you can hardly hear yourself think.'

'Imagine it being so busy,' says Amanda, cocktail cherry finally making it, 'that early in the morning on a Bank Holiday.'

'Not the road! It's the helicopter makin' all the noise: Mr T. Z. Wetherby on a flyin' visit.'

'Literally,' says Byron. 'All the way from Head Office in Hexham, Northumberland.'

'I've always thought Northumberland means exactly what it says,' says Shirlee.

'What?'

'North of the Humber.'

'Mm,' says Amanda.

'So?'

'Well, if Northumberland's to the north why's the helicopter coming in from the south?'

'Dunno. Might be some flight path they have to take. Maybe he wanted to see what Stetson Tex, Mackie Flowers done yesterday.'

'Did,' says Shirlee.

'Did,' I said.

'What *did* they do exactly?' says Amanda.

'Edale to Crowden. 15 mile.'

'Took them long enough, didn't it?'

'Par-ding?'

'I thought you said it took them ten hours or something.'

'Eight,' says Byron, tucking the menus under his arm as he gets to his feet. 'It's not bad in the circumstances, you know. Bog-trotting at best, side-tracking a lot of the time to find firmer ground. It's rough country. It's the watershed, for Pete's sake. Hey, Pete's sake: peat's sake. Get it? Seeing they kicked off with Kinder.'

'Hm, and I'll kick off with the prawn cocktail, thank you very much,' says Amanda. 'Shirlee?'

'Mm, garlic prawns for me.'

'Left us no choice, has she?' I said to Byron.'Get us some garlic bread so I can fight back.'

We're sat at this window seat in the Great Western on the A62 Huddersfield Road, the four of us, looking out across Redbrook Reservoir. Well, not Byron just at the moment, of course, because he's sloped off to order the starters. It isn't dark as yet, but it was gonna be a clear night when darkness come, and from where we're sat we'll have a clear view of the beacon on the Holme Moss television transmitter to the south-east, a mile or so beyond Black Hill. At 1908 feet, Black Hill is the highest land in Cheshire and the highest land we've stood on all day, me and Byron – a good five miles into the ten plus we've walked since breakfast. Also Raj and Milt and Cass, of course, who've surely reached the village of Colden above Hebden Bridge by now.

During the afternoon, the girls had borrowed Amanda's dad's Vauxhall CB Victor, picked up the Transit from Crowden Youth Hostel where we'd left it, and met up with us where we finished up (me and Byron on our own by now), at Brun Clough Reservoir next to Standedge Cut on the A62 Huddersfield Road, where six hundred feet below us there was three tunnels, each one of them over three miles long: the longest canal tunnel in the world plus a couple of railway tunnels too. All we stood in need of when the girls turned up was a pair of shoes and fresh clothes (the girls brung these with them), plus a bit of a wash (they brung soap and towels too). So there we was, a bit smelly, I suppose (if not exactly honking), but serviceable and starving, and just about ready to get stuck into a three course bar meal at the Great Western before heading off home again.

'You going to tell us you cheated after all that?' says Amanda.

'Cheated?'

'Yeah, Mr Wetherby fetch you in his helicopter instead of leaving you to walk it.'

'If he did,' says Byron, drinks in tow. 'He obviously crash landed on Black Moss.'

'Yeah, you seen the state of me boots and leggin's, didn't you?'

'You tell 'em, man,' says Byron. 'Helicopter comes over, sets down in the car park next to the camp site, and out steps Mr T. Z. Wetherby, MD, and . . . Oozit? What's his name, Dinchy – that transport manager of yours?'

'Eric Alport,' says Shirlee. 'He's nice, Eric.'

'He's okay,' I said. 'Eric's not in the helicopter. Eric's come by road – he's in that motor of his. What is it, Byron?'

'Farina line Oxford. Square, but trustworthy.'

'Eric to a tee,' says Shirlee.

'Yeah, Eric's parked up there waitin' for his nibs, and soon's the helicopter sets down, he come's runnin' over to where we're waitin' outside the youth hostel. His nibs keeps his distance, of course. All the way from the dizzy heights of Hadrian's Wall.'

'May've been dizzy heights when Hadrian built it,' says Byron. 'All of fifteen foot or so. Nowadays it's – what? – three, four feet high max. Let's put it this way: it's as high as the back of a farm cart. People who live round there took most of it away to build their farms with over the years.'

'Vandals!' says Amanda.

'Picts, I think you'll find,' says Byron, laughing. 'No, they were just survivors, love. There's not much up there even today. Few farms and that. Nice neck of the woods though. High, undulating landscape. Up there with the Scouts once upon a time.'

'Stoner or Eyeful,' I asked him as our starters turned up.

'Eyeful,' says Byron, making inroads on his homemade chicken liver pate.

Me and Byron and Huge had this coded way of talking about places we'd seen or visited, or maybe heard about from someone reliable who'd visited them and reported back. For instance, coming back from his Auntie Vera's in St Marychurch one time, Huge had begged his dad to drive to Stonehenge, which he did do – a pretty long overland slog from St Marychurch, Devon. And he was very disappointed indeed when Stonehenge turned out to be, as Huge reported:

'Heap of stones with a barbed wire fence round 'em on what's as bad as a traffic island between two busy main roads, and a rip-off entrance fee. Get in Pompeii for less.'

So, crap buildings and crummy landmarks was christened Stoners.

But the Eiffel Tower, Laura Pod told us – she'd holidayed in Paris with the school when daddy's business took off – 'the Eiffel Tower did not disappoint' (Laura's words). So famous places that 'did not disappoint' become Eyefuls.

The Grand Canyon, Eyeful; the Taj Mahal, Eyeful; the Isle of Capri, Stoner – 'boutique on a rock where they bill you for sitting down' (we had all this from Laura together with the gen on Pompeii), though Laura did say the chair lift on Capri from Anacapri to the summit is an Eyeful.

'What's an Eyeful?' Shirlee only has to go and ask.

'You are, gal,' says Byron.' Though I assume Dinchy's already told you that.' This had somehow come out sounding rougher than Byron meant it, I think. Shirlee coloured a bit.

'Well, that's quite enough of that, thank you very much,' says Amanda, giving him a clout. 'We'll have none of your rude bog-trotting ways in here, Marlfield.'

'Manners, Madam!' says Byron.

'Maketh the man!' says Amanda. 'And if you've got nothing better to do, you can pass me that menu again.'

The verdicts on the starters was fine, fine, fine, and – Amanda: okay (she supposed). Byron intended pigging out on the Great Western Mixed Grill (gammon, steak, sausages, lamb chop, liver, chips, egg, peas, onion rings, tomato and mushrooms). 'With an extra portion of chips,' says he.

'One potato more than a pig,' says Amanda, adding she thinks she'll go for the chicken fillet, *sauté aux champignons*.

'The mushrooms is nice too,' I told her, though she never heard us, being distracted by this fit of coughing from Byron when summat went down the wrong way. Besides, I was a bit distracted meself with Shirlee kicking us on the ankle by accident as she ordered her salmon steak with prawns and tarragon. I had deep fried wholetail scampi ('Sooty's pal,' so Byron informed us, and 'dog rough too,' said he.).

'No, what it boils down to is this, see,' Shirlee tells Amanda. 'Rapishaw Gap's not just some name they've dreamed up. It's an actual location on Hadrian's Wall. It's where the Pennine Way leaves the Wall and heads off north. See, the Pennine Way was opened almost exactly a year ago, so Mrs T. Z. Wether . . .'

'Meaning to ask you what the T. Z. stands for,' says Byron.

'Taduk Zygmunt,' I told him best I could.

'Well, that's more or less how it sounds, I suppose,' says Shirlee. 'Tadeusz.' (She spells this out, but not the rest of it.) 'His mother was Polish. He uses his initials so as not to confuse people.'

'Well, pardon me, but I'm still confused,' says Amanda. 'So Rapishaw Gap's somewhere on Hadrian's Wall and Mr T. Z. Wetherby owns Rapishaw Gap, the company . . .'

'Well, fifty-one per cent of it to be exact since it went public a couple of years back,' Byron tells her.

'Well, okay – but how does that get us halfway to Huddersfield on the Friday of the Easter Bank Holiday weekend?'

'Easy,' says Byron. 'You and Shirlee by road, Dinchy and yours truly on Shanks's pony.'

'Oh, you're so sharp you want to mind you don't cut yourself.'

'Like Shirlee says,' I told her. 'Early 1966, Mrs T. Z. Wetherby gets religion and decides Rapishaw Gap – that is, the people who work for Rapishaw Gap are gonna do this sponsored walk for charity – Cross Country, she calls it. In other words them that work for Rapishaw Gap will walk the Pennine Way in twenny stages from Edale in Derbyshire to . . . what's that Scotch place, Byron?'

'Kirk Yetholm in the Borders. Two hundred and fifty miles plus, split into twenty stages. All proceeds to go to a charity nominated by said Mr T. Z.-helicoptering-Wetherby and his missis.'

'What charity?' says Amanda.

'Save the Terrapins and Turtles of Tristan da Cunha,' says Byron.

'You're *joking*!'

'I jest, 'tis true,' he says.

'New Century-New Start,' says Shirlee when she can get a word in edgeways. 'They've done pretty well so far too. I don't know how they're doing further north as yet, but the two who did yesterday's section. . .'

'Stetson Tex and Mackie Flowers – Edale to Crowden,' I reminded them.

'They raised £55 between them.'

'We'll have somethin' like,' I said. 'Mind you, that's includin' Biffo that had to drop out. So there's three of us chippin' in, I suppose, countin' me an' Byron who done Crowden to Standedge

'Done?' says Shirlee.

'Well done, I hope,' says Byron as his mixed grill turns up.

'Flippin' hard done by,' said I, thinking about what Stetson Tex and Mackie Flowers had sprung on us.

'*Bien cui*!' says Shirlee, who had O Level French and Domestic Science on her CV.

They first sighted him at Crowden Great Brook, going north, at which juncture Dinchy began to show a bit of interest for the first time since leaving Crowden. Because somewhere in the dense thicket he called his head, Dinchy had begun to formulate a plan whereby this man would be their salvation.

They had made slow progress so far with Byron doing most of the work. Two miles uphill slog to Laddow Rocks where a path leaves the Pennine Way and runs north-westwards beside the Chew Reservoir and down to Greenfield. Dinchy had been thoroughly tiresome throughout, as he continued to be for the succeeding mile, a mile of descent now to the 1500 foot contour of Crowden Great Brook. The only good thing about it was the weather. It had been fine so far, though the sky remained ominously overcast,

Their departure had originally been timetabled for half past eight, but it was all of nine o'clock before they set off, an argument having broken out when it dawned on them what they were being asked to take with them.

'Stetson Tex and Mackie Flowers must be laughin' their bollocks off,' said Dinchy. 'They might of warned us.'

'How?' Byron had been much more reasonable about it.

'Phone,' said Dinchy.

'Oh, right,' said Byron. 'They finish their section six, seven o'clock last night. They're tired, dirty, hungry, footsore. You been in their shoes, that'd be the first thing on your mind, would it, Dinchy? Phoning us? Somehow I don't think so.'

Eric Alport was concerned at the prospect of Dinchy's showing him up in front of Mr T. Z. Wetherby who, so far at least, had kept his distance, staying with the pilot next to the helicopter in the car park.

'Look, lads, we don't want the governor coming over and sticking his oar in, do we now? It's one of the rules of the sponsorship deal. Right? It's got nothing to do with me. In a way, it's got nothing to do with Mr Wetherby either. His missis dreampt it all up, leaves T. Z. to organise it while she's ponceing about in the Holy Land somewhere. All you gotta do is raise twenty five quid a piece, rest of the lads the same. Twenty stages times two lads per stage makes a thousand quid, give or take a few quid. Now, be fair, lads. The sponsors Mr Wetherby's got lined up . . .' Eric Alport reeled off the names of a dozen companies, quoted and not quoted, large and small, local and national. 'The big boys have promised ten times that amount, provided the rules are obeyed. Rule Number One, you have to walk it; and, Rule Number Two, you have to hump the Cross Country Kit while you're about it. So you either hump it like Stetson Tex and Mackie Flowers did yesterday, or Mrs T. Z. Wetherby's favourite charity gets nowt – plus Mr T. Z. Wetherby gets a very bad name for himself with his business associates and a lot of earache at home too. So I'll put my cards on the table, lads: either you take the Cross Country Kit over the hills and far away, or I shouldn't think there's much of a future for you with Rapishaw Gap.'

'In case you've forgotten, man,' says Byron. 'I personally didn't have much of a future with Rapishaw Gap in the first place.'

Eric Alport laughed for the first time since he'd turned up that morning. He laughed long but not loud. Because Mr T. Z. Wetherby appeared to be looking over towards them now, and he appeared to be making motions that might signify he intended to don extra clothing prior to striding across to the youth hostel to enquire of Eric what the devil was going on, Alport.

‘Ha, ha, ha, ha, ha. Well, you’ve definitely drawn the short straw, haven’t you, mate?’ said Eric to Byron. ‘Biffo gets hauled into Christie’s for a check-up. Not before time, I might add. Twenty Capstan Full Strength a day for twenty years: seven thousand coffin nails! Surprised he hasn’t needed a chimney sweep before now. And you step in out of the goodness of your heart so Dinchy, here, won’t get egg on his face. Ends up Dinchy lets you down. Fine mate, he turned out to be, I must say.’

Dinchy responded with infinite bad grace. ‘All right, Eric, point taken. Where’ve they left the kin thing?

Eric went and fetched it from where it had spent the night – just inside the front door of the youth hostel, leaning up against the wall. It was the same height and width as the front door of the youth hostel and about half the weight, being constructed of two lengths of planed timber, the edges of which had been chamfered, the longer piece acting as the upright with the shorter one slotted in transversely about a third of the way down and secured with wood screws and glue. It was loam brown in colour (Leyland gloss, to be precise), and a car number plate (or rather, a part of one) had been affixed to the topmost section of the upright. This, in turn, bore a truncated registration consisting of four letters of the alphabet, displayed thus:

I N R I

‘*Iesus Nazarenus Rex Iudaeorum*,’ quoth Byron.

‘It’s purely symbolic,’ Eric Alport assured them.

‘I’ll kin sym-bollix yer,’ said Dinchy, unsmiling. Dinchy was reverting deeper into the peat bog of his Celtic roots the more this mood of his set in. Very begrudgingly indeed, he helped Byron shoulder the thing, indicating the encrusted grime on it where it had perhaps wrestled Stetson Tex or Mackie Flowers (or they it) over a peat hag and into one of the myriad groughs that pass for *terra firma* on the Kinder plateau. ‘That symbolic slutch, too?’ he asked Eric.

Wisely, Eric Alport treated the question as rhetorical. Inwardly, he sighed. But at least they were off at last, Byron with the Cross Country Kit on his back, Dinchy with a bit of a cob on his own.

Eric drew a copious draught of air into his lungs and, exhaling, puffed out his cheeks as he watched them go. He walked across to the helicopter to report in to Mr T. Z. Wetherby, then stood back as the helicopter took off again, whirling away towards the metropolis.

Eric Alport walked across to the Rose Taupe Morris Oxford saloon, opened the door and climbed into the driver's seat. He unscrewed the top of the Thermos flask of coffee that Mavis had prepared for him before he left home that morning and, pouring, began to drink. Five minutes passed before Eric wound the window fully down, watching for the lads again. He waited five minutes more before he was able to make them out in the distance.

The 800 foot contour . . . the 900 . . . a Pennine Way signpost with its distinctive acorn motif . . . a stile . . . a hut, another hut . . . alongside Black Tor now . . . a footbridge over a brook, the 1000 foot contour, the 1300 foot contour . . . Oakenclough Brook. Eric was glad he'd remembered to bring the Praktica 12 X 25 mm magnification binoculars Mavis had given him for his fiftieth birthday.

Oh, was that Dinchy taking over at long last? Well, wonders would never cease. The other bloke, his mate, the one with the odd name, he'd been making the running for – what was it now? Eric Alport checked his gold-plated Accurist quartz wristwatch, the one with the 9 carat gold strap like chain mail that Mavis had treated him to the Christmas before last. They'd been at it – what? (check the watch again) – thirty-five minutes already and they'd travelled – what? (check the OS Landranger map) – a mile at the most. Nah, Dinchy had got hold of the bloody thing all right, but he was dragging it along behind him like a red indian travois. He really did have a bit of a cob on, Dinchy, and no mistake.

Eric remembered now what some of the lads had said about him, Dinchy – what was it they called him now? The Roughie? The Rookie? The Rookie, that's it. Once he got a bee in his bonnet, The Rookie, they said, that was it, he was off. Well, he'd be off all right if he failed to come up with the goods here today. Oh, yes, he'd be off all right, getting wed later in the year or not. Nothing annoyed Eric Alport more than some arse hole who thought he could take him for a ride, thinking he was a soft touch because he tried to be half-way decent with the lads. Do your damnedest for Eric, and he'd do his damndest for you. Piss Eric about, and you just better be sure you had every bodily orifice caulked up tight, or you'd be crying Uncle before nightfall. Still, rather them than me, thought Eric. Transport, Eric Alport knew like the back of his hand; difficult terrain, he'd known some of that too – out in Mesopotamia and the Western Desert during the War. Italy after Anzio was no picnic either. D-Day dodging, was it? Pity no one had thought to tell the other side about that. Even so, Eric Alport would not have wanted to tackle Black Hill today, No, he wouldn't. Not even if he were given the option of crossing it like some latter day Caesar in a litter carried by four husky Nubians, never mind scrambling over it on foot with the Cross Country Kit to slow you down.

Presumably, Mr T. Z. Wetherby would have concurred with Eric Alport's point of view. Back at the helicopter he had screwed the cap back on the silver hip flask in tooled leather to which he had treated himself when he was last down at Newmarket for the racing, he'd checked the time on the gold Patek Philippe wristwatch he had purchased tax-free in the Cayman Islands, and – in the same instant in which he signalled for the pilot to start her up – he had given three sharp blasts on the klaxon he'd bought for fun at the Quorn Hunt in Leicestershire. 'Oh, do come on, Alport,' Mr T. Z. Wetherby had said to himself. 'It may be a Bank Holiday for you chaps, but I've urgent business to attend to back in Hexham, Northumberland.'

Beyond Laddow Rocks, Byron and Dinchy sank down to the ground, Dinchy slinging the Cross Country Kit like a caber so that it stuck, upside down, between a couple of rocks in a millstone grit outcrop. Checking his Timex, Dinchy realised it had taken them the best part of an hour to get this far. Dinchy's feet were beginning to match his mood. He threw down his rucksack too, took a package out of it, unwrapped it, and ate his way through a shelled hard-boiled egg, two cheese butties laced with Branston sauce, a packet of crisps, a Kiel biscuit, and a couple of Blue Riband.

'You hungry?' said Byron companionably.

'Mm, mm, mnm,' mumbled Dinchy. 'You want summat?'

'I'll have something later.'

'An army marches on its stomach,' said Dinchy absently, as he spotted the three figures in front of them, but far below. 'Who's that down there?' he said. 'Hey, come on, Byron.' Dinchy sprang to his feet without waiting for an answer and headed off, re-packing his rucksack as he went.

With an air of resignation Byron retrieved the Cross Country Kit, calling after Dinchy's retreating figure yomping ahead of him along the track. 'Hey, you don't take turns, Dinchy, I'm gonna . . .'

'You're gonna what?' said Dinchy, pausing momentarily to look back at Byron. He laughed once prior to shouldering his rucksack and travelling onward. 'What yer gonna do, Byron? Get *cross*? That what yer gonna do?'

By the time they reached Crowden Great Brook and the man whom Dinchy had decided was going to help them, the singularity of his victim's hill-walking inexperience had become only too clear. He wore brown brogues that were polished to a high ox-blood sheen and stone-coloured cavalry twill slacks, each leg of which retained an immaculate crease upwards to the hem of his Pakamac. Beneath this shower-proof apparel could be glimpsed – its being semi-transparent – the outline of a sports jacket in Prince of Wales check complete with pocket handkerchief. A knitted Tootal tie and a Tattersall check shirt buttoned at the neck completed his outfit. His supplies – that is, all the things he would need in order to make a successful 250 mile traverse of the Pennine Way between Edale in Derbyshire and Kirk Yetholm in the Scottish border country – these things were contained in their entirety in a Tesco bag that swung loosely from his right hand as he walked along. But his companions seemed to be seasoned trekkers: Milt from Milwaukee, as he introduced himself to them, and Cass from Castlemaine.

'The only way Raj was seasoned,' reminisced Dinchy in the Great Western on the evening of that same day, selecting condiments for his main course, 'was if he'd spilt salt at the breakfast table and thrown a pinch over his left shoulder for good luck.'

But Dinchy had made Raj feel he was an integral part of the enterprise right from the start.

'"Here, cop for this," says he,' says Byron, taking up the story along with the extra portion of chips on to his plate. 'And he grabs the Cross Country Kit off me and hands it to Raj.'

'You're new to these parts,' said Dinchy. 'Anyone doin' the Pennine Way's gotta take turns carryin' this thing. It's the rules, see. We've lugged it from Crowden. But share and share alike's what Eric says.'

'Who is this person, Eric, please?' Raj asks.

'Pennine big-wig,' said Dinchy. 'Eric says we're all to take turns. Me and him' – he pointed to Byron – 'we done our bit. So if you do this next stretch, we'll sort summat out when we hit the main drag.'

The main drag, as Dinchy called it, was the A635 Greenfield-Holmfirth road. By way of Black Hill, the A635 lay a good half dozen miles to the north-west from where they stood.

'And these are the rules, sir?' says Raj. 'Mr Tom Stephenson, he is saying nothing of this in his writings.'

''Fraid so, pal, these are the rules,' said Dinchy. 'Anyway, what's Stephenson know? He's a newcomer; he's not an old hand like me an' Byron – hey, like you after this.'

'Very well, sir,' says Raj, assuming something of his former cheerfulness as he shoulders the Kit. 'If these are indeed the rules, then so be it. But, but, I am wanting to make another enquiry, if I may.'

'Sure, fire away,' said Dinchy, looking away from him to scan the one thousand feet of rising ground that came with the approach to Black Hill.

'Perhaps, you will also be telling me, please, how I will be carrying this thing and also my impedimenta.'

'Eh?' said Dinchy.

'He means his bag,' says Byron.

'"This is not a problem, pal," said Dinchy,' says Byron, conveying the story to Shirlee and Amanda along with a final forkful of chips to his mouth. 'And he does no more than takes his Tesco bag off him and hooks it over the cross-member of the Cross Country Kit.'

Shirlee and Amanda did not seem best pleased with Dinchy at this juncture, though he contrived to pacify them somewhat, returning from the bar with a round of drinks that brought fancy cocktail sticks within the orbit of their scrutiny and discussion, enabling himself to escape it temporarily, though with the distinct impression that (as his Grandma Alma used to say of the creeps of the world – uncaring councillors, politicians on the make, foot-in-the-door salesmen and the like) 'he could have walked under a closed door with a tall hat on'.

Raj, the lads subsequently learned, had newly acquired an MA (Cantab.), his field of research being English conjunctions – a commodity St John's College deemed the Indian sub-continent to be in dire need of. He was walking the Pennine Way in celebratation of his success and eventual escape from the halls of academe. He was no slouch, it should be said, but even so, it was as if he were just tagging along with the other two ('Bummin' a ride', as Milt from Milwaukee succinctly put it, Cass from Castlemaine not demurring).

'Pair of perennially peregrinating pedestrians,' Byron so described these two to Amanda and Shirlee as he studied the menu for a third time. 'Using their outing into the Pennines, so they said, as a warm-up prior to spending the better part of the next decade on the Allegheny Trail and all points west, their final destination, come the bicentennial year of American Independence, being Baja California.'

Their initial suspicions about Raj were borne out via knowing glances and muttered asides as the five of them squelched across Grains Bar and Dun Hill. Raj continued to step out smartly, but (post-Grains Bar) the same could not be said of his footwear. Neither (post-Dun Hill) could his slacks any longer be described as stone-coloured – unless, by stone, was meant the Stygian-hued millstone grit indigenous to the region. He'd latched on to Milt and Cass at Crowden Youth Hostel, they learned, and was seemingly intent on dogging their tracks as far as Colden, a village in Calderdale, twenty-odd miles to the north-west where they intended to spend the night. For their part Milt and Cass were equally determined to shed him like a tick at the earliest opportunity. And, if truth be told, such an opportunity presented itself atop the summit of Black Hill where mist descended to consume them all and the heavens opened to show what was available in the stair-rods' department. But no easy escape was to be had – and not least because Dinchy had need of a porter this trip.

15

Friday, noon

A Sprite CI caravan dispenses steam, music and victuals in a lay-by to the northerly side of the A635 Greenfield-Holmfirth road. The steam billows from a rear window that vents it. The music ('El Paso') comes courtesy of Marty Robbins, acetatedly present on BBC Two on a transistor radio within. The victuals – cuppa/KitKat (Dinchy), beefburger, sausage barm (Milt and Cass, respectively), cuppa/shortbread biscuits, cuppa/chicken barm (Raj, Byron) – are relayed to each of them in turn by the hands (none too clean) of Barmy Boris, part-time car mechanic, odd job man, relief taxi driver, and currently caterer in charge of said Sprite CI caravan in the lay-by. Great big cheesy grins from all five, Raj and Byron hauling the Cross Country Kit upright. This, then, courtesy of the *Daily Mess* and Tommy Burnstones, press photographer *par excellence*, is the image that goes out to the world on the Saturday before Easter, 1966.

'Smile, please. Hold it. Okay! And one for good luck. Thanks, lads. That's your lot!' Tommy Burnstones takes their particulars along with his leave of them, and is already rattling south westwards towards the town of Uppermill in his Ford Cortina GT, hoping for an early bath. Tommy is remarkably sanguine about being scrambled at the last minute to do this job in the back of beyond, having been scheduled to attend a world class motor racing event at Oulton Park he'd been looking forward to all week. But that's Tommy Burnstones for you, that's just the way he is – which is precisely the reason why the boss asked for Tommy in the first place.

'Get me Tommy Burnstones, this job,' the boss had said. 'Job's a special. Get me Tommy Burnstones. I tell Tommy Burnstones I wanna shot the Queen's backside, Queen's backside I got. Most these jokers all I'd get, be obverse side a penny coin, bob at most, they feeling flush. Leave that kin Nantwich arse hole clickin' away Old Trafford. Hope to Christ Charlton drives a steamer in from the halfway line, misses, smashes his bastard Leica gear all over the shop, his front teeth too. Charlton doesn't, I'll do it myself next time I see the smarmy bastard. This job's a special, get me Tommy Burnstones!'

Mr T. Z. Wetherby had placed his call to the Chairman of the Manchester Chamber of Commerce at 9.05am precisely, and Mr T. Z. Wetherby had begun by reminding the Chairman of the Manchester Chamber of Commerce that he and several other captains of industry in the North-West (as Mr T. Z. Wetherby referred to his business acquaintances, prior to listing a good half dozen of his co-sponsors of the Cross Country charitable effort) that he (and they) considered the Cross Country story to be very newsworthy indeed, Mr Chairman. Yes, and particularly on the weekend of the Bank Holiday, Mr Chairman. Didn't he? It also occurred to Mr T. Z. Wetherby to mention that, As a matter of fact, Mr Chairman, it was Mr T. Z. Wetherby's considered opinion that the Cross Country story was every bit as newsworthy as the £2.5M plus that his Board of Directors intended to invest in an expansion of Rapishaw Gap's operations in the Greater Manchester area. Mr T. Z. Wetherby then went on to suggest that This was a not insignificant investment, as he was sure Mr Chairman would appreciate, and that he (Mr T. Z. Wetherby, that is) also thought, as Mr Chairman must surely do, that it would be unfortunate in the extreme if someone were to come along at this stage in the negotiations and persuade his Board of Directors to invest in, Well, let's for the sake of argument say East Anglia, for instance, from where there might be more scope for Rapishaw Gap's long hoped for expansion into Europe.

The Chairman of the Manchester Chamber of Commerce had felt inclined to agree with Mr T. Z. Wetherby about the undesirability of such an eventuality, and told him so. Privately, though, the Chairman of the Manchester Chamber of Commerce wondered whether the editor of the *Daily Mess* would see it in quite the same light. He wondered, too, whether there was any chance of his being able to contact the editor of the *Daily Mess* at home today. He knew he had the editor's home telephone number in his telephone index somewhere. The Chairman of the

Manchester Chamber of Commerce located his telephone index on his bedside cabinet next to the unopened tube of KY jelly. He seemed to remember the telephone number he required was near the front somewhere (under A for Alarums) rather than being listed alphabetically under the letter D.

Friday, 12.01pm

Mr T. Z. Wetherby is showering in the en suite facility in his private quarters at the headquarters of Rapishaw Gap – a newly constructed three-storey building in metal, glass, and russet-coloured, rough textured brickwork that is situated in what was until comparatively recently part of the green belt in the Tyne Green area of Hexham, Northumberland, south of the River Tyne. Two cocktail glasses, each containing a maraschino cherry in a Planter's Punch, have already been prepared by the only business Mr T. Z. Wetherby has in mind for the rest of the day.

Five feet nine inches tall in her stocking feet (supine or standing), thirty-eight D-cup (in house gown or not), endowed with very, very long blonde hair (her natural colouring, to which Mr T. Z. Wetherby could truthfully attest), Mr T. Z. Wetherby's business for the rest of the day answers to the name of Mirabelle wherever she is to be found at Mr T. Z. Wetherby's side – on Newmarket Heath, at the Quorn Hunt in Leicestershire, or taking her ease with him in a brace of spa towns, six European capital cities, Bermuda, Grand Cayman, or the Lesser Antilles. The only exception to the rule is Hexham, Northumberland. For Mirabelle St Henri will never be seen at Mr T. Z. Wetherby's side in Hexham, Northumberland, except in private. But then, because it *is* in private, there will only ever be Mr T. Z. Wetherby to see her, though Mr T. Z. Wetherby will, of course, see quite a lot of Mirabelle St Henri in Hexham, Northumberland, chronologically and quantitatively speaking too.

Many years of private practice have taught Mirabelle St Henri (*née* Gaynor Garrigill) to suppress any urge to socialise publicly in Hexham, Northumberland – the very same years of private practice that have helped her subdue an accent that still retains the slightest hint of Weardale and the South Tyne. And Mirabelle St

Henri is a girl whose age too, like her accent, is subject to no wearisome fluctuation. For Mirabelle has been twenty-four years of age for at least six of her last ten birthdays. Mirabelle could show you (though, of course, she will never do so) a safety deposit box in a vault at Brinks Matt that contains three diamond brooches and twice as many diamond rings to prove it. These trinkets were all bought as birthday presents by Mr T. Z. Wetherby, or by somebody very much like him. And, come December, Mirabelle St Henri fully expects to receive another such present for another of her birthdays – a brooch or a ring perhaps, either will do. In fact, earrings would be perfectly acceptable for Mirabelle's seventh or eighth twenty-fourth birthday, either from Mr T. Z. Wetherby, or from somebody very much like him. The provenance of her birthday presents doesn't matter to Mirabelle (with regard to donor, that is), though Mirabelle does have a very personal preference for purchases made at either Tiffany's or Asprey's. Mirabelle St Henri is far too professional a lady to worry about any other kind of provenance – just as long as the rings and the brooches and the earrings continue to accumulate in her safety deposit box at Brinks Matt until – well, until the swallows come back to Capistrano, as Mirabelle can remember Pat Boone singing when Gaynor Garrigill really was twenty-four years of age – or (in her heart of hearts Mirabelle, *née* Gaynor can be quite brutally honest about such things) till other birds come home to roost and crow's-feet walk all over her story.

Friday, 12.02pm

Eric Alport – overtired, overwrought, underpaid, and under-appreciated by all save one – is slumped in his favourite armchair, the G-Plan chair in the front sitting-room of his house on Stockport Road, Denton. The rental TV, the Murphy, that Eric picked up from Fred Dawes before last year's Cup Final is switched on and sport is in progress. Eric, alas, is out of it.

'Harlequins and bloomin' Old Etonians, running rings round each other. Where's ruddy Columbine, eh? That's what I want to know. Gimme togger anytime! If your dustbin's black, and you live within a cock-stride of Old Trafford, you ought to have no choice in the matter by law!' Eric would laugh then. But not today: Eric doesn't say anything today, and Eric doesn't laugh. Because Eric is out for the count. The *Daily Mess*, Thursday's, wide-open at its centre pages, shields Eric's eyes from the light of day. The daylight's not too bright, of course, but it would still keep him from having his nap.

Eric has completely forgotten he promised to take Mavis out for a meal today, though Mavis has not. But it doesn't matter to Mavis. It's not as if he means to forget. He works so hard, and he seems to be at the beck and call of every Tom, Dick and – well, Tadeusz. But he loves that job of his – just let her try to get him to stay off work when he's under the weather. Lead horse to water, make it drink a bucketful'd be easier than that. In any case, Mavis has cut the veg now – potatoes, carrots, parsnips, a bit of spring cabbage, and onions (Eric loves onions with his beef), and the joint will be ready in – what? – another half hour at the most. Time enough to wake him then if she has to. Give him time to have a snooze before the grandkids turn up. Oh, the youngest one, Donnie – what *was* he like?

Mavis turns the volume of the TV down to a whisper, but she doesn't switch it off – even that might disturb him. She goes through to the kitchen, opens the fridge and takes out a pint bottle of Newky Brown, as Eric calls it. How did he say that? New-ky Brown? New-*ky* Brown? She couldn't say it like Eric said it. He'd got a taste for Newcastle Brown when he was up north in Hexham that time. Mavis finds the bottle opener and takes the metal cap off the bottle of Newcastle Brown and returns to the sitting room with the opened pint bottle and a schooner glass. She places the bottle on the occasional table under the standard lamp, but beyond Eric's reach, in case he has that dream he sometimes has where Busby sticks him in goal at half time when Harry Gregg gets stretchered off. The schooner glass, Mavis inverts over the top of the bottle. Eric always has a raging thirst when he wakes up, when he's fallen asleep in the chair and maybe snored a bit; and though he likes his Newky Brown chilled, he much prefers it when it's lost the chill of the fridge.

Mavis thinks she may as well have a cup of tea whilst she's waiting. She gets the teapot down from the shelf, and as she opens the fridge to get the milk a thought strikes her: 'Waiting? Waiting for what? What am I waiting for? Waiting for the meat to do? Waiting for Julie to turn up with Neil and Jo and Donnie? And yes – thirty years on from day one – waiting for Eric.'

Friday, 12.03 pm

Fr Malchus is in his private quarters, the window of which looks out over an Assisi that, even this early in the year, simmers in a dusty heat. Fr Malchus is restive. *Lachryma Christi* is what Fr Malchus wants – craves, in fact. But this is not to be, not until midnight at the earliest. Midnight Thursday to midnight Friday: twenty-four hours of fasting and abstinence are decreed by Holy Mother Church. One good meal, perhaps a snack, no meat of any kind. But, for the friars, in addition to this discipline, there is to be no alcoholic intake whatsoever by decree of Father Guardian.

So there is nothing for it but to go cold turkey. And despite his present plight, the irony of the situation is not lost on Fr Malchus. No meat: truly, 'tis meet; no alcohol: go cold turkey. Nay, cold turkey is meat! Meet, indeed! More active than is its wont at midday, the mind of Fr Malchus continues to circle this wagon train of word play – meat, meet, mete out, and meat again. Not for the first time in recent years does Fr Malchus recognise his predicament. For Fr Malchus knows another hell: he cannot sleep in daylight – and he knows he must sleep now – for an hour at least, for ten minutes, for a few seconds even. How else will he manage to run the gauntlet of the 10,000-plus seconds before he joins the other friars at three? How else will he bridge the 43,000 seconds that stretch between the horrid present and the stroke of twelve midnight?

Fr Malchus crosses the room and opens the wardrobe door, and from the sandlewood scented interior, bottom right, where it stands next to the portable filing cabinet containing the Deepdale family documents and photographs that came from the old house when his mother died and his father was taken into the hospice, Fr

Malchus takes a soft Italian leather flight bag which contains the personal impedimenta of his many travels.

'Sleep, unbiddable, I bid thee – heel, sir!' trills Fr Malchus in a passable tenor to a ten-note melody of his own composition.

Fr Malchus seems a bit more relaxed now, for he knows of, indeed, he is very well-acquainted with an unfailing cure for daylight wakefulness, a cure he stumbled across many years before and quite by chance.

In those days Fr Malchus was still known as Shaun Deepdale (Drippy Deepdale, as he was unjustly labelled by the more alliteratively inclined amongst his peers) and he was studying English seventeenth-century History in VIth Form at De La Salle College, Sheffield. Sadly, there was a down side to Shaun Deepdale's VIth form studies. For a time it seemed likely they might interfere with two years of continuous party-going to which he had a prior commitment. Until, that is, Shaun Deepdale's studies and party-going ways received a unexpected boost from a new-found ability to fall asleep, like Churchill and Napoleon, at any time he so choose.

Fr Malchus releases the clasp of the pilot's flight bag and takes out a thickish volume which he has recently had re-bound in Moroccan leather. He checks the author and the title quite unnecessarily, because this is not less than the one hundredth time in the ten years since he was in VIth Form (his fifth in Holy Orders) that Fr Malchus has had recourse to this same volume. Fr Malchus settles back on his couch and opens the book at the only page he has ever succeeded in reading prior to apostatising to Morpheus. There may come a time, Fr Malchus anticipates in his more imaginative moments, when he may wish further to acquaint himself with Hilaire Belloc's life's-work. But about King James II of England, the last Stuart king, whose story lies ready to hand, Fr Malchus is for the time being content to know just this:

'ZZZzzzzzZZZ . . . ZZZzzzzzzZZZ . . . ZZZzzzzzzZZZ . . .'

*

Friday, 12.04 pm

Elinor Redmayne, recently *enceinte,* is still abed, a late night in convivial company the cause. Elinor lies on her back, looking lazily at the daylight that splays through the curtains on to the ceiling of her bedroom – a shifting light, brushed from corner to corner by the sweeping motion of the branches of a silver birch tree in the front garden. Even this late in the day there is still not much traffic to be heard, just the milk float and an occasional car. Elinor purrs a yawn, and her hands go instinctively to her stomach, to the tiny thing that – even as she lies here – is beginning to take shape and grow. There's no movement that she knows of, but it's early days as yet. How long is it before they begin to kick and turn and let you know they're there? She knows someone will tell her. Someone will say. Phil snorts, and Elinor digs him with her elbow.

'Hhw-nnn?' The master speaks.

'Time's the match?'

'Hhw-nnn-pa-hnn,' Phil tells his pillow.

'Hadn't you better get up then?'

The Kraken wakes, hauls itself up on its left elbow, looks at the clock on the bedside cabinet, turns the full baleful fury of the solitary eye it has managed to open upon Elinor Redmayne, and blinks. 'Mmm-mm.' The Kraken slides out of Elinor's bed and pads across her bedroom to the door.

'Phil.'

Blinks again, arrests its progress, turns towards her, blinks once more: wide-eyes a question.

'Dwinky,' says Elinor in the silly little voice she affects on occasion.

'D'y' wan'?'

'See if there's any of that orange juice left, will you?'

''kay.'

'And a Kraft cheese slice.'

'A *what*?'

We are back in the land of the living once more: the City of Salford, Lancashire, England, Europe, the UK: the land where Manchester City is almost sure to lose at home again; where the Triumph Herald that Elinor and Phil have nearly paid for will have received another scratch to its bodywork overnight; where death and taxes continue to retain a government-sponsored stranglehold on the population; where said population continues to get the politicians it deserves.

'A Kraft cheese *slice*?'

Smiling the while, Elinor nods her head vigorously like a child.

Splishings, splashings can soon be heard: clunks, a tap runs, the toilet flushes a second time. (Elinor has sneaked in there before Phil comes back. Then straight back to her nice, warm bed.) Brrr, Easter weather, thinks Elinor: bright and cold – always cold and not always bright.

Presently.

'You rang, Madame?'

Elinor takes the proferred Kraft cheese slice, folds it in two. 'Mmm. My compliments to the chef.' She takes a sip of orange juice, puts the cup down on the bedside cabinet next to the lamp, lies back down again. 'Oh, you're co-o-ld, Phil,' says Elinor.

'Well, you . . . smell of orange and cheese.'

'And you . . . smell of toothpay-th.'

'I' nicer than . . . orange and chee . . .'

'Not . . .'

''Tis.'

''Tisn't.'

''Tith.'

''Tith'n . . .'

Whatever the truth of the matter, at some time in the early afternoon for upwards of 1200 seconds and counting, the city of Salford knows no citizens more content with their lot than Elinor Redmayne and Phil, who, on their return to Planet Earth, will find themselves back in their council flat on Belvedere Road, Salford 5, somewhere between the Flemish Weaver and the Paddock, the latter being a Boddingtons' house at the junction of Belvedere Road and Cross Lane.

Friday, 12.25 pm

Tough Titty, Bernie to mother Marie, T to those who have the nerve to address themselves to him, pulls off Track One on the

Magpie taxi rank alongside the bottom gates of Boggart Hole Clough at the wheel of Car 27, the FX3 black cab that belongs to Line Bunratty.

Track One with a Track One job for once, thinks Titty to himself. About kin time too. Manchester job, take us down to Shude Hill, cut across to Piccadilly. Bound to be a caff open on the station approach, get a bit of breakfast at last. Breakfast? Kin dinner, more like. That kin hungry, belly thinks me throat's cut.

Good Friday – what's so kin good about it is what Titty wants to know when Magnus Piper turns up around tennish. Every kin shop closed, not even Dozy Dot open that rustles up Magpie's kin scran in Dotty's Diner three hundred and sixty-three days a kin year or summat. Is Dozy Dot a religious nut, or what, is something else Tough Titty wants to know.

But Dot is no more religious than anyone else in this God-forsaken neck of the woods, is what Mag Piper tells him. Dot needs her beauty sleep like anyone else. That's all.

More than anyone else, you ask Gib, is Gibraltar's (Gib's) opinion that's working the base today. Because, according to Gib, Dozy Dot still looks like a kin frog if she goes and gets some beauty sleep for twenny years or summat.

But Gib, Mag insists, can just cut it out, cunt. (Mag's wife, Myrtle, is Dozy Dot's sister's husband's cousin's mother's best friend, and Mag thinks this, plus Dot pays good rental monies to Mag for the catering concession, plus Mag gets free scran from Dot that the Revenue don't know about, entitles Dot to some show of loyalty.) Besides, Mag tells Gib, Dot only gets her beauty sleep once a week, don't she? (Meaning Sundays, when Barmy Boris stands in for her.)

Figures, given Dot's looks, is what Gib thinks.

So, Mag says to Shurrit, you, you cunt. He's already told Gib once, and he's not gonna tell him again. And Mag turns round to Titty then, and says: Bleed Nell, there's only two days a year apart from Sunday that Dot gets a lie in, Christmas Day and Good Friday. And If Titty's that hungry, Mag tells him, go get a nosebag downtown.

To which Titty says, You just bet he's hungry, he begun his day track at six, but there's no way he's *that* kin hungry. Because Line checks the mileage on the cab, and three miles on the clock to Line's way of thinking means five bob on the take. Titty goes downtown without a fare, that's nine miles return without a fare, so Line thinks Titty takes a quid he don't let on about. And Mag knows Line, right? No one never wants Line to get to thinking he's been had over. He'll get his breakfast, Titty. You just see if he don't. But he'll wait for the first kin fare that takes him down to town to get the bastard.

Titty is four and a half hours into his day track when he says this, and only coffee from a Thermos flask has passed his lips on the inward journey. Expletives by the score have passed them on the way out.

'Hey, T, ' Mag Piper says to Titty, pausing at the open window of the driver's door of Line's FX3 black cab, speaking *sotto voce* with the Manchester fare being on board. 'Watch your language in the kin cab.'

Sound advice which Titty appears to heed.

'Put the kin shed in gear, twat,' mouths Titty to the driver of a number 63 bus from Heywood as he overtakes it in the FX3 at the main gates to Boggart Hole Clough halfway up Valentine Brow. Titty gives the driver of the 63 a simultaneous two-fingered Churchillian salute lest he imagine Titty is maybe paying him a compliment. 'Kin bus drivers, wouldn't pay 'em in washers,' mutters Titty to himself.

Larry Gilderdale, a bus driver with fifteen years accident-free driving experience with Manchester Corporation Transport Department doesn't so much as bat an eyelid when Titty flicks him the vee. Larry Gilderdale is in his element at the wheel of his six year old 9.8 litres, Metro Cammell bodied, Orion design, Leyland Titan double decker in the red and white livery of MCTD. Larry smiles to himself as he selects third gear. Screwballs, the lot of them! He's seen them come and he's seen them go – one or two of the buggers in wooden boxes too. Black cab drivers, private hire, bus drivers even: the Jack-the-lads, the Wild Bill Hickocks, the Kings of the Wild Frontier – all the showy, full-of-themselves, free-wheeling, loud-mouthed braggarts you ever dreamed about in your worst nightmare: Mighty Joe Young with a driving licence; Tarzan flying a plane; Primo Carnera piloting the QEII. Heaven forfend! This is not for Larry Gilderdale, aged 39 only last week, with a wife and two kiddies he's fond of, and none on the way, thank God. No, not for Larry Gilderdale, the driver of the 63. Slow and steady wins the race, is Larry's opinion. Eight, nine hours a day, a bit of overtime now and then – spreadover if he really *has* to do it. That's quite enough for Larry Gilderdale. I mean to say (Larry's smiling to himself as the thought occurs to him), look at that fool in the black cab, there. We've travelled – what? All of three hundred yards? Yeah, three hundred yards at the most. And I'm already sitting on his tail at Moston Lane lights. That's without even trying. Hey, c'mon, Mr FX3-Screw-Loose, race us to the bus stop, why don'tcha? thinks Larry Gilderdale to himself.

Larry Gilderdale pulls up to let a woman with a kiddy get on at the stop outside the Harpurhey Con Club under the disdainful gaze of Benjamin Disraeli above the doorway and diagonally across the road from Bernard Manning's World Famous Embassy Club. Larry waits for the woman to stow the trolley, then eases away from the stop so as not to inconvenience her and the little one. Bernard Manning, talking to the cellarman on the pavement outside the club, gives Larry a wave which Larry acknowledges.

Larry Gilderdale is on the social committee at the MCTD's White House Club on Middleton Road where Bernard Manning did a sell-out charity concert last Shrove Tuesday. (Pancake Tuesday to Larry: he'd eat a ton of Marie's pancakes with Mixed Fruit jam on them if she'd let him.) Yeah, Larry Gilderdale's the bloke who requested a number called 'Boy, What You Do To Me', but Bernard Manning told him he didn't know that one, till Larry hummed a few bars for him. So Bernard told him No wonder he didn't know it, pillock. Because it was one of Perry Como's, and Bernard had never done much of Perry Como's stuff for the simple reason that kin Perry Como's stuff had never done much for him, Bernard being more of a big band man like Ol' Blue Eyes.

'But ears-a-mike, nothin' er-stop yer gerri-nupp-onner station sing nit,' Bernard told Larry. 'Lazy gennulmen, big hand ya very own Larry (what's yer name again, our Eli?), Larry Gi-i-lderdale with-a 'Boy, What Ya Do To Me', he tells us (you queer or what?), though it's 'Hot Diggity' to arrest her the world. Music, maestro, *please*!'

And Larry had brought the house down, even if Larry Gilderdale singing did sound like Lee Marvin yawning. And by the time Larry pulls up at the stop near the Bottom Derby at 12.27 pm that day, he is yawning like Lee Marvin again, singing (*sotto voce*) 'When Somebody Loves You', known to the rest of the world as 'All The Way', and which will take Larry Gilderdale as far as the Essoldo cinema opposite Eggington Street, smiling to himself at the memory of a good time had by all and £250 that the White House social committee had been able to donate to the burns unit at Booth Hall Children's Hospital.

Friday, 12.28 pm

No lights are burning in St Joseph of Cupertino's church because no lights are needed. Daylight is sufficient to see by, certainly for a congregation of one – a congregation that is also the celebrant: Fr Richard Bellis at his Daily Office. An open breviary in his left hand, Fr Bellis sits before the Lady Altar, third bench from the front. On occasion, he kneels. Fr Bellis has been here for half an hour now, and he will be back here, though on the high altar with his fellow priests, at three. A close observer (though none there is) would notice that Fr Bellis's lips are moving as he prays; a sharp ear might detect a whisper, the only sound in the church, save for the warbling of a wood pigeon somewhere on the outside of the building that can be heard from time to time.

A vaulted Norman arch framing the Lady Altar bears a Latin incription: VERBUM CARO FACTUM EST, the Word was made Flesh. Blue mosaic, glinting with gold mosaic stars, the ceiling shelves backwards from the archway to form an alcove within which there stands a small altar on which can be seen two unlighted candlesticks, a crucifix veiled with a purple cloth, and an empty tabernacle, its door standing ajar.

Fr Bellis stirs. He places his breviary on the bench beside him and takes from his breast pocket a slim booklet, grey in colour, the print on the front cover of which is red. *A Simple Prayer Book* was first published in 1886, and Fr Bellis's copy is perhaps the sixth he has owned over the years. A paperback, the prayer book disintegrates with frequent usage, and Fr Bellis uses his prayer book on a daily basis. As soon as he finishes the Divine Office, Fr Bellis always says the prayers he said for his mother when he was a child and she would take him on her knee. Fr Bellis still says the same prayers for his mother, though in a different sense, and for his father too. Fr Bellis would be the first to smile were you to refer to him as an orphan, but at the age of 45, this is precisely what (though by no means all) he has become.

'O Blessed Virgin Mary, Mother of God and our most gentle Queen and Mother . . .'

Fr Bellis pauses just long enough to waft away a crane fly that has begun to annoy him, drawn to the body heat he gives off. This slight effort calls for more oxygen. Fr Bellis breathes more deeply: an intake of air, an exhalation like a sigh. Never ceasing to pray, Fr Bellis breathes words and air in tandem:

'By thee it was that Jesus, our Saviour and our hope, was given unto the world; and He has given thee to us that we might hope still more . . . '

The wood pigeon is not to be outdone. It seems to be somewhere near the side door towards the back of the church.

Dinchy and Byron have often wondered whether Raj made it to the village of Colden near Heptonstall with Milt from Milwaukee and Cass from Castlemaine, and whether later that same evening the three of them sorted out a meal for themselves in the tap room of the New Delight Inn at Jack's Bridge. When he gets a certain mood on him, in fact, Dinchy has been known to speculate that Raj is with them still. Though what the truth of the matter is, they are never to find out of course.

Come quarter past twelve that day, Dinchy and Byron had had enough of Cross Country. They sank down beside the catering caravan in the lay-by off the A635, their anoraked backs to its nearside wheel with a raft of bacon barms (Byron), cheese and onion muffins (Dinchy). A brace of KitKats and two more cuppas rounded off their meal. In this way, a lazy hour was passed, and of Raj MA (Cantab.), authority on English conjunctions, porter of the Cross Country Kit from Crowden Great Brook to the A635 Greenfield-Holmfirth Road, this is the last they will see.

His hair is plastered to his head, his shirt collar sodden. Enthusiasm apparently undiminished, he alternates between talking volubly and slowly sipping tea from a polystyrene cup, steam rising from which has misted both lenses of his glasses. Thus does the simple scientific marvel of condensation spare him visual contemplation of the dire plateau that awaits him – that quagmire, that swamp, that veritable sump hole of a peat bog which some cartographical comedian in the employ of the Ordnance Survey has christened Featherbed Moss. Still, tackle it he must before Standedge is gained – as, indeed, must Milt and Cass, and (sixty minutes later) Byron and Dinchy. And Featherbed Moss will define for them quite unforgettably, as, indeed, it does for all fools who pass this way, the literal meaning of that gloriously onomatopaeic dialect word – *slutch*.

A lazy hour now passed, Byron and Dinchy rise, more unsteadily than before, to venture out on to Featherbed Moss, Cross Country kit in tow. Dinchy drags it along like a hobby horse now and then. Three miles to go, though not three miles of a picnic. Featherbed Moss first, then – the point of no return – into and across a ditch, which is all that remains of the Cotton Famine Road, a relict of unemployment relief from a time when the Union blockade of Confederate ports during the American Civil War (to which Mr Lincoln makes reference in his letter to Abel Heywood) threw local cotton operatives out of work. Over a brook now . . . White Moss, across two further brooks . . . Broadhead Moss, over another brook . . . Black Moss – and the sky clears. Along Black Moss Reservoir, across Rocher Moss. Then Redbrook Reservoir comes into view along with its yachts. Along Standedge Cut now to Brun Clough, which yields a view of Diggle to the south and, a much more welcome sight in the foreground, one Vauxhall HB Victor saloon, one Ford Transit van, and the girls.

*

Verdict on the main course at the Great Western: fine, fine, fine and – Amanda – she'd had worse; and about the desserts, ice cream for all four of them: fine, fine, fine and – Amanda – she'd had better.

'Mind you,' says Byron, 'what Mancunian, raised on Granelli's vanilla-flavoured treats, could not say the same?'

Away in the gathering darkness to the south-east, the beacon on the Holme Moss television transmitter beyond Black Hill returns Byron's solitary knowing wink.

16

Sometimes, you know, just sometimes, all the things you ever planned for fall into place like you wanted them to, and not long after we done the Cross Country walk me and Shirlee went after this house we'd seen and got it.

It wasn't far from where me Grandma Alma used to live. But where her house backed on to Boggart Hole Clough, this one me and Shirlee bought was across from there on Lewis Ave. A two up, two down, it was (I mean, *is*), with a back yard, and the end house of a block of terraced. So it was what they call a quasi-semi in estate agent speak. It had an inside toilet, and there wasn't a lot wrong with it neither except it was a bit run-down with it having belonged to an old lady who'd lived there since the Year Dot. So it needed a few mod cons, and decorating from top to bottom and a good lick of paint to bring it up to scratch, like.

Desmond Restorick ARICS from the Des Res estate agency on Moston Lane up near the Ben admitted as much. 'It's an absolute bargain,' he said when he took the For Sale sign down off the outside wall and stuck it in the back of his Merc. 'That's because it's not exactly in outstanding decorative order.'

'Mind you,' says Shirlee's dad when we come back to their house and reported in. 'House that's not seen kiddies has not seen many knocks neither. Oh, that's not to say you won't have to replace the odd window on account of the weather, or stick a new bathroom suite in, or update a few doors and what have you. But the interior woodwork and plasterwork should be sound enough, is what I mean.'

They was too, and like I say, it went like a dream.

We thought it over for twenny-four hours (slept on it, in fact) and spoke to one or two people about the jobs that might need doing – then we give Des Res our decision first thing next morning along with an holding deposit of fifty quid, subject to contract. We even found a good solicitor (contradiction in terms or not, we found one). So the job was a good un. We'd been saving up for over twelve months with the Leeds Permanent in this account Shirlee opened for us down on Mosley Street near the Art

Gallery in town. So we had enough for the deposit and a bit left over as well, and the Leeds give us a twenny-five year mortgage on the rest. By the end of July, the house was ours.

Bathroom suite (candy-coloured); kitchen units (jasmine); new windows, front and back; new front door (the one at the back was all right); re-wiring right through; central heating; bit of tiling; new interior doors; wall paper; paint – gloss and emulsion; carpets right through; new cooker. (We done without a fridge and a TV at first.) Yeah, I know it sounds a lot, but we got the house a lot cheaper with it looking a bit drab, and Byron Marlfield set us up with all the gear we needed.

Hey, that Byron! He either known someone who was a tradesman, or he known someone who known someone who was, or he known someone whose son-in-law was handy at doing summat, or he could get you summat himself dead cheap. So everything we got come at a discount. Every bit of it, even labour. Come the end of August, all that still needed to be done was the interior paintwork, carpets, and a bit of tiling in the bathroom. It was beginning to look like a little palace, it was, and I more or less moved in then with a camp bed and a tea pot and a kettle and got stuck into whatever painting I could do when I wasn't at work.

The decorators had done the outside paintwork already and papered the inside with that woodchip paper. But when the weather come up a bit sunnier than it had been, they'd shot off to do a bit of exterior work on a contract they had with Gus Demmy, the bookie. I expected them back in a week or so, or earlier if they was rained off. In the mean time I made a start on the emulsioning meself – weekends mostly, and doing as much as I could after work mid-week.

Come the weekend, I'd get the paint brushes and the roller and the Macpherson emulsion paint out and do the full stint: Friday night till ten pm; Saturday, seven am till ten; Sunday, ten till ten. I had the tranny for company and Shirlee would come round and keep us company every now and then – bring us a few butties, do this and that, like. But Shirlee was mostly charging about sorting out stuff that's a complete mystery to me, like soft furnishings and curtains and cutlery and crockery etc. (Byron again.) So I was on me own a lot of the time. But I'd get washed up for ten o'clock and Shirlee would call round and we'd maybe catch last orders in one of the pubs on Moston Lane – the Wellington, the Old Loom, the Brickies, the Mowers, the Museum or the Ben. Three or four weeks I was at it altogether, then one Saturday morning the tranny ups and dies on us.

I'd had it on from when I kicked off at seven, but I'd turned it off when I heard a knock at the front door (the delivery van with the mirror). And when I switched it on again: nowt. It had just died the death. And the worst of it was it needed one of them dirty big PP9 batteries and I'd no time to go out and get one. I'd of had to go down to Horridge's in Middleton, or Bailey's, up on Kenyon Lane near St Luke's church. Miles away in either case, and Shirlee'd took the car for the day. So I carried on working without it.

Funny things, empty houses, I always think, and I don't mean scary, though they can be – and I reckon you have to watch it if you're in an empty house on your own, exspecially if it's somewhere where you've been happy or sad, or where someone you cared about has left it or died.

Like Charlie Forrester, him that spewed up in the ratter twee at our Suzanne's christening, wotsit's brother – him with the dirty fingernails and the motor bikes, Gordon. Yeah, Charlie Forrester moved from Manchester to St Helens with his work (Pilkington's Glass, I think). Everything nice and bonny: good day for the move, big removal van from Pickfords: furniture, wife and three kids – just a few bits and bobs left to collect. Tea time, Charlie Forrester goes back to their old house for them bits and bobs; missis gets worried after a bit, panicky by midnight: calls the police. They found Charlie Forrester hanging in the stairwell with an hosepipe round his neck. Something had got to him. In his head, I mean. They never did find out what. He'd been dead for ten hours or summat by the time the police broke in.

Course, there was no scariness in our little house; I don't mean that. But I think it's sort of funny being in an empty house on your own like I was that Saturday, working away without the tranny on, and walking about on just the floorboards, then going up and down the ladders, say, and swishing up and down the walls and across the ceiling with the paint roller, and then maybe standing still for a bit and running the tap and filling the kettle and brewing a cuppa. Sort of echoey, it was, and then dead quiet, and then echoey again. Then I'd maybe hear a bit of clumping about next door where Keith and Sylvia lived – or a muffled shout, say, or voices on their radio downstairs, or Isobel's (their little girl's) voice out in the back yard, but shriller. Then it would be my turn again – up and down the ladders, walking about, swishing up and down the walls with the paint roller, or maybe just the sound of a letter or a circular dropping through the letter-box, or a car driving past in the street.

See, I got to thinking about things then. Not a lot of things: just one particular thing. Because it was like me mind had hopped on a sort of a treadmill and what I was thinking about just kept repeating itself over and over again. And that's what I mean about an empty house being funny. It's like it's not empty at all: it's like it's a part of you – hey, and a bigger part of you too. See, to my mind, an empty house can make the things you're worrying about get magnified out of all proportion (if you let it), or make you see the truth of things clearer than you ever seen it in the hole of your life. The trouble is, of course, how the hell do you sort out which is which? Which is the truth and which is just your mind playing tricks on you. And even if you known which is which, you've still got to decide whether it's worth worrying about in the first place. Hey, and I know it's a daft thing to say, but being in an empty house – exspecially working in it when there's no carpets or curtains or furniture to shut the echo up – well, the way I see it, it's like walking around inside your own head. I mean to say, God knows what Charlie Forrester come across in his head that day, but here's what I found in mine when the tranny went dead.

See, I'd always thought of Huge Jameson as me best mate. Yeah, that's exactly what I got to thinking about when the tranny went dead. Yeah, Huge, Shirlee's kid brother. Ever since we was kids at school. And even before that even, like when we was just playing out when we was kids. But he wasn't, you know. Nah, Huge Jameson wasn't me best mate at all; Byron Marlfield was that. In fact, Huge Jameson wasn't hardly a mate of mine no more.

Huge Jameson hadn't not been a mate of mine, not me best mate anyway, for – what? – six, seven years – if not more. And if I'm completely honest about it, I wasn't his best mate neither.

So why the hell had I went and asked him to be me best man? Course, the answer to that one's easy. Yeah, the answer to that one's Shirlee. Not that Shirlee made us, of course. It wasn't that way at all. But with me and Shirlee being like, well, with me and Shirlee being, like, wotsit, you know – well, that was the one and only thing that had kept Huge in the picture at all. Anyway that's what I got to thinking about in our little house that day when the tranny went dead.

Oh, and then I started thinking that maybe I should of asked Byron Marlfield to be me best man. I mean, it'd of made more sense in a way because I was seeing quite a lot of Byron at that time, what with the markets and that. In any case, after all Byron had done for us it would of been only fair too. Not that that is any way to choose your best man – going off what he done for you. But even so, what had Huge Jameson ever done for us? Sweet FA, that's what. Which is just not true at all, is it? I known that as soon as I thought it. Because to be fair to Huge, he *had* done summat for us, summat pretty special too – and he done it that same Saturday morning I got to thinking this way too. Well, sometime during the week anyway. Because what Huge done for us during the week is what had turned up with the carrier that morning (a rival outfit called Wells Cargo from out near Manchester Airport somewhere). Because Huge had only bought us this big gilt bevel-edged mirror for a wedding present (that I had better shift it quick, I thought, case it gets damaged) that Shirlee said she wanted, exactly like the one in her mam and dad's living-room at home.

I parked me stuff up then and put the kettle on again and picked up the mirror (still in its wrapping: corrugated paper, brown paper, twine) and took it upstairs where I left it in the spare bedroom so it wouldn't get under me feet while I was working. But I found meself thinking about the mirror now. Hey, and I caught meself singing a line out of that fairy tale, the one where the Wicked Queen thinks the princess is dead but she's only hid in the deepest part of the forest because the woodman had a change of heart and didn't do what the Wicked Queen told him to do. Snow White, is it? No, Cinderella? No, she's the one with the glass slipper, isn't she? Yeah, it's Snow White, isn't it? Snow White and the Seven Dweebs. And it was only when the water come to the boil and the tea was brewing in the pot and I'd shoved a Blue Riband biscuit in me gob and shut up singing that I realised what it was. It was this song called 'Mirror Mirror' that was in the charts that year and was also the last thing I'd heard on the tranny before it packed in. So I was back on the old treadmill again – mirror, mirror: Huge, Huge; mirror, mirror: Huge, Huge. That is, back to this song by Pinkerton's Assorted Colours that peaked at Number 9 in January, 1966 – and back to me best mate Huge Jameson. I mean, Huge Jameson, me best mate as was.

Oh, you know how he is, Huge, that is, Dee-Jay U.E. Jay, as he's better known to you. And you've only got yourself to blame too. Because, for about three hundred thousand million billion years, from the mid-sixties on, you and about three hundred thousand million billion pop pickers like you never was too keen on getting stuck into your Shreaded Wheat and grapefruit segments in the morning unless you was also tuned into Terry Wogan bejabersing it at the Beeb, Mike Sweeney dead-good-dead-hard-quizzing it on Piccadilly Radio, or your very own Dee-Jay U.E. Jay cock-a-doodle-doing it at Watchtower. Yeah, there you was on the stroke of seven each morning, Monday through Friday, chafing at the bit till you heard that acre-pellow voiceover or whatever they call it that brung Dee-Jay U.E. Jay to your breakfast table before you'd have to tear yourself away from hearth and home to catch the number 72 bus at Blackley Library to take you down to Newton Street.

Remember that? The jingle?

Wa-a-atchto-o-ower Ra-a-adio-o On Nine-Oh FM Ste-e-ere-e-o

Then even before you'd sprinkled the Sankey's sugar over your Puffed Wheat or splashed the Express semi-skimmed into your cereal bowl, you'd be joined at your breakfast table by the boy Jameson hisself, waxing poetic:

'Now, here's ya ol' pal, U.E. Jay with a toon to chase dem blues away!'

Then, Huge – sorry, ya ol' pal U.E. Jay – would dive straight in with that mouthy way he's got about him, chewing your lughole for up to two hours at a stretch, five days a week, two hundred and fifty odd times a year:

'Hi, me ol' toon tippers,/ how's things with you/ howdy-do, how'd-ya-do, how'd-ya-doodle-do!/Whadder want-cha to do is gimme a ring/ Da phone's right there, so pick up dat thing./C'mon, y'all/we need ya call/ U.E. Jay aims to have a ball!'

Or summat.

Mind you, he was pretty well established by that time, Huge. But the time I'm talking about, before me and Shirlee got wed, Huge was just beginning to make a name for hisself. Summer, he'd be down on the south coast somewhere; and in the winter, he'd have different residencies (as he called them) in the Greater Manchester area – or you might see him guesting at the Alma Lodge, or the Plaza, or the Twisted Wheel, or the Top Ten Club with Jimmy Savile at Belle Vue of a Sunday.

Hey, and do not get us wrong now, please. Me and Huge still got on great in them days. Well, whenever we seen one another, that is. Which wasn't that often no more, even then. No one's fault really. See, by that time me and Huge was already living maybe twenny miles apart (many miles apart nowadays). But, even in them days when we lived maybe twenny miles apart (me in Blackley, him out near the Ringway Airport somewhere) we was already living in different worlds. Yeah, the only time I seen Huge really would be at family do's and that, where we got on great just like we always done. (No, we did. Honest!) And I reckon the reason we still got on so well, me and Huge, was because I was never ever jealous of him like a lot of people was. Even people that had used to be his friends.

I heard this quack on Radio 4 the other day (Radio 4, eh? Dinchy's showing his age). And he was going on with hisself, this quack, about how constipation is the English disease. And I hope he gets bunged up for a fortnight, that quack, because he'd got it completely arse uppards. Because the real English disease (if there *is* an English disease) is jealousy – being jealous of someone else's success. And a hell of a lot of people was jealous of Huge like that, though I can honestly say with hand on heart that yours truly never was. On four counts too! Count One: I wasn't jealous of the job he had. No way could I of done what Huge done; wouldn't of known where to start. Count Two, I wasn't jealous of the boy's marriage neither. He got wed out in Gibraltar in 1965; separated after six months; wife and kiddy lived apart. Count Three: I wasn't jealous of Huge's lifestyle. You boring superannooated old get! Count Four: I wasn't one teeny-weeny bit jealous of the money he earned. Okay, so it was above the average, but no way was Huge Jameson major league.

See, loads of people have no imagination at all where money's concerned. If you got money; well, that's it, they think. You must of always had money. Yeah, always lived on Easy Street. Never had to work for it. Never had to give nowt up to earn that money. Hey, you don't even have no overheads.

Mag Piper – him that had Magpie, the taxi firm – Mag used to get that crack from the cabbies. Even Line who should of known better. (Though maybe it was just a wind-up with Line.) Yeah, they'd see Mag collecting his radio money of a Monday morning (£4 per cab X 30 black cabs = £120 a week: a very nice pick up in mid-sixties Great Britain when a decent wage was maybe twenny quid a week), and they'd think it all went in Mag's bin. Yeah, straight in Mag's bin, they thought, them black cab drivers: like, Mag had no shop rent to pay, no business rates, no electric bill, no phone bill, no car repairs, no base staff to pay, no insurance premiums, no overdraft at the bank, no thieving tax man to sort out, no hard graft all his flipping life while all the cabbies that worked at Magpie had been far too busy honing their business skills down the billiard hall that become the World Famous Embassy Club, or in the Top Derby every night of the week. Nah, straight in Mag Piper's bin all that radio money, they thought. Born with a silver Pye radio transceiver in his gob, Mag Piper (Mag's gob was big enough, I'll give 'em that); always had money, always will.

Absolute bollix! (As me Uncle Joe might say.)

And Huge got the exact same thing. People seen him with that flashy job he had, doing the adverts for the UCP tripe shop on TV, opening furniture shops on Oldham Street and garden parties at Booth Hall Children's Hospital or the Catholic Children's Rescue Home in Didsbury, appearing at that charity do at the World Famous Embassy Club after my oppo Biffo snuffed it and left a wife, ten kids, and an insurance policy not worth tuppence-ha'penny behind him. Yeah, people would see Huge doing all that stuff, and think: 'Oh, money, Dee-Jay U.E. Jay, he has!'

Bollix absolute! (As me Uncle Joe might also say.)

A moment's thought would have taught them the 1-2-3s of it. Item 1: a wife and kiddy living apart: that's two homes for starters, two sets of bills. Item 2: a different tart every night of the week: that takes gelt. Item 3: that lifestyle of his: pri-*cey*! What with Huge having to be seen at the centre of things and paying through the nose for the privilege in clubs and bars where they'd bill you for breathing if they could only find a way of doing it. Nah, Huge had no money to speak of. Oh, he had *income*, sure; and a pretty good income it was too. But Huge had no money to speak of. He was skint half the time. Drove his dad mad, that – seeing all the money Huge went through.

'The only money that counts, our Eugene,' Vic Jameson would tell him, 'is money that sticks.'

See, I was never jealous of Huge's money for the simple reason that he never had none. So I don't suppose I can claim too much credit for that. But even so, there *was* a time in the dim and distant past when I was jealous of me best mate Huge. (Yeah, I know I said I wasn't *never* jealous of him, but what I meant was I wasn't never jealous of the things that other people was jealous of – his money and his fame.) See, I was jealous of Huge in a very personal sense, me – and this was many years before he become famous. Still, if I'm gonna be hand-on-heart honest about it, this is the real reason why me and Huge was not best friends no more. It was nothing to do with different lifestyles or distance. And, like I say, this was a very long time ago I'm talking about. Yeah, I'm going back now to when we was fifteen, sixteen years of age or summat – to that time Huge pinched this bird I'd took a fancy to.

Mind you, even that's not the real, rock bottom, basic, ground zero reason I was jealous of Huge Jameson all them years ago, though it's part of it, of course. No, the real, rock bottom, basic, ground zero reason I was jealous of Eugene Jameson all them years ago – and I will thank, please, to kindly remember two things before I begin.

Thing One: this is two callow, pimply, zit-squeezing teenagers I have reference to who've got nothing better to do than the aforementioned zit-squeezing plus comb their hair three hundred thousand million billion times a day, thank you very much.

And Thing Two: this is many, many years before said callow, pimply, zit-squeezing, hair-combing teenagers have become the mature adults, citizens, taxpayers, and Euro-punters what they is today.

Right, here goes then: *Dah-dah-ah*! The real, rock bottom, basic, ground zero reason I was jealous of Eugene Jameson all them years ago in the past is because he was better looking than me and I had to find out the hard way.

It's this Sunday in July, see – hot and sunny and balmy and happy and free – and we're on the boating lake in Boggart Hole Clough, me and Huge, in this clinker-built rowing boat we've hired for half an hour with me on the oars as per usual, Huge never being inclined to turn his hand to physical activity of any kind. Anyway, there we is – sons of the sea – bobbing about on the Clough lake at the side of the island facing the fishing lake, me doing the rowing and Huge sort of lounging about on the back seat, his left leg crossed over his right, arms slung out sideways across the backrest, fag in his mouth; and as we get near to where there's this KEEP OFF notice on the island, we seen these birds not far off in a rowing boat of their own.

Four of them, there is. Two we never seen before, but the other two's Rhoda Rishworth, who's doing the rowing and is dog-rough ('in pretty poor shape, atheistically speaking,' as Byron once said, or summat), and Pamela Wembury, who's dead nice (as I'd noticed for the three hundred thousand million billionth time that year when I seen her go down to the altar rails at the half-ten Mass that morning). And these four birds is laughing and giggling away like people will laugh and giggle away on a nice summer Sunday afternoon when they're bobbing about on the water in the middle of Boggart Hole Clough boating lake with the sun on their backs, not a care in the world, the sound of voices all around them, and a monoplane tripping across the clear blue sky stringing a backcloth of happiness from Ferranti's, Hollinwood, to the ICI Dystuffs Division, Blackley. Yeah, just like that, they is, these four girls in their little rowing boat – and once or twice we seen them glance across at us and start giggling again.

'Hey, catch up with 'em, kidd-oh,' says Huge from his lounging position in the back seat: Horatio flipping Hornblower giving orders to a rating.

Still, I have me own good reasons for wanting to catch 'em up, so I pull hard on the left-hand oar, pushing with the right-hand one so as to position ourselves proper. Fleetingly, it occurs to us that a perceptive tart might well admire this particular rowing technique. (Fool! I should of known only horny-handed Rhoda Rishworth is into the finer points of rowing.) Then I pull both oars together and we is soon skittering across the water towards them. Meanwhile, Rhoda Rishworth is rowing away like a galley slave, and a bit stronger, I should think, what with her having more reserves to call upon. So with me rowing and Rhoda Rishworth rowing, and with Rhoda Rishworth having a real manly pull to her arms, well – BUMP-BUMP-BUMP – them two rowing boats end up colliding hard enough to jar your wisdom teeth.

Oh, there's all these shouts and screams from the girls' boat then, and one of them shouts: 'Oi, just look what yer bleedin' done, yer pillock.'

I turn round in me seat and look at them, shocked, but trying not to show it. I reckon this just has to be one of the two birds we never seen before, seeing how Rhoda Rishworth's got a deeper voice and Pamela Wembury is only three hours removed from the altar rails. Besides which, Pamela Wembury's dad (Weary Willie Wembury, as me dad calls him) is one of the good men of the parish who's in charge of switching the radiators on and off during Mass and answering the telephone during the Consecration. And sure enough, it's this other bird that's shouted, who's sat in the middle at the back, flapping her slack gob, and still going on with herself, pointing at summat in the water.

'Look – just look what you've done!'

I see then what she's on about then. There's a lady's handbag in the drink, a little blue number with a gold-coloured metal clasp like a letter P. It's still afloat, like, but looks dead set to do a Captain Nemo any second now. So I do no more than reach across and scoop it up and hand it to milady Pamela.

'Ta,' says she in a tone of voice that means just the opposite. And she snatches the handbag off of us and starts going tut-tut-tut-tut-tut as she wipes it down with her handkerchief. 'Oh, it's soaking wet,' she says. 'You're a public nuisance, you. You want to be more careful before you hurt someone.'

Choked, is not the word for what I am just then. 'I got it out for you, didn't I?' says Dinchy, grand master of wit and repartee.

'You wouldn't have had to if you hadn't made it fall in in the first place,' says milady Wembury.

Then, through the net curtain of me sheer embarrassment, I hear Huge say: 'Can we, ah, render any more assistance to you ladies?'

And the four of them is off again then, giggling away and going on with theirselves – hey, and Pamela Wembury's face is the picture I'd always imagined it to be close up.

'Why?' says this other tart I don't know. 'What of you got in mind?'

'Not you for a start, darling. You can be sure of that,' says Huge.

At which this tart clams right up and reddens. But, guess what – them other three (Pamela and Rhoda Rishworth and Slack Gob) only start giggling again..

I went right off her then – yeah, Pamela Wembury. Okay, call it sour grapes, if you like. But I really didn't care for them girls laughing at what Huge said to the other tart. If anyone slammed a mate of mine, I'd wanna dive straight in and defend him. Maybe tarts is different. No, they're not; I know they're not. So the only truth I can wrestle out of this situation is that maybe them four tarts, Rhoda Rishworth and Pamela Wembury and Slack Gob and What-of-Yer-Got-In-Mind is the ones that's different.

‘Hey,’ shouts Slack Gob to Huge then, ‘Pam thinks you look like Bobby Darin.’

Oh, trading insult for insult, I think. Which just goes to show what a fool I was. Because the way Huge took it, it was meant as a compliment.

Kin Bobby *Darin*! I’d rather look like Count Draclia!

Pamela Wembury was dead for me as of that moment (she’d have shot her bolt with Bobby Darin anyway), and my friendship with Eugene Jameson, such as it had been for the first sixteen years of my life – hey, such as it had been when we stepped into that clinker-built rowing boat on Boggart Hole Clough boating lake at nine minutes past two on that Sunday afternoon in July – my friendship with Eugene Jameson was dead as well. Dead in the water! Not that our friendship died at a stroke, like a spent rocket falling back from the sky. It was more like a Catherine Wheel, whimpering and wheezing and generally going on with itself before it give up the ghost, Shirlee being the pin that postponed its final plunge to *terror firmer*. Or summat.

Hey, and matters was not improved the night we ended up at that party in Crumpsall (that is, I think it was Crumpsall). Anyway, it was that party we went to that Huge brung Laura Pod to, and I took her home.

One New Year’s Eve at a party in New Moston, impecunious after the Christmas festivities and a job interview midweek with Cunard which had involved the expenditure of return rail fare to Southampton, Eugene Jameson took the detachable collar from his white poplin Van Heusen shirt and, fixing it back to front, emerged sober-suited and solemn from an upstairs front bedroom where his tie and Dot Harrytown (Dot perusing a Jess Conrad fanzine) awaited his return, and descended the stairs to take up a collection in a Quality Street toffee tin bereft of its original contents. This was before Eugene Jameson was famous, or rather, before he was famous for what he is famous for.

There were thirty-four people at the party in New Moston and, when the Quality Street toffee tin had done the rounds, Eugene

Jameson found himself in possession of £1. 4s. 5d. sterling, an Irish florin with the image of a fish on it, and a Praline Cracknel that the lady of the house had had second thoughts about eating. Apart from the Praline Cracknel, this constituted, in that Year of Our Lord, 1961, a welcome contribution to those in need, one of whom (the one who had taken up the collection in the Quality Street toffee tin) realised it would run to eighteen and a half pints of Boddington's Mild at vault prices in the Alliance, or a full year's membership at the Embassy Club with a couple of pints of Tetley's Bitter thrown in for good measure.

But Huge was out of smokes at the time and his subs for the Embassy Club were fully paid up, so this windfall lasted him till Twelfth Night, Players' Medium being his cigarette of preference. Besides, Huge already had somewhere to go of an evening (Dot Harrytown's parents were in Benidorm for the week), and a cigarette vending machine in Piccadilly bus station near the number 1 bus stop accepted the Irish florin with a handful of sterling and minimum fuss.

Normally, something like Huge taking up the collection at the party in New Moston would have enabled Dinchy to pinpoint the party in question – where it had taken place, who (within reason) had been present, what had happened there. But Dinchy never could sort out whether Huge had taken up the collection at the party on Northfield Road, near Ferranti's, Hollinwood, where Charlie Forrester threw his socks up in the E. P. Bowles crocus patch, or the party round the corner from the Manchester Dogs' Home where Idle Wild and Bernadette Holwick were justly accused of messing up the coats athwart Pamela Wembury's Slumberland bed and bending Rhoda Rishworth's golf umbrella in the process. There were other times too when it seemed to Dinchy that these things happened on the same night – and at another party altogether, at a house across the road from HMSO, Chadderton, though in reality this (the party across the road from HMSO, Chadderton) was the party where one of the French windows was pulled off its hinges when Himmler the Ted used it as a bottle opener once too often, where the police were called regarding Gordon Forrester's Norton 500 motorbike being stolen by a man wearing a Man City kit and a Viking helmet, and where brother Charlie puked in the piano.

Naturally, the passing of the years added to Dinchy's uncertainty about these matters. Even so, the sheer sameness of so many of the parties he attended at that time in his life made for uncertainty in the first place. There was a sameness of partygoer and location. Also, most of the parties he attended took place in and around north Manchester – and only on the periphery did the identities of the partygoers ever seem to change. There was a sameness of alcoholic intake too: they supped bargain basement booze at best (plonk and Party Fours), and far too much of it too. So no single party stood out as a separate entity in Dinchy's mind unless something happened on the night to make it different from the rest.

The 'something' need not be very much at all (an old man in a feather-trimmed trilby hat sitting by the fire reading *Dr Zhivago* and the *Football Pink* at a party on a farm in Pilsworth). And in the greater scheme of things the 'something' might be unimportant (Gordon Forrester riding his Norton 500 into a fish pond teeming with coy carp in the front garden of a little palace of a prefab on White Moss and flooring a dozen garden gnomes in the process). And there was a good chance the 'something' might be unsavoury (Cig Heil micturating from the upstairs front window of a public house in the village of Woodhouses on to Charlie Forrester's back as he up-chucked in the doorway). Nevertheless, it would be 'something' that Dinchy could latch on to, 'something' he could remember – and once Dinchy remembered the 'something', the different thing, he could usually remember the rest.

Item: Dinchy bumps into the Hunchfront of Newton Heath for the first time, Charlie Forrester throws up on an Ercol cottage suite, a taxi for the Airport turns up at midnight, courtesy of a bogus caller – ergo this was a twenty-first at a flat on Lord Lane.

Item: the fire brigade douses a chip pan fire, Dinchy alights on Miss Letting-Board, Charlie Forrester is sick on a Siamese cat that's Percy to its face and something quite indecipherable on paper – therefore, this was the engagement party at a Victorian end terrace on Mauldeth Road, Withington.

But the party in New Moston where Eugene Jameson took up the collection in the Quality Street toffee tin was one of two exceptions to Dinchy's rule about 'something'. The collection was certainly 'something', of course, so the party should have come quite clearly to mind. But there'd been a smell of chemicals in the night air, and whenever he'd try to remember the party in New Moston where Huge took up the collection in the Quality Street toffee tin, the smell of chemicals in the night air would interfere with his memory of it and lead him away from New Moston to other parties in other districts at other times – to Eccles, Irlam, and Cadishead, all of which are readily accessible via the A57 trunk road and the Manchester Ship Canal, but miles from New Moston.

The other exception to Dinchy's 'something' rule was the housewarming party in Crumpsall. Even so, Dinchy could remember most things about the housewarming party in Crumpsall – having good reason to remember them, two or three good reasons, two or three distinct 'somethings' to remind him.

Item: Charlie Forrester hauls a bird bath from garden to bathroom and promptly fills it with vomit.

Item: Huge Jameson – with Idle dancing close attendance – quaffs QC sherry in quantity, and turns nasty with Byron.

Item: Laura Pod having turned up with Huge, ends up (one chapter of accidents later) with Dinchy.

And again it is a smell in the night air that leaves Dinchy disoriented with regard to where the party took place. Of course, the smell in the night air on this occasion was the smell of the CWS biscuit works, which would seem to suggest that the party took place in Crumpsall. But Crumpsall – as far as Dinchy remembers it – is flat; and, as Dinchy remembers it too, the house where the housewarming party took place was set back high on a hill.

Laura links her arm in Dinchy's as they exit via a side door shortly after midnight, her perfume coming at him mixed with the smell of the biscuit works where the night shift is in progress. They cross the gravelled drive towards Laura's car, parked beneath a street lamp at the end of the street. The night air is warm, but

Laura shivers momentarily. Not for the first time, she wonders if he'll be all right, meaning Huge.

But Dinchy can honestly see no reason why not. Ginny's boyfriend is a doctor. Right? . . . Okay, a trick cyclist. But he's a doctor, Ginny's boyfriend. No? . . . All right, Gavin. So Gavin checks Huge over, soon as Ginny puts the spare bed up for him. By which time, Gavin's already stopped the bleedin'. Heck, the last Dinchy sees of him, Huge is sleepin' like a baby. No, Laura is not to give it a second thought: Huge will be all right. But Laura does give it a second thought. And one thing Laura worries about is why Byron goes and does a thing like that. Laura has never seen Huge so drunk, of course. But neither has she seen Byron so angry. But Dinchy says to just wait a minute, Laura. Because there is not one single thing that Byron does. Huge falls and bangs his head, right? . . . Well, okay, his conk. And this is before Byron can even get at him too . . . Yeah, Wotsit holds him back, doesn't he? Thingy, the teacher – what's his name? Mac? . . . Yeah, Mac holds Byron back. Because what Byron objects to, Laura, if Laura really wants to know (and who can blame Byron, Laura?) What Byron objects to is Huge shoutin' at the top of his voice that Byron (or 'Marlfield', as Huge puts it, Laura) that Byron is an effin' know-all, not to say an effin' black bastard too, begging Laura's pardon. Which Byron reckons is well out of order . . . No, Laura, Dinchy jokes not. Huge is drunk, remember – Huge is so drunk he's liverish . . . Well, okay, there's gotta be loads of questions like that, Laura. Like, for instance, why do Huge and Idle swig red wine and QC port in half pint tumblers like it's Vimto cordial goin' out of fashion? And while we're at it, Laura, why does Idle have the hat stand halfway up the stairs in the first place? Unless the reason for that is maybe the same reason why Huge is roarin' drunk on the first landin' with the standard lamp and six foot of flex trailin' behind him? (Hey, and isn't Laura glad she's went off with Ginny to sort out the buffy before the trouble kicks off, eh?) Still, there can be no question about Idle rippin' his pants when he fell, or about Huge lyin' at the foot of the stairs with his shirt tail hangin' out of his pants and his face all bloody – or about Byron laughin' his head off at the pair of drunken berks, AND, Laura (as was ever the way with Byron) sayin' summat clever, which Laura already knows anyway because that's exactly when she come through with the tray of canopies. Whereupon Laura quotes verbatim what Byron says:

What are these
So withered, and so wild in their attire,
That look not like th' inhabitants o' th' earth,
And yet are on't?

Which, Laura says (when Dinchy asks her what that is when it's owt), is from the Scottish play that Laura can't even say the name of because it's unlucky. So Dinchy tells Laura she can say that again! Because it's certainly unlucky for Huge, though not for me, thinks Dinchy to himself, as they come to Laura's car where it's parked at the edge of the high land where a little cinder track drops down through the fields and the dark and the trees, and where, leaning against the off-side front wing – they kiss . . . and . . . kiss . . . and pulling apart momentarily, hear the sound of voices, then breaking glass somewhere below them on the path beside the river, whereupon Dinchy murmurs (just to keep things light): 'If you go down to the woods tonight . . .' And Laura laughs, takes her car keys from her shoulder bag, unlocks the driver's door, slides behind the wheel, motions for Dinchy to jump in – and laughs again.

The engine of Laura's Chevrolet Camaro starts with a roar and Dinchy does as Laura bids him do. But for these two, Laura and Dinchy, their moment has passed. For, when Laura laughs and laughs again what Dinchy sees is not Laura's present laughter but a scene reprised from a late night movie of their distant past: *credits, reverse, fast rewind:*

A girl's scream . . . a frog *en bouche* . . . the hand that threw the frog . . . the hand that threw the frog that rolled the tyre . . . the hand that threw the frog that rolled the tyre that dug the mud . . . the hand that threw the frog that rolled the tyre that dug the mud that thrust the finger (CLOSE UP – *Idle's right index finger*. CUT TO CLOSE UP – *Idle's mucous-blocked nasal passageway*. CUT TO CLOSE UP – *right index finger and mucous-blocked nasal passageway*. CUE ACTION. *Repeat, repeat, repeat, repeat, repeat*).

*

Dinchy escorts Laura to her studio apartment in Prestwich village and partakes of victuals within. He listens attentively too, sitting next to Laura on the settee in Laura's apartment in the glow from a Tiffany standard lamp while Laura tells him about her little pony called Julia that is the best little pony for miles around and which, Laura tells him, could be shown except it has a blanket scald. No, Dinchy admits as much, he does not have a pony, except for Shanks's (ha, ha). But Dinchy says: In any case, he would not know a fetlock from a grommet if his life depends on it. But Dinchy is very interested, he tells Laura, to hear about Laura's brother, the optometrist, well, opthalmologist really, and about Laura's married sister who lives on a farm in Hampshire and would not be seen dead in anything but a Porsche Spyder. And Dinchy asks Laura, Isn't that what James Dean was seen dead in? Or was it somethin' else? And Well, no, not just at present, Dinchy hasn't, but that Mini Cooper Mr Podgorze (daddy, that is) is gonna buy Laura for her birthday sounds just the very thing for gettin' about town in much more easily than a Chevrolet Camaro import, and How fast will it go flat out? But Laura is sorry, because this she does not know; though something Laura does know is that her brand new Mini Cooper is the most scrumptious bronzey-gold sort of a colour with just this teeny-weeny hint of rouge in it. Which, Dinchy tells her, he is quite definitely of the opinion that it is exactly the right colour to go with Laura's dress and her complexion too; and Wherever does she go to get a nice tan like that, it's bein' such a wet summer this year? Why, the Seychelles, of course, is what Laura says. Where else? Then, a thought strikes Laura that it would be very mannerly of her if she asks Dinchy something about himself because she has not asked him one single thing yet except about his pony that he has not got and his car the same. So Laura says – eeny, meeny, miny, mo – she does so like Dinchy's midnight blue suit, but Are the shoulders all his? Yes, they is, Dinchy assures her – well, a good fifty per cent of them anyway (ha, ha), the rest belongin' to a gentleman's tailor, Walter Peart by name, though Dinchy has paid him good money to part with them and is payin' him the rest on the drip. And Dinchy says (shucks!): No, as a matter of fact, no one ever has told him he has laughin' eyes (whatever they is), but, in any case, Laura's smile is much much nicer by far. And then Laura and Dinchy *do* kiss, though only once or twice, but in doing so, they bend a perfectly good 45 rpm single called 'I'll Never Get Over You' by Johnny Kidd and The Pirates, though Laura is not to know the 45 is bent until the Tuesday after the August Bank Holiday Monday. Because when she goes and switches her Ferguson radiogram on, Dinchy says: No, perhaps not, seein' it is well past the witchin' hour, though he is always willin' to make an exception for Larry Williams whatever time of the day or night it is, but he doesn't suppose Laura has got anythin' by Larry Williams by any chance? And Dinchy supposes one hundred per cent correct, though Laura *does* have a record by a *Danny* Williams, and she wonders if this is Larry's brother by any chance. But Dinchy says, No, he thinks not, or Larry would have drownded him at birth in the river maybe – and he wouldn't of had to take him all the way to the moon to do so. (Joke.) No, Big Muddy would of done the job just fine . . . Well, okay, you say so, Laura - the Limpopo or the Thames maybe.

Then Dinchy makes his excuses and takes his leave of Laura, and Laura is glad to see him go. Not that Dinchy is sorry to be taking said leave. So even if Laura had managed to prevail upon Dinchy to give Johnny Kidd an audience that night, 'I'll Never Get Over You' would not have been saying a single thing about either one of them. Furthermore, at least with regard to Dinchy (no further information about Laura being ready to hand), Johnny Kidd's next single would be no nearer the mark.

Johnny Kidd's next single, 'Hungry For Love', was released in November, 1963, and according to the *Guinness Book of British Hit Singles* it peaked at number twenty in that same month. Similar information is available in *British Record Charts, 1955-1979*, except for the fact that the same record is shown as peaking exactly one month later.

But none of this matters overmuch in the Dinch scheme of things because Anthony Dismas Dinch (to give the fool his Sunday name) – idiot/grafter, dim wit/scrote, weed/dunce, ingrate/dope, friend/nutter, Mancunian/knucklehead, lame brain/vulgarian, dumb cluck/dope, pop freak/oik, unlettered and unread, head-banger and punter, running dog and coward, gobshite, layabout, looney tune, prospective lover, husband, father, ratepayer (if he really has to be), taxpayer (when he can't avoid it), voter (till new Labour comes along), Euro-punter, statistic . . . said Tony Dinch was involved with Eugene Jameson's sister Shirlee by the time 'Hungry For Love' was released. Indeed, if we were to say Dinchy was *enamoured* of her, we would not be stating the case too strongly – which emotion would appear (was the girl mad?) to have been reciprocated by Shirlee herself. And so it came to pass in the nineteenth year of his life on this planet, gratuitously and quite undeservedly, Dinchy knew hunger no more.

And neither did Johnny Kidd, though in a different sense – and not until that day which, at this point in time, is nearly three years in the future, when – returning from a gig at RAF Waddington in Cumbria in the early hours of the morning of 7 October, 1966 – he is killed in a car crash near Radcliffe on the outskirts of north Manchester.

Born Frederick Heath in Willesden, London, Johnny Kidd will be recognized by the *Record Mirror* and the *New Musical Express* as an important seminal influence on the British rock scene. Just 26 years of age at the time of his death, he had developed his trademark eye patch whilst wearing it to cover a pouk. Bass guitarist Nick Simper, travelling in the death car with him, is hospitalized with torn muscles and severe lacerations but, thankfully, survives.

17

I've been a bit unfair to Huge, you know. Oh, I don't mean Laura Pod: serve him right for getting palatic. No, saying he never done owt for us. Because he got us the mirror, didn't he? And it was Huge who swung us a good deal on our honeymoon pad.

We'd stayed at St Marychurch before, me and Shirlee, with her Auntie Vera who had the B&B. One Whitsun, it was, when Huge was D-Jaying down in Torbay. But by the time we got wed her Auntie Vera had snuffed it – took bad with the flu one Christmas and never recovered. Not that we'd of stayed with her Auntie Vera if she'd still been there, I don't think. Not on our honeymoon. Wouldn't of seemed right somehow. Or would it? I dunno, because it was summat we never discussed. But we both liked St Marychurch. It's busy enough and convenient, with shops and pubs and things, and the sea views above Oddicombe Beach have just gotta be the best on the South Coast. Anyway, we'd always planned to go back there, and knowing this, Huge swung us a good deal on this nice detached bungalow he known about.

All we had to do was divvy up up-front and hang on till the Sunday after the wedding to get the keys. But like I said to Shirlee at the time, it was right up our street in a way, because we could use them few days after the wedding to finish off the bits and bobs around the house that still needed doing. See, the good weather had held and the decorators come back from Gus Demmy's shop later than expected. So by the time they was finished painting our place we only just managed to get the carpet in the living-room and the front bedroom down before the Big Day. There was still the hall, stairs and landing and the spare bedroom to sort out, plus a bit of vinyl floor covering for the kitchen. So not being able to get the keys for the bungalow till the Sunday was a sort of a blessing in disguise. Or so it seemed to me.

See, what it was was this, see: Paula Petitor, what was Huge's girlfriend at the time, Paula Petitor lived in this bungalow in the back garden of her mum's guest house, but Paula would very kindly let us have the use of her bungalow for the week while she was over in France somewhere. (Britney, she said.) We'd have to do our own cooking or have our meals out, of course. But that wasn't a problem, and it sounded great the way Huge described it to us.

It was too.

Yeah, it was a smashing little place, that bungalow – nice and private with a lovely big garden and trees all around it so it wasn't overlooked from the guest house. And like I said to Shirlee when we come unstuck, you could hardly say it was Huge's fault because Paula Petitor changed her mind and never went to France after all but went across to Newquay instead, where Huge had this dee-jay residency that summer at The Cornish Chough – hey, and only for three days too (Paula, this is), and not for the full week as per our arrangement with her. And besides, as I pointed out to Shirlee when she was going on to some tune about it, at least Frau Schweinhundt (Paula's mum: that's not her real name, just how we found her) at least Frau Schweinhundt could fit us in for B&B in the guest house for the other four days after Paula come back. Hey, and it was hardly Huge's fault (was it? I said) that B&B accommodation costs more than self-catering accommodation That's just a fact of life, that. Like it's a fact of life that boyfriends and girlfriends is prone to have a barney from time to time – like Huge and Paula Petitor did down in Newquay when she went and dumped him on the Wednesday of that same week and come home to her little bungalow, fuming, when she found out about Huge and Trudy Trenance.

And Paula Petitor, well, Paula was in such a tizz when she come back from Newquay, we thought we better wait for the right opportunity to bring up the subject of a refund for the other four days we'd paid her for except that, as things turned out, the right opportunity never did present itself. But, like I said to Shirlee at the time:

'Not to worry, eh? It *is* our honeymoon after all, so hang the expense. Because you only get married once or twice in your life, don't you? (ha, ha)'

So Shirlee socked us one, but was laughing when she done it.

And the bungalow was really nice while it lasted. Yeah, it was. No, really. It had these two big rooms and a kitchen, and a toilet and bathroom combined – and, at the back there was this lovely sea view over Petitor Beach as well.

We'd drove down to Torbay on the Sunday. Took us all of nine hours, and it rained all the way. The roads was terrible, but at least there was no snarl-ups. See, in them days, coming from Manchester, you had to jump on the M6 at Mere Corner after tootling through Old Trafford, Sale and Altrincham, then you done this dog-leg round Birmingham to get on to the M5. And in them days too the M5 motorway stopped short of Exeter somewhere, so you had to go through all these piddling little towns and villages before you got to Torbay. Knackering, it was. Still, we made it without mishap, and the next day – the Monday – was glorious.

Course, we was still tired with all the travelling, but with the weather turning out nice we was up with the lark and got a breakfast in a cafe and used the funicular railway down to Oddicombe Beach and went out on the motor boats for an hour and over to Brixham in the afternoon on the open-top bus and had our dinner there. It was as if we didn't trust the good weather to last after all the rain we'd had. So we went on the Golden Hind in the harbour at Brixham, and done Kents Cavern on the way back. Then, come teatime, we had a cream tea in a cafe and a few drinks in a pub called The Drum. We'd decided to have a proper meal later on, but being tired after the drive and that, I wanted a bit of a kip first. So I left Shirlee in St Marychurch, looking round the shops, and cleared off back to the bungalow and crashed out for an hour.

An *hour* did he say? Bet it was more like three!

I zonked out soon's me head touched the pillow: never even made it under the covers. When I come to it was already going dark and I could hear Shirlee getting ready in the bathroom. She'd left the light on out in the passageway where it was etching this sort of soft white line round three sides of the bedroom door, the two uprights and the lintel. And I was flat out on top of the bed without a stitch on, barring me socks and me watch – the one with the luminous face that Shirlee bought us for me twenny-first that stopped for good when the water got in it that night. It was nineteen minutes to nine and I was just bursting for a pee. So there was nothing for it but.

I rolled out of kip, padded across the carpet and out into the passageway, and tapped on the bathroom door. No answer. Just the sound of running water. So I opened the door and went in.

'*Excoo-zay moy, silver plate*,' said I. 'Ay em *Mon-sewer* Sh-yee-may Rid-dell, an' Ay em sh-yoost dy-eeng four – 'ow you say eet, Eengleesh? – ay piece. May wee?'

No answer.

Carried on regardless. Done what had to be done, triple somersault, couple of backsprings, handstand, three hundred thousand million billion press-ups, the Drinking Song from *The Student Prince*, *Chorus of the Hebrew Slaves* (solo) – and I was on me way back out again when Shirlee sticks her head round the shower screen. 'I thought I heard something,' says she.

Now, them triple somersaults and backsprings is a bit noisy, I do admit. But three hundred thousand million billion press-ups is usually quiet as a church mouse on a Civil Service pension.

'So you're up at last, are you?' She looks like a ghost, with the steam all around her. 'Oh! . . . Oh, you are! Teddy's getting ready for a picnic.' The ghost giggles, reaches out to us.

'I'll get me socks wet,' says George Formby, watching water tracing scratch marks down her face.

She takes his wristwatch – slings it.

'Why?' he asks her.

So she tells him, but her words are foreign words, and he doesn't understand her till she kisses him, says again:

'I want every little bit of you!'

The words seem to be coming from somewhere between her teeth and bottom lip where gypsies have set up camp overnight.

'Oh, very Shakespearean, Dinchy!' This from Byron. 'What my old English teacher at North Manchester used to call "pathetic phalluses".'

Or summat.

Well, I ask you! (Eden Kane, 1961 – brother of Peter 'Where Do You Go To My Lovely' Sarstedt.) Hey, and I'll tell you where she goes to, My Lovely, meaning Shirlee Jameson (now Dinch): exactly nowhere. Well, not just yet she don't. Because Shirlee Jameson (now Dinch) is stood there in the vestibule of St Joseph of Cupertino's church in her wedding dress that she's took so much trouble with over the last twenny-four years (or so it seems to me), and with her hair done special for her earlier that morning somewhere up near Chain Bar. I dunno – Nina Drive, I think, opposite the Gardeners. And the girl is not alone neither. Because there's only three hundred thousand million billion Manpudlians crammed into the vestibule with her. And meanwhile, outside St Joseph of Cupertino's church, where there was this glorious Indian summer of a day when we arrived for the service an hour ago, the Manchester monsoon season has now set in with thunder and lightning sketching the SS runes in the skies above the ICI Dyeworks Division, Blackley, and buckets of rain getting chucked down by the cattery-full, not to mention the Manchester-Dogs'-Home-off-Church-Lane-kennel-full. And unless Henryk the Photographer (aka Henryk Bodinski, who spent his teenage years tired and dirty and lousy and hungry and cold back in his native Poland on the run from bastards like them that have now run their flag up in the skies above the ICI Dyeworks Division, Blackley), unless Henryk the Photographer can sort out an another backdrop for our wedding photographs instead of outside St Joseph of Cupertino's church as planned, it looks like Shirlee Jameson (now Dinch) is gonna get a right ducking when she's called upon to step outside and say Cheese.

Things are almost bound to go wrong at a time like that, aren't they? And of all the things that gang up on you at a time like that I think I'd be hard pressed to say which is worse – the flipping people or the flipping people.

Like Byron, trying to be funny and not succeeding.

Or me cousin Line: 'Look on the bright side, Dinchy. Yer on a cert tonight!'

Cheers, mate. Yeah, thanks for that!

Or some folk that never known how to behave proper in the first place and have no intention of changing the habit of a lifetime just because it's your wedding day. 'Hey, Dinchy, that van of yours from work. Reckon you could pick a fridge up from Grey Mare Lane Market for us?'

Hm, well, maybe not this afto, Idle.

Or flipping White Moss Taxis, where we'd booked the wedding cars, that turned out to be double-booked, so it's ten past eleven before Shirlee arrives at the church with the service scheduled for eleven.

Or Huge, the best man, turning up after Shirlee due to a personal double-booking that meant he'd had to get a cab all the way across town from Didsbury Village after opening the tripe shop.

Still, as luck would have it, I'd kept hold of the ring and the silver coins meself – a couple of Churchill crowns, though even that was a bit unlucky in a way because Huge only went and dropped them as I was passing them across to him – he was that het up after arriving in such a tearing hurry – and one of the coins rolled under the organ where we couldn't get it, but we still had the other one so it wasn't as bad as it could of been, I don't suppose.

Mind you, maybe that was my fault really because I was in a bit of a tizz, meself, with everything that had happened up till then. Like having to go down to Central Station at half past nine that morning to fetch Noreen Jessop and her three idiot children – Neev, Gnomie and Nut (or summat), who'd arrived from Southport without Uncle Pat but who couldn't manage to get no further without outside assistance. So Dinchy was elected to fetch them in the Countryman. And it was no consolation whatsoever when Nut shits hisself in Dinchy's car – 'bewrays hisself', as mum put it – and the only replacement pants we could find for him was emerald green and didn't go too well with his pale blue page boy outfit with frilly collar and cuffs, though the photos was in black and white, so even that wasn't as bad as it could of been.

Hey, and there was some good things that happened that day too. So I mustn't get too carried away with the other stuff. Like, me and Shirlee got wed, didn't we? Yeah. And like I said to Shirlee when we was signing the register in the sacristy: 'Well, they can't take this away from us, can they, pet?'

Which only goes to show just how wrong you can be, I suppose.

But Henryk done a wonderful job. No, he did, honest. He really was a smashing photographer, Henryk. See, instead of making us go outside where we'd of got a ducking, Henryk got us all back into the body of the church and the sacristy and took most of the snaps in there.

And Fr Bellis was very understanding about it all, as he had been all along – 'A walking saint, that man,' as me mam announced for the three hundred thousand million billionth time in her life when Fr Bellis had to show Neev, Gnomie, and Nut where the toilets was, and Charlie Forrester too, whose face had gone green. And then when the rain stopped for about two minutes or something, Henryk got us outside the front door of the church in the garden, with the Calvary as a backdrop, and took another raft of photographs, and a few more at St Joey's Club where the reception was.

And, of course, the reception itself went well. I mean, they don't normally serve food at St Joey's Mens' Club, but Huge had got them to do it as a favour through this contact he had, namely, Dot Harrytown, whose mum and dad was now the stewards. Yeah, all it took was cash up-front, and not too much of it neither. Okay, so Hetty Jameson and me Auntie Mary and one or two others was complaining about the chicken dinner being rabbit; and Noreen Jessop was heard to say it tasted like no chicken she'd ever ate, and maybe this was some of that chicken that was left over from the Davy Crocket hat craze in the 1950s when all them alley cats went missing in Middleton. But Hetty and Noreen was always complaining about something or other, and most people ate it, and I thought it tasted all right. Besides, Huge done a great job as best man.

Well, okay, I know there was some – Hetty and Noreen for starters – who took offence at that story he told about the bloke from Blackley that rode the Brahma bull into the ground at the Calgary Stampede after his missis had the whooping cough. But you get 'em, don't you? The Moaning Hetties is always with you. Hey, the Moaning Noreens too! I mean, like Shirlee said: No, of course not, Dinchy; it wasn't too bad at all, provided you covered your ears and hummed *Land of Hope and Glory* till Eugene had finished. But, like I said to Shirlee, It's not as though he used the eff word once, is it? So what's all the fuss about, that's what I want to know.

I mean to say, it was only after Harry, that played for Newton Heath Loco, and Johnno, Shirlee's cousin – him that turned out for Stalybridge Celtic – brought the house down with the mirror ball (well, the optics section of the bar really, and Dot Harrytown's mother's bee-hive hair-do). Yeah, it was only at this point that things begun to go downhill pretty quick. Well, uphill, to be exact, because there is three steps *up* out of St Joey's Men's Club on to Rochdale Road, Blackley, which is where we found ourselves – all one hundred and thirty-three of us – come half past six. Not that this was anything to do with the mirror ball, as Huge explained. True, the mishap with the mirror ball had not exactly endeared us to Mr and Mrs Harrytown, but there'd just been a bit of a misunderstanding over the booking, that's all.

See, the normal Wednesday night punters was expected at seven, and they was expecting a big turnout tonight, as it happened – a full-house, in fact. Because Douggie Carlingford, the comedian, was on (him that made Bernard Manning sound like a choirboy), and it was a sell-out, of course. Which, said Huge, was the one and only reason why the Jameson-Dinch wedding party (all one hundred and thirty-three of us) was chucked out of St Joey's Club at half past six in the evening and found ourselves scattered between the Farmyard Hotel, the Alliance Inn, the Top Derby, the Golden Tavern, the Grove Inn, the Red Lion, the New White Lion in the dip, Ye Golden Lion in Blackley Village, and home – no, not the Old House at Home on the ICI path, but back at our house, where the lid on the piano got broke.

'It wa' ship pwed'yush,' Huge told us when the bell went for last orders in the Farmyard. Meaning, that's what had kept us out of the New Inn on the corner of Moston Lane.

But Byron said there was no way 'sheer prejudice' had come into it. The fact of the matter was, said Byron, Huge Jameson was not the only one in the one hundred and thirty-three strong Jameson-Dinch wedding party who'd been unfit to cross Rochdale Road safely at Moston Lane traffic lights in order to access the New Inn.

Still, never mind, eh? Because the good things that happened on me wedding day is what I wanna concentrate on. Accentuate the positive, like the man said (said man being Byron). Because, quite apart from me and Shirlee getting wed (which was plenny good enough in itself), something really out of the ornery happened on me wedding day. Yeah, something happened on me wedding day that I don't never remember happening before in the hole of me life. Because what happened on me wedding day was this: *Dah-dahhhhhhh*! Me dad called us by me name.

Oh, go on then; go on and laugh if you're going to. And to be honest, I think it's pretty funny meself now I come to think of it. Because there's nowt to it, is there?

'Tony.'

Nah. Nowt to it at all. Except for this, of course: me dad had not never once called us by me name before the day I got wed. Before that it was always 'Oi!' or 'you!' or 'him' (this to me mam). Give us a flipping name (some of it stoopid: the Dismas bit) and never once used it till the day I got wed. Made no big deal about it then neither.

It was during the speeches, when I done me shivery shaky piece, and Huge done okay (apart from the bloke from Blackley at the Calgary Stampede) and the telegrams was read out, and Shirlee's dad said summat or other (dunno what – for once I was in agreement with Noreen Jessop: 'He should of spoke up!' But I seem to remember hearing mention of 'mickle' and 'muckle' and 'nest egg' and 'brass'). Then me dad got up on his hind legs and never got a chance to say much at all really, because, straight off, he upset all the Man U supporters with something he said. Summat about the Duke of Cumberland, for God's sake! Well, those weren't his exact words, of course – that's what Byron Marlfield told us when I asked him what Bloody Butcher me dad was going on about.

Anyway, the upshot was that Joe Bunratty and Line wouldn't let me dad say no more after this, and hit back with a bit of Stretford End chanting till Joe's voice (the wheedling Oirish one that was much in demand at the AG Club and the Kings Arms, Collyhurst) come clear above the chanting with this song called 'The Flowers of Manchester' that's about the Munich Air Disaster. Which meant me dad never did finish his speech – thank God, or I'd of died of shame. Because he'd already slipped me name in there. Hey, and for once in me life, I was sharing historic air space with his reminiscences about his Man City heroes – Bert Trautmann, Don Revie, Roy Paul, and them, though the boy Dinchy was not exactly on the hallowed turf at Maine Road or Wembley Stadium in the story me dad was trying to tell before me Uncle Joe cut him short, but on the Red Rec, Carisbrook Street, aged eleven, in his one and only appearance for St Joseph of Cupertino's Under-Elevens togger team.

Hey, and do not get us wrong now. Me dad wasn't talking about us, like I was a footballer or summat. No. That would of been too much to expect – for him to tell porkies about us. Nah, what he was doing was a bit of a put-down really. Which is why I was glad me Uncle Joe shut him up before he made it public. Still, at least he'd booted me name in the air for once in me life – like the loose ball that's got no connection whatsoever with the state of play but wins the Spot-the-Ball competition every time.

St Joseph of Cupertino's Under Elevens football team (royal blue and gold hoops/white shorts) had just three tactics when I was on the squad – that is, when I was on the squad, second reserve, safely removed from the field of play, but allowed to wear the kit.

Tactic One: St Joey's always used a Mitre Mouldmaster instead of a leather caseball, which give them a winning edge on the Red Rec, Carisbrook Street, (which was shale) over nesh opponents that was used to changing rooms (Moston Fields), grass to play upon (Hague Street: courtesy of Tootal's sports ground, Ten Acres Lane), or segments of orange to suck at half-time (St John Bosco's, White Moss: courtesy of Mr O'Connor, the caretaker).

But Tactics Two and Three was always kept dead secret until the kick-off, when they was shouted for the entire forty minutes (which is how long an Under Elevens' football match is supposed to last) by each and every feller who happened to have turned up to watch.

Tactic Two was: 'COME ON, LET'S GET INTO THIS GAME NOW!'

And Tactic Three was: 'GET UP, LAD, YOU'RE NOT HURT!'

Hey, and Tactic Three was a very, very important tactic too, exspecially on the Red Rec, Carisbrook Street, where you was not considered to be hurt with any injury short of a fracture – cheekbones and vertebrae notwithstanding, these being just midge bites.

But on the Saturday morning I'm talking about this kid called Denis Kisdon did *not* Get into this game (against All Vandals and Wreckers), seeing how Denis Kisdon never even turned up. Then just before half time, another kid called Owen Rowan said, No, he would *not* flipping-well Get up because he *was* flipping-hurt, seeing how he'd scrawped his right leg from armpit to ankle when he done this sliding tackle in the All Vandals' and Wreckers' goalmouth.

So, Ozzy had to call on *all* his reserves that day and, turning to Dinchy, Ozzy told Dinchy to Get into this game now.

Fame at last. (N.B. That's nowt I'm owed when Andy Warhol drops by to check.)

Hey, and to be fair to the boy Dinchy, he come on dead keen and done his best. Mind you, to be fairer still, the boy Dinchy's best was a heck of a lot worser than Denis Kisdon's worst – and no better than Owen Rowan's present best, said Owen Rowan being flat on his back by this time, using a muddy puddle as Savlon.

See, Dinchy's playing technique was to chase around the pitch from goal mouth to goal mouth like a scalded cat, trying to be wherever the ball happened to be at any particular moment in time. Oh, yeah, Dinchy really got into this game now, though whether this was of the standard that the fellers on the touchline was urging him on to, he had no way of knowing. Though maybe not, because the fellers on the touchline kept right on saying it. Then after a bit, Dinchy seen his dad stood on the touchline too, so Dinchy got into this game even more, using the two sets of goalposts like touchstones in a there-and-back race, stealing a glance at his dad every now and then to see how he was taking it, though there was no way Dinchy could tell. Then Dinchy got a chance to really show off.

It was about ten minutes from time when me and the ball just happened to find ourselves within a yard of each other and within striking distance of the All Vandals' and Wreckers' goalmouth –

hey, and slap-bang in the middle too. So I done no more than gather all me surplus energy into me right leg which transferred it to the toes of me right foot, and I let go with everything I'd got:

BLAM-M-M!

Whoa! Straight in the back of the net it went.

But the funny thing is, at the very moment I booted the ball this kid called Billy Swellands come up on the other side and connected with his left foot – and I swear to God the both of us kicked that ball at the same time and scored half a goal each. Or, so they told us, because me and Billy Swellands also connected head-wise, and the next thing I known I was flat out on the touchline next to Owen Rowan with Ozzy slapping me face with a wet sponge and a memory in me head that said:

'Oh! You really do see stars!' (Hey, you bet your sweet life you do: I was one of them, remember!)

When I got home after the match, I was grazed and sweaty, and feeling a bit sick with me head still throbbing, but dead, dead happy as well. And I seen me dad was already there, sat in his creaky-backed chair, eating his dinner. Tater-ash, it was, though I couldn't face it with the headache I'd got. But I hung around for a bit, hoping me dad'd say summat about me goal, but he never. Oh, I was just bursting for him to say summat about that goal of mine, so when I seen him push his plate back and pick up his paper and lean back in his chair and turn to the back page I couldn't contain meself no longer. I said:

'You see me goal, dad?'

He just sat there, reading the sports page, said nowt.

'You see that goal I scored?' I said, not quite so hearty now.

Me dad looked up at us with such a pitying look on his face I wished I'd never spoke. 'Goal?' he says. 'Billy Swellands banged that one in.'

'No. The other one, the second one.'

'Billy Swellands with his left foot.'

'An' me wi' me right.'

'Oh aye?' says me dad. 'Pull the other one, it's got bells on.'

'Ask Ozzy, yer don't believe us.'

'Ozzy? Who's he when he's owt? What is that team he runs anyway? First Blackley Nancy Boys?'

'What d' yer mean?'

'They're a load of flippin' bally dancers.'

Tears sprung to me eyes, blurring me vision. 'They're not,' I said. 'They're a good team. They're top of the league.'

'Oh, what league's that then? League for Distressed Gentlefolk? Listen, a football team's only as good as the men that's in it, and if one of 'em gets hisself stretchered off through pulling a daft stunt like you done, then you've got a team with an hole in it, and that's a team that loses.'

'But I scored a goal,' I said.

'Aye, so you keep tellin' us; and I say it was Billy Swellands. But be that as it may, what was the final score, eh?'

'Three, two.'

'Aye, for them. They scored the third two minutes from time while the man o' the match was lyin' around on the touchline doin' his Egyptian gymnastics. Now don't talk so daft, an' go an' wash your face.'

See, that's how he was, me dad – never used your name when he spoke to you, made you feel you was thick, a coward, summat worthless that was barely human. Very hurtful, it was, and it done you no good at all when he'd pass judgment on you like that. Because if you're thick you can't help it, and even a coward has his reasons. But it's maybe the worst thing in the world to be made to feel you amount to nothing in what you say or do, or the way you see the world on a/c of somebody that's got the power to do so treats you, like – well, like you're sub-human, like you're something beneath contempt.

'Blow an attitude like that up to national level,' says Byron one time I went to see his new pad over in Prestbury (there'd been this documentary on TV that night about the Bloody Sunday massacre in Northern Ireland), 'and you can bank on genocide before too long: the Sioux nation, the aborigines in Tasmania, six million Jews in World War Two, 4.7 million babies aborted in the UK in the last thirty years.'

Well, I dunno about that; this is just me dad I'm talking about.

Hey, and there was that other time he had us down in town with him too!

Look, I don't know what we was doing there. And I tell a lie, of course – we was waiting for the 17 bus on Cannon Street. But I don't know where we'd been is what I mean. You'd think I would too. Because I was only ever on me own in me dad's company about half a dozen times in the hole of me life. Anyway, we're waiting in this long queue for the 17 bus, like I said, one Sunday afternoon when I was a kid and a lot younger than I was when I was St Joey's second reserve, and this old tramp come right along the queue from the back to the front, begging.

Well, me dad bunged him summat, I dunno what. A tanner was a lot in them days. But he give him summat's what I mean – not a kick up the ash can like the other people in the queue seemed like they wouldn't of minded doing. Hey, you just watch him now, this tramp, they was muttering to one another, Why, you just watch this tramp dive in the first pub he comes to. Which he did do, of course: Sefton's Bar on the opposite side of Corporation Street. And as the tramp staggered into Sefton's doorway, this sort of a raggedy cheer went up from everyone in the queue, everyone except me dad, that is.

'Dad, dad,' I went, stood there in me hopsack short pants, joining in the fun. 'Dad, dad, he went in the pub. Yer give him some money, an' he went in the pub.'

Oh, real slow – oh, ever so slow, me dad looked down at us as if to say: No! This I don't believe. This I really do not believe. Here am I stood at the 17 bus stop on Cannon Street, Manchester, in this Year of Our Lord, 1949, and I've got my son with me – whatever his name is, I can never remember, I'm sure (maybe his mother will know) – and his hand . . . MY SON'S HAND . . . IS MADE OF DOG-SHIT! YUK!

Not that me dad said any of this; he just *looked* it. All he said was: 'He needed it, didn't he? Think I care why he needed it?'

See, he was always going on at you like that, see. Never happy with anything you said or done. Made you feel you was the lowest of the low: a tax man on commission, a DSS wallah who'd piss on someone in need, a police nark, a copper who'd stitch someone up, an Englishman in the pay of the enemy, a politician on the take, a traitor to the human race.

Like I say, the first time he ever called us by me name was on me wedding day. Hey, I can only remember him smiling at us the once. That is, I think he did. I mean, there was just this one time when I happened to glance round at him when he wasn't expecting us to, and I seen him smiling at us. Well, I mean, I think I did. Because when he seen us clock it, he made as if he wasn't, but was having a spot of trouble with his dentures. Mind you, that wasn't on me wedding day; that was a good few years before me wedding day. Yeah, that was on the evening of the day of St Joey's parish procession.

18

St Joey's held their parish procession on the third Sunday in June each year when all the people what lived in St Joey's parish would line up outside the church – the priests and the altar boys, the Agnesians and the Children of Mary, the Cubs and the Scouts and the Brownies and the Girl Guides, the 'scholars' (which is what the old folk called the school kids), the First Communicants and, the women and the men. And they'd head off on a sort of lap of honour round all four corners of the parish, lugging banners with them as they went and making a right to-do about it too with the the MacSwiney Pipe Band and the Kerries and the Beswick Prize Band and Middleton Brass Band and St Malachy's Fife Band slotted in at various points in the line-up.

Here's how they'd line up, see. Right up at the front, you'd have one of the older altar boys, carrying this big crucifix-thing they had, then behind him, in rows of four, come the rest of the altar boys with the four biggest at the front to share the job of carrying the crucifix, and behind the altar boys come the parish banner.

Now, this parish banner I'm talking about was red and green in colour, and said ST JOSEPH OF CUPERTINO in raised gold-faced script, and it had this dirty big picture of St Joey on it where he's doing that flying stunt of his, a bit more reserved than Captain Marvel, of course – sort of hovering a foot or two off the deck with his hands joined together and, like, a weather eye on the skies above him.

And it's funny what slips your mind till you think on, because the clergy come after the altar boys and before the banner. Four, there was, on the day I'm talking about: Fr Elrick, Fr Lancaster, Fr Bellis and Fr Selby, who was a newly-ordained priest that was only with us for a short time because, like me dad said afterwards, Fr Selby overstepped the mark that day (with me dad's assistance, of course).

Now, what you have to realise is that these four priests wasn't dressed like priests. Nah, not on the day of St Joey's procession. See, Mrs Parbold that lived next door but one to the Jamesons, Mrs Parbold said it was a crime or summat in England and Wales for a Roman Catholic priest to dress up as a priest in the street. Just as, if you was a Roman Catholic, you couldn't be Prime Minister or Lord Chancellor of England because you was disqualified by your religion. But, with England being a free country, Mrs Parbold said, and with things like this not to be took too serious unless you took them too serious, what you could do – hey, even if you was a Catholic – yeah, what you could do was set foot on the Queen's Highway, though if you was a priest, and wanted to set foot on the Queen's Highway for the purpose of walking in St Joey's parish procession, you had to wear an un-priestly uniform that shown everyone you was a priest, except this was not your normal priestly outfit that you would not have dreampt of wearing on the Queen's Highway in a month of Sundays, just like you would never have dreampt of becoming Prime Minister or Lord Chancellor of England because these was jobs for your equals what was more equal than you was.

Or summat.

So, what used to happen was this. On the day of St Joey's parish procession the clergy worn black suits like your great-grandad might of worn if he'd had enough dosh, that is. (So maybe not. Well, anyway, not my great-grandad, Mr Malachi Methuselah Finbarr Fingal Bunratty, what worked on the railway and got killed in Thompson Street Goods Yard). Yeah, waistcoats and frock coats and top hats is what the clergy worn, and what they would tip to anyone lining the route who seen through their disguise – as they was bound to do, unless the clergy also worn false moustaches and Raybans by law. In which case, of course, they might as well of stayed put in the presbytery with the lace curtains pulled shut instead of walking down Rochdale Road in St Joey's parish procession in front of a dirty big banner advertising that fact.

Oh, how can I explain what it was like that day? Because there is just nothing like it no more. And don't get us wrong now, maybe it's right that there shouldn't be nothing like it neither, the nutters there is nowadays. But it makes it hard to imagine what it was like. Because it was like a Bank Holiday, see? Well, yeah, it *was* a Bank Holiday, being a Sunday, of course, but Sundays was usually quiet in them days with church bells ringing in the morning and every shop but the off licence shut all day long and the pubs closing early after opening late. But the Sunday of St Joey's parish procession wasn't quiet. It was dead noisy. It was like when you've got everyone off work on a Bank Holiday except that they haven't all shot off to the seaside, or to the traffic jam where the M61 meets the M6 near Preston. And they've turned up at St Joey's parish procession instead. And everywhere you looked that day you'd see other people enjoying theirselves, and you felt sort of happy because of it. Because all your friends and relations and people that you never seen from one year's end to the next or out of doors during the winter would descend on St Joey's parish procession that day, and on you and your house. Yeah, just like you and your family would descend on their parish processions – Mount Carmel's, St Dunstan's, St Edmund's, St Peter's, Middleton – and on them and their houses on other Sunday afternoons throughout the summer, unless they was Italians, of course. Because Sunday evening was when the Italians walked, their parish being St Michael's, Ancoats.

On the day of St Joey's parish procession it was like you was all together in one big ocean liner or summat. Like the feeling you get when people are maybe huddled together in wartime, or in a thunder storm, or a great downpour of rain. Only these was no rough seas you was in, but blue water with the sun overhead and the sound of voices all around and people's faces bobbing about you instead of waves. Sometimes it'd rain, of course, though mostly it didn't. So all you remember are the sunny days – lovely and bright and clear and warm and blue as only June can be when it wants to be.

It was sunshine and a laughing crowd and kiddies shouting and maybe crying too, and old folk going on with theirselves – and some that never come out of doors all year long except for that one day in the year when they was pushed to the kerb in their wheelchairs. It was a sea of faces and voices and movement and shouts, with ice-cream vans bobbing above us like anchored buoys with their names in fancy colours and fairground script: Pandolfo, Rea, Meschia, Pessagno, Carlo, Granelli. (The Italians walked of a

Sunday night because Sunday afternoons was good for business.) It was the fragrance of flowers, the sweep of coloured streamers and flags, the skirl of the pipes, the little drum major mascot with the Kerries, and buses stuck on the hill. It was banners and litters and garlands and sashes and clothes of white and bright silk. It was everyone you'd ever known, all in holiday mood, in the procession or watching the procession, and – if they was watching the procession – well, racing like billy-oh from street to street for another sighting, a third, maybe a fourth. It was returning within the hour (walkers and watchers, both) and crowding into the flower-hung church to breathe hymns like a sigh. It was open house at home, and strawberries for tea.

And know what? Soon's you got that bit older, you was always trying to get out of it. Oh, you had your reasons, of course, though they was piddling and pretty vague. The lads out of the vault'd see you, that bird you trapped off with at Embo last night. So what? I think now. But when you're in your teens you don't always have that much upstairs to think with. Well, either that, or you're happy to let others do your thinking for you. Yeah, always following the crowd, you is; and never the main crowd neither. Oh no, not your crowd. Not your extra special crowd that is the best thing since street cred. Because your extra special crowd, with its crummy clothes and its crummy hair styles and its crummy way of talking and its crummy way of looking at things and its crummy way of treating people – oh, your extra special crowd is miles cleverer than two thousand years of European civilization ever was, your crowd is.

Me dad had my number all right. He'd say summat like:

'Might need your raincoat today.'

'What for?' I'd say, falling for it.

'Looks like rain. You don't wanna get caught out on Carisbrook Street if the heavens open.'

By which you known you had better be there, or else.

But this day, the day I'm on about, me dad come in from last Mass, and says: 'We're on the banner.'

'You what?' I said.

'You heard us. We're on the banner. You and me, Vic Jameson and his lad.' Meaning Huge.

Now, I can't tell you what a bombshell this was in our house. See, the banner me dad had reference to, the St Joseph of Cupertino's parish banner, was – well, some sarky devil not a million miles away from the Dinch breakfast table that morning (the same sarky devil who christened Pamela Wembury's dad Weary Willie Wembury) – some sarky devil had nicknamed the parish banner Col's Colours, seeing how Colin Leitrim and three of his good men of the parish cronies had baggsed it since Adam was a lad.

'What about His Lordship?' says me mam as she shoves me dad's bacon and eggs and three Bowyers pork sausages in front of him. 'He won't like it, you know.' Meaning Colin Leitrim.

'He can like it,' says me dad, prodding one the sausages with his fork, 'or he can lump it. It's all the same to me.' Me dad got his knife and slit the sausage lengthways, peeling back the skin. 'Nowt we can't handle. Where's the salt?'

'Even so, you can understand it, Alf. He thinks it's his after all this time.'

'Thinks what's his?' says me dad even though he known what her answer would be.

'The banner.'

'It's no one's flippin' banner,' says me dad, chewing and a bit muffled. (The only way you could ever get a point across with me dad was to put it to him when he had his mouth full.) He swallowed with difficulty. 'Damn, blast and bugger it! It's the parish banner an' we're parishioners, aren't we? Me and him, Vic Jameson and his lad? We're parishioners, aren't we?' He wipes his mouth with his hanky, and stabs sausage number two. 'Anyway, I don't give a monkey's what Colin Leitrim thinks. We're carrying the banner. Volunteered our services to Fr Selby after Mass, me and Vic. He was drawin' a rota up, very keen to look organised, bein' the new boy and that. So me an' Vic stuck our names down straight off. If His Lordship's that keen, he should of got his motty in first. Anyway, 'bout time Vic Jameson had a turn. Never away from church, is he? Lookin' at Hetty, it'll be the celibacy that attracts him, I shouldn't wonder.' Exit sausage number three.

When we went up to church that afto just before three – me and me dad, Huge and his dad – Colin Leitrim was already there, mooching about near the baptistry at the back of the church where the banner was kept. But we positioned ourselves either side of it so he never really stood a chance. Oh, he made a movement towards it, but me dad blocked him bodily. (If he'd had any further to go, he'd of run in with a sliding tackle, I'm sure.)

'Don't mither yourself, Mr Leitrim,' says me dad pleasantly enough. 'We'll manage just fine. Right, Vic?'

'No problem, Alf. Don't suppose you've got a bit of loose change you could let us have for the collection, have you, Alf?' Vic Jameson's faffing about with this half-moon purse he has. 'Thought I'd brought some with me but now I come to look I've only got an Immaculate Medal and a peseta they worked on me at the piety stall.'

Colin Leitrim looks from me dad to Vic Jameson, from Vic Jameson to me dad. 'Wha' . . . what're you doing?'

He gets no answer. The banner is tilted back so it'll fit through the door of the church (tilt it forward, you could knock a copper off an horse), and through the door it goes, and us with it, out on to Tudor Avenue at the side of the convent.

'Would . . . Would you mind telling me what's going on?' says Colin Leitrim, running after us.

Me dad acts daft-like. He looks up and down Tudor Avenue where the procession's lining up, waves to one or two people he knows – Mr Holwick, the caretaker from the youth club, Walter Jordan, does the door, studies the ranks of the Macswiney Pipers very closely indeed, points me cousin Cleet out to Vic Jameson (he's only joined this year, Cleet; they've stuck him on one of the kettle drums), then he turns back to Colin Leitrim, real slow: 'What's going *on*, Mr Leitrim? It's the parish procession, or hadn't you heard?'

'But the banner . . .'

'The banner?' Me dad inspects it, like it might be broke or summat.

'I carry the banner. I always ca . . .'

At this point (two minutes to three) the clergy come through the doorway from the church in a body. Fr Elrick breaks away from the other three priests, beaming down at us from his dizzy height with a smile that's broad as a side of beef. 'MMMmm, ah, good man, Colin, good man. Look here, I'm most terribly sorry, Colin, ah, there seems to have been . . . ah, what seems to have happened is, ah . . . well, Dinch, here, Jameson . . . good man, good man . . . ah, Dinch, Jameson very kindly offered, ah . . . ah . . . and Fr Selby . . . ah, perhaps unfortunate from your point of view, Colin, but . . . ah, now see here, Colin . . . good man . . . ah, have a word, Billy Wembury, there . . . Billy, ah, perhaps one of the stewards . . . ah, good man, good man . . . knew we could count on you, Colin . . . Billy . . .'

So Weary Willie Wembury digs out this blue satin sash with gold braid and frills on it and – hey presto! – Colin Leitrim is promoted to steward, and St Joey's procession is on its way at last.

Yep, there we is turning on to Rochdale Road with the Macswiney Pipe Band blasting away behind us ('Soldiers Are We' – the nerve of them on English soil!) and the onlookers at the kerbside are going mad. Me dad and Vic Jameson are carrying at the moment with me and Huge trotting along at the sides. Meanwhile Colin Leitrim – *dah, dahhhhhh* – steward, is keeping a bit in front of us, glancing round every now and then, walking backwards when the fancy takes him, flapping his arms about and signalling, like none of us known how to put one foot in front of the other. Couple of tennis table bats, he could of maybe HMS Ark Royal/Fleet Air Arm-ed it for England.

I mean to say, there was absolutely nothing to it. So, okay, maybe it was windy and the banner was jerking about a bit, but there was really nothing to it. You had this big pole affair at either side that the fellers carried and, from the tops of the poles, there was these, like, four braided cords that went out, two on each side, and these was held by four Children of Mary birds in white frocks and sky-blue cloaks: Rhoda Rishworth and Pamela Wembury on the Huge/Vic/Colin Leitrim side – two very demure young ladies that we've already met, whilst on our side (me and me dad's) we had Bernadette Holwick and Lorraine Walshaw, two birds that was not quite so demure when they was unfrocked of a Saturday night – that is, when they was dressed different and out at the Embassy Club on the razz. Hey, and there's Colin Leitrim showing all eight of us (me, me dad, Huge, his dad, and the four girls) how to walk up Rochdale Road in broad daylight without falling flat on your face – something, in any case, that would of been a physical impossibility for the Misses Holwick and Walshaw even if they'd of tried it.

Anyway, you get the picture? See, it's important I get everything in the right order here, because the accident didn't just happen like *that*.

All right, we'd changed over at Carisbrook Street on the way out, me taking me dad's pole and Huge taking his dad's. (Hey, you didn't just carry the pole in your bare hands, you know. No, you worn this, like, strapping-affair over your shoulders and the bottom of the pole was slotted into this leather holster-thing that dangled from the strapping in front of you.) Okay, the wind was getting up by this time, but we done all right, me and Huge, and we swapped over again on Upper Conran Street across the road from Armistead's bakery and the distorting mirror they had there to help the traffic. And we done this once more at the corner of Moston Lane near the New Inn. Oh dear! That's where so many things happened at once.

See, to turn that particular corner near the New Inn (well, to turn any corner really) one of yous has to walk a bit faster than the other one (me, in this case), and the other (Huge, as it happened) had to just sort of mark time till I sorted meself out. The trouble was, though, Huge was marking a bit more time than he maybe should of done, seeing how he'd been spotted by three tarts that was heathens from Holy Tripeshop and was stood outside the New Inn shouting:

'Oh, Eu-eu-eu-gene! Hold your lily up!' and other sayings of the sort.

Also, diagonally across the road from the New Inn outside the Golden Tavern, there was this gang of three hundred thousand million billion paddies and pretend-paddies that had been turfed out of Barnes Green Club after the dinner time session, me Uncle Joe and cousin Line amongst them. And these fellers from Barnes Green Club, being kith and kin to the paddies and pretend-paddies in the Macswiney Pipe Band, well, it was only natural that the

Macswineys (who'd stumped along like a centipede with a wooden leg with the sound of a me cousin Cleet's single kettle drum for company since leaving Upper Conran Street), yeah, it was only natural the Macswineys would want to serenade them. Which they did do, with an up-tempo version of 'The Wearing of the Green' which made the gang outside the Golden Tavern go madder than they already was, and made the procession (apart from Huge) put on a bit of a spurt all of a sudden. But what happened next was completely unexpected. Because this great gust of wind come out of Factory Lane from the Irwell valley at exactly the same moment that the Border collie from the Golden Tavern shot across the crown of the road chasing the ginger tom from the Top Derby between me legs.

'OOPS!'

Whoa! I thought I'd gone for a second, but I done a bit of fancy footwork and recovered. Still, as luck would have it, the dog from the Golden Tavern and the cat from the Top Derby just keep on going and end up doing a slalom through Rhoda Rishworth's legs too, which caused Rhoda to slacken off her cord, or let go of it maybe, because all of a sudden I felt this terrific extra strain on the pole I was holding before the buckle bust on me strapping. The second gust of wind was even stronger, and:

'CRIPES!'

The pole I'd been holding fell like a tree.

I'll say this for Rhoda Rishworth: she done her level best to stop it. But she was wrongly placed if anything, and being a big strong girl, she helped the pole to keep right on coming. Me dad dived headlong to catch it, and he caught it too – just in time to stop it landing as a bookmark in Fr Lancaster's open breviary. Even so, he'd not had first bite of the cherry, me dad. No, Colin Leitrim caught it before him. Right on the top of his head, it got him, me dad only catching it on the rebound. A minor hiccup: the St John's Ambulance Brigade swooped on Colin Leitrim, spreadeagled on the tarmac at the door of the New Inn. The procession moved on. Time, tide, and St Joseph of Cupertino's parish procession wait for no man.

*

Oh, you should of been at our house after the procession that day. There again, maybe you was and I never seen you, there was that many there. Me Uncle Joe was in attendance, of course, three sheets to the wind after an extended dinner time sesh with me cousin Line in Barnes Green Club. Me Auntie Annie was there too, Joe's missis, tut-tutting him whenever he spoke; and their Cleet was there too, and Line, and Line's missis, Marj – feeding her fat face from start to finish. Yeah, and me Auntie Kitty turned up after Benediction, that is, me mam's auntie's cousin's cousin, whose sole topic of conversation was how lovely the altar had looked with all the flowers and didn't we think the new priest looked like Robert Doughnut? (Whoever he is when he's owt, though me Uncle Joe said to me Uncle Bill: 'Jaze, not while de man's goth an hole in his arse, will I be havin' dat, begob.') And Mrs Parbold from next door but one to the Jamesons, called in for an hour and shifted an half bottle of Bristol Cream sherry whilst refusing to touch a drop. Then we had me Uncle Pat for once (all twenny-two stone of him) with Noreen Jessop and the three cretins, Neev, Gnomie, and Nut – Nut being just a babe in arms at the time. Hey, and me Uncle Bill was there, like I said, though he'd been warned to be on his best behaviour by Auntie Deirdre who had two kids she made sit on the sofa like they was paralysed and had had their tongues cut out. And there was maybe another three hundred thousand million billion bodies from all over Manchester, plus someone who was minding the Kerry Pipers' big drum for some reason I never did find out. Heaving, it was, with everyone guzzling and drinking tea out of the best china and sitting down and standing up again as soon as they'd sat down and sprawling around and getting under your feet and running around and charging up and down the stairs and in and out of the bathroom and slamming doors and opening them again and slamming them shut once more. Madhouse, it was, but happy. Well fed too.

Me Grandma Alma was there, of course, a bit quieter than the rest maybe, and in the other room at the back and the kitchen mostly, helping me mam get stuff ready, and bringing it in and passing it around and that, when me mam wasn't running to the front door to let people in, that is.

It was early evening before me Uncle Joe got his second wind and pushed his way through to the piano where he slung back the lid back and begun to play in that self-taught, shoulder-swaying, commanding way he had, slamming full-fathom five into one of them Irish tunes that go on for ever and ever:

Diddley-diddley-diddley-diddley-diddley-diddley-dih-dih-dih-dih

Anyway, this diddley-diddley tune went on for about three hundred thousand million billion years until it dominated the whole house so that, bit by bit, everyone drifted into the parlour where the piano was (God knows how they all squeezed in but they did), with me dad up at the front in his shirt sleeves and his braces messing about with this sheet music he had. Then me Uncle Joe begun to sing in this wheedling Oirish voice that was very well thought of at the Arthur Griffiths Club and the Kings Arms and the Spread Eagle, Collyhurst, and he made us have it with 'Macushla' and 'Danny Boy', and looked set to give us 'How Can You Buy Killarney?' till me mam come through from the front door where she'd been stood nattering to one of the neighbours and her voice cut quite shrill through Uncle Joe's estate agent's blather about Killarney and brung him up short of the Gap of Dunloe.

'Colin Leitrim's had an accident?' she says with some concern. 'Mrs Eshton from the presbytery says his both eyes are closed right up.'

'Ah!' says me Uncle Joe, vamping a couple of chords on the keyboard. 'Blest are dey dat have not seen ant yeth believe!'

Oh, the women was mortified, and Auntie Kitty blessed herself, and Uncle Joe had to be got out of the way quick on some errand by Auntie Annie. But it was already too late because Uncle Bill had forgot he was supposed to behave hisself, and barked laughter at the ceiling till he'd got everyone at it. At which point Uncle Bill got up to get one of the bottles Uncle Joe had come back with because he just couldn't stand being on his best behaviour no more, though he did take his tie off first so they wouldn't have to cut it off like the last time he was not on his best behaviour and give the kerb a Manchester kiss outside the Blue Bell, Moston. Uncle Bill was still laughing when Uncle Joe made a comeback and pounced on the keyboard to batter a dozen thunderous chords out of it before wheedling his way through 'If You're Irish Come Into The Parlour', glancing around the room every now and then to check no Aztecs or Etruscans had snook in.

Then, me Uncle Bill (three bottles of pale ale to the good) ruined Uncle Joe's avalanche of an introduction to 'The Mountains of Mourne' when he called across to me dad. 'Come on, Alf. Shift the bog monster and give us your party piece.'

A murmur of approval silenced Uncle Joe's fists and a piece of sheet music was found (me dad kept it alphabetical). Then a Mr Leslie Stuart got a mention too as the songwriter and one time organist at the Holy Name church, Oxford Road, by me Auntie Kitty before me dad treated us to his rendition of 'Soldiers of the Queen'. And when he was all done and dusted, me dad, and clapped into silence, Uncle Bill (six bottles of pale ale to the bad by now) calls across to where I was stood near the door, ready to get on me way: 'Right, your turn, Guy Mitchell,' says he. 'What's it gonna be? 'What A Crazy World We're Living In'?'

Then Uncle Joe vamped an intro on the piano, and everyone burst out laughing – hey, me included. Because like anyone else who don't know what he's on about, Uncle Bill had got it completely arse uppards, mixing up a singer and a song, neither one of which was my cup of tea. In any case, like I say, I was ready for the off, but as I went to go out the door I sort of turned round to shake me head, sort of as if to say: 'Mm, maybe not, Uncle Bill. Not this time.' And in that split second I seen this look on me dad's face.

Yeah, he was stood there, leant on the piano as if he was cock o' the walk, me dad, with this look on his face like as if to say:

'Hm, that bloomin' berk! You'll get nowt out of him, I can tell yer!'

It was a smug look, a self-satisfied look – a bloody know-all's look. And I wanted to tear it off his face with me fingernails, roll it up in a towel for him, and tell him to: 'Piss off home, old man – you've been in the plunge too long and your fingers is not the only thing that's wrinkly!'

She'd brushed past us almost before I known it. They both of them had, coming through from the kitchen when the music stopped, and as me mam crossed the room towards a couple of spare chairs, me Grandma Alma following her, she sort of turns her head, me Grandma Alma, and asks us for a light, her lighter being lost. Then inhaling just the once, she whispers her request.

Hey, and that wasn't me cup of tea neither. No, not by a long chalk, me real cup of tea being three guitars minimum, a set of drums, speakers, amps to me eyeballs, a group of backing singers from the Mississippi delta, very understanding neighbours, and a better voice than I've got when I was giving it welly in the bath or the entrance to Blackley Library where there was a lovely echo once upon a time. But me Grandma Alma always was a lady I couldn't find it in me heart to say no to. So I done some thinking about that request of hers, and I got to thinking about me dad too.

See, when I was a kid there was this programme on the wireless of a Sunday night called *Grand Hotel.* And maybe I'm misremembering it, but as I *seem* to remember it, it featured Max Jaffa and the Palm Court Orchestra. Now, *Grand Hotel* wasn't me cup of tea neither, so maybe that's why I'm maybe misremembering it. But I make no mistake about this – many's the time Max Jaffa and the Palm Court Orchestra done a rendition of a particular tune that would set me dad back in that creaky-backed chair of his, humming softly to hisself, his eyes looking blindly I known not where.

Anyway, that's the song me Grandma Alma had asked us for. It was easy enough to find it too. Right there, under 'R'. And when I'd opened it up and stuck it on the piano in front of Uncle Joe, and cleared me throat, and made sure I focused on Mrs Parbold's front door across the street to hide me embarrassment – well, the Singing Dingo struck again. I socked it to 'em good and proper, I did. Well, proper anyway. Because it goes without saying me voice was nowt to write home about. But I got the words right, is what I mean, seeing they was right there under me nose. Yeah, I give it to them straight from the shoulder, I did. No trills. And maybe Little Eva would of duetted with us if she'd been around that day. Though on second thoughts, maybe not. Because the song me Grandma Alma requested what I sung in our front room on the day of St Joey's parish procession was fifty years old if it was a day. Yeah, it's been around since 1912, that song (credits: Frederic Edward Weatherly and Haydn Wood), though the lyrics maybe took on a whole new meaning once another few years had passed. Sheet music from the Year Dot, I'm talking about. But if The Byrds can chart in the 1960s with a song that's two thousand years old ('Turn, Turn, Turn' being from the Bible, so Byron tells us), well, maybe it's okay for the Singing Dingo to use sheet music with dog-eared corners and olde-worlde print, which is only to be expected, I suppose, with a song called 'Roses of Picardy', which was all of fifty years old on the evening of the day of St Joey's parish procession.

Hey, I really did have to go then, having arranged to meet Lorraine Walshaw at Blackley Tram Office. So I was out in the lobby then, ready for the off, when I seen . . . I seen me dad smiling at us. That is, I think I did. Because, like I say, soon's he seen us clock it, he cracked on he wasn't, of course, but was having a spot of trouble with his dentures. But I seen . . . Well, I seen summat. It was only for a second, like. But it was sort of nice, and . . . Well, it'll do for me.

It'll flipping-well *have to*, won't it?

Why is it, I wonder, you can really hate someone all your life and miss them when they're gone. Even though you know full well that even if they was to come ran-tan-tanning at your front door this very day, hale and hearty, a blooming miracle like Lazarus, things would be just the same as they always was between you, with you hating him and him treating you like a pillock.

I dunno.

Yeah, summat else Dinchy don't know. But I done a bit of thinking about it, all the same. And know what? It don't make a lot of sense even then.

See, it seems to me there's a kind of love that's not a bit like they say in the songs. It's not bitter or sweet, it's not warm or cold, it's not selfish or selfless: it's just lasting, then dying. Yeah, it seems to me there's a kind of love that won't never be set to music, or given words that singers will wanna sing, or people find easy to remember or want to. Because there's a kind of love that is just plain hard. Oh, it's no less a love for that, of course, but it's doled out like medicine for medicinal purposes, and like medicine, it is never enjoyed or dreampt about, or fondly remembered.

Hard love is hard as hell. Hard love is a kick in the pants when you done wrong, and sometimes when you haven't, just in case. Hard love is hydrogen peroxide dripped on an open wound to stop it from turning septic. Hard love bawls Turn-the-damned-thing-down! when you're listening to music, it shouts Get up! when you fall down – and when you speak, it says to Shurrit! Hard love don't seem to notice you most of the time, then curses you for getting under its feet. Hard love is rain in your face on a windswept street with the buses not running and no shop doorways for shelter. Hard love is what me dad had to offer. Me dad's love was that hard I never seen it for what it was while I was having to endure it.

I see it now though. Hey, I don't hate him now neither. To tell the truth, I find meself wondering if I ever did, or only thought I did. Yeah, I know it's daft, but I've begun to think that maybe what I hated all them years was meself. I mean, what I hated was maybe the part of me I seen in him. And if summat as daft as that is true for me, it might just as easy of been true for him. What I mean to say is this, see – maybe what me dad was inflicting his love on for all them years was a part of hisself he seen in me.

Like I say, I dunno. Though I do know this: I don't hate me dad no more. I mean, how could I hate him now even if I ever done? How could I hate him now I know what his hard love done for us? What I mean to say is this, see – hard love makes you appreciate things you might not never of done if left to your own devices. The windswept street makes you long for the cosy hearth; it's never the other way around. So appreciation of what I've got is me inheritance from hard love. And it's a priceless one at that. For though it's a magical thing to stumble across a better love, a warm love, it's magical too to know it for what it is when you find it, to know you won't never let go.

19

I think it's strange, me, sort of uncanny. You're sat there for ages, see? Maybe you're reading the paper and she's ironing. Or maybe you're not – it could be anything, see. Maybe she's stripping the living-room wallpaper off and you're doing your crochet work. Or it could be you're just sat there, buffing your nails with your Carmen electric rollers in, while she's minting up this AJS Porcupine she got for a song out of the *Exchange and Mart*. On the other hand, maybe she's lay there in her dungarees on the sheepskin rug in front of the fire, with her slide rule and her Open University text books all over the shop, boning up on open cast mining in the anthracite region of Pennsylvania; hey, and you're close-up to the mirror – the big bevel-edged one that Huge bought yous for a wedding present – squeezing a blackhead or putting your false eyelashes in place. It don't really matter, see. The thing is you're there for ages, the both of yous, and you're silent, not talking or owt. You've not fallen out or anything: you're just silent – companionable. Yeah, that's the word: companionable.

Then what happens?

Well, you've only been at it all night, whatever it is you're doing, so you've only had about three hundred thousand million billion milliseconds to choose from, but all of a sudden the both of yous speak at once. Hey, and get this: you both say the same flipping thing. Well, either that, or she slams shut this hard back copy of *Das Kapital* that's two weeks overdue at Queen's Park Library, and says summat. So you lay your mascara aside, and you say:

'Funny that. I was just thinkin' the exact same thing!'

Or maybe you just look at her after ages and ages and ages, and at the same moment – for no reason either of yous can pin down – she switches off her oxy-acetylene gear, whips the visor up over the top of her Man U bobble hat, and looks at you – hey, maybe smiles too. Old married couples I'm talking about – and that's exactly what happened with me and Shirlee that night.

Shirlee says she fancies the Canadian Charcoal Steak House on Princess Street, meaning to celebrate our wedding anniversary –

our seventh as it happens. And I told her I'd just been thinking the exact same thing. Though I hadn't. Oh, I'd been thinking about food all right, but I'd been thinking I fancied a Chicken Chop Suey with Cashew Nuts and all the trimmings at the Sun Ya down the bottom end of Portland Street. Still, Shirlee says she fancies the Canadian Charcoal Steak house, so why argue?

We had this great arrangement with Keith and Sylvia next door. Course, they moved on a long time ago, Keith and Sylvia, when it got that way they needed three beds, but in them days when Shirlee was here and our Suzanne was only (what would she be at the time?) four years old, maybe – yeah, four, she was, and their Isobel had just started school, we used to babysit for one another by moving the kiddies from our house to theirs or vice versa, letting them sleep over with one another. It was really handy, that, exspecially with Keith and Sylvia being a decent couple and not too demanding like some you can get.

So, there we is on our seventh wedding anniversary, late September, 1973, and our Suzanne is already bedded down for the night at Keith and Sylvia's, and Shirlee's upstairs getting ready to go out: washing her hair, showering for about three hours, putting her make-up on and that, and I'm sat downstairs in the living-room in me best whistle (nowt flash, Burton's the Tailor: light grey, bell bottom trousers, wide lapels, kipper tie, pink shirt), ready for the off. I've brewed meself a cuppa, like, and I'm having a drag (Embassy Regal, Senior being too expensive for us nowadays, and being untipped, akin to dicing with death). And the house is nice and quiet with our Suzanne being out, and I'm sat there watching TV when, as luck would have it, this western comes on, and it's only me favourite western of all time called *3.10 To Yuma*. An old black and white film, it is, but so's *High Noon* and *3.10 To Yuma* is tons better than *High Noon*, for my money.

'Elmore Leonard,' says Byron when I told him about it later.

But it wasn't, you know, it was Glenn Ford. Yeah, it's Glenn Ford in, *3.10 To Yuma*. See, Glenn Ford in *3.10 to Yuma*, well, he's just an ornery feller, Glenn, minding his own business, not to mention a wife and kiddy, out in Arizona Territory somewhere when these baddies get right up his nose for some reason I'm not sure why now. And Glenn Ford, well, Glenn does what any ornery feller minding his own business with a wife and kiddy to support always does in circumstances like that, which is to say to hisself, Glenn, that maybe he shouldn't be minding his own business when there is more important issues at stake, and never mind what the missis thinks about maybe being left to bring up a kiddy all on her own in the wild and woolly West without no bloke to bring home the bacon, or the beef, as the case may be – although Glenn Ford, I once seen him bring home the New Zealand lamb, but that was in a different film. Anyway, to cut a long story short, Glenn Ford decides that it *is* an ornery feller's business not to mind his own business and to make sure that the boss of these three hundred thousand million billion baddies does not miss the train (the 3.10, get it?) that will take him to Yuma (this prison out in Arizona). Mind you, I've told you the whole story now, but it took a bit longer than that for the actual film to be shown. And after about half an hour or so, Shirlee pops her head round the living-room door, and says:

'Right, I'm ready.'

'Yeah, let's just see this bit.'

Now, at nine o'clock the news come on, right in the middle of the film and Shirlee's brewed herself a cuppa by this time and then the film comes on again after the news.

'Okay if I watch this bit?' I asked her.

'Sure,' says Shirlee, who's sat in an armchair now, reading the *Daily Mess.*

Well, the film continues, and I won't go into all that again because I've already explained it. (Oh, yeah, Van Hefflin was the boss of the baddies.) And then the film finished about a quarter to ten, and I got up and switched the telly off.

'Okay?' I said to an empty room.

No Shirlee.

When I went upstairs I found she'd got in bed, and I don't care to dwell on the conversation that then took place. But the gist of it was this: No, Shirlee Dinch (*née* Jameson) would *not* be going out to celebrate our seventh wedding anniversary tonight, thank you very much, though Dinchy could, of course, go if he wanted to, though in that case Dinchy would be celebrating our seventh wedding anniversary on his todd. (Which would be very good practice for Dinchy, as it happens – though Dinchy never known this at the time. Because Dinchy was only gonna to have to do that exact same thing for the rest of his natural, God help him!) So, like the bastard Dinchy was – and *is*, that's exactly what Dinchy done.

See, while he'd been watching Glenn Ford and Van Hefflin going at it Dinchy had got the taste of charcoal steak in his mouth. (And by the way, Glenn Ford was the baddie in *3.10 to Yuma* because Glenn worn the black hat; Van Hefflin being the good guy.) And to the best of Dinchy's knowledge, charcoal steak such as Dinchy now had the taste of in his mouth was available nowhere else in Manchester in September, 1973, other than at the Canadian Charcoal Steak House on Princess Street. For instance, it most certainly was not available chez Dinch, the front door of which Dinchy slammed hard when he went out. Hey, you just bet he did. And Dinchy would have took the car too except the air filter was bunged up, summat else Dinchy had messed up on his seventh wedding anniversary. So Dinchy jumped a private hire cab outside the Farmyard Hotel on Rochdale Road. And for all Dinchy cared as he tootled townwards, Shirlee Veronica Dinch (as of seven years – Jameson, for twenny-four years before that) could stew in her own juices – unlike the 12 oz charcoal steak that Dinchy saw hisself eating within the hour at the Canadian Charcoal Steak House on Princess Street, opposite the College of Commerce.

Then, one very tasty 12 oz. steak, a few too many nice drinkies, and two cabs later (got a black cab from Piccadilly), I was home again where I crashed out on the settee in the living-room. When I woke up next day at noon, she'd gone. I presumed she'd took Suzanne with her, but checked with Sylvia just in case – give her some spiel about Suzanne's teddy bear, Teddy Boy. Yeah, she had: she'd took the bab. I don't mean packed and gone, I mean gone off somewhere – her mum's maybe. Hey, so what? Yeah, who cares? Well, I did, to be honest. But even so, I reckoned I'd earned the right to nurse me hurt feelings for a bit.

I went upstairs to bed then and went out like a light. It was five o' clock before I woke up, and they still wasn't back. But I was still feeling ratty, so I went out.

It wasn't too bad, out, now the rain had left off. So I walked across Lewis Rec at a fast pace to get a bit of air and down into Boggart Hole Clough past the fountain and up to the boating lake and across the running track and the football pitches, trying to clear me head. The fresh air helped us there, of course. Then I come down Oliver Brow to the shop in the valley, and turned down the little track to the right that follows the brook past the little waterfall and the bandstand (as was) and come out at the gates at the bottom of Valentine Brow near the bus stop and the Magpie rank.

Magpie's radio base was in this brick building that was a private school till the Council killed it off with double yellow lines. Not that double-yellows worried Magpie: they parked anywhere they wanted. And there was public conveniences there too, and in the middle, on the same level as the base, there was Dot's Diner, this greasy spoon the cabbies used all year round, barring Christmas and Easter.

Now, this Magpie I'm talking about is the same mob I tracked out with that time I drove for me cousin Line when I needed some extra dosh when our Suzanne was born and Byron didn't need us on the markets no more, seeing I'd jacked it when we got married and Byron's brother Pearson and Huey, Duey and Louie was now old enough and keen enough to muck in with him. Anyway the taxis was a change from what I normally done is the way I looked at it at the time.

Hey, and when I come out of the Clough that afternoon and drawn level with Magpie, I seen there was one or two of the lads I known that worked there, hanging about in their cabs. Black cabs, that is, though Magpie had some normal saloon cars as well that done weddings and that. There was a few more of them inside the base too, swigging that lousy coffee from the machine. And after me forced march through the Clough and over the top fields, not to mention all the boozing and arguing and snoring I'd done in the last twelve hours or so, I felt as if I could really murder a cup of lousy coffee, so I went in. Oh, and this big cheer went up soon as they seen us. Sort of jokey, you know. Yeah, they was all there as usual, the Saturday night track crowd: Ben Gunn, Zapata, the Buffalo Soldier, Quatermas, Einstein, Keyhole, Gibraltar, Mag Piper, and them. And when they give over cheering, I done this little dance sort of thing to gee 'em up, going:

'Ta-ra-rahhhhhh!' Like a ragman's trumpet announcing a grand entrance.

'Hey up,' says Mag Piper. 'Watch your bleedin' pockets, yous lot.'

Laughter.

'You're after a track,' says Mag. 'Town Hall job's been took.'

Laughter again, more than before. Had to laugh meself in view of what had happened that time. Sometimes you've just gotta laugh, otherwise you'd cry.

'It's not all that's been took neither,' says Ben Gunn, milking it for all it was worth from where he's working the base with this tart called Janice.

'Come in, Car 2.' Janice is speaking into her mouthpiece now.

'*ZZZZQuackkiterpppklikfff . . . ogithyzzztooopzx*!' come this voice from Outer Space.

'Roger, Car 2,' says Janice, then: 'Car 6?'

'*QwwXxx*!'

'Slow down, Car 6,' says Janice: 'You've got Car 13 on your tail.'

'*Rqhyg*!'

Car 13 being the bogies, of course.

'Come in, Car 27,' mimics Quatermas. 'Car 13 thinks you can help 'em with their enquiries.'

Which has them off again, laughing their bollocks off – Car 27 being the call sign of me cousin Line's cab, the one I had used to drive. Not that Car 27 still belonged to Line, of course. Nah, Marj sold Car 27, the plate too, when Line done a disappearing act for a couple of years. Hey, and don't get us wrong now, please. I'm not saying Line done it. I prefer to keep an open mind, me. I don't care what anyone else says. Even though everyone else says he done it.

'All right, all right,' says Mag, waving his arms about for a bit of hush, because by this time the laughter's drowning out the base calls. 'Hey, Dinchy,' he says. 'Don't fancy a turn on base, do you?'

'What? Tonight?' I thought he was jossing us like before. 'You're jokin'.'

'No, straight up.'

'Start now, you mean?'

'Well, yeah. Gunner should be tracking 15, but we're one down on the base wi' Bonehead havin' flu.'

'What? Do the monte?'

'No, Janice is there. Just answer the phones and that. You know the crack. Bit of money off the lads at the end of the night, and . . .' (Mag addresses the room in general) '. . . there's always the lousy coffee.'

Laughter again, and from Zapata, the sound of a drunk throwing up.

Well, it certainly answered me bed for the night problem. Besides which, after all the sleep I'd had in the last twelve hours, I didn't need a bed. And with having a day's holiday booked off work for the Monday, I known I'd be able to catch up on any kip I missed out on.

'Okay, you're on,' I told Mag. 'Hey, Keyhole. You're passin' a chippy, get us an atom bomb, will yer.'

'Eh?'

'Fission chips. You havin' owt, Janice?'

Hey, you ever drove a cab? I mean a black cab, the FX4? Because I have, that time I drove for me cousin Line. Well, okay, the FX3, as it was called. They don't suit everyone, of course. No, there's some that would rather drive around in an ornery saloon car all day long – just as there's some that would never take to cabbying in the first place, not if it was the last job on earth. But if you take to cabbying, that's what I'd have if I was you – a black cab, a nice shiny FX4, 5, 6, or whatever the hell it is they call them nowadays.

See, for one thing, in a black cab you're high up off of the road, so the visibility's great. You're not as high up as a lorry, of course, but you can see right down the road in front of you, and when you're in traffic you can read the road conditions for miles ahead. The mpg's good too. Yeah, you'll get thirty-two-ish to the gallon with a black cab, which is not bad considering a black cab maybe weighs a ton and half. Mind you, they've gotta be in good nick if you wanna good mpg. I mean, I've known black cabs that was rough as hell, and they certainly didn't return thirty-two to the gall.

Like one night when Line's cab was laid up having new injectors put in or summat, and Mag Piper says: 'Why, Dinchy, me old mate, yer short of a track, you're welcome to drive Car 3.' Meaning one of his cabs.

And needing the money, I took him up on his offer. Never again. It was hanging, Car 3. Rough as a bear's botty, stiff on the steering, off-side front headlight out, horn not working, driver's door window too strongly sprung so it nearly took your nose off if you forgot and stuck your head out to ask a passer-by for directions. Yeah, it was knackering to drive, Car 3 – and the gears was that stiff I couldn't even lie on me left side in kip when I finished me night track with me arm being sore.

'The worst of it was,' I said to Line when I picked Car 27 up, complete with new injectors the following week. 'The worst of it was Car 3 needs new injectors or summat.'

'How d'you work that one out?' says Line, because he known I known nowt about mechanics.

'Every second job you was on, the engine'd cut out and you'd have to crack open one of the injectors with a spanner, crank the starter till the fuel come through. She'd start then.'

'Bent derv,' says Line.

'Par-ding?'

'He's usin' bent derv, the pillock.'

'Why? What's wrong with it?'

'Oh, there's nowt wrong with it,' says Line. 'Well, yeah, there is, of course. But there's nowt wrong with it as such, is what I mean. There's a lot less duty on agricultural derv, see. But what happens is Mag's gone and bought it off some bloke, don't give a monkey's, and he's bunged it in an old five gallon can with water at the bottom of it, or a bit of crap floatin' about in it. Serves him kin right. Mag ought to know better. Catch us usin' bent derv! Lose more than you gain in the long run. 'Less you can pump it straight from sauce, of course.'

'From *sauce*?'

'From the pump, pillock.'

See, Line's cab was always in good nick. What with Tough Titty who drove Car 27 full-time being a fairish mechanic and Line hisself being dead keen on how his cab was turned out. Yeah, Car 27 was a dream to drive.

Weekend tracks is what I done – Friday night, Sunday day, while Titty had a break. And just to climb into Car 27, start her up and hear the engine, throaty but smooth, and pull away from the rank with your first fare and the steering nice and light – well, you felt as if you really wanted to drive Car 27. Getting paid for it was like a bonus.

We went half the bag, me and Line. That is, once I'd put the fuel in at the end of the track (we worked on thirties) we divvied up, and split what was left over between us. I never coughed up me tips, mind, though Line hinted strongly that maybe I should. But I worked hard and honest, and there wasn't too many cabbies done that. Yeah, to hear Einstein talk, he never broke twenny quid on a Friday night – and him out from six in the evening till four next morning. They reckoned Mag only kept him on because he was a careful driver and didn't smash the cab up for him. Well, only the once anyroad.

And it wasn't that bad a job when you got the hang of it neither. But you had to get the hang of it first. I mean, you can't just get up out of your armchair one night, switch the *Magic Roundabout* off, have a good long stretch, stow your *Daily Mess* in the magazine rack and go out cabbying for the first time in your life, and expect to make a butty. Nah, you've gotta know where the streets is for starters. And that's not the half of it neither, as I was to discover that first Sunday I tracked out.

'Nice, easy day track for you,' Line tells us. 'Roads are clear, no chargin' about. Be like, well, dippin' your toe in the water.'

Yeah, like as if.

It was that flipping bad I didn't know if I was coming or going. And mostly I wasn't doing neither, but was sat stationary on the rank, five cabs deep, with me the fourth in line. This tart's voice – Janice – this tart's voice kept coming over on the radio, saying stuff, like:

'Car for Leroy.' Then: 'Free Call for Leroy.' Then, maybe she'd say: 'Assistance Leroy.'

I'd no idea what she was on about, me. Took us a few weeks to get the drift.

See, 'Car for Leroy,' meant Janice was inviting any cab that happened to be near Leroy Drive to bid for this job she'd got booked. Now, suppose I'd gone: 'Car 27, Grange Park,' well, Janice might of come back with: 'Car 27, Grange Park. Anyone nearer?' Then you might of heard her say: 'Car 12, Booth Hall. Anyone nearer?' And, if no one else blown in, then Car 12 would get the job, because any fool knows Booth Hall Children's Hospital is nearer to Leroy Drive than Grange Park Road is. Except for this fool, of course. Meaning Dinchy on his first Sunday day track.

Mind you, even that wasn't the end of it sometimes. See, the bidding might go on and on. Grange Park, Booth Hall, Charlestown Road, Polefield, Leander Close, on location Leroy, in the front garden of the address you want, in the lobby of that same address, sat in their front room watching TV, in bed with the lady of the house . . . Then other times, you'd get nowt.

'Car for Leroy,' Janice might say.

Nowt.

So, then Janice would say: 'Free call, Leroy.' Which meant you could blow for Leroy from wherever you happened to be in the Solar System. Mind you, there might still be an auction like before:

'Car 2, the Planet Venus . . . Car 17, the Outer Atmosphere . . . Car 21, coming in to land, west of the Windward Islands . . .'

Even so, there might still be nowt. So Janice would go:

'Assistance, Leroy.'

And, if you nipped in quick then, on 'assistance' and was the first to blow, well, the job was yours and no argument whatsoever. Because if Leroy went to assistance and you got it, not even Fr Christmas with his reindeers ready on the roof of that Leroy address would be allowed to pinch that job off of you.

Right-ho, let's get out there, do a day track and make a bit of moolah . . . What? . . . Oh, you're not quite ready for it yet? Well, what d'ya know! Thought you might be raring to go, earn a bit of easy money, money for jam, money for nothing. Still, I can't pretend I'm not personally acquainted with that slightly confused feeling that come over you just then, Because the boy Dinchy spent most of his first Sunday day track feeling the very same way. Sat on the rank, not moving – not knowing how to flipping-well move.

Ten years passed by before I got to track one – that is, before I got to the head of the rank where the first fare to turn up would be mine. Then another five years passed by before this feller with a duffel bag comes toddling across from the Tram Office, opens the near side passenger door, and clambers aboard. *Ah, this is it!* I remember thinking. *Off at last!* And I turned the taxi meter on as the pages of the World Gazeteer flicked over in me head: Manchester city centre at least, the Airport, Altrincham, Leamington Spa – the villages of the Garden of England. What a wonderful dream while it lasted! And it lasted just as far as the gates to Boggart Hole Clough at the foot of Valentine Brow. Because the punter wanted Sandhutton Street. Flipping walking distance! I could have spit that far! The taxi meter never so much as clicked over once.

Still, never mind, I was free, on the open road at last – the Queen's Highway prepared to unfold itself before me.

I tootled around and back to near the base when I'd dropped the fare off, but the work coming over the radio was for everywhere I wasn't. You want work, you go where the work is. Right? Well, yeah, but not that day it seemed, not on Dinchy's first day track.

A job was blown for Vicky Avenue, so I shot up there, but by the time I got there they was wanting cabs in Crumpsall. No problem, I dropped down to Crumpsall, by which time they was screaming for cabs in Moston. So I drove across to Moston only to find the lazy pigs in Cheetham Hill had tumbled out of their pits at last and found theirselves desperate for cabs all of a sudden. Agh! I give it up as a bad job then and went back on the rank. And by the time me day track ended at 6 pm I'd read the print off me

Sunday Spurt, I'd had two separate bacon butty breakfasts off Barmy Boris in Dot's Diner, I'd used the gents' convenience three hundred thousand million billion times, I'd got out to stretch me legs once or twice, I'd had a bit of a kip around half past two, I'd grown three wisdom teeth, and aged twenny years. Worst of it was, at the end of me first day track there was best part of ninety miles on the clock – three gallons of fuel! – and I'd only took a fiver.

'Hey, not bad for a beginner, Dinchy,' says Line when he clocked me mileage. But it was a different story when I weighed in. Give us a right old fashioned look, he did. 'Kinnell!' he says, snatching the take off us. 'Decide to take the family to the Blackpool instead, did yer?'

But I got better.

First off, you get to know where things is, see. I mean, the streets are a doddle because you've got the A to Z map. It's the pubs that's the bugger, and the punters will keep going to them – hey, and coming home from them too when they've rung for last orders. And that's even worse, because there's no pubs listed in the A to Z. But even so, once you learn where things is, you're on your way. (Hey, literally!)

See, what you're aiming at is to watch your mileage so your fuel bill is somewhere between a quarter and a sixth of your take. A sixth is excellent; quarter you can live with. Course, a sixth is only possible if you get some good clock and a half work after midnight, or at Christmas and New Year – or if you touch lucky at the normal tariff. Like, if you get some lazy tart like her off Winterdyne Street near the Dogs' Home that leaves you with the clock ticking over while she does her weekend shopping at the little off licence at the corner of Ringley Street. And make no mistake about it, there is some people like that, with nowt in their heads but sawdust – and nowt in their purses neither once me and the little off licence on the corner of Ringley Street had finished with them.

Normally though, you won't do as good as that. Still, you won't do too bad because you get to know where it's best to be depending on the time of day. It's common sense really. I mean, it's no use being outside ASDA's when the pubs are chucking out; and it's no use being outside the Bottom Derby on the last shopping day before Christmas. Hey, you get so well attuned to taxiing you can spot a fare at two hundred yards – even before that fare of yours knows he wants a cab.

This fare of yours – that is, this fare that don't even know he wants a cab as yet – this fare of yours is just a vague human shape on the horizon when you select him. He's stood there on the corner of Southdown Crescent, say, enjoying the night air after tumbling rat-legged out of the Charlestown Hotel where the bloke with the stutter sung 'Wimoweh' one Friday night, and he's whistling to hisself with his hands in his trouser pockets, this fare of yours. Oh, he don't have a care in the world, this fare of yours, least of all the fact that what he needs pretty desperate is a cab. Because he don't need a cab – well, not yet he don't. But you, on the other hand, in the comfort of Car 27 known different. Yeah, you in the comfort of Car 27 known it for a fact that this pedestrian – separated from you though he be by six hundred feet of evening air – this pedestrian is the very man who would give his kingdom for a cab.

'Well, kingdom such as it is,' says Byron, that night we was in Middleton on Dewey's twenny-first. 'Apprenticeship at Ferranti's, Hollinwood; talent competition at the Charlestown of a Friday night; Chinese supper from Dirty Lil's when the mood takes him; Yankee with Sammy Faithful of a Saturday afternoon; haircut, Blackley Village every six weeks or so; nosebag at the Pukka Vindaloo Balti House, Cheetham Village of a Bank Holiday Monday; clothes from Studd menswear in Middleton; holiday at Butlin's Pwllheli when he can't afford the Costa; weddings and funerals courtesy of Chain Bar Methodist!'

Bad weather helps, of course, though it's not absolutely necessary. Heat makes the punters flag too. ('Flag': get it?) So, let's get Billy Bunter in from the cold, eh? I mean, it is not by any stretch of the imagination cold, of course, except that Billy Bunter is cold to you. He's not even seen you as yet, so that's the first thing: switch your headlights on, make sure he sees you.

Done.

A touch of full beam will not go amiss, or you can flash an invisible dog, say, or that car coming the opposite way. That's got him guessing – the driver of the car, that is. There's no guessing with Billy Bunter: he's seen you all right. (N.B. squeaky brakes is dead handy too if it's an awkward punter that's got his back to you; a good old rev on the accelerator does the same trick). So there he is – he's seen you, he's heard you, you've got him hooked. All you gotta do now is land him.

A slowish speed is a definite must. You're not kerb crawling slow, but you is slowish rather than fast. If you was an horse and not a black cab you would be cantering – like, as if you had some definite destination in mind, see. Yep, somewhere in the great blue yonder where Mr & Mrs Pre-booked Punters is awaiting your timely arrival. Billy Bunter's your destination, of course, but you never let him know that. You're playing hard to get, see? Change down a gear at fifty yards, give that invisible dog a second warning. Right, now change up a gear and rev a lot whilst you're about it. And, who'd-a thought it? Look there he is, Billy ex-pedestrian Bunter – jumping up and down, flapping his arms about like an albatross going for take-off, whistling like a boiling kettle, and ready to do an Emily Davison under your front wheels any minute now in one last desperate effort to get you to stop.

Yeah, cabbying is a doddle if you take to it, though you get good days and you get bad. Some days you just sit there, bored to flipping tears; other days you can't get where you want to get fast enough, and when you've got there there's always somewhere else to go, and: Oh, pull the stops out, please do? When it's snowing it's like that, and most of the cabs go off the road when it's snowing and most of the traffic does too. But that was a favourite time of mine, in the snow – taking it easy, not clogging it, nice and easy, using the gears instead of the brake pedal. Car 27 paid in well when it was snowing.

'Hey, Dinchy,' says Line after one winter's night track when I got them flaggers for Lancaster. 'Cop for another track like that, fetch her in for a short service around midnight.' (Joke.)

You had loads of laughs on the cabs too. See, most people is smashing, honest. But a lot depends on how you treat them. Make 'em feel comfortable, that's the trick. People generally don't ask too much, you know. All they want you to do is treat them like – well, like people, that's all. Not too much to ask, is it? Gee the old girls up: 'Steady on, ma, this was a nice quiet cab till yous lot got in.' Let a younger bird talk if she wants to, otherwise don't crowd her. Get the blokes talking about the beer in the Grove or the score at the close of play. Get the old blokes going on about the roadworks on Lightbowne Road. You're a face in the crowd, a shoulder to cry on, a voice in the wilderness. See, it's a kind of a privilege to be sat in your cab as close to someone as you would be in their own living-room. Hey, and that's summat else you must never forget: while he's paying for it, it's the fare's living-room, not yours. Cabbies that forget this is very soon treated to a knuckle sandwich or a Manchester kiss.

Course, that's not to say you won't get the odd berk from time to time. Like this young arsehole I dropped off on Victoria Avenue one night, who spewed his ring up in the back of the cab. SPLAT – the full monty, it was: a pavement pizza once removed. All over the back seat, it went, one of the little dicky seats that fold up when not in use, the off-side passenger door, the glass divider. Everywhere, it was, a right flipping mess. You could tell what he'd had for his elevenses last Tuesday week.

'Cost you a fiver, that,' I told him when he got out, looking for his money.

That was the rule, see? I'd have to take the cab off the road, give it a good cleaning out and disinfect it. Half past eleven of a Friday night this happened so that was me track finished because the cab'd take a while to dry out and the bulk of the fares was always picked up when the pubs kicked out. I reckoned it'd be half past midnight at least before I got it back on the road.

'Fiver?' says the spewer. 'Wha' sonner clock?'

'Never mind what's on the clock,' I told him. 'In fact, forget it.' It wasn't much, I know: I'd only fetched him from The Millstone in Blackley Village. 'Just give us a fiver.'

'A kin fiver?'

'I've gotta clean it out.'

'Yer job, innit?'

'Give us a fiver an' piss off 'ome,' I told him. 'You'll feel better in the mornin'.'

''K off,' he tells us, like a doctor testing me bollocks, and he slings a bit of shrapnel through the open window of the cab, so that goes on the floor too. Hey, and he's off then, over their front gate like an antelope, key in the door, straight in, slams the door shut, and won't open up again when I give the knocker a bit of welly. Wasted another ten minutes doing that.

Oh, Line was none too pleased about it, I can tell you. The take was well down. I missed out on a lot of work that Friday night.

'Who done it?' Line wants to know.

'Dunno his name. Youngish bloke, denim jacket.'

'Where's he live?'

'Vicky Avvy. It's that one, you know – the one with the sunflower and the windmill-thing. We take her down to bingo at the Cintra of a Friday. Always goin' on about her dahlias and chrysants.'

'Spoiled your night,' says Line. 'You was doin' all right till then from the looks o' things.'

Hey, that nosey bugger, Keyhole, Sunday week, this is – things is a bit quiet on the rank and Keyhole hauls hisself up into the back of Car 27 for a natter.

''T were you 'ad spewer t'other neet, weren't it, Dinchy?' says he.

'Yeah.'

'Yo bastard, heh, heh, heh.'

'Eh?'

'Yo, heh, heh, heh.'

I sort of half-turned round to him in the driver's seat, hooking me elbow over the bottom channel of the glass divider. 'What's that supposed to mean?'

'Pullin' stunt like that.'

'Like what?' I shifted round some more, folded me *Sunday Spurt* in half, shoved it under the driver's seat.

'Heh, heh, heh, oh, gi' o'er actin'daft, heh.'

'You on about?'

'Heh, heh, heh, oh, heh, heh, heh.'

'You gonna tell us or what?'

'As if tha didn't know.'

'Look, I don't know nowt. Right?'

'Well, 'appen somebody does. I jus' picked t'auld feller up from the ICI Club.'

'What old feller?'

'*'E's* auld feller, spewer's. Spittin' fevvers, he were.'

'Oh, was he now?'

'Yeah, heh, heh, heh. Be lucky to grow dock leaves next year, never mind bleedin' dahlias. Sat'dy neet, it were. Some bugger tipped a load o' diesel o'er 'is flowerbeds'

But mostly you'd have some good laughs on the cabs, funny things that happened. Like, getting stuck on White Moss Road with an Indian someone had ordered and I'd paid for – oh, they do that, the punters: get you to buy 'em a curry at the Andaz and fetch it round the house for 'em – and then finding these punters wasn't at home when I turned up with it, but I made that much noise knocking at the front door that the next door neighbour come out to see what was going on and bought it off us herself when she heard it was Rogan Josh.

Hey, and swinging round that corner near the White Lion, Blackley Village, into Market Street on a clear dry night at such a speed that I dislodged this fat councillor, Alderman Addlecock, off the little dickey seat and he fell – SMACK – on his fat backside and bit through this King Edward cigar he'd just lit.

And this slag that flagged us down outside this club down Shude Hill one night and give us an address near Harp Lager. And, by the time I'm tootling past Lewis's window on Fountain Street, it's only got its bra off and its thingies out and is going on about how's about waiving the fare in consideration of favours received. So what with it not being very nice to insult a lady even if she is a slag, I told her: 'Sorry, love. You got nowt smaller?' and got me fare after all. No tip, mind. Still she did pay us the fare in full: one pound two shillings and sixpence, as I recall.

Hey, and most of the cabbies wasn't bad blokes neither, though the hours was long (a 72 hour week being normal for a cabby) and there was a lot of bent work about too. So if you wasn't a miserable bastard when you took up cabbying at Magpie, it was a knocking bet you'd be a miserable bastard by the time you left off. And one or two of them cabbies was bastards anyway. Like Herb Landaff, for instance, him we called Wrexham after he went and wrote his cab off one Christmas Eve going down Factory brow. Yeah, and Wrexham's driver, Nobby Castleton, who we called Godiva because, when Piggott won the Derby that time, Nobby was the only one who had nowt on him. Yeah, them two bastards, Wrexham and Godiva's the reason I thought of jacking the cabs in the first place.

See, some cabbies is just bag-swingers. Which is what Wrexham and Godiva was: bag-swingers. Tossers in other words. Yeah, they was the sort of cabbies that was always swinging their moneybags about as if that's what taxiing's all about. Hey, and for nine months in the year they was happy as Larry too, doing as little as they could get away with doing. Driving about in the cab when it suited them, reading the *Daily Mess* for eight hours at a stretch when that suited them, and when it suited them too, why, they'd go and grab theirselves a bacon butty at Dot's Diner – always provided they had took enough money to buy a bacon butty since they come on that morning.

And most of the time, it seemed to suit Wrexham and Godiva right down to the ground to sit drinking that lousy coffee in the base all day long instead of getting out on the street and doing a bit of graft. And just sometimes, of course, it might even suit them to have a run out to the Airport, or, come summer, to sit around in the sun on the rank, reading the *Daily Mess*. But come summer, of course, a bagswinger's lifestyle is threatened somewhat.

See, for maybe nine months out of the twelve a bag-swinger can get away with not doing much graft at all, reason being he'll have a missis at home that's a damn good grafter and tips up a good butty from her full-time job at ASDA's, or the school dinners, or bar work at the North Parade, or childminding for anybody and everybody in the street. Yeah, nine times out of ten a bagswinger will have a good missis that works eight hours a day, five days a week, fifty weeks a year, plus she does the shopping, the cleaning, the washing, the cooking, looks after the kids, and generally makes herself available for any other whims that might occur to her lord and master in them rare moments twixt slumber and sleep.

A bag-swinger makes sufficient money only unto his needs.

Depends on him what his needs are, of course, but since his main needs is met by the grafter he once upon a time had the good sense to marry, a bagswinger may just need his beer money (Wrexham), though you do get the odd visionary who has set his sights on a fortnight in Benidorm (Wrexham and Godiva), or he might be a womanizer (Godiva) who's got the transport to hand and the lack of supervision that suits his hobby. But they was, both of them, being bagswingers, affected by summer.

See, trade goes down a bit in good weather, so bagswingers start to feel the pinch. And then they maybe get to thinking that, well, if there was no part-timers on the rank (Dinchy, for example), there might be enough work to keep them in the bagswinging style to which they've become accustomed. And what happens then is they make the job a pain. Yeah, that's what they done, them bastards – they made the job a pain.

Friday, I'd get home from work, bolt me tea down me neck, and go tracking out. Sunday, I'd get up at six, skip me breakfast, and go tracking out. All I wanted to do was work. Not much to ask, is it? Hey, no such luck, pal. All of a sudden I found meself stuck with no-job after no-job. I'd drive to an address I'd been give only to find they never ordered no cab, or it was an empty house, or there was no such address. And this is not just once or twice, I'm talking about, but time after time after time after time. It really ground me down, that. Me fuel bill was up, plus I was out of pocket too because I'd of missed out on whatever genuine work was going. If I was on the rank, I'd never get off it when I needed to get off it because they'd have us blocked in while they'd gone off for a bacon butty. Out on the road I learned never to blow me call sign, just 'caller', or I'd would never get any job I blown for because there was always someone nearer to it than I was, even if they was not nearer. Yeah, they made the job I liked, the job I done well, the job that used to earn us a good butty an absolute pain in the bum. Then what happened was I begun to overhear threats of damage to the vehicle – not never to me face, of course (nothing is ever to your face), but under cover of darkness: whisperings, things hinted at: tonight . . . parked up . . . windscreen . . . bodywork . . . acid . . . tyres . . . It was all very vague, of course, but I was left with the distinct impression that Car 27 would be made unsightly at best, and, at worst, unsafe.

'I've had enough of it,' I said to Shirlee when I got in after one really bad Friday track when I'd got dragged from the shops at White Moss to Paul and Smart's on Bottomley Side for yet another fare that wasn't there. 'I'm jackin' it. I'll tell Line when I weigh in, Monday.'

20

When I went round to Line's house on the Monday night I found him flat out on the sofa in the living-room, watching *The High Chaparral*. It was that episode where Blue Boy and Mano and Uncle Buck have stayed too long in Tucson instead of going straight back to the ranch to ride point. Hey, and Big John Cannon's none too pleased about it neither, so Victoria's got herself in a bit of a tizz, trying to calm him down and that, and meanwhile these Ay-patch indians (as Uncle Buck calls them) that's led by Choc Ice, the Ay-patch chief, are raiding Senor Montoya's arsey-ender where Victoria grown up. Or summat. But I know it was enough to make you forget your own troubles, bad as they was, though what happened next I never did find out because Line switched the telly off just as Blue Boy knocked this feller twice his size into an horse trough and the middle of next week.

'Ma-arj!' Line bawls. (Marj is in the kitchen.) 'Ma-a-arj!' he bawls again. Then when she pops her fat head round the door: 'Do us another cuppa, will you, love? One with, one without, oh, and Marj you haven't got, couple o' pieces, that wimberry tart left, have you? Thanks, love.' Line stretches and gives this stupendous yawn that fills the room like an airbag. He fluffs up the cushions, flops back on the couch and nods towards the armchair beside the standard lamp. 'Load off your feet, Dinchy. So what's it all about, then?'

Well, I give him the bare bones of it. I'd had just about enough of being pissed about so I wanted to finish. 'I mean, suppose summat happens to the cab because of me,' I said.

'Because of *you*?'

'Because of them, I mean.'

Line laughs. Another airbag hits the ceiling.

Marj, smiling, comes through with the tea things on a plastic tray with a picture of a dozen Queen Elizabeth roses on it. Line positions this guitar-shaped glass and wrought-iron coffee table between us, and Marj sets the tray down on it. Cups, saucers, plates, teaspoons – there's two of everything except for the teapot, milk jug and sugar bowl. The teapot's like a model of a thatched house, the teaspoons are holiday souvenirs (one each from Blackpool and Douglas, IOM), and the crockery's got pictures of bluebells on it. The plates are stacked one on top of the other, the top plate holding two pieces of wimberry tart. Line plays mum, but I'd just had me tea so I waved away the piece of wimberry tart he offers us. Line scoffs it in two bites before he spoke.

'Hoof noon hut?' he says through a gobful of wimberry tart

'Eh?'

'Who's doin' it?' His lips is ringed with pastry crumbs.

I mentioned a couple of names, but they was just sheep and Line known it.

'Nah, the main players,' he says, wiping his mouth with a hanky. 'The ringleaders.'

So I told him.

'Hm, might of guessed as much.' Line's making inroads on the other piece of wimberry tart when the cuckoo in the clock on the wall next to the picture of Constable's *Haywain* in the bamboo frame shows its face and calls nine times. From where he's sat on the sofa, Line slings his left arm backwards like he's swimming back crawl at Harpurhey Baths. He grabs the telephone off the window ledge and hauls it across the back of the sofa and on to his knees. He belches, lifts the receiver, dials seven digits, and waits.

'Go to the top, Dinchy. That's what I always says,' says Line, breaking off from humming 'The Wonder of You' while he waits for a reply. Then: 'That you, Herbert? . . . Line . . . Linus Bunratty, ye heathen bastard . . . Line, yeah . . . Oh, fine, Herbert, yeah, fine. You? . . . Good, good, glad to hear it, boyo . . . You don't know how glad I am to hear that, Herbert . . . Well, okay, Herb, you say so, Herbert. I mean, Herb . . . No, nah, nothin' much at all really . . . On my life, Herb. No, what it is is this, see. I just happened to call into Paton's today . . . Paton's. You gone deaf, your old age, Herb? . . . Yeah, Paton's. An' I was just sat here, havin' me tea – lovely piece of sirloin the wife does of a Monday: mushrooms, onions, all the trimmings – and the thought suddenly strikes us, like: Oh, dearie, dearie me, I was thinkin' to meself. Oh, dearie, dearie me, I thought. I wonder if Herbert, that is, Herb,

I wonder if Herb has any idea what they're askin' for a replacement windscreen these days . . . You do? . . . Oh, of course, the write-off you had that time. Me forgettin' a thing like that. Let's see if I've got it right now. It was round about the time you blown for the Leeds fare that T blown for and you was not where you said you was, you naughty boy. Yeah, you blown Slattocks but – well, I won't say who it was, but you was seen outside Woolco's, wasn't you? One Christmas, as I recall? . . . Hm, that long ago, is it? How time flies when you're havin' fun. . . . Mm, you reckoned someone had tampered with the brake line, didn't you? Nasty thought, Herb? I mean, who'd wanna do, thing like that? . . . Still, that's all water under the bridge now, but look, that windscreen of yours . . . Sure, I mean the cab. Why? What other motor you got? . . . Notta tall, Herb . . . No, nothin' of the sort. Look, just hear us out, will you?' Line pauses and takes the little finger of his right hand to this crumb of pastry that's clinging to the corner of his mouth. 'No, no, no, no, no . . . You got us all wrong, pal. I don't mean no such thing. No, Herb. I mean, we're all in this together, aren't we? Cut one and the rest bleed. No, Herb . . . Herb, I want you to hear me now. Because I wanna tell you I know exactly how you feel, mate. Yeah, course I do. Same's I'd feel, some naughty boy was to do summat, uh, reckless to Car 27 . . . Yeah, the cab, Herb. Car 27, *my* Car 27 that T drives full-time and Dinchy drives Friday night, Sunday day. Be like, well, be like strikin' me personal . . . That's right, pal. Yeah? . . . Well, lemme tell you I really appreciate that, Herb . . . Sure, me too . . . And my very best regards to your good lady . . . You too, pal . . . Yeah, be sein' you, Herb. See you on the ice . . . Herbert.'

Line replaces the receiver and drains his cup. He stands up, stretches, and airbags a yawn. 'Well, now, Dinchy. You can jack if you wannoo, but I think you'll find things just a bit more relaxed down the rank from now on.'

Hey, they was too, and I begun turning over a fair bit of money again. But the message still hadn't filtered through to Nobby Castleton. No, Godiva was still at it, blocking us in when he got a chance to, phoning the no-jobs in when the fancy took him. Like, Friday night, right at the death, it was, he phoned in this no job that I copped for up on the Heywood stretch: farm track with a mad Great Dane on the loose at the end of it, and no one who'd ordered a cab in the first place. And Godiva only had to hang around and watch the fun; seen him in me rear view mirror on me way back, parked up in the car park of the Gardeners Arms, Hollin Lane.

'Yeah, tons better,' I told Line when I weighed in on the Monday. 'Apart from Godiva, of course.'

'No problem then.'

'Nah.'

Hey, it wasn't neither; Godiva was just a little fart of a feller, had to show off to feel big. Breath of wind would have blown him over; good shit would of killed him.

Following week, I done me Friday night track as normal, and I done well for mid-summer. I was in the middle of me Sunday day track, tracking one, when I seen Line and Titty roll up in that breakdown truck of Line's, like a cut-away Land Rover with an hook at the back. Then this old dear waddles across and gets in and I pulled off to run her down to Crumpsall Hospital for visiting. There was no rank to speak of when I got back. Police everywhere and firemen hosing diesel fuel away. All the black cabs bar one was parked up down the dip across from the White Lion

'Jeesh! Jee-zozz H. *Christ*!' this Zapata bloke's going when I climbed in the back of Gibraltar's cab. 'Jeesh! The look on Nobby's face, it was a picture. Just wings him up and over. Line on the hook and Titty on the winch. Crash, bang, wallop. Jeez! And there's Nobby tryin' to scramble out like . . . Jeez! Hey, Gibraltar . . .'

'Shut your face,' says Gib.

'Yeah, but . . . Jeesh!'

'Shut yer stoopid face.'

'Yeah, but you can't, heh, heh, you can't keep summat like that quiet,' says Keyhole.

'Why? Who's gonna say owt?'

'Oh, not me, Gib. Not me, heh, heh, heh.'

'He had it comin', didn't he?'

'He did that, Gib.'

'Anyway, what's there to say? Anyone says owt, they was helpin' him change a wheel, and things got a bit out of hand.'

'Jeesh!' says Zapata. 'Kin wheel-nuts wasn't even loosened!'

'Shut yer stoopid face,' says Gib.

Now, things really did get very relaxed for a time after that, and I started to cop for some good long distance work for a change, what with Line hinting very strongly to Mag Piper that bent work was also something he did not regard too kindly, unless it was bent his way, that is, and with Mag Piper proving to be very obliging in this respect, being only too keen to keep Line happy. Yeah, the job was fine: it was me that went wrong.

See, if you just toddle along in a part time job it can last you for years, I reckon, but if you tear at it like a bull at a gate, like I done, you burn yourself out. Well, that's what I think, for what it's worth, because there come a day when I just didn't wanna do it no more. Yeah, it was the anniversary of when me and Shirlee first went out together that done for us, and I was sat on the rank, tracking ten, and I suddenly thought:

'Hey, get you, you berk. Five years ago tonight you was doing exactly what you wanted to do and you was with exactly who you wanted to be with too, and you would not have wanted to change places with anyone else in the hole wide world. And now look at you. Eight years on, and what have you got? A bit of extra money in your pocket, but you hardly ever get to see her. Or our Suzanne. So what's it all about, eh? I mean, you won't even get a decent night's kip, for Pete's sake . . . No, not for Pete's sake, I thought to meself, for kin Line's sake!

So, I jacked it. Don't hang about, me. Give Line one week's notice, jacked the black cabs for good.

Line jacked it hisself six months later. What I mean to say is Line done a runner six months later, leaving Marj to manage the black cab and sell it for him. Same time Titty cleared off, just as soon as the police investigation into the Council wages snatch got under way. Okay, so Line had a damn sight more than I had when he jacked it, and there's a difference of opinion about how he come by it too. See, there's some who'll tell you Line had money no one known about; then there's others who reckon he got an half share of the Council wages snatch. Still, money isn't everything, they say – summat you'll always hear people say when they've got none. But what's the betting they'll change their tune PDQ if that lottery win ever turns up?

Yeah, like as if.

Look, I know nowt, me. No, honest! Shirlee'd say I was daft sometimes because I don't never notice nothing even if it's going on right under me nose. So all I can tell you about Line and Titty and the Council wages snatch is what I've heard from other cabbies who reckon they know what went on. That's not saying it's true though. Because a lot of them cabbies had an axe to grind anyway. Besides, I've more or less had to make-do and piece the story together because it only come to us in snippets.

There was a full report in the *Daily Mess*, of course, but I don't get the *Mess* every day and I missed that issue. So the only newspaper report I seen about the Council wages snatch was in the *Hebers & Tonge Telegraph* in Tommy's Chippy in Middleton Gardens, and I had to read it quick too because they was getting ready to wrap this feller's cheese and onion, chips and peas in it. Hey, I have never read anything so quick in the hole of me life, though as luck would have it, the feller was waiting for a fresh load of chips to cook.

The trouble is, though, them reports in the *Hebers & Tonge Telegraph* is not always very accurate. See, it's only a local paper so you can't expect too much. Mind you, they do try their level best to get everything completely arse uppards like the *Daily Mess* does. Also, by the time I read about the Council wages snatch in the *Hebers & Tonge Telegraph* I'd already heard a bit from Keyhole who was in the Old Boar's Head one night when me and Shirlee was in.

'Contract we had wi' t' Council, heh, heh, heh, runnin' wages clurk round wi' t' money, Thursday mornin's, heh, heh, heh. Grand job, heh, heh, heh, done it on a rota basis, heh, heh, heh, till it were 27's turn . . .'

And this report I read in the *Hebers & Tonge* Telegraph in Tommy's chippy before they wrapped up this feller's cheese and onion, chips and peas off Hereford Way, Boarshaw, where we used to run him from the Vasa Club had this to say:

"*Everything proceeded as per usual until they reached Jim Allen Court where Mr Wain Hardy, a wages clerk with the Treasurer's Department, duly made his call. On his return to the cab Mr Herdy realised he had left his raincoat on the premises, so he placed the briefcase containing the money on the back seat of the cab and returned to the building to retrieve his coat.*

"*Mr Bernard Tiffield, the driver of the cab, failed to notice this because he was reading the*

HEBERS & TONGE TELEGRAPH
(EASTER BONNET EDITION – only 30p)

"*The first thing Mr Trafford knew about the matter was when Mr Heidi asked him where the briefcase had gone. Mr Triffid distinctly remembers hearing the rear door of the cab being opened prior to Mr Hurdy's return, but he had thought this was Mr Howdy coming back. Mr Trifle had not thought to look round at the time because Mr Hitler was in the habit of doing his paperwork before proceeding to Turnus Grove Primary School, the next call on the Council wages itinerary. When informed by Mr Hitman that the briefcase had disappeared, Mr Truffle telephoned the police immediately.*

"*A spokesman for the City Treasurer's Department estimates that 'a sum of money in the region of six thousand pounds is still unaccounted for'.*"

'Heh, heh, heh, t' were Line that done it, him an' T. Heh, heh, heh. Mind you, provin' it's another matter. Yeah, provin' it, heh, heh, heh. Seems Line were fishin' wi' Mag Piper up at Slattocks at the time, heh, heh, heh. Can you beat that? Three-way split, the lads reckon, heh, heh, heh. Maybe four if the Council feller was in on it. Grand contract we lost too, heh, heh, heh, oh, a grand contract, heh, heh, heh . . .'

Like I say, I don't know the truth of it either way. And I couldn't have asked Line for a good eighteen months anyway, even if I'd of wanted to – well, not without bearding him (yeah, he grown one for a while) at the Bar Humbug English Bar that him and T set up in Marbella. Course, that was only until the police investigation died down. Because Line come back then to invest what money he had with Mag Piper with a view to changing Magpie's name to Bee Line when Mag took early retirement (so Gib said). And this was around the same time that Titty come back from the Costa too and took up a half share in a roadhouse near Tenby in partnership with Dot Harrytown's dad who had experience as a licensed victualler but not enough of the readies.

'Richard Harris's dream of heaven, if you think on,' I reminded Byron. 'Nymphomaniac whose father owns a pub.'

'I'd settle for Denzo in the dentist's chair, way my guts feel at the moment.'

This is that same night we was celebrating Dewey's twenny-first in Middleton: Joiners, Archer, Dusty, Roebuck, Brit, Assheton Arms, New Inn, Brickies – and a curry at the Akash to finish off with. Afterwards, we jumped a Bee Line cab on Market Place to fetch us back to Byron's house on Polefield.

'You ever get to the bottom of that wage snatch business, Dinchy?' Pearson asks us while we're stuck at the Avenue lights on the way back. 'Was it them, like the man says?'

'Never asked 'em, mate.' Made no bones about it, me. 'Marbella . . . Tenby. Either one, always seemed helluva long way to go to get a knuckle sandwich for askin' stoopid questions!

21

Still, that was then and this is now. I mean, what I'm on about now is that time I done the base for Mag one Saturday night when Shirlee fell out with us on our seventh wedding anniversary. Well, two days after it, I suppose it was. Because this is the Sunday morning I'm talking about – the morning after the night before. Well, two mornings, to tell the truth.

I finished on the Magpie base at six when Motormouth come on. But I hung around for a bit playing three-card with them that was on, seeing I didn't have no home to go to. Oh, the bricks and mortar was still there. Don't get us wrong. There'd been no Heinkels or Junkers overhead for thirty-odd years or more. No, what I mean is – well, you know very well what I mean, don't you?

There's not that many on at Magpie early on of a Sunday morning. Three that day – no four: Motormouth, Shane, Kipper and Felix. And the reason for this is because there's not much doing at Magpie early on of a Sunday morning unless you cop for an airport, say, or you've got a booking you already known about – like Kipper who was gonna pick this fare up that was due in from Faro that he'd took out to Ringway a week last Sunday. It was about seven before I got away. Yeah, it was – seven exactly. Because Kipper had tootled off to the airport for his half seven pick-up. (What you done was you phoned up to check the ETA, then set off as soon as you heard they'd landed, because by the time they was through with customs and that you'd be ready and waiting for them, and not hanging about too long because parking was piss-poor at Ringway. Still is. Anyway, I know it was seven, because when I come out of Magpie and went and got some fags and a paper at Brian Short's newsagent's near the zebra, and was walking back to Dot's Diner for me brekky with a cig between me lips and a *Sunday Spurt* under me arm, I can remember hearing the clock at St Bartholomew's on Bottomley Side giving it six ding-dongs, seeing they'd never got around to putting the clock on for BST at the end of March.

Bacon barm, two of – with brown sauce, if you don't mind, Boris (that is, Barmy Boris what stood in for Dot of a Sunday),

Wagon Wheel, Caramel Wafer, pint mug of tea. Famished, I was, and thirsty too. Besides which, I didn't want to go home just yet. Well, yeah, of course, I wanted to go home (I'd not changed that much overnight), but I didn't wanna go home to an empty house or an argument is what I mean.

It was a nice bright September morning with sunlight slanting down, sharp, but filtered through the ash trees in the Clough behind the base beneath this bit of an incline we used to call the Cresta Run when we was kids, tobogganing down it on a KitKat tea tray belonging to Huge's mum. Peaceful, it was, and sort of quiet too because there was no one about as yet. And Barmy Boris had the radio on in the galley there, but not loud – like background music, and a bit tinny too. Then when the early news come on (dead boring as usual) Boris slides the back window open overlooking the Clough and this breath of fresh air wafts into the diner where, before, there'd just been steamed up windows and the hot stove and the smell of bacon rashers sizzling on the grill and sausages and coffee and tea, and the sound of water bubbling away in the shiny silver urn on the counter top.

So, I had a nice leisurely breakfast all on me todd and I read me paper and drunk me tea and ate me biscuits and had a smoke. Oh, them bacon barms Boris done was a treat – bacon a bit on the rough side, salty, lean, crisp, and with brown sauce thrown in. Just right. Well, just right for me anyway: bacon served up the way I like it.

And I'm not too sure about this – I mean, I'm not exactly certain when it was is what I mean. But, at some point in the proceedings, while I was sat there – sipping me tea, reading me paper, eating me biscuits, having a smoke (like I say, I'm not exactly sure when it was, but), at some point in the proceedings, I begun to feel – well, I dunno. Uneasy, I suppose you could say. Yeah, sort of uneasy.

Now, it may of been when I'd scoffed me bacon barms and pushed me plate back and sat back with me mug of tea and lit up. Like I say, I dunno. There again, maybe it was when I dropped cigarette ash in me lap and asked Barmy Boris to sling us an ashtray, for Pete's sake, Boris. But be that as it may, at some point in the proceedings while I was sat there – pushing me plate back, taking a sip of tea, reading me paper, puffing away on a fag (me umpteenth) – at some point in the proceedings I got this very uneasy sort of a feeling. Not anxious, just uneasy. Like, as if there was summat I should of done that I'd forgot to do, or, like, I should of been getting ready to do summat but I'd forgot what it was, or, like . . .

Well, I dunno.

It was the sort of feeling you get when you're trying to remember somebody's name, say, or a word for a crossword, or the answer to a question, and it's right there on the tip of your tongue, but it just won't come. Or like when you seen someone in the street you know really really well but you can't for the life of you think where you know them from because they are not wearing the white coat they normally wear or the policeman's uniform you're used to seeing them in, or they're not stood behind the shop counter in Balf's chemist's shop in their white coat, or dishing out curry and chips in Tommy's chippy, or working the petrol pump at the ICI garage on Church Lane like they're usually doing when you seen them.

Strange it was, a funny sort of feeling. And it took us a bit before I twigged what it was. Because it was only the boy Jameson's voice I could hear. Yeah, Huge. Jameson, me best mate as was: Dee-Jay U.E. Jay, as you known him for all them years, but very very faint, he was, far off in the background on this radio Barmy Boris had on in the galley, there.

Yeah, it was me old mucker Huge Jameson on the radio there, doing his regular Sunday morning stint in the studio at Watchtower and, judging by the time it was (7.19 am precisely by this Reflex wristwatch I bought on Conran Street Market for a fiver), he must of been yattering away for the better part of ten minutes. Huge, because this Sunday morning show of his begun right after the news and Huge is already into what he calls his Disco Dig'n' Delve ('Hey, turn it up a bit, can't you?' I said to Boris), playing stuff that would of grabbed me attention anywhere: 'Searchin'', being undertaken by The Coasters; Frankie Ford, sailing away on a 'Sea Cruise'; and Larry Williams, going down with 'Rockin' Pneumonia and the Boogie Woogie Flu'. Then

Huge whizzes us bang up to date with Van Morrison's 'Brown-Eyed Girl'. (Never charted, that record, would you believe it?) Hey, I reckon I'd of had to be dead from the neck up to miss out on that lot.

And then Huge bungs this other record on ('Hey! *Mucho Fantabulastico*!' as Huge so describes it. With which sentiment I happen to agree, as a matter of fact!), though where the hell he's managed to get hold of a copy of that one, I'll never know. Because it's only local Blackley lad made good, Tony Auton and The Trauma singing 'All I Want to Do'. WOW! And that particular number only whizzes us right back to the very first time I'd went out with Shirlee all them years before . . .

The Bottom Derby of a Friday night with free entertainment thrown in – said Tony Auton and The Trauma, up on stage there, giving it bags of welly – and three-hundred thousand million billion boozed-up Manpudlians crammed into the downstairs room like maggots in a tin at half past ten at night when the bell goes for last orders and, as per usual, it goes off in there. Cig Heil calls us a f&#kin' c#nt for stepping on his blue suede shoes when I'm applauding Tony and the lads . . . so Idle Wild tips a pint of Chesters Dark Mild over Cig Heil's head because Tony Auton is only Avis Henstone's mother's cousin's auntie's best friend's next-door neighbour's painter and decorator, and Avis thinks it's Tony Auton Cig Heil's calling a f&#kin' c#nt, and Idle disagrees . . . so Himmler the Ted makes off with the snare drum . . . so Stan and Jed, who's stood around waiting for Burke's Law to get the drinks in, floors the pair of them . . . so the landlord bars Stan and Jed *and* Burke's Law, notwithstanding the fact that Burke's Law is Sammy Faithful's uncle's cousin's nephew's brother-in-law who the landlord owes a fiver to for a foreigner he done earlier that day when he very kindly replaced the window that Line put through at Rhoda Rishworth's Twenny-First the night before . . . so Barry Brick-Shithouse-In-A-Suit goes ballistic because one of the drinks Burke's Law is ordering is his . . . so Barry Brick-Shithouse-In-A-Suit decks Gordon Forrester who's waiting on that night and carrying a full tray of drinks to Pamela

Wembury's table, and belts Gordon's brother Charlie for good measure (who pukes in The Hunchfront's lap) . . . so Barry Brick-Shithouse-In-A-Suit goes to lamp Charlie again, but misses on the repeat puke (Lorraine Walshaw copping for this one), and puts the window in again . . . so Bernadette Holwick starts screaming blue murder and Slack Gob the same . . . so Dot Harrytown's dad grabs this Chubb fire extinguisher off the wall and turns it on all three hundred thousand million billion Manpudlians that's in the Botton Derby that Friday night except for me and Shirlee and Stan and Jed and Burke's Law, who back out of the Bottom Derby PDQ (Stan with a chair leg in his hand, Jed with a broken bar stool, me with Shirlee's brollie with the duck's head handle, and Burke's Law with a crate of Mackeson he finds in the lobby . . . so Tough Titty, who pulls up outside the Bottom Derby in Car 27 with the engine running, having just brung the landlady back from A&E at Crumpsall on crutches – Tough Titty tells us to jump in quick, does a U-turn in moving traffic in front of a 72 bus, and drops us off at the World Famous Embassy Club for last orders . . . while the band plays on.

'Oi, Dar-*tan*-yun!' (Cripes! I've still got Shirlee's brolly in me hand, and Manning clocks it straight off: *laughter*) 'Or is it the C#nt of Monty Christo, may Hi h-ask?' (*More laughter, ripple of small talk*) 'Oozat wi' yer? Kin Long John Silver?' (*Laughter: Stan's still got hold of the chair leg.*) '

Jed puts the bar stool down and sits on it, quick.

'Kin feller, there (*points Jed out*), queer he is: city nonner fortune an' dozen kin know it.' (*Laughter, laughter, laughter, laughter, laughter.*)

Ah, happy days, eh?

And then Huge – I mean Dee-Jay U.E. Jay on Watchtower, there – yeah, ya ol' pal Dee-Jay U.E. Jay, well, he does no more than dives straight into all that silly boingy-oingy, bubbly-wubbly, ding-a-ling-donging he was in the habit of socking to you of a Sunday morning before he'd introduce his Extra-Wextra Ambi-Dexter Special Request Slot that was three hundred thousand million billion times more sloppier and boring than Two-Way Family Favourites ever was, and would just bore the pants off you because Dee-Jay U.E. Jay's Extra-Wextra Ambi-Dexter Special Request Slot is always going on about some soppy tart (called Shirlee or summat) who wants Dee-Jay U.E. Jay to give out some soppy message over the air to some absolute arse hole of a feller (called Dinchy or summat), saying how she is . . .

Well, okay, that's about the gist of it, because that's where Dee-Jay U.E. Jay comes in with the music again, which is this song by the Impalas, called 'Sorry', which is fourteen years past its sell-by date if it's a day.

Had us up on me feet though.

See, 'Sorry' is just one word out of seven that go to make up that song title. Because in brackets it says: 'I Ran All The Way Home'.

Forget it! There's no way I'm admitting to that one!

'PUT WOOD IN T' 'OLE!'

Barmy isn't in it. Voice like a flipping foghorn. I can still hear the barmy bugger going on with hisself from over by the Clough gates at the bottom of Valentine Brow.

She done us a cooked breakfast when I got in. Yeah, another one – and, like the pig I am, I ate it. We drunk a good few cuppas too, and (okay, there's a down side to everything) I had to look at these cushion covers she'd bought on Grey Mare Lane Market yesterday afternoon. We took our Suzanne out in the Rec then and to see her grandparents (two sets) and ate our tea quite late and watched TV. Shirlee said she was tired. But I'd had enough sleep for two. I said I'd be up in a bit.

Another film, it was, first time on TV: *The Night of the Generals* where Peter O'Toole plays this nutty Nazi general (so what's new?), and Donald Pleasance plays an halfway decent one (hey, like as if), and Omar Sharif gets shot at point blank range halfway through the picture, and Tom Courtenay goes on the run for thirty years, Otley Pursued (Joke.). Anyway it was after midnight by the time the film goes off, so I went upstairs, using just the landing light in case I disturb her. She's fast asleep, sort of half in and half out of the covers, and pale in the moonlight, like something from another world.

'You okay?' I said, whispered, I suppose..

'Mm.

'Have a shower, 'f you're hot?'

'Mm, no' ho' now.'

'Suzanne's fast,' I said.

She moves against us, cooler now. ''S cold ou' the covers, ' she says. 'Soon gets cold out . . .'

'Yea-h,' I said. Then: '*Hh-hhn*!' before she ate us.

'Oh, there you is,' I said to them sweet lips. 'There you really an' truly is.'

Shirlee says, Yeah, if you want, she'll pick the air filter up from Volmax on Great Ancoats Street, but I'd better write the number down just to be on the safe side. We had this Hillman Californian by then – the Imp, you know, with the rear engine, but the estate version. The air filters on them things was right at the back of the engine compartment, so they always got skipped on the service.

Next morning, this is.

'*Mwa*! Gimme one!' She's off then, reminding us for the three hundred thousand million billionth time that I'll have to pick Suzanne up from nursery at three and get the tea on.

No problem.

Like I say, I'd booked a day off that was due to us, so if Shirlee got us the thingy, we'd be all right for the Tuesday . . .

All right for the Tuesday!

Dear God, we was never gonna be all right again!

And if I live to be an hundred I'll never know what possessed her to go all the way across town into Manchester Arndale Centre instead of coming straight home to us on the 72 like she always done.

I picked our Suzanne up from the Nursery at ten past three that afternoon (Bunty Bra-Straps, as Shirlee christened her, always made a point of keeping you waiting an extra ten minutes) and Isobel from Year One at half-past (Felicity Fograt, as Sylvia always called her, had a wristwatch that kept better time). We done loads of stuff like that for one another, me and Shirlee and Keith and Sylvia.

'Daddy, daddy, daddy, dad, dad, dad,' says our Suzanne, skipping down the path. 'Idobel have her tea my youse?'

'Yeah, okay. If mummy says she can. Come an' hold me hand.'

'Mummy say she can, daddy,' says Suzanne, doing as she's told for once in her life. 'Idobel have her tea my youse, my bird-day.'

'No, pet, Isobel's gotta ask *her* mummy's what I mean.'

'You have your tea, me, my youse, Idobel?'

'We yav mitten potato pie?'

'Mean potato pie,' Suzanne tells us.

'Me *ten* pot-ato pie,' says Isobel carefully.

'Meat an' potato pie comin' up,' I said.

'No. Me not, daddy. Me wan' beans.'

'Okay then. No need to throw your bag down. Mean potato pie an' beans, it is.'

'No, daddy. Wan' beans. No' mean potato.'

'It's not *really* mean, you know.' Struck us maybe the name she'd give it was the problem. Suzanne would never cross the road with Mrs Snape, the lollipop lady, till Shirlee called her Marlene instead, realising Suzanne thought 'Snape' was 'snake'.

'Wan' beans, daddy. Wan' beans, wan' beans, wan' beans.'

Isobel giggled.

'All right, Miss Keck.' Now, where's she get that from, I wondered, though not really. 'Mitten potato pie for Isobel, and for Suzanne May Dinch, good girl seldom, human beans.'

They giggled.

'What are you?'

'Goo' girl theldom.You thilly, daddy.'

'Human beanth ith thillier.'

They giggled again, looked like they wanted us to say something just as daft.

'How about Welsh rabbit?'

More giggles

'Snake an' pygmy pie?'

Another hit. The old ones are the best.

They'd finished their tea by half past five – well, as much as they were going to eat of it anyway, and Isobel went off home when the Granada news come on. Suzanne settled down to some crayoning while I got cheese and onion pies and peas and boiled potatoes and a couple of treacle puddings sorted out for me and Shirlee. Then I bathed Suzanne. Come seven o'clock, Shirlee still hadn't turned up and I was getting a bit annoyed now. Suzanne was fast sleep on the settee when the front door bell went.

Now, this I do wanna hear, I thought – and it had better be good too! Like, where's her front door key for starters?

One of the coppers, the younger one, he wasn't much more than a cadet, I don't suppose, I known him slightly – Benny Wessenden, kept goal for the Clough Hotel of a Sunday. Easter before last, cup tie on North End, Benny had put the New Inn centre forward in hospital for a fortnight with a greenstick fracture and a pair of crutches to hobble about on for twelve months after. Another time he booked Byron for parking on the kerb outside the Alliance when he'd beat him at Don one night. Benny the Bastard, as they called him, was removing his cap when I opened the door. The uniform with him, the older one, the one who used me Sunday name, he'd already got his cap tucked under his arm.

Me mam and dad come and stayed with Suzanne overnight with her already being asleep. There was so much that had to be done. There was still a lot to do the next day, but by mid-afternoon we'd done as much as we could do for the time being. They'd took Suzanne round to me mam's during the morning, then Shirlee's dad brung us home in his car about half past four. I got out the back passenger door on the kerbside, picked Suzanne up and give her a hug. She was sleepy again and she didn't really know what was going on. I leant back inside to get Teddy Boy from where she'd dropped him in the foot well, and when I stood up again I seen Sylvia stood at their front door.

'Tony, I'm so . . .'

There was music coming out of Sylvia's front door. Dave Edmunds was stood in Sylvia's lobby with his guitar and his band. Dave Edmunds was singing 'Baby, I Love You' in Sylvia's lobby that day.

'Rockfield label,' I told Sylvia.

'Daddy, daddy.'

'Tony, I'm so, so . . .'

Did I tell you Dave Edmunds was singing in Sylvia's lobby that day?

'*Hoo-hoo, hoop-hoop.*' This wasn't Dave Edmunds, this was Dinchy when Dave Edmunds was singing in Sylvia's lobby that day. A different Dinchy: not singing, not singing, not singing no more.

'Daddy, daddy . . . *dad*-dy!'

I said to Sylvia: 'Our Suzanne's got no mummy, Sylvia. Has your Isobel got a mummy, Sylvia?'

Suzanne begun to cry and someone took her off of us. But I wouldn't let go of Teddy Boy – no, NO! – not till they sat us on the settee in our front room and brung us a cup of tea while they phoned Dr Dryburn.

Me tea was miles too sweet. I told Shirlee. I said: 'Ugh! Shirlee, this tea's miles too sweet.' I was smiling when I said it, but Shirlee had the funnies and wouldn't talk to us.

'*Hoo-hoo, hoop-hoop,*' I told Shirlee.

Shirlee was maybe mithered with Dr Dryburn having to be called out again. She wouldn't give us a ciggy neither. Her dad went round to the off licence on James Street and threw us a packet of Senior when he come back. But I'd forgot how to smoke.

You pull the cellophane off a packet of twenny Senior. You push the card container up with Tommy Thumb. You open the foil wrapper, take a cigarette out, and stick it between your lips. Then you light up. Easy peasy, lemon squeezy! But every time I'd get about halfway down, me cigarette was always straggly with me face being wet.

The inquest into the death of Shirlee Veronica Dinch, aged 32, was not, as it turned out, referred to Mr Leonard Gorodkin, the Coroner for the city of Manchester. A holiday was in the offing for Mr Gorodkin: a holiday that was many months overdue.

For some considerable time Mr Gorodkin had entertained the idea of a sojourn at Treetops, the safari hotel in Kenya where Her Majesty Queen Elizabeth II had been a guest some twenty-one years before when, on the death of her father, King George VI,

Her Majesty Queen Elizabeth II had actually become Her Majesty Queen Elizabeth II. Enquiries were duly made with Pzazz Playaway, a local travel agent which specialised in once in a lifetime holidays for the outgoing, the adventurous, the extravagant, the flamboyant, the outrageous, the rumbustious, the hell-raiser, the chancer, the individualist, and the decidedly odd. In the event, though, Mr Gorodkin proved to be nothing more excessive than individualistic and socially-outgoing, and the rumpus stirred up by Idi Amin in Kampala, though it was a world away from Nairobi, decided him against the trip, and he flew out to Seattle and was gone for a month, sighting sperm whales and seals as far north as the Aleutian Islands and a narwhal and walrus off Nome. Accordingly, the inquest into the death of Shirlee Veronica Dinch was conducted by Mr Barry Etherow-Ashe, LLB, MPhil who had been 'borrowed on tick', as Mr Etherow-Ashe laughingly put it, from Truro, the county town of Cornwall.

Larry Gilderdale, Mr Etherow-Ashe was informed, was a married man of exemplary character and reputation, the father of two children, a boy and a girl, aged 15 years and 10 years, respectively. Aged 46, Larry Gilderdale (Laurence Kelton Gilderdale, which name Larry had answered to on being called to make his statement before the court) had worked as a bus driver in the employ of Selnec since it was set up in 1968. Prior to that, and for a further sixteen years, he had been employed as a bus driver with Manchester Corporation Transport Department. Moreover, Larry Gilderdale had never, previously to this, been involved in a traffic accident during the twenty-five years he had held a full driving licence – and for no fewer than twenty-one of those years Larry Gilderdale had driven a public service vehicle in the north Manchester area, working out of Queen's Road bus depot. Larry Gilderdale, it was said, was well liked by his colleagues and by his employers. His employment record was second to none, and as a member of the social committee at the White House Club, Middleton Road, Larry Gilderdale had played his part in raising more than £1500 for the burns unit at Booth Hall Children's Hospital.

The Court was told that when Larry began driving buses in the early 1950s he had driven a Crossley Type 7 8.4 litres double decker, and he had done so for upwards of five years. MCTD had been impressed with Larry's work record, so Larry was one of the first in its employ to be given the opportunity of driving, successively, the 9.8 litres Leyland Titan, that is, the PD/12 with the Metro Cammell body, the PD/40 with the Burlington bodywork, and its successor, the Leyland Titan PD/34. Then when the new Atlantean, which could carry 95 passengers (43 on the upper deck, 32 on the lower one plus 20 standing) was put into service in Selnec's distinctive Sunglow orange/Mancunian white livery, Larry Gilderdale was again amongst the first of its drivers to be invited to drive one of what MCTD now regarded as its flagship and, again, he did so out of Queen's Road bus depot.

It was a dream to drive, the Atlantean, Larry Gilderdale told the Coroner. Well, comparatively speaking, sir, that is. It had a kerbside weight of more than nine and a half tons, of course. So it was over a ton heavier than the Titan, but you had an extra three litres of power under the bonnet to compensate for that. Well, not the bonnet exactly, Larry explained, because the new Atlantean was rear engined. But the engine was 11.1 litres, so the power was certainly there.

So, Mr Gilderdale enjoyed driving the, ah, Atalantean Mancunian? Mr Etherow-Ashe sought clarification on this point.

Very much so, Larry Gilderdale assured him. The Atlantean was (that is, in Larry's opinion, it was) a vast improvement on the Titan. It had a semi-automatic gearbox, for one thing. So it was a lot smoother on the up-take and less tiring to drive too.

And what was the, ah, extent of Mr Gilderdale's working day, the Coroner wanted to know. To which Larry Gilderdale replied that he worked between eight and nine hours a day on a regular basis. Whereupon Mr Etherow-Ashe enquired as to whether Mr Gilderdale was in the habit of taking the normal rest-days and statutory holidays. Well, yes, he was indeed, Larry Gilderdale affirmed. Slow and steady wins the race, that had always been Larry's motto. Larry worked his normal shift, and was very reluctant to take any overtime on. There again, Larry hardly ever had any time off work, of course. (His employers were able to confirm this.) Larry said he could count on the fingers of one hand, sir, the number of days he had had off work in twice as many years. (Again, his employers were able to confirm this point, though only as far back as 1968.) He loved his job, said Larry, and it was his fervent wish that he might be allowed to continue in that job despite the tragic circumstances in which he now found himself, and which, he assured the Court through his solicitor, he did most sincerely regret from the bottom of his heart.

The Court adjourned for a short break at this point when Mr Etherow-Ashe said that 'as a visitor to this fair city from the sea coves of Kernow' he would need to avail himself of more detailed information on certain matters that had arisen in the course of Mr Gilderdale's testimony. Accordingly, representatives of Mr Gilderdale and of the Selnec transport authority were invited to join him in his chambers. And when the Court re-convened at eleven o'clock, Mr Etherow-Ashe reiterated something he had already made clear at the commencement of the proceedings, namely, that it was not the duty of the Coroner's Court to apportion blame for what had occurred, but rather to seek out the full facts of the matter. This was not to say, said Mr Etherow-Ashe, that other proceedings in other courts might not result from the findings of the Coroner's Court. But this was a matter for the Crown Prosecution Service, and was entirely dependent upon the nature of those findings. No, the duty of the Coroner's Court, declared Mr Etherow-Ashe, was to determine as precisely as possible exactly what had caused the sudden and tragic death of a young woman, Shirlee Veronica Dinch, a wife and mother in the prime of life.

Thereupon, Mr Etherow-Ashe turned to Laurence Gilderdale (reported on the Granada news as appearing 'pale and wan' at this juncture – Avril Hazelgarth, the lady presenter, a graduate of St Hilda's College, Oxford, having recently had a verse published in *Granta*), and he thanked him for the clear and forthright way in which he had addressed the Court so far. He now urged Mr Gilderdale to proceed with similar clarity and calm, so that the Court might do its duty in the interests of all concerned. So perhaps Mr Gilderdale would begin by telling the Court in his own words exactly what had happened on the afternoon of the day in question.

Larry Gilderdale had already spent three quarters of an hour giving evidence before the Court. He looked shaken, a little unsteady on his feet perhaps.

Mr Etherow-Ashe enquired if he would care to be provided with a chair.

Larry thanked him, but responded in the negative.

'You may proceed then,' Mr Etherow-Ashe told him. 'In your own words, and in your own time.'

Laurence Kelton Gilderdale drew a deep breath before proceeding, and exhaled slowly. He had been down for spreadover that Monday, he told the Court, whereupon the Coroner stopped him immediately and asked him to define that word or, indeed, words. What was 'spreadover' the Coroner wanted to know. Well, 'spreadover', Larry explained, was when a bus driver might have to do maybe four hours in the morning – the rush hour, schools and that – and the same sort of thing in the late afternoon. Like a split shift, it was. Yes, that's exactly what it was, Larry supposed. It was a split shift. And, in view of his normal work routine, the Coroner asked him, did Mr Gilderdale perhaps consider, ah, spreadover to be an, ah, imposition? Whereupon Larry Gilderdale begged the Coroner's pardon. Did Mr Gilderdale find, said Mr Etherow-Ashe, that spreadover was, ah, personally inconvenient, should he say? To be honest, he did, Larry admitted. Especially now they were operating these new one man buses where the driver had to take the fares as well as doing the driving. 'You done the rush hour in the morning and the rush hour in the afternoon, and even though you had the rest of the day off, you felt' – well, he certainly did, that is, Larry Gilderdale certainly did, 'that you couldn't properly relax. It was like – what was it like? – it was like being on stand-by. Yes, that's what it was like. It was like being on stand-by, only all day long.' This was just Larry's personal opinion, of course, as Larry was at pains to point out. Whereupon Mr Etherow-Ashe again asked Larry Gilderdale to tell the Court exactly what had happened on the day in question.

Well – Larry coughed twice to clear his throat and took a sip of water from the tumbler that lay ready to hand – Larry had been on spreadover that day, like he said. He'd been on the 63 route, driving an Antlantean. He'd driven it to Heywood town centre and back to Manchester a couple of times that afternoon, and he'd pulled into the bus station at the Manchester Arndale Centre at ten minutes past six in the evening and parked up at Stand J behind another Atlantean, the number 17. Immediately the passengers had alighted, Larry had closed the doors behind them and taken his wallet out of his breast pocket to try and sort it out a bit better, and – and he'd dropped it.

'You dropped your wallet, Mr Gilderdale?

'Yes, sir.'

'And where did it fall?'

'On the floor, sir.'

'On the floor of the bus?'

'Yes, sir, on the floor of the driver's cabin between the pedals.'

'The clutch pedal? The foot brake? The accelerator perhaps?'

'There's no clutch, your honour . . . sir.'

'Ah, yes, the Atlantean is semi-automatic. You select the gears by hand without use of a foot pedal?'

'That is correct, sir.'

'So, the wallet fell . . .?'

'Between the pedals, sir.'

'Mr Gilderdale?'

'Between the brake and the accelerator, sir.'

'And, ah, was the bus in gear when you dropped your, ah, wallet?' Mr Etherow-Ashe then asked.

'Yes.' Larry Gilderdale sighed rather than spoke the word. 'Yes, sir, it was.' Larry had been parked behind the number 17, and he'd been in second gear.

'You had not applied the, ah, hand brake, Mr Gilderdale?'

'No, sir. . . It was an oversight on my part.'

'Tell us, Mr Gilderdale,' said the Coroner – Mr Etherow-Ashe glanced towards the body of the Court as if to draw those present into his confidence –'would it perhaps be true to say that this was not in accordance with, ah, normal procedure? That is to say that the, ah, non-application of the handbrake whilst an omnibus is stationary with the ignition switched on is, ah, contrary to Selnec regulations?'

'Yes, sir.'

'Mr Gilderdale?'

'It is not in accordance with . . . It was an oversight on my part, sir. I was tired, I dunno, It was late in the day, I was distracted. I'd only had chance to apply the footbrake when . . . Well, I bent down to get the wallet, sort of instinctively. And . . . well, I must of taken the pressure off the footbrake because . . .'

'Mr Gilderdale?'

'Because the bus crept forward, sir. You get a sort of a forward creep with a semi-auto . . . I mean, she wasn't there one minute, and the next . . . *ha-a-ah*!' Larry Gilderdale paused to compose himself. 'It sort of nudged her, sir. The bus nudged her, it never hit her . . . It nudged her against the bus in front, sir . . . I seen her face. . . I was out like a shot when she fell . . . The other lads . . . *ha-a-ah*! There was nothing we could do, sir. There was nothing none of us could do . . .'

Dr Gayle Langdon, a Home Office pathologist, gave evidence to the effect that Shirlee Veronica Dinch had been dead on arrival at the hospital. There had been no mark of any kind on the body apart from a slight issue of blood adjacent to the left ear. (Mr Etherow-Ashe interrupted Dr Langdon's testimony at this point just long enough to allow relatives of the deceased to escort the husband to a rest area outside the courtroom.) Trauma to the chest was in evidence and the damage caused to the internal organs had been heavy. The stomach, liver, lungs, spleen . . . (Dr Langdon listed a series of internal organs.) Had Shirlee Veronica Dinch still been alive on arrival at the Manchester Royal Infirmary, where she was taken that day, she could not, in the opinion of Dr Gayle Langdon, have survived injuries such as those she had sustained in the accident.

The funeral arrangements for Shirlee Veronica Dinch were handled by a long established firm of undertakers, Fyans and Gordon at New Cross. The funeral service was held in her home parish of St Joseph of Cupertino, Fr Richard Bellis officiating. The interment took place at Blackley Cemetery in a plot that lies within sight of the Post Office tower in Heaton Park and behind which, in season, bloom magenta-flowered rhododendrons – a plot upon which, before the year was out, Mr Owen McGarry, a monumental mason with a business address on Moston Lane, was commissioned to erect a headstone of black granite bearing ten dozen letters in Art Nouveau script.

In the privacy of the fourth funeral car which she shared with Niamh, Naomi and Mrs Parbold, who lived next door but one to the Jamesons (Knut did not attend), Noreen Jessop was heard to observe that it was better weather than she'd seen at many a funeral she'd had to attend, Mrs Parbold. And Marjorie Bunratty, in the privacy of the third funeral car she shared with her husband Linus, the late Bill Bunratty's wife, Deirdre, her twenty-five year old brother-in-law, Cletus, and his fiance, Astrid Wembury (whose elder sister Pamela had recently appeared on the Lifebuoy soap advert on TV – the one in which Pamela had showered wearing lipstick, mascara, and a smile), Marjorie Bunratty said she'd heard Noreen Jessop would have had her husband Pat cremated when he died last June, Deirdre, except for the fact that Pat had been so well acquainted with a bottle of Bushmill's she'd been afraid he'd set the flue alight.

Then, upon being deposited simultaneously at the Galleon Restaurant on Kenyon Lane, Moston, for the funeral breakfast, Noreen Jessop told Marjorie Bunratty, *sotto voce*, that If that Tony Dinch showed any signs of shedding a tear (the hard-faced young divil), to please let her know, Marjorie, because in that eventuality she fully intended to contact Fr Frank Tetlow, the PP of St Dunstan's, across from the Ben Brierley, there, and get him to run up the Union Jack alongside the Irish Tricolour in celebration of that fact. Oh, and by the way, Marjorie, she hoped it wasn't gonna be chicken again like the last Jameson-Dinch do they'd been to. She was sure she'd never forget it. Oh-ho, Noreen could be as catty as she needed to be when occasion demanded it, Marjorie, but she'd never felt called upon to be quite as catty as that.

*

When industrial designers were invited to contribute to the design of the new British Leyland Atlantean omnibus, they are reported to have agreed that: 'A bus is a box, and an honest shape. Why disguise it with false peaks and domes?' The same could be said of a coffin, of course. And it would perhaps be reasonable to suppose that, had they known of this quotation, it might well have occurred to either Noreen or Marjorie to mention it. But the quotation in question was unknown to both women, and quite possibly because it never has been featured in the pages of *Woman's Realm*, *The Weekly News*, *Titbits*, *Living*, *True Confessions*, *TV Times*, *The Crusader*, or *Ireland's Own*.

22

One day he heard the phone. He
said: Yes, he was that Tony
to the voice of Penny Kirkham
where Shirlee used to work, and
he thanked her most profusely –
No, he couldn't do till Tuesday:
he had Suzanne to see to.
Sure, drop in when he's free to.
Don't pop it in the post, don't do:
He'd bring his sick note, that was due.

It took a month of Tuesdays before Dinchy even thought of visiting Rapishaw Gap to see Penny Kirkham. Meanwhile, his mother took it upon herself to post sick notes on his behalf.

23

Editor's Note

Only where they relate to the location of events in what is here recorded should the parts of speech be taken to possess the full weight of normal meaning. Elsewhere caution should be exercised, particularly where a connection with any one of the five senses is indicated. Thus, an apparently innocuous form of expression such as 'I see' is not to be taken on trust, nor should it be understood to suggest that it might have been possible to photograph what was 'seen' – still less to point it out to a companion. But on the other hand, neither should it be imagined that there is one word of a lie in anything I here relate. For what follows is exactly what Dinchy told me. That he was somewhat overwrought at the time is true – he had been so for some considerable time. But I pressed him on this point, and can confirm that he gave me his firm assurances that to the best of his knowledge and understanding he would try to be as objective as possible in everything he chose to relate.

In the weeks that followed Shirlee's death, Dinchy would get up on a Sunday morning, get himself and Suzanne ready, and make something of an outing out of going to Sunday Mass. He stopped going to his home parish of St Joseph's soon enough. There were too many memories for him there, and too many well-meaning words of condolence for far too long. More often than not, they'd walk up Lewis Avenue, the two of them, and along Worsley Avenue if the weather was fine, and end up at St Dunstan's near the Ben Brierley; or, when Suzanne got a bit older, continue along Moston Lane and across Broadhurst Fields to St John Vianney's on Poynter Street. After Mass, they might have a pub lunch together, or catch a bus into town and eat there. At one time Barnaby Rudge on Old Bank Street was a favourite of theirs, and The Mariner's Restaurant across the way from it. On some occasions they were very nearly in town anyway if they'd perhaps decided to catch a bus down Rochdale Road to St Malachy's, or to

St Patrick's, Collyhurst. Just occasionally though, Mount Carmel would be accessed via a short walk across Lewis Rec. But having walked across the Rec, they'd more often than not catch a bus going northwards. If the 60 came first they'd go to St Clare's, Higher Blackley (just the once), or to St Chad's, Cheetham (which they preferred). The 63 would take them to St Joseph's, Heywood; the 121 to St Mary's, Langley, the number 17 to St Peter's in Middleton. The 63 would have taken them to St Peter's too, but they would invariably let the 63 take them into Heywood where, after Mass – again if the weather was fine – they might catch another bus to Bamford and go down into Ashworth Valley to the Carr Wood Tearooms. It was at St Peter's, Middleton, that Dinchy saw Mr and Mrs Irlam.

It is the eleven o'clock Mass on a bright Sunday morning in May. St Peter's has a full congregation as usual, with Fr Cassidy officiating. Vincent Irlam, Dinchy's old teacher, recently retired deputy head of St Joseph of Cupertino's school, is one of two special ministers of the Eucharist going about their post-Communion duties on the sanctuary when Mrs Irlam appears at his side. Conchita seems to be in some distress. She follows Vincent Irlam off the altar and out into the body of the church and back to his place where he kneels by the twelfth station. Vincent Irlam seems unaware of his wife's agitation, or, indeed, of her presence. It is as if his thoughts are elsewhere – and, given the circumstances, this is perfectly understandable. For it is scarcely a fortnight since Dinchy's dad had telephoned him to say he'd seen Conchita Irlam's name listed under the Deaths in the *Manchester Evening News*: family flowers only, please; donations to Cafod preferred.

It was almost exactly a month to the day since he had heard from Penny Kirkham that he called in to see her at Rapishaw Gap. Dinchy entered the office through the Despatch Yard off Every Street as five notes of an air-horned *La Cucaracha* signaled Stetson Tex's V-signed greeting and imminent departure for Hawes in Wensleydale. Then, with the door of the office closing behind him, Dinchy fell back against it, wide-eyed at what awaited him within

This office where Shirlee had worked for sixteen years, Rapishaw Gap's Manchester office on Every Street, was simultaneously empty yet full. Nowhere was Penny Kirkham to be seen, and neither were any of the other works personnel – the office junior (Dinchy never could remember her name: Janine was it?), the lad from Despatch (Mitch) who fancied her and was forever getting under their feet (so Shirlee had told him) because he was forever inventing reasons to call in and see her. Neither was there any office furniture in the room – no desks or filing cabinets, no clock on the window wall which might truthfully have said (had there been a clock where usually there was a clock) one minute past two precisely. Gone too were the shredder, the brace of battleship grey waste paper baskets, the telephone (bright red in accordance with Penny Kirkham's association football affiliation), the safe bearing the Chubb trademark, and – from the wall nearest to where Shirlee's desk had once stood – the calendar from Withers and Pratt's with the colour photograph of the Free Trade Hall on Peter Street. All of this – the office furniture, the tools of the clerical trade, the temporal and locational impedimenta of this Ancoats-based business premises – every last bit of it had gone, or, had at least fallen back behind the touchline of this present visitor's narrowed field of vision and muddled consciousness.

And in their place – in place of these items, betwixt floor and ceiling, and spilling through into the staff room, the rest-room, the back office, the strongroom (the door of which stood ajar), all Dinchy could see were hatboxes – hatboxes that went on *ad infinitum*: hatbox after hatbox after hatbox filling to the full every inch of the available office floor space.

Some of the hatboxes were open, up-ended. Their lids tossed carelessly aside, their tissue paper wrappings were plainly visible within, their former contents being giddily disgorged to lie where they had fallen, creating a linear pathway across the room from where Dinchy remained standing, transfixed. But most of the hatboxes remained closed, their lids set firmly in place. These were the hatboxes which, stacked one upon the other towards the far wall, rose tier upon tier, row upon row to form the solitary elevation of a millinery ziggurat that climbed up and away from him towards the ornate oak-leaf and ivy patterned cornice crowning the length of the window wall of Rapishaw Gap's Manchester office on Every Street.

Suddenly, Penny Kirkham, opening the office door from the outside, nudged against him, and Dinchy, laughing uncertainly at his own clumsiness in standing so close to the door, stood to one side to let her come through with her sandwiches and a paper bag, corners twisted, that contained an eclair. Their hellos were quickly out of the way as Penny went behind the counter where she placed her packages on her desk.

The hatboxes, Dinchy noticed, were no longer in evidence. Everything had returned to normality – a normality that now encompassed a trio of beech wood office desks, three chairs to match, two banks of filing cabinets, and a Westclox clock on the window wall which gave the time as two minutes past two precisely. The wastepaper baskets, the shredder, the calendar from Withers and Pratt's, the safe, the red telephone handset (which now began to ring) – all these things conspired together to pretend they had never left the room.

Penny Kirkham took a sealed A5 manila envelope from her desk drawer and, coming back to the counter with it, set it down in front of him on the counter top as she turned to answer the phone.

'I'm so glad you could come,' she said at last. 'I was beginning to think . . .' Penny Kirkham did not enlarge upon what she had been beginning to think. Instead, she indicated the nearest bank of filing cabinets, then the envelope which Dinchy now held, unopened, in his hands. 'It turned up in Shirlee's section during stocktaking. And with it having your name on it . . . 'Again Penny left her thoughts unspoken. 'Why ever would she file it under 'E'? Misfiled, I suppose. Still, it's not . . . I mean, I can't say it was like Shirlee to misfile things.'

Short of opening the envelope on the spot, Dinchy was unable to enlighten her. And since he was still somewhat bemused at the thought of a road transport office overrun with hatboxes, it didn't occur to him to open the envelope just then. He muttered a thank you, repeated himself, and asked Penny how she was doing, without registering a single word of her volubly cheerful reply. Finally, alluding briefly, boringly, and predictably (rain was suddenly stair-rodding the office windows) to the weather, ever a convenient conversational stand-by in the Greater Manchester conurbation, Dinchy took his leave of Penny Kirkham, and of Rapishaw Gap too. The relevance of the letter 'E' would remain unclear to him until later that day. And, even then, he would have been unable to speak with any degree certainty, though he would at least have been prepared to hazard a guess.

He knew exactly *what* it was as soon he opened the envelope, though at first he imagined the 'E' stood for 'emerald'. Because the envelope contained that verse, so long disremembered, which Dinchy had once upon a time prevailed upon a friend of his to write for him.

'Yeah, I know I can buy her somethin',' Dinchy had told his friend that day. (This was shortly before they stood the markets together.) 'Hey, and I will do too. Wristwatch maybe, somethin' of the sort. But with it bein', well, with the ring bein', like, a freebie. It was me Grandma Alma's ring, see. Well, it feels like cheatin', if you know what I mean. I mean, Shirlee seen it before I even had it cleaned up for her. So I'd like her to have a bit of a surprise to sort of make up for it. I mean, I'll get her a wristwatch or a bracelet or somethin'. Depends what she wants. But, wi' this . . . Well, wi' this she'll have somethin' she'd never even of dreampt of havin'. Okay, *okay*, I know it's daft, but it's only a word or two, innit? Roses are red, sort of thing.'

'That's all you want, whyn't you do it yourself?'

'Because I can't.'

'And I can?'

'Yeah. Well, better than me anyway.'

'What? Me write it for Shirlee, you mean?'

'No, for me. I mean, write it for me for Shirlee. Like wotsit.'

'Wotsit?'

'Him wi' the big conk.'

'Par-ding?'

'Fingy,' said Dinchy, a bit muffled with his mouth being full of cheesburger.

'Thingy?'

'Him who done a bit o' writin', Nose you could put on a sandwich.'

'*Cyrano de Bergerac*?'

'One potato more than a pig, you.' Dinchy wound the passenger door window down PDQ. 'Think I'd rather have you hungry than replete, pal. But no, you have to order the king-size. Shirlee reckons it's all them onions they give you. '

When Suzanne was safely tucked up in bed for the night, when the pterodactyls and the Dirty Yellows had all been banished and the landing light left on, Dinchy went downstairs again and got the envelope from the letter-rack on the sideboard. Then, the afternoon and early evening having been taken up in supervising Suzanne's comings and goings – from school, to the doctor's after school, to the chemist's for a cough mixture subsequent to that – he took the sheet of paper out of the envelope for the first time since Penny Kirkham had given it to him that afternoon

Dinchy sat down in his favourite armchair with its back to the window wall under Shirlee's gaze, as it were. To his right, the Shirlee Dinchy loved in the photograph that showed her outside Kendals department store off Deansgate – the photograph which Shirlee herself had never liked very much at all; whilst to his left (similarly framed in one and a half inch Ital by Clive Bradley of Manor Arts, Middleton) was the Shirlee Dinchy himself had never liked very much at all – or, to be more precise, a girl who looked very much like the Shirlee Dinchy had never liked very much at all: that is, the young girl with the hoop and stick in the right foreground of the print of *Les Parapluies* from the painting by Pierre August Renoir, which Dinchy had come across in the second week of his bereavement on a stall facing Trisian's Cafe on Harpurhey Flea Market.

Then Dinchy began to read, mouthing the words to himself as he read them:

If in the mirror of my eyes
Your image cease to glister –
If never more I breathe or sigh,
Nor words of love may whisper;
If bones, all sinew, nerves, lie still,
I'll speak clear from your finger –
I loved you, love you now, and will
This proof with you to linger.'

He was reading from memory before he'd finished, because Dinchy was feeling sorry for himself all of a sudden, as indeed, Dinchy felt sorry for himself pretty much all of the time these days. He laid the paper down on the coffee table, sat back and wiped his eyes. But if anything, the action of wiping them seemed to make his eyes wetter. Dinchy wiped his eyes again. His eyes felt wetter still.

There was a box of Kleenex in the top drawer of the sideboard but, when Dinchy got up and went across to get one, he caught sight of his reflection in the big gilt bevel-edged mirror on the wall above the sideboard and saw – his eyes were *bleeding*.

He did a quick double take, leaning in towards the mirror, checking his eyes in panic. No. No, of course, his eyes weren't bleeding. There was blood *on* them though. The right eye in particular. Yes, it certainly looked like it was bleeding. And it was at this point Dinchy realised it was his hand that was bleeding, his right hand – the hand (more precisely, the right index finger) with which he had sought to wipe away his tears.

He went through to the kitchen and got himself cleaned up at the sink. It was the tiniest of cuts about a third of the way down his right index finger. How on earth had that happened, he wondered. He backtracked in his mind as he washed and dried it, applying an Elastoplast to the infinitesimal wound.

Then, un-bloodied, cleaned up, dried off, Dinchy returned to his favourite chair by the window wall. He now made as if to hold the sheet of paper that contained the verse in exactly the same way he had previously held it. This was what he'd been doing. Right? Holding it like this – right? Okay, maybe a bit more firmly. Like this, yeah?

And Dinchy noticed something now, something which, in his hurry to re-read the verse, he had previously missed completely. To the side of the verse, top right, there was an item attached to the paper which, Dinchy knew, had not been attached to the paper when he had first gifted it to Shirlee along with the ring. What was attached to the paper, he now saw, was a brass stationery clip. In holding the paper perhaps too tightly, he had somehow contrived to cut himself on its prongs. Yes, there was blood on the paper, there – see!

Ha-a-ah!

And even before he checked to see he knew what he would find.

It's a childish trick to cross the prongs on a brass stationery clip. For to do so is to profess to believe that a brass stationery clip may thereby be transformed into a love pin as if by magic. Anyone above school age will tell you that – anyone that's daft enough, that is. But not just anyone could tell you that Shirlee Dinch (*née* Jameson) had crossed the prongs on this particular brass stationary clip – the brass stationary clip that came as an extra on the sheet of paper with Dinchy's verse on it. Of course not. That would take someone who's daft enough to be a looney tune. And anyone who's daft enough to be a looney tune may be daft enough to tell you too that 'E' is not necessarily for 'emerald'. Maybe what it stands for is 'eternal', 'evermore' and 'everlasting'. 'Ever-loving' too.

24

'I think I've been a bit unfair to you over the years, Tony,' said a lady who looked like Shirlee's mum, though she was very much older than Shirlee's mum had ever been and looked as if she'd been crying. 'You loved her very much, didn't you?'

'No!' he said, then shouted it: 'NO!'

The lady fell back as if she'd been stabbed.

'I never loved her enough,' he said.

He had to stop himself then because someone was laughing like a looney tune.

'I love her now though,' said the looney tune. 'I love her like there's no tomorrow.'

There was always tomorrow, of course, though very often it came before today, and just occasionally too, it wouldn't come for a year or so, but when it did, it could last all week and be twice as black as night. Our Suzanne was part of tomorrow, and a Cannon gas cooker, and inoculations, and new carpets from Carpetworld, and appointments with the dentist to be made, and nursery school, and Suzanne's bath at half-past seven every night. There was an infant school tomorrow, where every one of them teachers known exactly what was right for our Suzanne and an unmarried single parent like me. There was a Matsui microwave and a Hoover vacuum cleaner and housework tomorrow – and once a year at Easter a fun fair in Boggart Hole Clough where I kept tight hold of our Suzanne's hand, you just bet. There was shopping to do at ASDA's of a Saturday and the grotto at Lewis's at Christmas, and one tomorrow took us to Blackpool to see the illuminations, while another one brung us back from Rhodes Wood with oak leaves and acorns and conkers and helicopter-things off a sycamore tree for the nature table in Mrs Wytham's class in Junior Two. Our Suzanne cut her leg one tomorrow and we had to go to Booth Hall Hospital for a stitch. Another tomorrow saw Rapishaw Gap and me part company, because no one wants a zombie at the wheel. And for a time then all the tomorrows rolled into today and all the todays fell back into last week, and one day I slept for a year.

Tomorrow I got a job at the Post Office, delivering yesterday's post today. Our Suzanne went to high school on a Tuesday, left on a Wednesday, started work on a Thursday, met Ian on a Friday, moved in with him on a Saturday, and had their little Stephanie on a Sunday. She had *our* little Stephanie, I mean. I'll be seeing the girls tomorrow. *Our* girls, I mean to say, that is.

PART TWO

That which has been is now; and that which
is to be has already been.

Ecc. 3:15

Not long to go now, the Millennium behind us and counting — *Hah*! the Millennium plus one or two, depending how you look at things.

The good news is, of course, I won't get out of this one alive. The century, I mean, never mind the Millennium. The year if I'm lucky. *Hah*! And the bad news – well, the bad news is I'm not out of it yet.

I'm okay, I suppose, though I fly on a wing and a prayer. Because all that keeps us alive nowadays is an item you'll find in any cottage garden in the country – the humble foxglove, no less. Digitalis, as it's otherwise known (Byron), or, in its tablet form, Digoxin (Dr Stanegate). Yep, 250 mcg of Digoxin per day (as prescribed by Dr Stanegate three hundred thousand million billion years in the past, Dr Dryburn being long retired to his native County Durham, puts the fluence on Dinchy's irregular heartbeat – that is to say, on Dinchy's atrial fibrillation (Dr Stanegate wrote it down for us).

'Oh, dearie, dearie me,' I hear you mutter. 'How ever did poor old Dinchy cop for a complaint like this un?'

Well, poor old Dinchy, as you is unkind enough to call him, copped for said complaint not long after Shirlee died when he took up residence in his very own Crackpot Hall (there being a very real Crackpot Hall in Swaledale: see Alfred Wainwright's *Coast to Coast Walk*, pub. Frances Lincoln). So somebody or other (Dr Dryburn, Dr Haylands, Dr Hardraw, Dr Ure – I was seeing a lot of quacks in them days – anyway, someone with an MD after his name prescribed Pro . . . well, anyway, Summat-You-Can't-Say-Too-Easily to calm poor old Dinchy's nerves, what with poor old Dinchy being so clearly out of his tree.

'There aren't any,' Dr Dryburn, Haylands, Hardraw, or Ure told him when poor old Dinchy asked about the possible side effects. But side effects, there is, see: witness poor old Dinchy with a dodgy ticker that he's had for years now. See, whatever it was he give us calmed us down a treat, but 'would seem to have triggered' – Dr Stanegate, this – 'this atrial fibrillation'. So poor old Dinchy, Dr Stanegate also said: 'Must of been damaged goods in the ticker department to begin with' (Broken hearted! *H-ah*!)

'otherwise Wotchermakrite-on-Stilts would not never have give old Dinchy said wonky ticker.'

So, that's all right then!

'Now, whatever you do, Mr Dinch,' Dr Stanegate also told poor old Dinchy, 'never ever double up on the doseage' – Digoxin, this – 'because Digoxin has a long half-life, and too big a dosage could really balls it up for yer.'

Or summat.

So, *there's* some more good news: Digoxin could actually *stop* poor old Dinchy's ticker ticking altogether, always providing he bungs enough of it down his neck. Not that poor old Dinchy would ever do a thing like that. Well, not on purpose anyroad. Because there's our Suzanne to think about, and our little Stephanie too.

Oh, what a blinder of a smile! Poor old Dinchy should look so cute without his top set in. Good lad, too, Ian. Only wish I could say he was her husband (Suzanne's) because she'd go a long way to find a better one. Still, that's the way they is these days, though why they is that way, I couldn't even begin to say.

They're going out to see Huge at Easter, the three of them. Gran Canaria or somewhere. I dunno. Somewhere in the Cannery Islands anyway. He's lived out there for years, Huge. He had this bar out there at one time; rents it out now, keeps hisself busy with other stuff – little bit of this, little bit of that (like the Birdy Song. *H-ah*!). Oh, he's often said for us to come out and visit, like. But it's not for me. No, home is where the heart is. And this old heart of mine (Isley Brothers. *Ha-ah*!), irregular though it be in the heartbeat department ('Heartbeat': Buddy Holly with Tommy Allsup on lead guitar. *Ha-a-ah*!), well, this old heart of mine belongs right here where it's always belonged, going to a very particular spot that's close at hand whenever Digoxin decides it's high time it give up the ghost on poor old Dinchy at long last.

Hey, and don't get us wrong now. I'm a lot better off than some I could mention. I do all right, me. Watch a bit of TV of a night. I was into *The Bill* at one time when Frank Burnside was in it, but not any more. Nah! And not because I don't have a telly neither. No, I've got this whopping big 32-inch Sanyo widescreen from Argos: nice to watch and, like I said to Joyce next door but one, if

I get burglars breaking in like they did all the way down Goodman Street and Cobden Street that time, well, they're welcome to help theirselves to that 32-inch Sanyo of mine because (*Ha-a-a-ah*!) they can help theirselves to a double hernia while they're about it too! No, what it is with *The Bill* is – well, if *The Bill* that's on TV nowadays is what the police are like, I think I'd rather be burgled.

I still get to call in the pub most nights too – Alliance, Farmyard, Grove, Bluebell, Thatched maybe. So that's something else to be thankful for. Because a lot of folk – well, older ones anyway, they can't get out no more. Leastways not of a night. But I'll usually have Derek to walk back with from the Thatched or the Bluebell – Derek Keld, Joyce's husband, works down the sorting office, bottom of Oldham Road. Hey, and sometimes when I'm in the pub, there, some nosey parker (Clem Hardiker maybe; Derek when he's got 'em on him, because he's had two bites of the cherry, has Derek), some nosey parker'll maybe ask, though not as much as they done when our Suzanne was still at home:

'You not get wed again, Dinchy?'

'Nah, once bitten!' I tell 'em. And, as God is my judge, these are the only three words I have ever spoke on the subject. And very useful words I've always found them too. Because they don't say what I was bitten with.

Still am! *H-ah*!

I never go hungry, though I do have a thirst. I am never ever cold. I am tidily, though not trendily, dressed. I look after meself without spoiling meself. I keep body and soul together, the wolf from the door, me own counsel, meself to meself, mum – and I don't vote. What for? *This* lot? Tell you, I don't even bother turning out to spoil me ballot paper like Byron says I really ought to make a point of doing if I feel as bad as that about 'em.

Tossers!

You know our house, don't you? Well, my house, as it is now – end terraced, across the Rec from where me Grandma Alma used to live. I mean, Lewis Rec's still there if I fancy a stroll, of course, though the tennis shelters are long gone; though birch saplings grow thick and fast where there used to be two putting greens for the use of, though just one of the two bowling greens is still in good nick (because it's padlocked). Not that I wanna play bowls, not that I hanker after a game of putting – not that I could play a game of tennis to save me flipping life, I don't suppose. But what I do bewail (and often, when I get me soapbox out in the pub at night) is the way this piss poor quality of life has been foisted on us all. I mean, the IRA blown Corporation Street apart so Manchester city centre gets a three hundred thousand million billion pound face-lift, thank you very much. But Boggart Hole Clough hasn't got a clinker-built rowing boat to its name no more, though it had a full fleet of them and skiffs and a working motor boat too when me dad was working for four quid a week, and Frank Swift could earn a tenner a week in Man City's goalmouth – and (ooh!) could pick up a extra couple of quid for hisself (you lucky boy, Frank) if City won. Which City did do sometimes in them days, so you can tell I'm talking history.

And I still walk through Boggart Hole Clough too when the weather's fine – over the Rec from our house, down to the brook, up past the shop that got fired, and as far as the bashed angel on the hill. Then I'll check to see (in vain so far) if the angel on the hill still looks out over a bandstand in the valley like she done when I was a kid, or if it's just a cinder track she sees below her with Manchester poplar trees and a church tower rising above them, reaching skywards towards the far south-west.

The poxy powers-that-be couldn't change this woodland scene without a logging team to help them, though I wouldn't put it past them to try. But so far at least, in our internetted, whiz-bang, get knotted Manpudlian new Millennium, the angel on the hill (bashed though she be) still stands guard over – well, Nutwood's what I like to think of it as, where Rupert Bear may still be found, and women and children and old uns walk safe and secure even at dead of night.

Stoopid, eh?

Well, maybe it is. But it's a free country, and in a free country anything's possible, and I'm entitled to dream.

Hey, and here's another fairy tale while I'm about it too: I read a bit nowadays, me. You believe that, do you? Old Dinchy read? Well, yeah, old Dinchy does read, as a matter of fact. Not a lot, mind. But of a Sunday I'll maybe go down to Waterstone's in town – though, if truth be told, I'll do it as much to have some excuse for walking through Parsonage Gardens at the back of Kendals and maybe sit there with me memories for the space of a cigarette or two. But I'll usually pick something up from Waterstone's while I'm about it too.

Whatever it is has to have a good few pictures in it to suit us, of course. (Like Wainwright's *Coast to Coast* book that I mentioned.) Also, the books I go for are non-fiction in the main. I mean, they *are* non-fiction, is what I mean – non-fiction pure and simple. Like, local history's a favourite of mine, or anything to do with the county (by which I mean Lancs), or the North. For instance, last time out I bought another of Wainwright's books about the Pennine Way, big coffee table thing that's got piles of colour photos by Derry Brabbs in it. An absolute gem, it is. And I think I got *The Moston Story* from Waterstone's too. Or was that Menzies? I mean, W.H. Smith's. I dunno. Anyway, it's this book about north Manchester by Fr Brian Seale, the parish priest at St John Vianney's where I go to Mass of a Sunday, walking there and back like I used to do when our Suzanne was still at home. (You'd think a postman would have had enough of walking during the week, wouldn't you? Still, it all depends on what the weather's doing.)

This other book I bought is about Manchester as it used to be. *The Jackie Brown Story*, I call it, though it isn't the same *Jackie Brown* they made a film of that was a book called *Rum Punch* (Byron) that was set in Miami before they moved it to Los Angeles for the film version. No, this *Jackie Brown Story* I'm on about was wrote by a bloke called Brian Hughes, trains local boxers. *Jackie Brown – the Man, the Myth, the Legend* is what it's really called. And it's the story of a Manchester boxer of that name (Jackie Brown, that is) – world champion boxer, no less! – what lived in Collyhurst years ago, and I used to deliver his *Evening Chron* on me paper round when Jackie Brown was retired and living on Tudor Avenue (now Blackley Park Road) near Lewis Rec.

'Oh, there never was such a brawny, battlin', bustlin', livin'-

and-breathin', boisterous book about Manchester in the 1920s and '30s!'

'Whoa, Dinchy!' Byron tells us, hearing me going on like this. 'You never read *Fame Is The Spur*, *Magnolia Street – Our Kid et al?*'

WHAM-OH! This rocket takes off over Oxford Road Station like a maroon out at sea.

'Ate *Al*?' I said. 'Sounds like *An American Werewolf in London*.'

I'd give Byron the *Jackie Brown* book for his Christmas present. (Me buy Byron a book!) Mind you, he'd had to wait till I seen him at his New Year's Eve do.)

WHOO-OO-OO-OOM-STR-R-R-I-I-I-I-I-ITS! Roman candles arcing – red, orange, yellow, green, blue, and two shades of purple – over the Ritz. Every colour of the plectrum!

'*High Hopes*, *Going Places*."

'Hm, sequels, I suppose, knowing you.'

'As a matter of fact they are.'

'Told yer.'

'Piss off, clever 'ole!' says Byron, too pissed to say owt else; too wary to get into that same old argument as Amanda comes back with a tray of goodies.

BLAMM-M-M! Again: BLAMM-M-M-M! No light in the sky – an explosion followed by another, followed by a bit of cheering in the street below.

Amanda the Clubbable, as Byron nowadays tells me she is (thought he was talking about wife-beating at first), Amanda brings us coffee and mints. Byron plays mum – decaff for him ('hygienic mud', says he), Joe Lyons for Amanda and me.

BLOO-OO-OO-OOM-SH-SH-SH! An almighty racket, three repeats, sparks like the light of day.

'Odd, don'tcha think?' Byron picks up an After Eight mint, holds it an inch from his gob. 'Your life, Dinchy – t'would appear to be regulated by two Brians: one spiritual; the other physical.'

'I wouldn't say that, Byron.'

'Let's have it right, man. You *couldn't* say that.'

HA, HA, HA, HA, HA. Someone down on the street thinks

something somewhere is very funny indeed. HA, HA, HA, HA, HA.

Hah! Me and Byron are laughing at the laughter itself before it's finished. Then three hundred thousand million billion people are laughing and cheering like they're all in on the joke. What joke?

ACKER-YACKER-ACKER-YACKER-S-S-KIRR-R-R-R-R-R-R-R-R! Noise – noise without light.

'Nah. Local history's the connection. I think I'm a bit like you, Byron. Wanna know where I've come from. Don't never wanna forget it. Because I know where I'm goin'. An' if I know where I've come from, I can always check to see I'm still on the right track. Guard against being led astray by any Tom, Dick, Adolf, Margaret or Tony.'

'I take it you mean the Phoney One – Tony "I'm-All-Right-Jack-Sod-the-Students" PM?'

'Well, I don't mean *mwa mem*, pal. That's for sure!'

'Well, okay, fine. But tell me, Dinchy – where *are* you going exactly?'

'Downhill, on pack ice, PDQ.'

FLASH-SH-SH-SH-SH-SH! Lightning strike without thunder.

'I mean, you with us with New Century-New Start?'

I told him I'd give it a coat of looking at. That's all.

See, Byron had been prattling on all night about this New Century-New Start stuff, and I was tired. It was eighteen minutes past three by this time, and there was just the three of us left. But earlier on when the party was in full swing (they was mostly business bods that Byron known), Byron had been pushing these crazy ideas of his. Well, not Byron's personal crazy ideas, of course, and for all I know maybe they wasn't so crazy after all. But it was the same sort of stuff about the UK and Third World debt that I'd first had me lugholes chewed about by Fr Human in St Joseph of Cupertino's church thirty-odd years before.

Item One (according to New Century-New Start): every wage earner in the UK should take an unemployed school leaver under his wing at work for a full twelve months.

Item Two: every wage earner in the UK should covenant 0.7% of his income to the Third World so as to shame the government into doing what the UK should have been doing since 1970, but never has as yet.

'Hey, that's not just me talking. That's UN Resolution 2626, according to which the developed nations of the world promised . . .'

'Oh, *cat* it out,' says Amanda, sharply. She stifles a yawn, wraps her dressing-gown tight around her and gets up from the settee. Thought she was maybe gonna check.

'You allowed to have pets?' I asked Byron.

'Par-ding?'

'Can you keep pets in here?'

'What?'

'In the apartment?'

'Pets? Keep what the hell I want, man. Boa constrictor, anteater, kin AJS Porcupine, if I've a mind to. I own the ruddy place. Why?'

'Oh, just wondered.' There was no sign of a cat from what I could see.

DER-DER-*DER*-DER-*DER*-DER! A police car and an ambulance join in the New Year celebrations, blue and orange strobe lights running the length of the Palace Theatre from Oxford Street to Oxford Road towards the MRI.

Amanda crosses to the windows overlooking Whitworth Street and pulls a drawstring, closing the blinds. She comes back across the room, very graceful in this ankle length silk kimono dressing-gown that Byron brung back from a business trip to Hiroshima. (Don't ask us what Byron's business is. What Byron does is he sells what he hasn't got yet – summat I will never be able to get me head round if I live to be an hundred.) Amanda pauses for a second at an occasional table and flicks a button on a remote control handset before plonking herself back down on the settee as muzak begins to trickle down all four walls to the floor.

'Time to go, said Dougal,' said Dinchy. Nice food, plenny of it; plenny to drink too. Even so, time to go. 'Been meanin' to say,' I stood up, none too steadily, asked Amanda for me coat. 'Suzanne bought us your house for Christmas.'

'Eh?

'*Oxford Road* by Adolphe Valette. Shows the Refuge buildin' goin' up.'

'Whoa! Think she'd sort one out for me? Pay her, of course.'

I felt sure she would. 'Framed up?' I asked him.

'Whatever. Why? What've you got? The two-inch Ital?'

'Is the Pope Catholic?' I asked him. 'Does a bear do pooh-poohs?'

I took me coat from Amanda when she fetches it through, really tired all of a sudden, and swinging it round to shove me right arm through the sleeve I got that pain I'd been getting on and off all week that I'd been bunging Andrews Liver Salts, Milk of Magnesia, and Beecham's Pills down me neck by the ton, trying to get it to shift.

Hah! Dead sharp now. Then sharper. '*Ha-a-a-ah*!'

'You okay?' Byron this.

'Bit of indigestion. You got any mints?'

He found us a packet of Polo.

'No, keep them. Give you a bell through the week, okay?

I'd twice refused his offer to call us a cab. 'Cabs galore in town. Be home in twenny minutes.'

Did I heck get a cab: walked it. If you're used to walking all day long, what harm's another walk? Went across town at a fair lick: Portland Street, Piccadilly, Shudehill, past Thompson Street, and straight up Rochdale Road. I'd walked as far as Eggington Street before I got mugged.

Two of them, come out of nowhere. Well, come out of where I wasn't looking anyway. Big Un pushes us, stiff arm. It's only the NCL junction box outside St Oswald's that stops us going down, which is when me Uncle Joe gets in on the act:

St Patrick was an Oirishman and so were all his people,
He built a church on Livesey Street, a church without a steeple.
St Oswald was an Englishman, his church it had a clock,
He built a church on Rochdale Road, a church without a flock.

Gee, thanks for that, Uncle Joe! More's the pity the thought won't stand us in good stead in a street fight. Because Little Legs comes at us then with Big Un urging him on. Me Uncle Joe was choc full of suggestions:

Oh, me Uncle Mick, he had a big stick
To belt 'em where he didn't ought t'.
He'd belt 'em, then,
He'd belt 'em once again
If they wouldn't give a dollar for a quarter.

No stick had I, but what I did have was cash in hand. Because I reached in me trouser pocket, grabbed a pocketful of shrapnel in me right fist, and when Little Legs run in at us, smashed him right in the kite. Correction – soggy kite. Me fist was wet with blood, his blood. I think his top set had gone. Poor little sod, talk about seven stone weaklings! He was no bigger than a thr'upenny rabbit. Like a rat-fink stood up on its hind legs, moaning away now – burbling blood too.

'*Ha-a-a-a-ah*!'

Kin heartburn. Don't go down, Dinchy! Don't go down!

'Want some more, do yer?' Hey, I'm doing the asking now, like I'm just dying to dish it out. Bluster, sheer bluster. Bluster that worked though. Because Little Legs turns and runs. My mistake was to . . .

'*Ha-a-a-a-ah*!'

My mistake was to watch him. Because Big Un hasn't gone, Big Un that picks up a brick and hits us with it.

BUL-LUNG!

'*If a brick and a half weighs a pound and a half* . . .'

And I've got news for Unzo, if we ever meet in hell: a brick and a half weighs a ton and a half. Because the brick Big Un hit us with was a ton weight. Felt like a chimney pot had fell on us from a dizzy height. I never went down, mind. But the back of me head was just killing us when this screech of brakes seen Big Un off. I have never in all my life been so pleased to see a private hire cab touting for a fare.

'Is everything okey-dokey, my friend?' The driver's leant across the passenger seat, calling through the open passenger window of a white Nissan Primera saloon car, hazards blinking, that says MAHOUT MINICABS in orange letters down the side. The driver's a brother to Raj, who'd helped us out in the hills three hundred thousand million billion years in the past.

'Yeah. Yeah, think so, mate.' Walking towards him now, feeling the back of me head where there's blood running free. Take me hanky to it: drenched; fold it double. Take me shirt off, hold that to it.

'It may or may not be anything,' says Krishna, his taxi badge so informing us. 'But if you are wanting a doctor to take a Gandhi at it, I can be running you down to Crumpsall A&E in two shakes of a lamb's tail, innit?'

'Nah, take us home, mate. Just take us home.'

'Strictly speaking,' says Krishna, me tumbling in beside him now, 'this is something I really ought not to be doing unless pre-booked. But I cannot see Lord High Chancellor keelhauling me over the coals in present circumstance.'

No, it was me who threw a wobbler: when Krishna stiffs us for clock and half on Lewis Avenue. Hey, and let's have it right: it *was* New Year's Day, and it *was* five o' clock in the morning with no buses running – and I *was* very very glad of the lift home. And another thing: it was worth clock and half just to hear, courtesy of Watchtower Radio on Krishna's in-car stereo, David McWilliams' 'Days of Pearly Spencer'. In fact, it was hearing 'Pearly Spencer' that put us in the mood for what I done next, soon's I got in and got meself cleaned up and stopped the bleeding and got meself a whisky (bottle of) and got the Beecham's Powders out of the bathroom cabinet because I felt like I had a real stinker of a cold coming on us now.

You know, once upon a time when I was a kid at school, all I had to play me records on was this Dansette portable me Grandma Alma bought us one Christmas, and then this Philco that I bought off Huge when he moved down to Torbay.

Not nowadays though.

No, nowadays I've got this Aiwa Z-R700 Digital Audio System with Dolby and Super T-Bass that I picked up at Curry's – as is only right, I might add, for my collection of 3,000-plus 7-inch vinyl singles I've amassed over the years, plus 200 LP's going back to the Year Dot. (No, please do not mither poor old Dinchy just now! Go and ask your grumpy old grandad what an LP is when it's owt!) And though it's true that the Stereo Full Automatic Turntable System (PX-E 850) that goes with me Aiwa Z-R700 Digital Audio System is an absolute treat, well, awkward old curmudgeon that poor old Dinchy is, he only went and got his old Philco portable out of the loft, give it a bit of a dust down with a J Cloth and took it through into the living-room where he switched it on, leaving the arm right back so anything poor old Dinchy wanted to listen to a second time he could listen to a second time by just waiting for the gubbins to do its own reprise.

This is not to say I prefer the old Philco to the Aiwa. But there is some records I prefer to listen to in mono because that's exactly how I heard them the very first time they give us the old goosepimples or made the hairs on the back of me neck stand up. Like, The Bea . . .'

'*Ha-a-a-a-ah*!'

Like, The Beatles, for instance. Yeah, for my money, mono is the only way to listen to the Beatles. Yep, that's how I come in; and it's how I intend to go out too.

'When I snuff it,' I said to our Suzanne one time I was feeling a bit low (night they took Joe Bunratty into St Joseph of Cupertino's church before the funeral and left him there overnight), 'when my time comes, Suzanne, don't leave us in church overnight. Stick us in our front room here with me Beatles' records on.'

'Sure, pops,' says Miss Teenage Dirtbag Suzanne May Dinch. 'You can have your headphones on too.'

So, there I am this morning, and very early in the morning it is too. Half past five in the morning on New Year's Day. And I'm in the living-room, right? And the Beatles is on the turntable of the old Philco; and a good few other records is on the turntable from time to time too: I'm sort of trawling through the alphabet, like . . . Chuck Berry, 'Talkin' 'bout You' – play it, reprise . . . Buddy Holly, 'Reminiscing' – play it, whiz it . . . Percy Sledge, 'Warm and Tender Love' – play it, wing it . . . Edwin Starr, '25 Miles' – play it, reprise . . .

Now, look here. I wouldn't mind going out on a bit of a high note here, the night it's been. I mean, see this water I've got here . . .

'*Ha-a-a-a-ah*!'

Yeah, this water – this ASDA's Sparkling Fountain Head Spring Water, no less? 18p for a two litre bottle, and very nice it is too when combined with Tesco's cheap Scotch at less than seven quid a bottle, though there's no need for that tha neet, seeing I've got this pint bottle of Bell's our Suzanne bought us for Christmas. Well, a pint as was, that is; an half pint now, more like. Yup, half a pint! Well, this *hic* water I've got here, this Sparkling Fountain Head Spring Water from *hic* ASDA's, Harpurhey, that I'm now using very *hic* sparingly indeed. Well, how's about we give this Sparkling Fountain Head Spring Water a *hic* mention in my beloved Blackley-ese?

Yeah, this water. Why not?

What I mean to say is this, see. How's about we give this *hic* here *van de payee* – this *hic* water – the Queen's Manpudlian English treatment, that is to say *hic*: 'Wa'er' – 'water' without the tee. Because 'water' without the tee (that is, 'wa'er') happens to be a very old north Manchester custom, and is something – nay, *summat* – that me mam would not never let us say when I was a kid and she was learning us to talk proper. Not that it ever worried me Grandma Alma.

'Oh, we don't need the tee in water, do we, chuck? Because the tea's already in't pot.'

So, to say 'wa'er' just this *hic* once would upset me Grandma Alma not one bit, and besides, would be a *hic* great freedom for us – like Mel Gibson shouting: 'Freedom!' at the end of *Braveheart*, say. Anyroad, here goes me little bit of Manpudlian freedom for what it's worth.

'Wa'er!'

Nah!

WA'ER! See? Like this: WA'ER! WA-A'ER! Purra bitter life into it!

'WA-A-A'ER!' See? Now, come on!

'WA-A-A-A'ER!'

Hey, that's not bad. No, that's not bad at all. I think we're getting somewhere. And, look, if it's any help at all, I do not rule out the possibility of Moston joining in with us here, or Collyhurst, or Newton Heath, or Clayton even. Yeah, you're all welcome, I'm sure. Because it's . . .

Ha-a-a-a-ah!

Because it's open house at our house tha neet though, sadly, there's no strawberries for tea.

And look, I do not draw the line at the likes of Middleton and Heywood joining in. Notta tall. And I do not I rule out anyone beyond the Tropic of Didsbury Village. No, the only qualification for admission to our house tha neet is . . .

Ha-a-a-a-ah!

Ya gotta spikka da lingo, *comprenez*? Like, WA'ER! See? WA-A'ER! So, one more time, eh? *Parley-voo*? I wanna hear ya roll your R's (*Carry On* crew, on your bike! '*Oo-ooh! Do you ride tandem*?') See, there's no need to be shy. I mean, it's not as if Bernard Manning's gonna poke fun at you. ('Feller over here. See him? Poor man's Barry Manilow. Seen him, Midland Bank, yesterday. *Oh, is that so, Elmer Fudd? Well, HSBC, my arse, as George Roper said to the Harley Street Brain Surgeon*!') Hey, and it's not as if the BBC Talk-Proper Police is gonna baton charge you. Nah, the BBC's gonna be far too busy looking for us in Blakk-ley, wherever that is when it's owt. So one more time now. From the top – and let's make it flipping Clough Top while we're about it.

'WA-A'E-R-R-R-R!' (Roll 'em!) 'WA-A-A'E-R-R-R-R-R!' A one, two, three, a-four – the big un: 'WA-A-A-A-A-A-A-ER-ER-ER-ER-ER-ER!'

'*Ha-a-a-a-ah*!''

Smashing! No, really. It was smashing, that. Yeah, it was just like the old days when rowing boats was clinker built and a park had a bandstand in it and old fogies could walk home of a night without getting mugged, and maybe Shirlee and me would . . .

Ha-a-a-a-ah!

Right – deserve a treat, yous lot do.

Crackle of stylus on vinyl.

Ready? You ready for it?

'GET A KIN MOVE ON, WILL YER!'

Ah, thank you, sir. Spoken like a native of, er, Clayton, I'd imagine. Right, with no more ado then . . . Lazy gentlemen, your host, poor old Dinchy, what you already knows, poor old Dinchy, pr-r-oudly pr-r-esents for your hennertainment . . . Dinchy and Ringo . . .

Yeah, Ringo Starr. Why not? Poor old Dinchy on the unopened packet of Beecham's Powders (two taps), his nibs on the upturned dustbin. (Some packet of Beecham's Powders! Some – WHACK-WHACK – dustbin!)

Hey, and lezz have a big hand for George, here, who's bang on time, like I told him to be . . .

Yeah, George Harrison. Why not?

See, like I told him earlier: 'Look, George,' I said. 'You've gotta be bang on time with this. I mean, this is Blackley, and we won't put up with none of your Litherland-Town-Hall-I've-got-blisters-on-me-fingers malarkey!'

'You mean, *The White Album*?' says George. 'That was him, thur.' Ooh, and George strikes this right ratty chord, like he done all the way through 'Taxman' that he wrote. Yeah, and George passes the buck to this one, front left, that's stood there like he done when he sung 'Twist and Shout' on Granada all them years ago – sort of bow-legged and with the rhythm guitar tucked up tight beneath his chin.

'I believe you, George,' I told him. 'Thing is, there's only three hundred thousand million billion Blackley folk out there, plus a Clayton clodhopper that may not be quite so understandin' . . .'

Ha-a-a-a-ah!'

'You laughing at me, man.'

'Notta tall, George. Notta tall. Feelin' a bit ropey, that's all. No, all I'm askin', George, is for you sock it to us, nice and true, like only you knows how with one of the best guitar licks known to man.'

BLEE-EE-EE-EE-EEB-BLEEB-EE-LEEB-eeb-eeb-eeb-eeb

'Ah, sweet: 'Free As a Bird'! . . . Little Richard! You doin' here?'

'Havin' a ball, man, like ah allus do.' And he gives us this great big cheesy grin. 'An' 'Early One Morning' jus' as soon's these nass white baws is finch.'

'Mr Penniman, pull the lead out, will ya?' yells this one front left.

'Ooh, yessah, Mass' Lennon! Yes, sirr-ee! Lucille, she say: "Ah sho' nuff lack a mairn tha's firm!"'

(Get these *Carry On*-ers off the stage! Security: groupies! Shift 'em, will ya?)

BU-LUB-UH-LEEB-EE-LEEB-eeb-eeb-eeb-eeb

'Buddy! Tommy with you? Waylon?

'Waylon's on-a next flight. Cain't rightly say 'bout Tom.'

BU-LUB-BU-LUB-BU-LEEB-BEE-LEEB

'Buddy, you know 'em all, right? Seen a photo once upon a time, you wi' Milad-oh. . .'

'Mm, done a cover version, same song one time.'

'You got the words wrong, right?'

'Yuh noticed, huh?'

'Mm. 'Baby I Don't Care': the rhyme's the clue. He says "Dance steps that are *new*" to rhyme with *do*. You say: "Dance steps that I *do*." He's gotta be right.'

'Hey, what ya don' know's I done drove seven-ah-farv miles a-Clovis, Noo Mexico, 'fore that take.'

'That him there with Roy?'

'Whoo-ee!' Buddy whistles, clocking him, and the Big O in the shades still, then he gives the D string of his Strat this little bit of a last second tuning tweak. 'Git along home, Cindy. Oh, ye-e-e-s, sir. Got one helluva full house here tonight, that's for sure.'

Sheer lunacy! Eh? Sheer bloody lunacy!

I mean, let's have it right. Presley's not sung for twenny-odd years or more; Beatles for a few years before that; Buddy Holly ten years prior – *Monsewer* Anthony Dismas Dinch (the acclaimed lip-synch air guitar, the unplugged organ, the thumb-in-mouth sax) for twenny-seven years if it's a day.

Yeah, Dinchy. Why not?

'*Ha-a-a-a-ah*!'

But we is all, every one of us, bang on time like George. Though Dinchy is miles too late in another sense, many years too late.

Hah! Story of Dinchy's life, I suppose. Unless he's quick about it.
Beatles' track comes off, whiz it. Another 45 goes on . . .
Ha-a-a-a-a-a-h!

It is Dinchy's favourite Valette, a study in blue – blue and bluer. It hangs on the chimney breast in his living-room. The background, a blue wash, shows a building with many windows, a building bigger far than any building in the city past or present, its lower floors wreathed in smog and smoke and mist and steam. It is a building heavy with symbolism, an allegory perhaps for the dominance of industry, of the city, of the state, of the media, of a political movement, of institutionalism for its own sake, of the *zeitgeist* – an allegory for the dominance of anything that seeks to do just that: to dominate. But it is only a background, of course.

The water between the buildings is bluer, the buildings on either side are bluer still, though where water finishes and air begins, where buildings stand in city dirt, or are reflections in the water, it is impossible to say. Also, it is impossible to say with absolute certainty which city this is. One building (front left) suggests Venice, though this cannot be. In other respects the city would appear to be Manchester – witness the signs of industry in the background: steam again, smoke, a modern bridge, ramps, the pitched roof of a building that can only be a warehouse, a pair of canal barges, one with two funnels; witness the name of the artist: Adolphe Valette, L. S. Lowry's teacher. The title of the painting – or, in the case of the illustration that hangs on the chimney-breast in Dinchy' living-room, the print – is *India House*.

Silently, dead as night, inexorably, the canal barge with two funnels slinks towards us, its destination clear as day. It veers towards the Venetian side of the canal as though intending to deceive, but there can be little doubt about the direction it will take. The canal barge with two funnels is heading for an archway, blue as the ocean deep, an archway that frames the entire scene. In real life this archway straddles one of the Manchester canals – the Rochdale, the Bridgewater, or the Ashton – and it affords access to other towns in the industrial north. But not today. Today the archway throws its shade – blue mosaic within yards (unseen), glinting with gold mosaic stars (again, unseen) – across a canal barge with two funnels that sails to Avalon or Far Cathay.

As he embarks Dinchy's lips are seen to move: he murmurs something, something whispered at most, something that could not be heard were Dinchy to shout it – if he were still capable of shouting, that is. For a record is playing on the turntable of the Philco record player in Dinchy's living-room, and the record that is playing on the turntable of the Philco record player in Dinchy's living-room is revolving beneath the stylus at a continuous 45 revolutions per minute; and the music that is coming from the single speaker of the Philco record player in Dinchy's living-room, though tonally tinny, is loud enough to drown out whatever it is that Dinchy is trying to say. But, from the little we know about Dinchy, it would perhaps not be unreasonable to suppose that, as it was in the beginning, so it is now, and ever shall be – and what Dinchy is saying is: 'Shir . . . lee!

EPILOGUE

'Silly bugger! Pissed probably. I don't care what the coroner says. What's he know anyway? Quacks and lawyers! In it for what they can get, the lot of 'em. Seen too much of it over the years, me. They all piss in the same pot. There's not a one of them knows his arse from his elbow . . . Yeah, between three an' four thousand – scattered all over the shop. Sat on some of 'em, twat. Some on top of the gas fire, full on. I mean, it's the daughter I feel sorry for, Arthur . . . Suzanne, yeah. Goes round there at dinner with it being New Year's Day and that. She's got the little un with her too. Senses there's summat wrong straight off. Miles too warm, for one thing. Gas fire full on, like I say. Bit of a whiff about the place too. Hey, and the same old record's playin' away there, over and over again on this crappy little record player he's got, like summat out of the Ark . . . As God is my judge, Arthur. Anyroad, she goes in, takes Derek with her from two doors up . . . As a dodo. Absolute bloody fortune in original Beatles' albums, well, fifty quid's worth, melted on top of the fire. Well, that's where they'd started off, I suppose. By this time they look like that Spanish feller painted 'em . . . How do *I* know what kin Spanish feller? They all draws meltin' watches and burnin' giraffes, them dagoes. All they're good for, you ask me . . . Dally, yeah, that's him, Arthur. Yeah, he's the one done the drippy watches, isn't he? Scorched a giraffe or two in his time, unless I'm very much mistaken. I dilly, I dally, I dally and I dilly . . . Same again, Arthur . . . Turntable? What was on the *turn*table? I don't kin know, do I? You bloody pop-pickers get me, you do. What *are* you like? Suzanne's the same, silly tart. Some shite, I dunno. What's she say now? Some shite. 'White Christmas'? Nah. Wait a minute. It'll come. Hang on – no, wait a minute. Yeah, that's it, Arthur: 'New Year's Day'. Well, anyway, that's what Suzanne said . . . Me too? Oh, you are *so* wrong, Arthur. Nah, not me. You would not believe how wrong you are, my son. I'm no pop-picker . . . Sorry . . . Oh, *U2*! . . . What? Oh, they're the ones that done it, are they? U2, eh? Ooh! get you! Regular little Jimmy Savile, you are, Arthur. Missed your way, you ask me. No, really. What y'doing stuck behind a bar all day long when you could be out there guys-and-gals-ing it on Radio One? Beats me, it does . . . An' if that phone's for me, tell 'em to piss off. Hours I've put in in me time, reckon I've earned the right to enjoy me Sunday dinner time sesh undisturbed before I go off home and get stuck into that nice beef dinner of Marj's that she does. Hey, and by the way, if it's that new kid mitherin' about an early finish, tell him an early finish at Bee Line's midnight on the dot unless he wants a broken back that I'll see to personal . . . Blood yell, Arthur, what's this shite you've give us. Tastes like you've strained it through a sweaty jock strap? Pull us a proper pint, come on, pull us a proper kin pint . . . Nah! Won't know till Tuesday, the earliest – Coroner's Court and all that fartin' about to do. But yer reckon to this? They've seen the will, of course, an' it says Suzanne's not to have her mum's engagement ring. Nice one, it is too. Emerald. Nah, her mum's ring's to go to this New Sentry-Newfart thing . . . Search me. Some kin charity. Plus the same kin charity gets some piddlin' percentage out of his estate. Hey, an' how's this for a game of soldiers? If their Suzanne don't bury him with his missis in Blackley, the charity gets the lot . . . You heard us. The kin *lot*! Mind you, there's no danger of that, of course. They'll chuck him in with the missis all right, would of done anyway . . . Yeah. Oh, yeah, Shirlee . . . Yeah, Shirlee, her name was . . . Well, you wouldn't, do, would you? I mean, how long you been here now? What is it? Six, seven years? . . . Eight, eh? How time flies when you're having fun! Even so, it's a bit before your time, Arthur. Yeah, Shirlee's been dead – oof! – must be thirty years Shirlee's been . . . Well, gettin' on that way anyway. Let's see. I'd just bought in with Mag Piper . . . Course you do, clown whose missis topped herself, he moved in with that tart on French Barn Lane, what's her name now? . . . Nah, can't think. But I know I'd just bought in with Mag Piper when Shirlee died. Yeah, Marj had just got rid of that carbuncle on her . . . Yeah, must be twenny-seven years since Shirlee snuffed it. Now there's another barmy bugger, ever there was one . . .'